EMMANUEL APPADOCCA;

OR,

BLIGHTED LIFE.

EMMANUEL APPADOCCA;

OR,

BLIGHTED LIFE.

A Tale of the Boucaneers

MAXWELL PHILIP

Edited with an afterword by Selwyn R. Cudjoe
Introduction and annotations by William E. Cain

UNIVERSITY OF MASSACHUSETTS PRESS

AMHERST

Introduction and annotations © 1997
by William E. Cain
Afterword © 1997 by Selwyn R. Cudjoe

LC 96-47786
ISBN 1-55849-075-2 (cloth); 076-0 (pbk.)
Designed by Jack Harrison
Set in ITC Bodoni Book by Keystone Typesetting, Inc.
Printed and bound by Braun-Brumfield, Inc.

Library of Congress Cataloging-in-Publication Data
Philip, Maxwell, 1829–1888.
Emmanuel Appadocca, or, Blighted life : a tale of the boucaneers /
Maxwell Philip ; edited with an afterword by Selwyn R. Cudjoe ;
introduction and annotations by William E. Cain.
p.   cm.
Includes bibliographical references (p.   ),
ISBN 1-55849-075-2 (cloth : alk. paper). – ISBN 1-55849-076-0
(pbk. : alk. paper)
I. Cudjoe, Selwyn Reginald. II. Cain, William E., 1952-   .
III. Title.
PR9272.9.P48E66   1997
813–dc21   96-47786
                                      CIP

British Library Cataloguing in Publication data are available.

Excerpts from Euripides, *Hecuba*, translated by William Arrowsmith from volume 3 of *The Complete Greek Tragedies*, general editors David Grene and Richard Lattimore, copyright 1960, are used by permission of the University of Chicago Press. The map on page viii is from Herbert S. Klein, *African Slavery in Latin America and the Caribbean* (New York: Oxford University Press, 1986).

Acknowledgments

We are indebted to Bruce Wilcox, Pam Wilkinson, and Catlin Murphy of the University of Massachusetts Press for their encouragement and support of this project. We owe thanks too to our Wellesley College colleagues Tim Peltason for advice about the Introduction and Mary Lefkowitz and Lorraine Roses for help with several annotations.

Contents

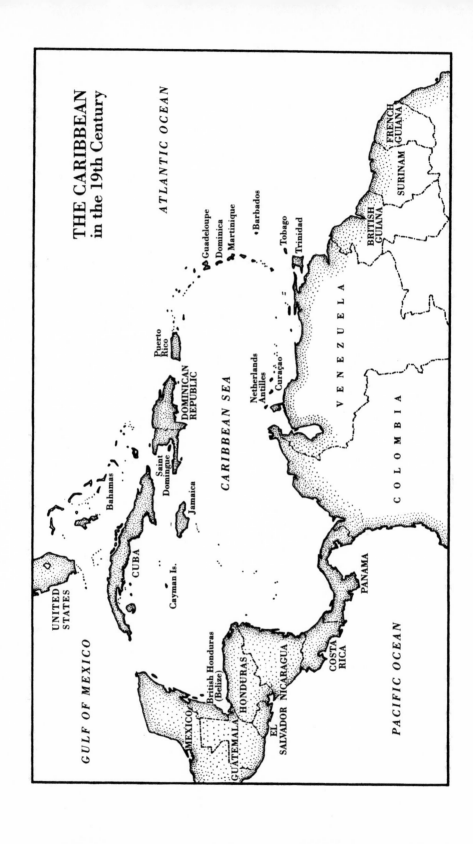

THE CARIBBEAN
in the 19th Century

ATLANTIC OCEAN

Guadeloupe
Dominica
Martinique
• Barbados

• Tobago
Trinidad

Puerto
Rico

CARIBBEAN SEA

DOMINICAN
REPUBLIC

Saint
Domingue

Bahamas

Jamaica

CUBA

Cayman Is.

UNITED
STATES

GULF OF MEXICO

Netherlands
Antilles
Curaçao

VENEZUELA

COLOMBIA

BRITISH
GUIANA

SURINAM

FRENCH
GUIANA

PANAMA

COSTA
RICA

NICARAGUA

HONDURAS

British Honduras
(Belize)

GUATEMALA

EL
SALVADOR

MEXICO

PACIFIC OCEAN

Preface

SELWYN R. CUDJOE

Described by C. L. R. James as "the most brilliant native of his time and within memory,"[1] Michel Maxwell Philip (1829-88) was born in Trinidad during the era of slavery. He was a member of the fourth generation of the Philip family, a family that had its origins in "a dynasty of Black women, heirs to estates on Carriacou, Grenada, and the entire island of Petite Martinique" and who through their radical activities and public service fought against discriminatory and racist practices in Grenada and Trinidad.

At the head of the family was Jeanette Philip (?-1784), a "free negro woman," who inherited an estate of 464 acres and eighty-nine slaves when Honore Philip, a Frenchman with whom she cohabited, died sometime before 1775. The family's wealth gave the descendants "the opportunity for schooling which resulted in a class of well trained people versed in the classics and in possession of literary skills." As Lorna McDaniel notes, a good number of them acquired an "elitist education in European universities."[2]

Yet despite their social privilege and elitist education, many members of the Philip family were involved in the radical political activities of their society, such as the Fédon Rebellion of 1795.[3] During that rebellion, Jo-

1. C. L. R. James, "Michel Maxwell Philip: 1829-1888," in *From Trinidad: An Anthology of Early West Indian Writing,* ed. Reinhard W. Sander (New York: Africana Publishing, 1978), 255.

2. Lorna McDaniel, "The Philips: A 'Free Mulatto' Family of Grenada," *Journal of Caribbean History* 24, no. 2 (1990): 179-80, 183-84.

3. Julie Fédon, the son of a French Grenadian planter and an enslaved African woman, organized a rebellion of slaves and freemen who held the island of Grenada for sixteen months. The insurrectionary activities of Fédon and his comrades were important in the revolutionary overthrow of European slavery in the Caribbean and were part of the international struggle for the liberation of black people. As Robin Blackburn notes, the wars waged by "the black revolutionaries of the eastern Caribbean tied up more British troops and warships than the campaign in San Domingo. French propaganda of word and deed inspired slave revolts in Venezuela, Cuba, Jamaica, and Brazil" ("*The Black Jacobins* and New World Slavery," in *C. L. R. James: His Intellectual Legacies,* ed. Selwyn R. Cudjoe and William E. Cain (Amherst: University of Massachusetts Press, 1995), 91. See also chapter 4 of Edward L. Cox, *Free Coloreds in the Slave Societies of St. Kitts and Grenada, 1763-833* (Knoxville: University of Tennessee Press, 1984) for an analysis of Fédon's rebellion.

achim Philip, son of Jeanette, was one of the leaders of Grenada's free
coloreds who "attempted to gain full citizenship as promised to their breth-
ren in French territories by rising in arms against island whites, whom they
perceived to be responsible for their degrading sociopolitical status."[4] Indeed, Joachim, a chief emissary of Julien Fédon, was among those who
"burst into the British meeting room along Charles Nogues with a flag and a
declaration of truce. They were uniformed in short blue coat[s], with white
edgings, flaming golden epaulets, and large helmets on their heads, bearing the inscription–*La mort ou la liberté!*"[5] The French Revolution had
reached the eastern Caribbean.

Maxwell Philip belonged to a branch of the family that relocated to Trinidad because Joachim's political involvement with Fédon's rebellion limited
its economic opportunities in Grenada. Joachim's brother, Louis, migrated
to Trinidad and acquired estates in the Naparimas between 1793 and 1796.
According to McDaniel, he "operated the largest slave-holding sugar plantations there."[6]

Born on the Cooper Grange estate in South Naparima on October 12,
1829, Maxwell Philip was named after Frederic Maxwell, a young slave who
had accompanied Louis to Trinidad and, after manumission, became the
manager of the Phillipine estate. L. B. Tronchin, principal of the Port of
Spain Model School and one of the leading critics and intellectuals of the
latter part of the nineteenth century, notes that Philip was indeed a member
of the Philip family. Bridget Brereton identifies him as "the son of a coloured woman of the Philip family," and according to C. L. R. James, who
undoubtedly spoke to older Trinidadians acquainted with Philip, "he was an
illegitimate child, the offspring of a white owner and a coloured woman on
the estate."[7]

As a member of the Philip family, Maxwell Philip received the best education of the day. He attended the public school of San Fernando until the age
of fourteen when he was sent to St. Mary's Catholic College, Blairs, Scotland, for six years, where he received a classical education. On his return to
Trinidad in 1849, he was attached to Henry Hart Anderson, solicitor-at-law,
to prepare for legal studies in England. After two years in Trinidad, Philip
returned to England, entered Middle Temple, and was called to the bar in

---

4. Cox, *Free Coloreds in the Slave Societies of St. Kitts and Grenada,* 76.

5. McDaniel, "The Philips," 186–87.

6. Ibid., 187–88.

7. Bridget Brereton, *Race Relations in Colonial Trinidad, 1870–1900* (Cambridge: Cambridge University Press, 1979), p. 87; James, "Michel Maxwell Philip," 254.

1854. It was during this English period that he composed and published his one literary work, *Emmanuel Appadocca; or, Blighted Life. A Tale of the Boucaneers* (1854).

At the time, Philip was serving as the London correspondent for the Trinidad *Free Press,* and evidence suggests he had a well-developed interest in literature. Tronchin notes that while Philip was in Trinidad he was influenced by the romantic novels of Sir Walter Scott, "which absorbed all of his leisure time. His youthful and ardent imagination was kindled by the recitals of the deeds of daring, love and danger, which are described so graphically by the greatest novelist of Scotland."[8] In England, Philip studied the works of Virgil, Horace, Euripides, and Sophocles, as well as the eloquent discourses of Demosthenes. Evidence of such classical influences becomes apparent when we note that the epigraph at the beginning of *Emmanuel Appadocca* is taken from Euripides' *Hecuba.* Having already mastered several modern languages, Philip was so brilliant and intellectually inquisitive that "when he started to practice at the bar, seeing that Hindustani would be useful to him he soon mastered it."[9] In 1850, he participated in the local literary scene and was one of the most active promoters of the Trinidad Literary Association "in whose weekly debates he distinguished himself as a promising young orator, and received the warm congratulations of the most eminent members of that society."[10]

After completing his work at Middle Temple, Philip visited several European cities "in order to improve his knowledge of men, places and things; and also to gain an insight into the most noted institutions to which he might refer in the discharge of his duties as a lawyer."[11] When Philip returned to Trinidad in January 1855, his reputation was well established; he was known as "a literary character and an eloquent speaker."[12]

Until his death in 1888, Philip devoted his life to the practice of law and to public service, distinguishing himself in both fields. He served as inspector of schools, mayor of Port of Spain, unofficial member of the legislative council, solicitor general, and on seven occasions acting attorney general. He was also a member of the board of health, board of education, a college council, and various commissions. As a lawyer, he built a reputation for lucid and eloquent expression, astute and thorough cross-examination, and

8. L. B. Tronchin, "The Great West Indian Orator," *Public Opinion,* December 18, 1888, 5.
9. James, "Michel Maxwell Philip," 255.
10. Tronchin, "The Great West Indian Orator," 5.
11. Ibid.
12. José Bodu, *Trinidadiana* (Port of Spain: A. C. Blondel, 1890), 83.

unparalleled knowledge of the law. Indeed, he was reputed to be *the author-ity* on the old Laws of Spain which prevailed in Trinidad during most of the time he practiced. In 1888 he played a prominent part in the debate on the annexation of Tobago to Trinidad.

Yet Philip always rued the fact that he never received the recognition he deserved and would have received had he been white. Although all accounts indicate that he was the most distinguished jurist of his time, he never attained the post of attorney general of Trinidad, which he coveted and to which he had a legitimate claim. Tronchin notes that "his raciality as a creole and his descendence from the African blood were formidable obsta-cles in the way of his promotion."[13] Toward the end of his life, he was offered the chief justiceship of the Gold Coast, but he turned it down be-cause he did not want to leave his home and start all over again at an advanced age. Philip died on June 30, 1888, after a long struggle with Bright's disease. In an editorial, *Public Opinion* described the British gov-ernment's treatment of him as the "callous and hard-hearted neglect of one of Trinidad's favorite sons." It continued:

> The Colonial Office cares little for the wishes of the people of those distant colonies. The vast majority of the people wished to see Mr. Philip elevated to the Bench, but the people of Crown Colonies might as well command the tide not to rise, or the wind to cease blowing, as to impress the Colonial Office with what they know to be for their own good and what the Colonial Office knows nothing of and cares less for unless it be the preferment of its own favorites.[14]

Even in death, Philip failed to receive justice. His heirs had tremendous problems in securing the gratuity that should have come to them and which his predecessor had received. Philip was married to Eliza Englehart, who died in 1870, and was the father of two daughters. His utter disregard for finances left his family in poverty. James notes that "he was extravagant to absurdity. Money meant nothing to him. He made it and he spent it. Unfor-tunately he spent more than he made."[15] Apparently he was also careless with public funds. Brereton observes that he did not serve out his third term as mayor of Port of Spain because of allegations of "gross carelessness and extravagance in spending public funds."[16] One of Philip's daughters, who was living in a state of destitution, was able eventually to secure a gratuity

13. Ibid., 5.
14. "The Late Hon. Maxwell Philip," *Public Opinion,* July 3, 1888.
15. James, "Michel Maxwell Philip," 263.
16. Bridget Brereton, "Michael Maxwell Philip (1829–1888): Servant of the Centurion," *Antilia . . . : Journal of the Faculty of Arts* (University of the West Indies) 1, no. 3 (1988): 10.

of £100 from the colonial authorities in recognition of her father's long service. The editor of *Public Opinion* described this as an "extremely paltry" sum for someone who had served as solicitor general for upwards of eighteen years and had been described by the governor of the island as "not only a safe and wise Counsellor but [a] trusty and loyal adviser."[17]

Philip's chief legacy is *Emmanuel Appadocca,* a novel that blends elements of historical romance, the African American slave narrative, and the ideology of organized piracy. The plot concerns the desertion of the protagonist's mulatto mother by his father, a wealthy white sugar planter from Trinidad, and his subsequent attempt to vindicate his mother's dishonor. Although it is an adventure story, it can also be read as a meditation of how an enslaved person ought to behave under the crushing weight of slavery. Much more will be said about this fascinating text in William Cain's introduction and my afterword. Although *Emmanuel Appadocca* has been virtually unknown for more than one hundred years, it remains a significant achievement in Caribbean and African American literature and intellectual thought. Scholars and students of Caribbean, African American, and American literature would do well to engage this remarkable book as they attempt to expand and refashion the meaning of the Atlantic sensibility.

A Note on the Text

Although there are references to *Emmanuel Appadocca* in works such as C. L. R. James's essay on Philip and José M. Bodu's *Trinidadiana* (both cited above), I did not see a copy of this text until I discovered it at the British Library in 1980.[18] When, therefore, in 1988 I claimed that A. R. F. Webber's *Those That Be in Bondage* (1917), was "the first novel of Trinidad and Tobago" I really sought to distinguish between the novel proper and the romance, the category in which I placed *Emmanuel Appadocca* initially.[19] In retrospect, such a distinction seems somewhat pedantic and not terribly meaningful. *Emmanuel Appadocca* is really the first Anglo-Caribbean

17. "The Late Hon. M. M. Philip," *Public Opinion*, December 4, 1888; "Michel Maxwell Philip," in *Emmanuel Appadocca: Blighted Life* (Port of Spain: Mole, Brothers, 1893). A sketch of Philip's life is included in this printing of the novel and is reproduced in the present edition.

18. In his introduction to this work, William Cain notes that three libraries in the United States (Library of Congress, New York Public Library and the University of Rochester) own copies of *Emmanuel Appadocca.*

19. See A. R. F. Webber, *Those That Be in Bondage* (Wellesley, Mass: Calaloux Publications, 1988).

novel even though the author draws on romantic formulations. *Emmanuel Appadocca* certainly predates Tom Redcam's *Becka's Buckra Baby* (1903), which Kenneth Ramchand, in his pioneering work, *The West Indian Novel and Its Background,* claimed to be "the earliest known work of West Indian prose fiction."[20] And although one wishes to give some pride of place to Mary Prince's narrative that she dictated to Mary Pringle,[21] *Emmanuel Appadocca* certainly stands as the first piece of prose fiction in the Anglo-Caribbean literary tradition. As Wilson Harris observed when he spoke of *Those That Be in Bondage:*

> When one reflects on the distinguished body of writing that has come from Trinidadian-born authors, who include C. L. R. James, Alfred Mendes, Ralph de Bossière, V. S. Naipaul, Samuel Selvon, Earl Lovelace, and others, one looks to the 'first' in such a faculty of design for seeds of impulse both ominous and instructive within the medium of the twentieth century that spans areas of colonialism and postcolonialism, empires and revolutions.[22]

Were he speaking of the Caribbean, Harris would have extended his list to include creative writers such as Derek Walcott, George Lamming, John Hearne, Erna Brodber, Merle Hodge, Roger Mais, Edgar Mittleholzer, and, perhaps, even Caryl Philips. Suffice it to say that Michel Maxwell Philip was the first writer in the Anglophone Caribbean to offer us a sustained and eloquent novel and for that pioneering act of imagination we will be in his debt always.

20. Kenneth Ramchand, *The West Indian Novel and Its Background* (London: Heinemann, 1983), 3.
21. See *The History of Mary Prince,* ed. with an introduction by Moira Ferguson (London: Pandora, 1987).
22. Wilson Harris, "Afterword" to *Those That Be in Bondage,* 237.

Introduction:
Emmanuel Appadocca
in Its American Context

WILLIAM E. CAIN

In the preface to *Emmanuel Appadocca,* Maxwell Philip, writing in London, links his novel to the slavery crisis in the United States, in particular to the sexual exploitation of black women and the callous treatment of their children by white slavemaster fathers. Philip declares that his book "has been written at a moment when the feelings of the Author are roused up to a high pitch of indignant excitement, by a statement of the cruel manner in which the slave holders of America deal with their slave-children." But he no sooner connects the novel to American slavery than he says that it is based on "the known history of the Boucaneers," its scenes "laid principally" in the author's "native isle" of Trinidad. The United States, England, Trinidad: there are three important, interrelated geographical markers for this author and the text he has composed, a text located within the literary, cultural, and socioeconomic contexts of the Atlantic world system.

Philip complicates his preface still further by stressing that *Emmanuel Appadocca* is a work of the imagination, a fictional inquiry into the likely conduct of "a high-spirited and sensitive person" who is the offspring of a white father and slave mother. This blend of realism and romance about racial and sexual themes is heightened in the sentence with which the preface concludes, where Philip tells of his hope that he will be buried in the same high ground of Trinidad, looking out over the sea, that already contains the body of the woman – probably his mother, though he does not give her name or relationship to him – who was "the object of his deep love and high veneration."

Philip's opening words to the reader are notable for their mixture of emphases and tones – historical, personal, analytical, sentimental – and for the balancing of truth and fiction that the writer professes he will perform. But it is also a bold preface for a twenty-four-year-old law student to present. *Emmanuel Appadocca* is from its preface forward not only an ambitiously conceived triangulated text that binds the United States, England, and the Caribbean, but a text whose lofty literary aims are heralded in the epigraph on the title-page from Euripides–given in Greek–and in the epigraph from Shakespeare's *Richard III* that opens the first chapter. These references, and many others that follow, indicate the classic and canonical literary and cultural touchstones according to which Philip orients his book, as well as the renowned names in the Western tradition that Philip wants readers to bear in mind while reading the book that he has written.

On one level, to be sure, Philip's literary self-conception will strike readers today as ironic, for *Emmanuel Appadocca* is almost unknown. Apparently it did enjoy success at the time of its publication. A nineteenth-century report on Philip's career states that the novel was "well received in the literary world" and that the royalties were of great benefit to Philip as he worked under "difficult circumstances" toward the completion of his legal studies; another more recent one notes that the novel was so successful that it supplied Philip with the funds to tour Europe.[1] Very little is known in detail beyond this: *Emmanuel Appadocca* has not figured in literary history. The eminent Trinidadian intellectual and Marxist theorist C. L. R. James did call attention to Philip's importance in an article published in *The Beacon* (September 1931), but with little effect. James refers to *Emmanuel Appadocca* and suggests that this story of an embittered son mirrors Philip's own anger toward his neglectful father. He remarks, however, that he will save discussion of Philip's novel for another time, and it appears that he did not return to it.[2]

Occasionally *Emmanuel Appadocca* receives a passing mention.[3] But it is rarely cited by critics and is not taught in English and American colleges and universities. There has been no detailed study of the text, nor has Philip's distinguished legal career in Trinidad been traced. This holds true not only for scholarship on American and African American literary and cultural history, but for studies of Caribbean and West Indian literatures as well.[4]

1. See L. B. Tronchin, principal of Port of Spain Model School, in his essay "The Great West Indian Orator," *Public Opinion,* December 18 and 21, 1888; and *The Book of Trinidad,* ed. Gerard Besson and Bridget Brereton, 2d ed. (Port of Spain: Paria Publishing, 1992), 331.

2. C. L. R. James, "Michel Maxwell Philip: 1829–1888," in *From Trinidad: An Anthology of Early West Indian Writing,* ed. Reinhard W. Sander (New York: Africana Publishing Company, 1978), 255. *The Beacon* was a literary, cultural, and political magazine published in Trinidad from March 1931 through November 1933.

3. For example, Reinhard W. Sander, *The Trinidad Awakening: West Indian Literature of the Nineteen-Thirties* (Westport: Greenwood Press, 1988), 7.

4. Speaking of the literary situation in the nineteenth century, in *The West Indian Novel and Its Background,* 2d ed. (London: Heinemann, 1983), Kenneth Ramchand states that "the

The recovery of *Emmanuel Appadocca* is, then, a significant literary event, and, as the book becomes more widely read and examined, it will prove a seminal text for histories of West Indian and Caribbean literatures, and, furthermore, for the new histories of American literature that are being written. These histories seek to enlarge "American" literature beyond its traditional canon by including many texts by women, African Americans, and other minorities. In addition, they define this literature in the midst of its historical context and, beyond that, within the literary, cultural, social, and political history of the Americas, North and South, and the past and present patterns of trade, commerce, cross-cultural relationships, European domination and subjugation of other races.

With *Emmanuel Appadocca* before us, it is tempting to propose that our new object of study should be not "American" but "Atlantic" literature–the literature of the Atlantic world as it has been shaped by the slave trade, slavery, race, and racism. As the cultural critic Paul Gilroy has argued, it is time for critics, historians, and teachers to recognize "the inescapable hybridity and intermixture of ideas" that have circulated within the Atlantic system. "The Atlantic," he states, should serve "as one single, complex unit of analysis in discussions of the modern world" and should be used "to produce an explicitly transnational and intercultural perspective."[5]

---

period appears to have produced no novelists, only a handful of minor poets" (31). Neither Michael Gilkes, *The West Indian Novel* (Boston: Twayne, 1981), nor O. R. Dathorne, *Dark Ancestor: The Literature of the Black Man in the Caribbean* (Baton Rouge: Louisiana State University Press, 1981), cites Philip's book. In *The Evolution of the West Indian's Image in the Afro-American Novel* (Millwood, N.Y.: Associated Faculty Press, 1986), Melvin B. Rahming states that the West Indian novel "begins in 1903 with the publication of Tom Redcam's *Becka's Buckra Baby*" (xvi). The entry on the Caribbean novel in the *Encyclopedia of Post-Colonial Literatures in English*, ed. Eugene Benson and L. W. Conolly, 2 vols. (New York: Routledge, 1994), making no reference to Philip, similarly states that "the first notable landmark in the Caribbean novel" is the Jamaican Redcam's book (2:1119). Only three U.S. libraries (Library of Congress, New York Public Library, University of Rochester) own copies of *Emmanuel Appadocca*.

5. Paul Gilroy, *The Black Atlantic: Modernity and Double Consciousness* (Cambridge: Harvard University Press, 1993), xi, 15. See also the discussion and helpful bibliographies in Philip D. Curtin, *The Rise and Fall of the Plantation Complex: Essays in Atlantic History* (New York: Cambridge University Press, 1990). My own approach has been shaped not only by Gilroy, but also by the promising leads in this "Atlantic" direction given by Eric J. Sundquist, "*Benito Cereno* and New World Slavery," in *Reconstructing American Literary History*, ed. Sacvan Bercovitch (Cambridge: Harvard University Press, 1986), 93–122; Keith A. Sandiford, *Measuring the Moment: Strategies of Protest in Eighteenth-Century Afro-English Writing* (Cranbury, N.J.: Associated University Presses, 1988); Lawrence Buell, "Melville and the Question of American Decolonization," *American Literature* 64 (June 1992): 215–37; Buell, "American Literary Emergence as a Postcolonial Phenomenon," *American Literary History* 4 (Fall 1992): 411–42; Renata R. Mautner Wasserman, *Exotic Nations: Literature and Cultural*

This argument for the relationship between geography and culture, though it has gained many supporters, still meets with much opposition, largely because of the painful, contested political and historical issues that it raises. Many scholars are inclined to resist the notion that the monuments of high culture emerged within–indeed, were made possible by–violence, war, colonialism, racial oppression, and human bondage, and it is often hard to gain a hearing for contextualizing them, for returning them to history. As Edward W. Said has observed, "the curricular study of a national language and literature fairly enjoins an appreciation for that culture that regularly induces assent, loyalty, and an unusually rarified sense of from where the culture really springs and in what complicating circumstances its monuments derive."[6] Yet the evidence for the dependence of culture on harsh historical realities is close to the surface once one begins to look for it.

As an instance pertinent to Philip's book, with its context of North American-Caribbean slavery, consider the life and career of Hans Sloane (1660-1753), who served as secretary of the Royal Society from 1693 to 1712, and later as its president, from 1727 to 1741, in addition to holding the presidency of the Royal College of Physicians. His superb library and collection of 80,000 artifacts and specimens, purchased by the government at the time of Sloane's death, were the foundation for the British Museum, one of the great expressions of British culture and nationalism. Sloane's

---

Identity in the United States and Brazil, 1830-1930 (Ithaca: Cornell University Press, 1994); and, in a somewhat differently focused piece, Antonio Benitez-Rojo, "The Polyrhythmic Paradigm: The Caribbean and the Postmodern Era," in *Race, Discourse, and the Origin of the Americas: A New World View,* ed. Vera Lawrence Hyatt and Rex Nettleford (Washington, D.C.: Smithsonian Institution Press, 1995), 255-67. Also pertinent are Reed Way Dasenbrock, "English Department Geography," *ADE Bulletin* 86 (Spring 1987): 16-23; Dasenbrock, "What to Teach When the Canon Closes Down: Toward a New Essentialism," in *Reorientations: Critical Theories and Pedagogies,* ed. Bruce Henricksen and Thais E. Morgan (Urbana: University of Illinois Press, 1990), 63-76; and Michael Valdez Moses, *The Novel and the Globalization of Culture* (New York: Oxford University Press, 1995).

6. Edward W. Said, "Nationalism, Human Rights, and Interpretation," in *Freedom and Interpretation: The Oxford Amnesty Lectures, 1992,* ed. Barbara Johnson (New York: Basic Books, 1993), 189. See also Earl Lewis, "To Turn as on a Pivot: Writing African Americans into a History of Overlapping Diasporas," *American Historical Review* 100 (June 1995): 765-87; and Michael Geyer and Charles Bright, "World History in a Global Age," *American Historical Review* 100 (October 1995): 1034-60. For students in literary and cultural studies, helpful secondary sources include: Betsy Erkkila, "Ethnicity, Literary Theory, and the Grounds of Resistance," *American Quarterly* 47 (December 1995): 563-94; and David Roediger, "*Guineas, Wiggers,* and the Dramas of Racialized Culture," *American Literary History* 7 (Winter 1995): 654-68.

wealth and worldwide connections and contacts were principally the result of his experiences in Jamaica, the slave colony where he worked as physician to the governor from 1687 to 1689. In the 1690s, Sloane married Elizabeth Rose, who was the widow of a wealthy planter, and it was the income he accrued from sugar and tobacco on his slave plantations that enabled him to make his vast purchases.[7]

The pressure of historical knowledge has impelled critics such as Gilroy and Said, in *Orientalism* (1978) and *Culture and Imperialism* (1993), to reexamine the origin and development of cultural discourses and institutions and to recast and redefine the field of literary and cultural studies. This process of critique and analysis is one that I think *Emmanuel Appadocca* both epitomizes and reinforces. As one reads Philip's book, it seems simultaneously English, American, and Caribbean (or, more precisely, Trinidadian). It is a multicultural, polyphonic "Atlantic" book that challenges, even as it capitalizes upon, traditional notions of what a "national" literature is and includes.

This dimension of *Emmanuel Appadocca*–its challenge to traditional, unduly narrow and highly nationalistic conceptions of the field–becomes clearer when we consider its date of publication and ponder its location in literary history. The novel was published in 1854, which for modern readers of American literature puts it in the midst of the "American Renaissance" of 1850-55, the period that takes its name from the title of the Harvard scholar F. O. Matthiessen's magisterial study published in 1941. In his book Matthiessen surveyed this five-year span of writings–an "extraordinarily concentrated moment of expression," he explained–that "saw the appearance" of Emerson's *Representative Men* (1850), Hawthorne's *The Scarlet*

---

7. See *Sir Hans Sloane: Collector, Scientist, Antiquary, Founding Father of the British Museum,* ed. Arthur Macgregor (London: British Museum, 1994). In *Stand the Storm: A History of the Atlantic Slave Trade* (1985; Chicago: Ivan R. Dee, 1993), Edward Reynolds points out that by 1700, English plantations in the Caribbean islands were producing half of the sugar consumed in Europe (65). See also Bryan Edwards, *The History, Civil and Commercial, of the British Colonies in the West Indies,* 2 vols. (London, 1793-94); and Richard B. Sheridan, *Sugar and Slavery: An Economic History of the British West Indies, 1623-1775* (Baltimore: Johns Hopkins University Press, 1974). Other valuable studies include: Leslie B. Rout, Jr., *The African Experience in Spanish America, 1502 to the Present Day* (Cambridge: Cambridge University Press, 1976); and Herbert S. Klein, *African Slavery in Latin America and the Caribbean* (New York: Oxford University Press, 1986). For the intellectual history of the region: Gordon K. Lewis, *Main Currents in Caribbean Thought: The Historical Evolution of Caribbean Society in Its Ideological Aspects, 1492-1900* (Baltimore: Johns Hopkins University Press, 1983). On Trinidad and Tobago: Bridget Brereton, *A History of Modern Trinidad, 1783-1962* (Exeter, N.H.: Heinemann, 1981).

Letter (1850) and *The House of the Seven Gables* (1851), Melville's *Moby-Dick* (1851) and *Pierre* (1852), Thoreau's *Walden* (1854), and Whitman's *Leaves of Grass* (1855).[8] Matthiessen's influence endured for several decades, and in certain respects—for example, his account of Emerson's theory of poetic language and his commentary on Melville's *Moby-Dick*—*American Renaissance* remains an essential source. But revisionists have disputed Matthiessen's canon and approach and have added to his list a range of texts that he neglected, did not know about, or else referred to only to set them to the side.

The American Renaissance now includes not only the books that Matthiessen honored, but also Susan Warner's *The Wide, Wide World* (1850), Harriet Beecher Stowe's *Uncle Tom's Cabin* (1852), Maria Cummins's *The Lamplighter* (1854), and Fanny Fern [Sara Payson Willis]'s *Ruth Hall* (1855).[9] Scholars have also delved into the popular culture of the period, into such texts as Ik Marvel [Donald Grant Mitchell]'s wistful *Reveries of a Bachelor* (1850) and T. S. Arthur's temperance novel, *Ten Nights in a Bar-Room* (1854).[10] There has also been innovative work on Anglo-American literary and cultural relations and on American texts' resemblances to and differences from European literatures. American writers were reading, responding to, feeling the influence of European and, especially, English authors formed by a richer, denser, fuller, and more fertile literary tradition.[11]

---

8. F. O. Matthiessen, *American Renaissance: Art and Expression in the Age of Emerson and Whitman* (1941; reprint, New York: Oxford University Press, 1972), vii. For background, see William E. Cain, *F. O. Matthiessen and the Politics of Criticism* (Madison: University of Wisconsin Press, 1988).

9. For influential studies of women's writing in the period, see Nina Baym, *Woman's Fiction: A Guide to Novels by and about Women in America, 1820–1870* (Ithaca: Cornell University Press, 1978); Mary Kelley, *Private Woman, Public Stage: Literary Domesticity in Nineteenth-Century America* (New York: Oxford University Press, 1984); and Jane Tompkins, *Sensational Designs: The Cultural Work of American Fiction, 1790–1860* (New York: Oxford University Press, 1985).

10. See David S. Reynolds, *Beneath the American Renaissance: The Subversive Imagination in the Age of Emerson and Melville* (1988; Cambridge: Harvard University Press, 1989); and Sheila Post-Lauria, *Correspondent Colorings: Melville in the Marketplace* (Amherst: University of Massachusetts Press, 1996).

11. For the argument that English and American literatures need to be studied as a single body of texts, see William C. Spengemann, *A Mirror for Americanists: Reflections on the Idea of American Literature* (Hanover, N.H.: University Press of New England, 1989). For related analyses, see Donald A. Ringe, *American Gothic: Imagination and Reason in Nineteenth-Century Fiction* (Lexington: University Press of Kentucky, 1982); Robert Weisbuch, *Atlantic Double-Cross: American Literature and British Influence in the Age of Emerson* (Chicago:

The "renaissance" of writing in America coincided with the production of the following texts in England, and the well-read Maxwell Philip likely would have known about all or most of them:

Dickens, *David Copperfield* (1850), *Bleak House* (1853), *Hard Times* (1854)
Elizabeth Barrett Browning, *Sonnets from the Portuguese* (1850)
Wordsworth, *The Prelude* (1850)
Tennyson, *In Memoriam* (1850) and *Maud and Other Poems* (1855)
Ruskin, *The Stones of Venice* (1851–53)
Thackeray, *The History of Henry Esmond* (1852)
Arnold, *Empedocles on Etna, and Other Poems* (1852)
Charlotte Brontë, *Villette* (1853)
Trollope, *The Warden* (1855)
Robert Browning, *Men and Women* (1855)

But when dealing with the American Renaissance and other familiar periods, it is not enough to gesture toward the convergence–or dissolution–of national literatures as they become reconceptualized as Atlantic rather than American or English. In the community of scholars, even more significant has been the return of American, and especially, American Renaissance texts to American and Atlantic *history,* above all to the history of the slave trade, slavery, and abolition.

Neither Matthiessen nor the scholars influenced by his work examined the consequences of slavery debate, discussion, and agitation for the production of literature. As a result, many texts by both whites and African Americans were excluded, and cross-cultural Anglo-American and Caribbean encounters were not perceived. Yet in the 1850s, slavery and abolition were immediate, momentous issues and the point of origin for a massive outpouring of texts of many kinds. In fact, when the Boston abolitionist Wendell Phillips summarized the "philosophy of the abolition movement" in 1853, he claimed that the speeches and writings that had flowed from the antislavery cause answered the appeals that had long been made for a dis-

University of Chicago Press, 1986); Leon Chai, *The Romantic Foundations of the American Renaissance* (Ithaca: Cornell University Press, 1987); Alden T. Vaughan and Virginia Mason Vaughan, *Shakespeare's Caliban: A Cultural History* (New York: Cambridge University Press, 1991); and Stephen Fender, *Sea Changes: British Emigration and American Literature* (New York: Cambridge University Press, 1992). On the connections between American literature and European political history, Larry J. Reynolds's *European Revolutions and the American Literary Renaissance* (New Haven: Yale University Press, 1988) is a valuable source.

tinctive literature for the new nation. "This discussion has been one of the noblest contributions to a literature really American," Phillips stated. Two years later, in his own review of the antislavery movement, Frederick Douglass declared that the 1850s would "be looked to by after-coming generations, as the age of anti-slavery literature."[12]

Among the important books written from 1850 to 1855 by white authors active in antislavery were Harriet Beecher Stowe's *Uncle Tom's Cabin* (1852), the radical minister Theodore Parker's *Speeches, Addresses, and Occasional Sermons,* 2 vols. (1852), the abolitionist William Lloyd Garrison's *Selections from the Writings and Speeches* (1852), and the abolitionist editor and intellectual Lydia Maria Child's *Isaac T. Hopper* (1854), a biography of a saintly Quaker who aided fugitive slaves. Aligned in opposition to these texts, and forming a potent if perverse counterdiscourse, were books, pamphlets, and articles written in defense of slavery, including *The Pro-Slavery Argument as Maintained by the Most Distinguished Writers of the Southern States* (1852), the South Carolina lawyer-politician William Grayson's didactic poem *The Hireling and the Slave* (1854), and the Virginia lawyer George Fitzhugh's *Sociology for the South; or, The Failure of Free Society* (1854).

African Americans, too, contributed to the literature of antislavery and had their own cluster of texts published between 1850 and 1855:

Daniel Payne, *Pleasures and Other Miscellaneous Poems* (1850)

Frederick Douglass, *Lectures on American Slavery* (1851) and *My Bondage and My Freedom* (1855)

Martin R. Delany, *The Condition, Elevation, Emigration and Destiny of the Colored People of the United States* (1852)

William C. Nell, *Services of Colored Americans in the Wars of 1775 and 1812* (1852; revised, 1855)

William Wells Brown, *Three Years in Europe; or, Places I Have Seen and People I Have Met* (1852); and *Clotel, or, The President's Daughter* (1853)

Solomon Northrup, *Twelve Years a Slave* (1853)

Frances Ellen Harper, *Poems on Miscellaneous Subjects* (1854)

12. Wendell Phillips, "Philosophy of the Abolition Movement," 1853, in *Wendell Phillips on Civil Rights and Freedom,* ed. Louis Filler (New York: Hill and Wang, 1965), 51; and Frederick Douglass, "The Anti-Slavery Movement," 1855, *The Life and Writings of Frederick Douglass,* ed. Philip S. Foner, 5 vols. (New York: International Publishers, 1950–75), 2:356. See also John Mercer Langston, "The World's Anti-Slavery Movement" (August 1858), in *Freedom and Citizenship: Selected Lectures and Addresses* (Washington, D.C.: Darby, 1883), 61.

These listings of American, English, and African American texts itemize and map the literary work done in the period and illuminate the cultural conjunctions and literary relationships that have altered older envisionings of the field of American literature; and they point to the body of knowledge that scholars and students should seek to master–the texts that the slavery crisis directly generated, and the texts not directly tied to it but nonetheless published at the same historical moment and touched by it. But for each "new" text, such as *Emmanuel Appadocca,* that we manage to recover, the contexts must be rearticulated and renewed through the patient accumulation of historical and literary detail. How should *Emmanuel Appadocca* be read and interpreted? What does it teach us about the literature, history, and culture of the 1850s and, especially, about the personal, familial, and political crisis that slavery and abolition triggered?[13]

Philip signals us how to begin the work of knowing *Emmanuel Appadocca* when he refers in its preface to the impact of American slavery on black mothers and their children as it seared his consciousness in the early 1850s. The events of the 1840s and 1850s intensified the sectional crisis in the United States and spurred the growth of antislavery sentiment, and these established the context within which Philip constructed his book. After disputes between the United States and Mexico over the annexation of Texas to the Union in 1845, and several incidents along the border, President James K. Polk asked Congress for a declaration of war. U.S. troops soon won major victories that led to the cessation of hostilities in February 1848 and to the acquisition of extensive lands in the southwest through the Treaty of Guadalupe Hidalgo. To many abolitionists, the purpose of the war,

13. For examples of revisionary work with which my commentary here might be compared, see *Slavery and the Literary Imagination,* ed. Deborah E. McDowell and Arnold Rampersad (Baltimore: Johns Hopkins University Press, 1989). For more general context: *Within the Circle: An Anthology of African American Literary Criticism from the Harlem Renaissance to the Present,* ed. Angelyn Mitchell (Durham, N.C.: Duke University Press, 1994). See also Moira Ferguson, *Colonialism and Gender Relations from Mary Wollstonecraft to Jamaica Kincaid: East Caribbean Connections* (New York: Columbia University Press, 1993); Sandra Adell, *Double-Consciousness/Double Bind: Theoretical Issues in Twentieth-Century Black Literature* (Urbana: University of Illinois Press, 1994); Michael North, *The Dialect of Modernism: Race, Language, and Twentieth-Century Literature* (New York: Oxford University Press, 1994); Lorna Valerie Williams, *The Representation of Slavery in Cuban Fiction* (Columbia: University of Missouri Press, 1994); Laura Doyle, *Bordering on the Body: The Racial Matrix of Modern Fiction and Culture* (New York: Oxford University Press, 1994); *The Discourse of Slavery: From Aphra Behn to Toni Morrison,* ed. Carl Plasa and Betty J. Ring (New York: Routledge, 1994); Craig Hansen Werner, *Playing the Changes: From Afro-Modernism to the Jazz Impulse* (Urbana: University of Illinois Press, 1994); and Geta Leseur, *Ten Is the Age of Darkness: The Black Bildungsroman* (Columbia: University of Missouri Press, 1995).

waged by a pro-South Democratic president, was to enlarge the domain of slavery. It proved that the South controlled the national government and made clear to them – at least to radicals like Garrison – the folly of relying on political means to bring about emancipation.

Yet it is important to note that one of the main opponents of slavery expansion was a congressman, an antislavery Democrat from Pennsylvania, David Wilmot, who introduced a measure in the House (the so-called Wilmot Proviso) in August 1846, that would have prohibited slavery in any territory acquired during the war. This measure was debated for years (it never received congressional approval), and it showed the cracks in political parties that the battles over slavery had caused. By the late 1840s, slavery was steadily becoming an issue that, somehow, was going to be focused and decided politically, in the midst of congressional debates and laws, party conventions, state and national elections.[14]

The Compromise of 1850 reinforced this point, and it is the piece of legislation that lies behind Philip's words in his preface. Supported by the distinguished U.S. senators Henry Clay, Stephen A. Douglas, and Daniel Webster, the Compromise was intended to resolve the strife between the North and South that slavery had engendered. It included provisions favorable to antislavery: the slave trade was prohibited in the District of Columbia, and California was admitted to the Union as a free state. But the Compromise also enacted a severe fugitive slave law (passed in September 1850) that denied a jury trial to, and prohibited the testimony of, escaped slaves and that imposed penalties on anyone who aided them.

This law imperiled all African American men and women; as the historian John Hope Franklin has said, "virtually every free person of color was in imminent danger of being taken up and placed in slavery with no opportunity whatever to establish a valid claim to freedom."[15] It enraged many whites in the North, for it mandated that all citizens assist in the capture of runaways and, inevitably, in the breakup of African American families in the northern free states. It brought slavery home to white men and women who may not have supported it but who had concluded that it was really a

14. On the Mexican war, see Alfred Hoyt Bill, *Rehearsal for Conflict: The War with Mexico, 1846–1848* (New York: Knopf, 1947); and Robert W. Johannsen, *To the Halls of the Montezumas: The Mexican War in the American Imagination* (New York: Oxford University Press, 1985). On the Wilmot Proviso, see Chaplain W. Morrison, *Democratic Politics and Sectionalism: The Wilmot Proviso Controversy* (Chapel Hill: University of North Carolina Press, 1967).

15. John Hope Franklin, "Race and the Constitution in the Nineteenth Century," in *African Americans and the Living Constitution,* ed. John Hope Franklin and Genna Rae McNeil (Washington, D.C.: Smithsonian Institution Press, 1995), 25.

social problem that bedeviled another region. Ralph Waldo Emerson called the law a "filthy enactment," adding "I will not obey it, by God."[16] Speaking on May 3, 1851, to the citizens of Concord, Massachusetts, Emerson declared: "An immoral law makes it a man's duty to break it, at every hazard. . . . If resistance to this law is not right, there is no right."[17]

The crucial, vexed term here is "resistance." What did resistance mean? Could it justifiably include violence? What was the difference, if any, between resistance and rebellion? Were African Americans, on their own or with the assistance of whites, within their rights to *fight* for freedom and take arms against their enslavers and captors? This set of questions engaged Garrison, Emerson, and other radicals and reformers, and it is this same set that is explored in Philip's *Emmanuel Appadocca,* published in the immediate aftermath of the Fugitive Slave Law and the heated debates and violent outbreaks of resistance that it sparked.[18]

Speaking in Ithaca, New York, on October 14, 1852, Frederick Douglass stated that the Fugitive Slave Law had taken away the excuse, previously tendered by Northerners, that slavery was southern and sectional, not national: "If it never was before, [slavery] is now an American institution, to be maintained by all the powers of the American government. . . . There is not one spot in the Republic sacred to freedom; but every inch of soil is given up to slavery, slave-hunting, slave-catching, and slaveholding."[19]

The former slave Douglass knew all too well how deeply entrenched slavery had become in America. During the period from 1780 to 1810, almost as many Africans were shipped to the United States as in the 160 years from 1620 to 1780. The slave population expanded by 33 percent between 1800 and 1810, and by another 29 percent between 1810 and 1820. Despite the Atlantic slave trade's termination in 1808, the slave

16. Ralph Waldo Emerson, *Emerson in His Journals,* ed. Joel Porte (Cambridge: Harvard University Press, 1982), 429.

17. Ralph Waldo Emerson, "Address to the Citizens of Concord on the Fugitive Slave Law," in *Emerson's Anti-Slavery Writings,* ed. Len Gougeon and Joel Myerson (New Haven: Yale University Press, 1995), 57. See Len Gougeon, *Virtue's Hero: Emerson, Antislavery, and Reform* (Athens: University of Georgia, 1990).

18. The importance of the term "resistance" for the analysis of southern and Caribbean slavery has been developed by my coeditor, Selwyn R. Cudjoe, in his pioneering book, *Resistance and Caribbean Literature* (Athens: Ohio University Press, 1980). For further articulations of this theme, see also Cudjoe, *V. S. Naipaul: A Materialist Reading* (Amherst: University of Massachusetts Press, 1988); and *Eric Williams Speaks: Essays on Colonialism and Independence,* ed. Selwyn R. Cudjoe (Wellesley: Calaloux Publications; distributed by the University of Massachusetts Press, 1993).

19. Foner, *Life and Writings,* 5:260.

population in the United States soared, its number boosted by illegal trading and slave breeding and interstate slave trading. Between 1808 and 1860, the slave population tripled; and the profit from investment in slaves averaged an impressive 10 percent during the 1840s and 1850s. Slaves were "capital assets" that brought a return equal to or exceeding other kinds of investments; and by the 1850s, slaveowners in the East were shipping and selling 25,000 slaves to the West each year.[20]

Between the 1770s and the 1850s, slavery simultaneously diminished and grew, dying out in the North and West and enlarging in the South and consequently in the body politic. By the 1850s, the decade of the American Renaissance and the historical moment when Phillip wrote *Emmanuel Appadocca,* four million slaves lived in the South, compared to five hundred thousand in the colonies at the outset of the Revolution in 1775-76. The British Parliament had passed its own Slave Emancipation Act in 1833, but twenty years later, when Philip was writing, slavery in the southern states was "flourishing as never before."[21]

Philip's preface cries out against the brutalities inflicted on slave women and their children. Their suffering was a bitter point for many African American abolitionists—Douglass highlighted it repeatedly in his autobiographies and speeches—and it inflamed their activism and, increasingly, their calls for resistance. Between 1820 and 1860, two million blacks were sold; and 25 percent of all slave families were disrupted by the sale of at least one member of the family. Masters claimed that they sought to keep slave families together; to an extent they did, and this led to family and kinship networks on single plantations and those nearby. But "slave family" for the

20. Roger L. Ransom and Richard Sutch, "Who Pays for Slavery?" in *The Wealth of Races: The Present Value of Benefits from Past Injustices,* ed. Richard F. America (Westport: Greenwood, 1990), 31. For other statistics cited in this paragraph, see Steven Mintz, ed., *African-American Voices: The Life Cycle of Slavery* (St. James, N.Y.: Brandywine, 1993); David Northrup, *The Atlantic Slave Trade* (Lexington, Mass.: D. C. Heath, 1994); and Richard H. Sewell, *A House Divided: Sectionalism and Civil War, 1848-1865* (Baltimore: Johns Hopkins University Press, 1988). It is estimated that ten million Africans survived the transatlantic journey (the "middle passage") to slavery. Most were sent to Brazil and the West Indies; only 4 to 6 percent of the total were delivered to the American colonies. But by 1860, 66 percent of the slaves in the New World were in the American South.

21. C. Vann Woodward, *The Future of the Past* (New York: Oxford University Press, 1989), 181. Abolitionists in the United States faced a difficult challenge; unlike their colleagues in Great Britain, who took up the cause of slaves far away in the Caribbean, they had to argue for emancipation and *then* explain what should be done with (and for) the millions of African Americans who would be freed. Many Americans supported slavery; many who opposed it on moral grounds could not imagine the United States as a biracial society in which white and black races would be equal.

master usually meant a mother and her children, not the father.[22] Families were torn apart, and the chances of freedom (and restoration of family) by the master's initiative declined with each decade. As the scholar Richard Bardolph has noted, "the chances for the freeing of a slave living in Virginia . . . in the generation preceding 1800 were about one in ten; in 1800 to 1832 about one in twenty; in 1832 to 1860 and one in fifty."[23]

Black women were sexually exposed to, and victimized by, their white owners, as Philip's novel bears witness; and black men who sought to protect their women faced reprisals and legal punishments. Domestic slaves were especially at risk, and, as James Walvin indicates in his study of colonial slavery, the result was often complicatedly painful: "slave children, offspring of white masters and their slaves, became servants to their half-brothers and sisters."[24]

The constant threat and frequent reality of attacks and separations of loved ones describe only part of a complex story. The family was an institution that black men, women, and children cherished and fought to preserve; it was central to their lives, and, when it did suffer violation, when family members were separated, it remained keenly alive in memory. The slave family, Walvin concludes, "provided an immediate and wider network for all stages of slave life," and in colonial America it "emerged from the most unpromising of circumstances to become the most durable and resilient of slave institutions."[25] It was precisely because the family as an institution was highly valued that African Americans were willing to defend their families with resolve and courage against extreme odds.

Slavery's assault on the African American family had always been featured in antislavery and abolitionist arguments, and Philip's point of departure thus has ample precedent. In, for example, the preamble to a measure

22. See Deborah Gray White, *Ar'n't I a Woman: Female Slaves in the Plantation South* (New York: Norton, 1985), 145; and Douglas R. Egerton, *Gabriel's Rebellion: The Virginia Slave Conspiracies of 1800 and 1802* (Chapel Hill: University of North Carolina Press, 1993), 16-17. See also two important contemporary writings: Harriet Wilson, *Our Nig* (1859), and Harriet Jacobs, *Incidents in the Life of a Slave Girl* (1860). Also noteworthy are Aphra Behn's *Oroonoko* (1688, and frequently reprinted thereafter), which tells of a slave's murder of his pregnant wife; and Elizabeth Barrett Browning's "The Runaway Slave at Pilgrim's Point," first published in *The Liberty Bell*, 1848, in which a black woman relates her murder of a mulatto child whom she conceived when she was violated by her master. See *The Complete Poetical Works of Elizabeth Barrett Browning* (Boston: Houghton, Mifflin, 1900), 191-95.

23. Richard Bardolph, *The Negro Vanguard* (New York: Vintage, 1959), 56.

24. James Walvin, *Black Ivory: A History of British Slavery* (1992; Washington, D.C.: Howard University Press, 1994), 131-32.

25. Ibid., 207.

passed by the Pennsylvania Assembly, March 1, 1780, which was one of the
first calls for the emancipation of slaves in America, the author or authors
(one of whom may have been Thomas Paine) emphasized that bondage not
only deprived slaves "of the common blessings that they were by nature
entitled to, but has cast them into the deepest afflictions, by an unnatural
separation and sale of husband and wife from each other and from their
children, an injury, the greatness of which can only be conceived by supposing that we were in the same unhappy case."[26] Half a century later, in 1835,
the Unitarian minister William Ellery Channing reaffirmed this judgment:
"Slavery virtually dissolves the domestic relations. It ruptures the most
sacred ties on earth. It violates home. It lacerates the best affections. . . .
The slave's home is desecrated."[27] In *Letters on American Slavery* (1837),
John Rankin, a Presbyterian minister in Ohio, concluded: "In the boasted
land of freedom . . . you may hear the clankings of the chains that bind
innocent husbands, and wives, and parents, and children, in order that they
are to be forever separated from the objects of their affections, and all that is
dear to them in life!"[28]

At the dawn of the organized abolitionist movement in the 1830s, many
believed that by making such abuses of the African American family widely
known, they could create the impetus for peaceful emancipation. But it
quickly became clear that few in the South would heed appeals to end the
sufferings that slave families endured. Garrison observed, for example, in a
November 6, 1837, letter to Elizabeth Pease, a Quaker abolitionist in England: "Upon the slaveholding States, we make no perceptible impression.
No opponent of slavery can tread upon their soil, as an abolitionist, without
the risk of martyrdom. I have relinquished the expectation, that they will
ever, by mere moral suasion, consent to emancipate their victims. I believe
that nothing but the exterminating judgments of heaven can shatter the
chain of the slave, and destroy the power of his oppressor."[29]

Garrison placed his faith in God, but some African Americans were less
trusting of divine intervention, as a noteworthy exchange between Douglass

26. *The Complete Writings of Thomas Paine,* ed. Philip S. Foner, 2 vols. (New York: Citadel,
1945), 2:22. On the question of Paine's authorship, see John Keane, *Tom Paine: A Political
Life* (Boston: Little, Brown, 1995), 572–73.

27. *The Works of William E. Channing* (Boston: American Unitarian Association, 1888),
711.

28. John Rankin, *Letters on American Slavery* (1837; reprint, Westport: Negro Universities
Press, 1970), 44.

29. *The Letters of William Lloyd Garrison,* ed. Walter M. Merrill and Louis Ruchames,
6 vols. (Cambridge: Harvard University Press, 1971–81), 2:324.

and the African American Presbyterian clergyman and abolitionist Henry Highland Garnet at the National Convention of Colored Citizens, Buffalo, August 15-19, 1843, demonstrated. Douglass–at that time close to Garrison in his views–objected to Garnet's emphasis on "physical force," saying that he was "for trying moral means a little longer" and warning of the danger to the blacks of any "insurrection" they might launch against the slaveholding power. Garnet said in reply that he simply was advising slaves "to go to their masters and tell them they wanted their liberty, and had come to ask for it; and if the master refused it, to tell them, then we shall take it, let the consequence be what it may."[30]

Emmanuel Appadocca confronts the meaning of *taking* liberty and the slave's right to resist and remedy the exploitation and oppression of black women and their offspring. For Philip, as for others, morality dictated not that African Americans wait patiently on God's will, but, rather, that they abide by the higher law–the law higher than any made by the State–that God had inscribed in the hearts of all persons. Many reformers and abolitionists clung to higher law doctrine, though they differed in their response to its implications. Some of them, such as Garnet, coupled it to violent resistance, whereas others, such as Garrison and Henry David Thoreau, defined it in terms of nonviolent civil disobedience.

It was in fact an antislavery U.S. senator from New York, William H. Seward, who thrust this "higher law" view into sociopolitical discourse in a March 11, 1850, speech in the Senate: "There is no human enactment which is just that is not a re-enactment of the law of God. . . . Wherever I find a law of God, or a law of nature disregarded or in danger of being disregarded, there I shall vote to reaffirm it, with all the sanction of the civil authority."[31]

These were astonishing words for a statesman to utter, and they shocked supporters of slavery and many moderates as well. As the historian David Brion Davis has shown, Southerners connected the defense of their peculiar institution to the laws of the nation, reaching back to the proslavery clauses of the Constitution. "Unlike the planters of the Caribbean," Davis states,

30. *Minutes of the Proceedings of the National Negro Conventions, 1830–1864,* ed. Howard Holman Bell (New York: Arno, 1969), 13. When Garnet published his speech five years later, he toned down its insurrectionary sentiments, counseling resistance but adding "we do not advise you to attempt a revolution with the sword." Cited in Blyden Jackson, *A History of Afro-American Literature,* vol. 1 (Baton Rouge: Louisiana State University Press, 1989), 194.

31. Frederic Bancroft, *The Life of William H. Seward,* 2 vols. (New York: Harper, 1900), 1:247.

"southern slaveholders held a fixed bastion within the national government; their political power drew sanction from the supreme law of the land."[32] Many others who opposed slavery on principle nonetheless averred that the law of the land had to be respected, for otherwise the Constitution would be subverted and the Union placed in grave danger.

Yet it was unclear exactly what Seward's position was. Did he mean that the Fugitive Slave Law should be disobeyed? Or was he making a rhetorical point, stating a theoretical tenet while not necessarily counseling action? Was violent opposition to the law warranted? Should laws that conflicted with higher law be set aside, flouted, countered if need be by force of arms? Seward answered that he did not mean any of these things; he said he was making explicit what everybody already knew–that the Fugitive Slave Law could not be enforced and that legitimate "civil authority" could be invoked to justify resistance to forms of civil authority that were morally indefensible.[33]

"Resistance" was a charged, complex idea that involved issues of law and justice. It could connote refusal to obey law; it could suggest forcible response to unjust law; or it could be deployed to justify seizing and protecting freedom by violent means. As the example of Emmanuel Appadocca in Philip's novel reveals, it could also mean vengeance–bloody retaliatory action taken to punish the sins that slaveholders had committed.[34]

32. David Brion Davis, *The Problem of Slavery in an Age of Revolution, 1770–1823* (Ithaca: Cornell University Press, 1975), 107.

33. Bancroft, *Life,* 1:259. For studies of violence, nonresistance, and abolition, see Merle Curti, "Non-Resistance in New England," *New England Quarterly* 2 (January 1929): 34–57; L. D. Turner, "Antislavery Sentiment in Literature: The Second Period of Militant Abolitionism, 1850–1861," *Journal of Negro History* 14 (October 1929): 440–75; Herbert Aptheker, "Militant Abolitionism," *Journal of Negro History* 26 (October 1941): 438–84; Howard Bell, "Expressions of Negro Militancy in the North, 1840–1860," *Journal of Negro History* 45 (January 1960): 11–20; John Demos, "The Antislavery Movement and the Problem of Violent Means," *New England Quarterly* 37 (December 1964): 501–26; William H. Pease and Jane H. Pease, "Confrontation and Abolition in the 1850s," *Journal of American History* 58 (March 1972): 923–37; Bertram Wyatt-Brown, "John Brown, Weathermen, and the Psychology of Antinomian Violence," *Soundings* 58 (Winter 1975): 425–41; Charles B. Dew, "Black Ironworkers and the Slave Insurrection Panic of 1856," *Journal of Southern History* 61 (1975): 321–38; Lawrence J. Friedman, "Antebellum American Abolitionism and the Problem of Violent Means," *Psychohistory Review* 9 (Fall 1980): 23–58; and John R. McKivigan, "James Redpath, John Brown, and Abolitionist Advocacy of Slave Insurrection," *Civil War History* 37 (1991): 293–313.

34. Student of the classics that he was, Philip may have interpreted the higher law in the context of Greek tragedy and philosophy. See, for example, Sophocles' Antigone, who declares that Creon must abide by the law behind the law: "All your strength is weakness itself against/The immortal unrecorded laws of God" (*Antigone,* scene 2). In his address on the

The events of the early 1850s drove abolitionists toward understanding resistance as involving violence. One can see this in Theodore Parker's sermons and writings following the passage of the Fugitive Slave Law. In his "Sermon on the Function and Place of Conscience," in Boston, September 1850, Parker declared: "The fugitive has the same natural right to defend himself against the slave-catcher, or his constitutional tool, that he has against a murderer or a wolf. The man who attacks me to reduce me to slavery, in that moment of attack alienates his right to life, and if I were the fugitive, and could escape in no other way, I would kill him with as little compunction as I would drive a mosquito from my face."[35] In another sermon in Boston, titled "The State of the Nation," November 28, 1850, Parker said that the United States was caught in a struggle between democracy and despotism. "Which," he asked, "shall recede? which be extended? Freedom or slavery?" These questions, he explained, could only be answered by fidelity to the higher law and opposition to any human law that was substituted for it: "Ambitious men, in an act of passion, make iniquity into a law, and then demand that you and I, in our act of prayer, shall submit to it and make it our daily life; that we shall not try to repeal and discuss and agitate it! This false idea lies at the basis of every despot's throne, the idea that men can make right wrong, and wrong right."[36]

On April 12, 1852, Parker spoke on the first anniversary of the remanding of Thomas Sims, an African American who had been living in Boston and who had fallen victim to the Fugitive Slave Law. "I am a friend of law," Parker averred, "but such an outrage on all law and right I will not obey. I will tear it in pieces and trample it underfoot."[37] In a letter he wrote on September 25, 1852, to the abolitionist Samuel May, Parker noted: "I respect the statutes which men have made only so far as they embody Justice and conserve the Unalienable Rights of men. When statutes fail thereof, or go beyond that, I have no respect for them."[38]

Samuel May had already preached against the law, most notably in a

---

Fugitive Slave Law (May 3, 1851), Emerson stated that he had identified precedents for the idea of "Higher Law" in Cicero, Grotius, Blackstone, Montesquieu, Burke, and Jefferson. See *Anti-slavery Writings,* 59. See also Ainsworth Spofford, *The Higher Law Tried by Reason and Authority* (New York: S. W. Benedict, 1851).

35. See *The Trial of Theodore Parker* (Boston, 1855), 186.

36. Theodore Parker, "The State of the Nation," Sermon for Thanksgiving Day, November 28, 1850 (Boston, 1851), 20, 24.

37. Theodore Parker, in *The Liberator,* April 16, 1852.

38. Cited in Michael Fellman, "Theodore Parker and the Abolitionist Role in the 1850s," *Journal of American History* 61 (December 1974): 670.

sermon he delivered in October 1850, in Syracuse, Rochester, and Oswego, New York. Again the emphasis was on the higher law: "The assumption of Mr. Webster and his abettors–that there is no higher law than an enactment of our Congress or the Constitution of the United States–is glaringly *atheistical,* inasmuch as it denies the supremacy of the Divine Author of the *moral constitution* of man." May said that he was a nonresistant himself but knew why others believed that force was now warranted, so grievous was the Fugitive Slave Law as an offense against God's law:

> If you are fully persuaded that it would be right for you to maim or kill the kidnapper who had laid hands upon your wife, son, or daughter, or should be attempting to drag yourself away to be enslaved, I see not how you can excuse yourself from helping, by the same degree of violence, to rescue the fugitive slave from the like outrage. . . . Before all men, I declare that you are, every one of you, under the highest obligation to disobey this law,–nay, oppose to the utmost the execution of it. If you know of no better way to do this than by force of arms, then you are bound to use force and arms to prevent a fellow-being from being enslaved. There never was, there cannot be, a more righteous cause for revolution than the demands made upon us by this law. It would make you kidnappers, men-stealers, bloodhounds.[39]

These sentiments are even more starkly evident in writings by African Americans, who were, as the historian Curtis D. Johnson has stated, "more open to violent solutions than were their white counterparts" and who turned to "Old Testament examples of divinely sanctioned destruction and New Testament apocalyptic hope" to buttress their arguments in favor of violent means.[40]

American political rhetoric was also a powerful source for the justification of violence, and African Americans frequently invoked the Founding Fathers and heroes of 1776. For example, in an October 1, 1850, letter to Douglass's paper, the *North Star,* William P. Newman announced that the fight for freedom by slaves and the protection of their families could justifiably reach even to the killing of the president: "I am proud to say that Patrick Henry's motto is mine–'Give me Liberty or give me Death.' . . . It is my fixed and changeless purpose to kill any so-called man who attempts to enslave me or mine, if possible, though it be Millard Fillmore himself."[41]

---

39. Samuel May, *Some Recollections on Our Anti-Slavery Conflict* (1869; Miami: Mnemosyne, 1969), 361–62.

40. Curtis D. Johnson, *Redeeming America: Evangelicals and the Road to Civil War* (Chicago: Ivan R. Dee, 1993), 138.

41. William P. Newman, in *The Black Abolitionist Papers,* ed. C. Peter Ripley et al., 5 vols. (Chapel Hill: University of North Carolina Press, 1985–92), 4:64. For discussion of the links

Charles H. Langston, at the "Convention of the Colored Citizens of Ohio," in Columbus, Ohio, January 15-18, 1851, drew upon the Declaration of Independence while attacking the Constitution as proslavery, as "made to foster and uphold that abominable, vampirish and bloody system of American slavery." Langston said he "would call on every slave, from Maryland to Texas, to arise and assert their *liberties,* and cut their masters' throats if they attempt again to reduce them to slavery."[42] Douglass, in a speech on the Fugitive Slave Law, at the National Free Soil Convention, Pittsburgh, August 11, 1852, professed that "the only way to make the Fugitive Slave Law a dead letter is to make half a dozen or more dead kidnappers."[43]

These calls by African Americans for violent resistance in defense of freedom and family developed and carried forward a pattern of militant argument that the Boston abolitionist David Walker had expressed in his fiery *Appeal,* published in 1829 and reissued in 1830.

> Now, I ask you, had you not rather be killed than to be a slave to a tyrant, who takes the life of your mother, wife, and dear little children? Look upon your mother, wife and children, and answer God Almighty! and believe this, that it is no more harm for you to kill a man, who is trying to kill you, than it is for you to take a drink of water when thirsty; in fact, the man who will stand still and let another murder him, is worse than an infidel, and, if he has common sense, ought not to be pitied.[44]

---

between revolutionary discourse and abolition, see R. A. Yoder, "The First Romantics and the Last Revolution," *Studies in Romanticism* 15 (Fall 1976): 493-529; George B. Forgie, *Patricide in the House Divided: A Psychological Interpretation of Lincoln and His Age* (New York: Norton, 1979); Kenneth M. Stampp, *The Imperiled Union: Essays on the Background of the Civil War* (New York: Oxford University Press, 1980), 3-36; and Eric J. Sundquist, "Slavery, Revolution, and the American Renaissance," in *The American Renaissance Reconsidered,* ed. Walter Benn Michaels and Donald Pease (Baltimore: Johns Hopkins University Press, 1985), 1-33.

42. Charles H. Langston, in *Proceedings of the Black State Conventions, 1840-1865,* ed. Philip S. Foner and George E. Walker, 2 vols. (Philadelphia: Temple University Press, 1979), 1:263. See also William J. Watkins, June 2, 1854, editorial in *Frederick Douglass' Paper;* and Dr. John S. Rock, March 5, 1858, address in Boston, in *A Documentary History of the Negro People in the United States: From Colonial Times Through the Civil War,* ed. Herbert Aptheker (1951; New York: Citadel, 1967), 402-5.

43. Frederick Douglass, "Speech on the Fugitive Slave Law," in *Life and Writings,* 2:207. Three years earlier, in a speech in Boston in 1849, Douglass said: "I should welcome the intelligence tomorrow, should it come, that the slaves had risen in the South, and that the sable arms which had been engaged in beautifying and adorning the South, were engaged in spreading death and devastation." Cited in William S. McFeely, *Frederick Douglass* (New York: Norton, 1991), 192.

44. David Walker, *"One Continual Cry": David Walker's "Appeal to the Colored Citizens of the World"* (1829; 3rd. ed., 1830), ed. Herbert Aptheker (New York: Humanities, 1980), 89.

Garrison published parts of Walker's text in early issues of *The Liberator,* begun in Boston in January 1831. Walker's position, circulated widely, was very controversial and alarmed many abolitionists as well as supporters of slavery. Garrison, a pacifist himself, insisted he was always opposed to violence, yet he conceded that if violence could be used by whites for their defense of liberty, then it could equally well be used by black slaves. The lessons of the American Revolution, in other words, applied to all persons, not to one privileged race only. In his January 8, 1831, issue, Garrison noted the contradiction that white Americans were unwilling to deal with: "A white man, who kills a tyrant, is a hero, and deserves a monument. If a slave kills his master, he is a murderer, and deserves to be burnt."[45]

Eight months later, in Southampton County, Virginia, Nat Turner and a small band of followers rebelled against their white masters, rallied dozens of slaves to their side, and killed sixty whites. Not long afterward reports began to arrive of a massive slave revolt in Jamaica in December 1831, which evoked for many in the United States and abroad the terrors of the rebellion by black slaves in Saint Domingue (the western part of Haiti) in the Caribbean in August 1791, and the recollection of plans for insurrection in Virginia (1800), Louisiana (1811), and South Carolina (1822). These revolts and conspiracies heightened fears in the white population about the consequences of easing or ending slavery, and they formed a disturbing background for the invocations of, and responses to, the idea of violent slave resistance in the 1850s. Whenever white and African American abolitionists called for violence, or, like Philip's Emmanuel Appadocca, espoused revenge and retaliation, they rekindled the images of murder, rape, and the violation of white families that African American and Caribbean slaves had proposed or undertaken.[46]

---

45. Reprinted in *William Lloyd Garrison and the Fight against Slavery: Selections from "The Liberator,"* ed. William E. Cain (Boston: Bedford Books, 1995), 75.

46. On Nat Turner, see Herbert Aptheker, *Nat Turner's Slave Rebellion* (New York: Humanities Press, 1966); Stephen B. Oates, *The Fires of Jubilee: Nat Turner's Fierce Rebellion* (New York: New American Library, 1975); and Henry Irving Tragle, ed., *The Southampton Slave Revolt of 1831: A Compilation of Source Material* (Amherst: University of Massachusetts Press, 1971). On slave revolts in general, see Herbert Aptheker, *American Negro Slave Revolts* (1943; New York: International, 1974); Eugene D. Genovese, *From Rebellion to Revolution: Afro-American Slave Revolts in the Making of the Modern World* (Baton Rouge: Louisiana State University Press, 1979); and Robin Blackburn, *The Overthrow of Colonial Slavery* (London: Verso, 1988). Also relevant are Emilia Viotti da Costa, *Crowns of Glory, Tears of Blood: The Demerara Slave Rebellion of 1823* (New York: Oxford University Press, 1994), which describes the revolt of ten to twenty thousand slaves in the British colony of Demerara (now Guyana); and Abigail B. Bakan, *Ideology and Class Conflict in Jamaica: The Politics of*

In the aftermath of the failed Southampton revolt of the prior year, a white Jamaican wrote to the governor in 1832, using phrasing relevant to the situation in the southern states: "The question will not be left to the arbitrament of a long angry discussion between the Government and the planter. The slave himself has been taught that there is a third party, and that party [is] himself. He knows his strength, and will assert his claim to freedom. Even at this moment, unawed by the late failure, he discusses the question with a fixed determination."[47] By the 1850s, whites in the United States as well as in the Caribbean recognized that the slave could be an agent, indeed a bloody one, in his seizure of freedom and defense of mothers and children.

One way of explaining the extraordinary impact of Stowe's *Uncle Tom's Cabin,* published in 1852, two years before *Emmanuel Appadocca,* is that it ratified long-lingering fears of slave revolt and insurrection even as it presented alternatives to them. Tom triumphs through Christian meekness over his diabolic tormentor Simon Legree, who learned his horrid tortures, according to the mulatto slave Cassy, "among the pirates in the West Indies." Stowe depicts Tom's heroism alongside another, more problematic and disturbing kind, embodied in the mulatto George Harris, who makes his "declaration of independence" against the slavehunters who pursue him, firing his pistol and saying, like Patrick Henry, that he will fight for liberty or die in the attempt. Stowe compares Harris not only to the patriots of 1776 but to the Hungarian freedom fighters of 1848–49 whose revolution many Americans had celebrated.

Later, Augustine St. Clare tells his brother Alfred that the mulattoes among the slaves will lead the Africans' quest and campaign for freedom, and he connects his prophecy to the slave rebellion in Saint Domingue in the 1790s: "If ever the San Domingo hour comes, Anglo Saxon blood will lead on the day. Sons of white fathers, with all our haughty feelings burning in their veins, will not always be bought and sold and traded. They will rise, and raise with them their mother's race."[48]

Rebellion (Montreal: McGill-Queens University Press, 1990), which examines the Jamaica revolt of 1831.

47. Cited in Eric Williams, *From Columbus to Castro: The History of the Caribbean* (1970; New York: Vintage, 1984), 325.

48. Harriet Beecher Stowe, *Uncle Tom's Cabin* (1852; New York: Penguin, 1982), 534, 298–99, 392. See also William Wells Brown, *Clotel, or, the President's Daughter* (1853; reprint, New York: Arno, 1969), 211. On the mulatto figure in literature, see Jules Zanger, "The 'Tragic Octoroon' in Pre-Civil War Fiction," *American Quarterly* 18 (Spring 1966): 63–70;

Stowe presents Tom as the hero of her book; he is a "black saint."[49] But her portrait of George Harris, whose violence she evokes and then tries to control and contain in an acceptable rhetorical form (comparing him to the heroes of 1776), shows her awareness of the limits of Tom's heroism. As the literary critic Theophus H. Smith has acutely pointed out in discussing Stowe's text, "evidence of the innocence or virtues of a victim is far from constituting a bar to victimization; they can ironically activate and even attract scapegoating attacks."[50] Tom practices Christian piety: this is his strength, but it does not ward off victimization; it may even invite it, as Legree's ever-intensifying brutality toward Tom illustrates. Tom receives his reward in heaven for his Christian fortitude and submissiveness. But George Harris is rewarded, too: he does not suffer for fighting for *his* freedom. He survives and prospers with his family, though Stowe does at the conclusion locate their future as lying outside the United States, in the colony of Liberia.

Emmanuel Appadocca, like George Harris, is the son of a white father, and in this respect and in others, Philip positions his novel in relation to slavery in America, with its crimes against the family and the demands for violent response to them.[51] But this point needs to be qualified somewhat, and in a way that brings out one of *Emmanuel Appadocca*'s most intriguing

---

Judith R. Berzon, *Neither White nor Black: The Mulatto Character in American Fiction* (New York: New York University Press, 1978); and Wernor Sollors, " 'Never Was Born': The Mulatto, An American Tragedy," *Massachusetts Review* 27 (1986): 293–316. Also helpful are Lorenzo Dow Turner, *Anti-Slavery Sentiment in American Literature Prior to 1865* (1929; Port Washington, N.Y.: Kennikat Press, 1966); Jean Fagan Yellin, *The Intricate Knot: Black Figures in American Literature, 1776–1863* (New York: New York University Press, 1972); and James Kinney, *Amalgamation!: Race, Sex, and Rhetoric in the Nineteenth-Century American Novel* (Westport: Greenwood, 1985). For recent criticism on *Uncle Tom's Cabin*, see *New Essays on "Uncle Tom's Cabin,"* ed. Eric J. Sundquist (New York: Cambridge University Press, 1986); and *The Stowe Debate: Rhetorical Strategies in "Uncle Tom's Cabin,"* ed. Mason I. Lowance, Jr., Ellen E. Westbrook, and R. C. De Prospo (Amherst: University of Massachusetts Press, 1994). For a suggestive commentary on Stowe and stage adaptations of *Uncle Tom's Cabin,* which treats race, class, and politics, see Eric Lott, *Love and Theft: Blackface Minstrelsy and the American Working Class* (New York: Oxford University Press, 1993), 211–33.

49. Edwin Cady, " 'As Through a Glass Eye, Darkly': The Bible in the Nineteenth-Century Novel," in *The Bible and American Arts and Letters,* ed. Giles Gunn (Philadelphia: Fortress Press, 1983), 40.

50. Theophus H. Smith, *Conjuring Culture: Biblical Formations of Black America* (New York: Oxford University Press, 1994), 194.

51. The U.S. census of 1850 lists 159,095 mulattoes as "free Negro," and 246,656 as "slave." This suggests that although many white fathers had freed their mixed-race offspring, an even larger number had not. See James Hugo Johnston, *Race Relations in Virginia and Miscegenation in the South, 1776–1860* (Amherst: University of Massachusetts Press, 1970), 236.

features. Slavery is condemned by the action of the novel but it is not often, and not often explicitly, *named* in it. Given the wounded tone of the preface, one might have expected that Philip would saturate the text with repeated overt references to, and denunciations of, slavery and the evils that it has wrought. This would have made *Emmanuel Appadocca* a companion piece to such manifestly antislavery texts as *Uncle Tom's Cabin* and Douglass's *The Heroic Slave,* another tale of African American resistance on the model of 1776 that was included in the important collection *Autographs for Freedom,* published in 1853. For modern scholars, it might also then seem a prophetic preview of Melville's *Benito Cereno,* a tale of slave revolt at sea published in *Putnam's Monthly* in October–November 1855, and Martin R. Delany's *Blake; or the Huts of America,* a novel about a planned insurrection by Cuban slaves published serially in 1861–62 (sections had appeared earlier, in 1859).

Although *Emmanuel Appadocca* has affinities with these texts, it is, again, a different kind of book, one that both does and does not derive and develop its meanings from slavery and abolition. Philip's novel is forthrightly antislavery in its implications, and its potent critique would be missed if today's readers were unaware of its historical contexts. Yet *Emmanuel Appadocca* is more metaphysical than this designation implies, for its intent is to dramatize issues of philosophy, ethics, and religion that are only partially tied to slavery. This goal is in keeping with Philip's conception of his literary performance articulated in his preface and through his epigraphs and webs of classical allusion and reference.

Emmanuel Appadocca is everywhere "about" slavery, yet is at the same time distanced from it. When, for example, Appadocca confronts his white father, he says nothing about slavery. For him, the crime his father perpetrated was cruelly abandoning his offspring, a violation of nature that Appadocca describes in graphic terms (61–63). Several chapters later, Philip refers to slave ships in the St. Thomas harbor, but he devotes only a few short sentences to them. He mentions the "slavers" (87; 113–14)–ships built for high speed; alludes to the "nefarious traffic" in which such ships engage; and ironically places them near a "majestic British ship of war," intimating the contrast between imperial splendor, technological ingenuity, and the grim truth of the warfare against black persons that slave trading perpetuates. These are the only references to slavery as such in the novel.

Indeed, *Emmanuel Appadocca* may appear to some readers as less like *Uncle Tom's Cabin,* less like a text that belongs with either American or English abolitionist writings (e.g., in England, Maria Edgeworth's "The Grateful Negro," 1802, and Harriet Martineau's novel about the Haitian

Revolution, *The Hour and the Man,* 1841), than one that belongs alongside the sea adventure stories of Daniel Defoe (e.g., *Captain Singleton,* 1720; *Colonel Jack,* 1722), Tobias Smollett (e.g., *The Adventures of Roderick Random,* 1748), Richard Henry Dana, Edgar Allan Poe, Melville, and Frederick Marryat; the romances of Walter Scott and James Fenimore Cooper; and a host of Romantic poems and dramas about revenge, retribution (and sometimes parricide), and justice, including Coleridge's *Rime of the Ancient Mariner* (1798), Byron's *Manfred* (1817), Keats's *Hyperion* (1819-20), and Shelley's *The Cenci* (1819) and *Prometheus Unbound* (1820).[52]

Here, one recalls Philip's epigraph from Euripides–whom Erich Auerbach has identified as "the most revolutionary of the Greek tragic poets"– and the placement of *Emmanuel Appadocca* within the Western canon that Euripides' work inaugurates.[53] Each chapter opens with an epigraph from Shakespeare; and the novel is filled with well-placed mentionings of writers in the great tradition, as when Philip describes the "darkness visible" of the *Black Schooner*'s torture room in which the suffering British officer undergoes the "torments of hell" (156)–an evocation of the "darkness visible" of Milton's Hell in *Paradise Lost.*

Details in Philip's plot also parallel those in classic texts and myths. At the conclusion of the novel, for example, Appadocca commits suicide by "jump[ing] from the rock" and throwing himself into the "thundering waves" of the ocean (244). This death is akin to the fate of Hecuba, wife of Priam (the king of Troy) and mother of many children, who, after exacting revenge for the murder of a son, is turned into a dog and throws herself into the sea. The allusion is especially worth noting because Philip takes his main epigraph from Euripides' play, *Hecuba,* and two of his Shakespearean epigraphs from *Hamlet,* another play about revenge and one in which the protagonist, after hearing the Player tell of Hecuba, assails himself as "a rogue and peasant slave" for his failure to avenge his father's murder.[54]

52. *The Cenci,* for example, like Philip's novel, deals with the theme of parricide, though in this instance the plot is centered in the crime of incest that a father commits upon his daughter. For a pertinent discussion of *The Cenci,* see Earl R. Wasserman, *Shelley: A Critical Reading* (Baltimore: Johns Hopkins University Press, 1971), 84-128. For additional background: Joan Baum, *Mind Forg'd Manacles: Slavery and the English Romantic Poets* (Hamden, Conn.: Archon, 1994); and Deborah A. Thomas, *Thackeray and Slavery* (Athens: Ohio University Press, 1993). See also *America and the Sea,* ed. Haskell Springer (Athens: University of Georgia Press, 1995).

53. Erich Auerbach, *Mimesis: The Representation of Reality in Western Literature* (1946; Princeton: Princeton University Press, 1973), 324.

54. From the mid-1820s through the early 1850s, one of the leading lights of the English theater was the African American actor Ira Aldridge, whose roles included Shakespeare's tragic heroes. See Herbert Marshall and Mildred Stock, *Ira Aldridge: The Negro Tragedian*

Philip contributed to antislavery literature by designing a text that the historical moment has motivated. But this is also a text produced within (and informed by) the classic tradition, a text that cites and refers to Euripides, Shakespeare, and Milton, that echoes Elizabethan and Jacobean revenge tragedies, and that, while written in the form of a novel, rivals such bold, provocative Romantic and Transcendentalist symbolic masterpieces as Thomas Carlyle's *Sartor Resartus* (1833–34).

This network of intertextual reference, allusion, and explicit and implicit thematic connections is, in part, a means for Philip to achieve "authentication," to demonstrate his command of literary materials known to and valued by his readers, and to confirm his own authority to speak and write within the culture.[55] But his strategy is also defamiliarizing–"making strange" and unsettling the tradition and renewing attentiveness to its powers and properties–as he situates the language of the classics in contexts where it has not been formerly located.[56]

Even more, Philip seeks through allusion and textual reference to grapple with and overcome "the reality of unequal racial identities between black and white."[57] He adapts for his own purposes the cultural property of the white, Western world, making it equally his as a resource for the composition of literature that both will and will not be part of the classic tradition. The result is *Emmanuel Appadocca,* a dazzling and singular unorthodox text, akin to many texts and yet unlike any of them.

(1958; Carbondale: Southern Illinois University Press, 1968). Perhaps Philip saw, or knew of, his performances. One wonders, too, whether Philip read Matthew Arnold's "Empedocles on Etna," published anonymously in October 1852. At the poem's climax, Empedocles hurls himself into a volcano, saying: "Ah, boil up, ye vapours!/Leap and roar, thou sea of fire!/My soul glows to meet you" (*Arnold: The Complete Poems,* ed. Kenneth Allott; second edition by Miriam Allott [London: Longman, 1979], 203–4).

55. For a discussion of strategies for "authentication" in slave narratives, see Robert B. Stepto, *From Behind the Veil: A Study of Afro-American Narrative,* 2d ed. (Urbana: University of Illinois Press, 1991), 3–31.

56. On "defamiliarization," see Tony Bennett, *Formalism and Marxism* (New York: Methuen, 1979), 20–25, 49–58. See also Herbert N. Schneidau's commentary on texts that have "layers of purpose," which are sometimes radically at odds with themselves, pushing readers in different directions, perhaps doing so to achieve a new synthesis, in *Sacred Discontent: The Bible and Western Tradition* (Berkeley: University of California Press, 1977), 212; John P. McWilliams, Jr.'s account of Melville's "polytonal improvising" in *Moby-Dick,* in *The American Epic: Transforming a Genre, 1770–1860* (New York: Cambridge University Press, 1989), 187–216; and Tejumola Olaniyan, *Scars of Conquest/Masks of Resistance: The Invention of Cultural Identities in African, African-American, and Caribbean Drama* (New York: Oxford University Press, 1995).

57. Manning Marable, "History and Black Consciousness: The Political Culture of Black America," *Monthly Review* 47 (July–August 1995): 71.

Philip's goals are all the more striking when one remembers the doubts in the nineteenth century about African Americans' capacity for authorship, particularly in poetry and fiction. In *The Philosophy of History,* first published in English in 1837 (though based on lectures in the 1820s), G. W. F. Hegel presented a dismissive account of the "African character": "In Negro life the characteristic point is the fact that consciousness has not yet attained to the realization of any substantial objective existence—as for example, God or Law—in which the interest of man's volition is involved and in which he realizes his own being."[58] Many American critics, journalists, intellectuals, scientists, ministers, and political economists, including some who were sympathetic to antislavery, raised similar questions about African and African American intelligence, intellect, and potential for literary and cultural achievement.

These doubts were expressed in England as well, before and after the Emancipation Act of 1833. The writer and diplomat Edward Long, for example, in the *History of Jamaica* (1774), observed about "Negro" men and women in Africa: "In general they are void of genius and seem almost incapable of making any progress in civility or science. They have no plan or system of morality among them." The writer Robert Charles Dallas stated in his *History of the Maroons* (1803) that "tyrant and slave is the only government among savages"; he added, invoking a common theme in proslavery argument, that the Caribbean "colonists rescue these unfortunate blacks from a state of horrid and savage slavery [in Africa], to place them in a mild and civilised state of servitude; they snatch them from the most degrading idolatry and lead them to the benevolent system of the Gospel of Christ." Rev. G. W. Bridges, in *The Annals of Jamaica* (1828) justified West Indian slavery by concluding:

> The imported Africans were wild, savage, and barbarous, in the extreme; their untractable passions, and ferocious temperament, rendered severity necessary; they provoked the iron rule of harsh authority; and the earliest laws

58. G. W. F. Hegel, *The Philosophy of History* (New York: Dover, 1956), 93. This is a more accurate translation than the original 1837 edition. For analysis of Hume, Kant, Jefferson, and Hegel on "blackness" and racial identity, see Henry Louis Gates, Jr., *Figures in Black: Words, Signs, and the "Racial" Self* (New York: Oxford University Press, 1987), 3–58. Examples of books published in the late eighteenth and nineteenth century that were more sympathetic to black potential and capacity for achievement include the French journalist and historian Abbé Raynal, *Histoire philosophique et politique des éstablissemens et du commerce des européens dans les deux Indes,* 4 vols. (1770; English translation, 1776); and the abolitionist Thomas Clarkson's pamphlets and books, such as *An Essay on the Slavery and Commerce of the Human Species, Particularly the African* (1786) and *The History of the Rise, Progress, and Accomplishment of the Abolition of the African Slave Trade by the British Parliament,* 2 vols. (1808).

constructed to restrain their unexampled atrocities, were rigid and inclement. They exhibited, in fact, such depravity of nature and deformity of mind, as gave colour to the prevailing belief in a natural inferiority of intellect.[59]

The novelist Anthony Trollope visited the West Indies in 1858 and, in a book about his travels published the following year, he took for granted that "when white men and black men are together the white man will order and the black man will obey. . . . The negro's idea of emancipation," he declared, "was and is emancipation not from slavery but from work. To lie in the sun and eat breadfruit and yams is his idea of being free."[60]

English writers stated their negative judgments about Caribbean blacks with particular confidence and force during the very period when Philip resided in London and pursued his study of law and literature. And there were if anything fewer positive accounts to counter this trend than there had been in the past. As the historian Douglas A. Lorimer has shown, "the 1850s and 1860s saw the birth of scientific racism and a change in English racial attitudes from the humanitarian response of the early nineteenth century to the racialism of the imperialist era at the close of the Victorian age."[61] An article in *Fraser's Magazine* in 1853, for instance, described emancipated blacks in the British West Indies as "suspicious, slothful, filthy, and half-clad."[62] The novelist William Makepeace Thackeray, although opposed to slavery, observed in a March 14-19, 1853, letter, that, having seen blacks in the United States, it had become clear to him that "they are no more fit for freedom than a child of 10 years old is fit to compete in the struggle for life with grown up folks."[63]

This context of racism and demeaning racialism suggests that *Emmanuel*

59. Edward Long, *History of Jamaica*, 3 vols. (London, 1774), 2:253; Robert Charles Dallas, *History of the Maroons*, 2 vols. (London, 1803), 2:392-93; Rev. G. W. Bridges, *The Annals of Jamaica*, 2 vols. (London, 1828), 1:508.

60. Anthony Trollope, *The West Indies and the Spanish Main* (1859; 2d ed., London, 1860), 89, 92.

61. Douglas A. Lorimer, *Colour, Class, and the Victorians: English Attitudes to the Negro in the Mid-Nineteenth Century* (Leicester, England: Leicester University Press, 1978), 13.

62. "Concerning Free British Negroes," *Fraser's Magazine* 47 (1853): 116. In this same year, Carlyle published *Occasional Discourse on the Nigger Question*, which was a version of a notorious racist essay that had first appeared in 1849 (*Fraser's Magazine* 40 [1849]: 670-79). John Stuart Mill replied in "The Negro Question," *Fraser's Magazine* 41 (1850): 25-31. Later in the century, Carlyle's biographer, the English man-of-letters J. A. Froude, wrote a racist history of the area that Philip depicts, *The English in the West Indies, or, The Bow of Ulysses* (London, 1888). For cogent discussion, see Simon Gikandi, "Englishness, Travel, and Theory: Writing the West Indies in the Nineteenth-Century," *Nineteenth-Century Contexts* 18 (1994): 49-70.

63. *The Letters and Private Papers of William Makepeace Thackeray*, ed. Gordon N. Ray, 4 vols. (Cambridge: Harvard University Press, 1945-46), 3:242.

Appadocca is not only about a character of imposing strength of will, but also is itself, as a text, intended as an act of will against the claims that persons of African descent are incapable of authorship and lack the judgment, understanding, and talent to exercise command over the master's language. This gives yet another dimension to Appadocca's anger and bitter determination to gain sway over the father who has mistreated him. He wants vengeance for the mother whom his father abandoned; and he is determined to face down paternal authority and punish and displace the figure who has denied him.

After Appadocca is taken prisoner, the commander of the ship cites Scripture against the violent revenge that Appadocca seeks:

> "Young man . . . it was wrong, on your part, to treat your parent in this manner. If what you say is correct, he has treated you unnaturally, but there is One above us to punish such sins, and it is not yours to arrogate the right of taking vengeance, even when you consider yourself injured–recollect," he said solemnly, "recollect–'Vengeance is mine, saith the Lord.'"

Appadocca is unmoved:

> "You speak, my lord," replied the captain, "as I should expect you to do; but you are scarcely a judge in this matter: you have not had to endure what I had. I can read in you, my lord,–pardon the personality–something which tells me that, if you had found yourself in my place, you would have acted in the same manner." (95-96)

Both the Old and New Testament dwell upon types of vengeance and retribution. But in general the scriptural texts stress that ultimate justice will transpire through God's agency: men and women therefore should not commit acts that only divine will can perform. In Genesis, the Lord declares: "whosoever slayeth Cain, vengeance shall be taken on him sevenfold" (4:15). Paul, in his epistle to the Romans, states: "Dearly beloved, avenge not yourselves, but rather give place unto wrath: for it is written, Vengeance is mine; I will repay, saith the Lord" (12:19; see also Deuteronomy 32:35; Hebrews 10:30).

Vengeance in this sense is tied to God's presence in history. His faithful may suffer but should be consoled by the knowledge that there will be a day of final judgment when all wrongs will be righted. In *Uncle Tom's Cabin,* Stowe sounds this note often, as when her narrator says of Legree, after he has nearly killed Tom and (so he believes) silenced the slave's voice at last: "Yes, Legree; but who shall shut up that voice in thy soul? that soul, past repentance, past prayer, past hope, in whom the fire that never shall be quenched is already burning!" On the final page of her book, Stowe issues a warning to her readers: "Christians! every time that you pray that the kingdom of Christ may come, can you forget that prophecy associates, in dread fellowship, the *day of vengeance* with the year of his redeemed?"[64]

Though the connection is impossible to prove, it is very likely that Philip not only read *Uncle Tom's Cabin,* but, furthermore, aimed in his novel to articulate an alternative to it–his vision of vengeance and retribution. In one sense the context is historical: how to deal with the fact of slavery? In another, it is literary: how to deal with slavery given the formidable presence, already *there,* of Stowe's text? It is her text that Philip must resist and reimagine to make way for his own.

Uncle Tom's Cabin was a phenomenal success, read and discussed, it seems, by everybody, and Stowe and her book were powerful presences for any later author who sought to contribute to the literature of antislavery. The five thousand copies of the first United States edition sold out in forty-eight hours, and for the next two years the presses never caught up with the demand, with three hundred thousand copies sold in 1852. Total sales in the United States reached a million in the next seven years; for students of the London-dweller Philip's work, even more noteworthy is that sales were extraordinary in Great Britain, too–about a million and a half copies in the first year alone.

Stowe herself journeyed to England, arriving in Liverpool in April 1853, and she stayed until early June in order to advance the antislavery cause and capitalize upon the triumph of *Uncle Tom's Cabin.* As a sign of their respect for her achievement, her English readers prepared a grand petition, one that was initiated by a number of prominent British women, including the duchess of Sutherland, the duchess of Argyll, Viscountess Palmerston, Mrs. Tennyson, and Mrs. Dickens. They titled it, "An Affectionate and Christian Address of Many Thousands of Women of Great Britain and Ireland to Their Sisters, the Women of the United States of America." Nearly five hundred thousand signatures were collected, and they were gathered in twenty-six black leather folio volumes.[65] Stowe was honored in public meetings held in Liverpool, Glasgow, Edinburgh, Dundee, and London. The petition itself was delivered to her on May 7 at Stafford House, the residence of the duchess of Sutherland; and, with the exception of Queen Victoria, every important English man and woman of rank and distinction was in attendance.[66]

Stowe's account of divine justice is a basic tenet of Christianity, yet her

---

64. Stowe, *Uncle Tom's Cabin,* 584, 629.

65. Thomas F. Gossett, *"Uncle Tom's Cabin" and American Culture* (Dallas: Southern Methodist University Press, 1985), 254–55.

66. Joan D. Hedrick, *Harriet Beecher Stowe: A Life* (New York: Oxford University Press, 1994), 238, 245.

expression of it also reflects a concern about African Americans taking justice into their own hands, reenacting, in the worst case, the scenes of Saint Domingue in the 1790s and early 1800s. In a letter about the August 1791 slave revolt in Saint Domingue, Thomas Paine had pointed out: "It is the natural consequence of Slavery and must be expected every where. The Negroes are enraged at the opposition made to their relief and are determined, if not to relieve themselves to punish their enemies."[67] By the late 1840s and 1850s, as the slavery crisis intensified, African Americans escalated their calls for violent resistance into direct demands for punishment, retribution, and justice–justice that they could no longer wait for God to administer, *racial* justice impelled by memories of injustice done to individual slaves and their families.[68]

Frederick Douglass–who had seen his own family members and friends brutalized in bondage–made the point with stunning precision. Ridding America of slavery, he explained, required that "a little St. Domingo [be] put in the coffee of our Georgia slaveholders." In reply to this, the white abolitionist Lewis Tappan rebuked Douglass's " 'vengeance is mine' attitude." But vengeance was something that African Americans now were affirming they desired.[69]

In *Clotel,* Williams Wells Brown describes the African swamp-dweller Picquilo, a member of Nat Turner's band: "He was a bold, turbulent spirit; and from revenge imbrued his hands in the blood of all the whites he could meet."[70] Frank J. Webb, in *The Garies and Their Friends,* a novel about mixed racial identity and northern racial hypocrisy published in London (as was *Clotel*) in 1857, tells of Caddy Ellis's anger after a mob beats and mutilates her father: "What those white devils will have to answer for! When I think of how much injury they have done us, I *hate* them! I know it's wrong to hate anybody–but I can't help it; and I believe God hates them as

---

67. Paine, *Complete Writings,* 2:1321.

68. See the recent collection, *History and Memory in African-American Culture,* ed. Genevieve Fabre and Robert O'Meally (New York: Oxford University Press, 1994), and also the treatment of slave rebellion, religious revivalism, and charismatic leadership in J. C. D. Clark, *The Language of Liberty, 1660–1832: Political Discourse and Social Dynamics in the Anglo-American World* (New York: Cambridge University Press, 1994), 251-53.

69. For these citations, see David W. Blight, *Frederick Douglass' Civil War: Keeping Faith in Jubilee* (Baton Rouge: Louisiana State University Press, 1989), 95.

70. Brown, *Clotel,* 213. In his play, *The Escape; or, A Leap For Freedom* (1858), Brown gives his slave protagonist Glen the following prophetic words: "There is a volcano pent up in the hearts of the slaves of these Southern States that will burst forth ere long. When that day comes, wo to those whom its unpitying fury may devour" (4.1). Included in *Black Theater USA,* ed. James V. Hatch (New York: Free Press, 1974), 51.

much as I do!"[71] Martin R. Delany, in *Blake,* portrays the leader of the black "Army of Emancipation," the West Indian slave Henry Blake, who prepares for insurrection in Cuba by declaring: "I am for war–war upon the whites." Gondolier, a black cook who wields a huge carving knife, says in the same vein: "We have a race of devils to deal with that would make an angel swear. Educated devils that's capable of everything hellish under the name of religion, law, politics, social regulations, and the higher civilization; so that the helpless victim be of the black race. Curse them! I hate 'em! Let me into the streets and give me but half a chance and I'll unjoint them faster than ever I did a roast pig for the palace dinner table."[72]

The idea propounded in all of these texts is that whites should be murdered: this is the punishment they deserve for the crimes that they have committed. Such vengeance or, better, legitimate retribution, is, from one perspective, a principle of Old Testament law, one that fell under the jurisdiction of judges, as the young lawyer Philip no doubt was aware. The well-known passage in Exodus asserts: "Eye for eye, tooth for tooth, hand for hand, foot for foot" (21:23–24; see also Deuteronomy 19:21). This is severe, and Jesus explicitly rejects it (Matthew 5:38–42; see also Luke 6:29). But it is less severe than the private vengeance, undertaken by the "avenger of blood," in cases of evil done to a family–though even here there were rules and limits to blood feud (Numbers 35:9–28).

"Eye for eye" is the *lex talionis,* the law of equivalent retribution, and in philosophy and religion, the nature of such codified revenge and punishment has been the subject of interpretation and dispute for centuries.[73] Many of the West's leading thinkers have explored it, including Lucretius, Aquinas, Kant, Bentham, Hegel, and J. S. Mill. But for *Emmanuel Appadocca,* Aristotle and Bacon are perhaps more relevant since Philip refers to them directly; when Lorenzo enters Appadocca's cabin, he finds that his captain has been reading both Bacon and Aristotle (24). Aristotle, in *Nio-*

---

71. Frank J. Webb, *The Garies and Their Friends* (1857; New York: Arno, 1969), 267. The Massachusetts Anti-Slavery Society examined and debated slave insurrection during its January 1857 convention. See the record of the proceedings, *The Liberator,* February 13, 1857.

72. Martin R. Delany, *Blake; or The Huts of America* (1859, 1861–62; Boston: Beacon, 1970), 290, 312. See also 19–20, 305.

73. For further discussion and bibliography, see *The Anchor Bible Dictionary,* ed. David Noel Freedman, 6 vols. (New York: Doubleday, 1992), 4:321–22. Northrop Frye, in *The Great Code: The Bible and Literature* (New York: Harcourt Brace Jovanovich, 1982), comments on the relation between *lex talionis* and the *nemesis* of Greek drama, which depicts justice as connected to "the tendency of nature to recover its balance after an act of human aggression" (120).

machean Ethics, states: "For it is by proportionate requital that the city holds together. Men seek to return either evil for evil–and if they cannot do so, think their position mere slavery–or good for good–and if they cannot do so there is no exchange, but it is by exchange that they hold together."[74] Francis Bacon, in his essay "Of Revenge" (1625), reflects that "revenge is a kind of wild justice, which the more a man's nature runs to, the more ought law to weed it out; for as for the first wrong, it doth but offend the law, but the revenge of that wrong, putteth the law out of office."[75]

The problem with the law of retaliation is how to bring vengeful deeds to closure and thereby prevent the specter of widespread death and destruction that are evident in the passages I have cited from Douglass, William Wells Brown, Webb, and Delany. It is the need for limits that Aristotle and Bacon treat in their classic texts, and that other philosophers, however different their purposes, emphasize as well. Thomas Hobbes, in *Leviathan* (1651), contends "That in Revenges, (that is, retribution of Evil for Evil), *Men look not at the greatnesse of the evill past, but the greatnesse of the good to follow.* Whereby we are forbidden to inflict punishment with any other designe, than for correction of the offender, or direction of others."[76] In his *Enquiry Concerning Political Justice* (1793), William Godwin distinguishes punishment from vengeance, emphasizing that punishment must not result from vengeance, but only from the desire to prevent future evils. To punish the guilty man "for what is past and irrecoverable, and for the consideration of that only, must be ranked among the most pernicious exhibitions of an untutored barbarism."[77]

The context of slavery and its consequences gives added charge and depth to Philip's commentary on this theme of retribution. Appadocca seeks to punish his father, but in the process he participates with his men in cruel acts of piracy and bloodshed. Whenever a person of African descent com-

74. *The Basic Works of Aristotle,* ed. Richard M. McKeon (New York: Random Hous, 1941), 1010.

75. Francis Bacon, "Of Revenge" (1625 ed.), in *"Essays" and "New Atlantis"* (New York: Black, 1942), 17.

76. Thomas Hobbes, *Leviathan* (1651; London: Penguin, 1977), 210.

77. William Godwin, *Enquiry Concerning Political Justice* (1793; New York: Penguin, 1985), 635. The "venerable Judge" in Walter Scott's "The Two Drovers," in *Chronicles of the Canongate* (1827), declares: "The law says to the subjects, . . . with a voice only inferior to that of the Deity, 'Vengeance is mine.'" See also the former slave Mesty's story of a terrible cycle of African tribal vengeance in Frederick Marryat's *Mr. Midshipman Easy* (1836), chapter fifteen. My commentary on the law of *lex talionis* emerges from conversations with my coeditor, Selwyn R. Cudjoe, who drew my attention to its importance in the novel. See also Cudjoe's afterword, below.

mitted murder, whatever the rationale for it, he evoked for American and English audiences the specter of race war, which meant war of unparalleled ferocity and savagery. A single crime by a black person, or any attempt by him or her to compensate for an injustice, symbolized the fierce wrath that the entire race was capable of, if not restrained by slavery.[78] Most immediately, such wars were connected to slave uprisings in the Caribbean and the United States. But lying behind them for North American readers, in a merging of history and cultural myth that reached back to the earliest decades of settlement, were the realities, fears, rumors, and stories of war between the whites and the Indians.

According to the cultural critic Richard Slotkin,

> the story of American progress and expansion took the form of a fable of race war, pitting the symbolic opposites of savagery and civilization, primitivism and progress, paganism and Christianity against each other. Quite early in the history of white-Indian relations, a conception of Indian warfare developed that tended to represent the struggle as necessarily genocidal. "Savage war" was distinguished from "civilized warfare" in its lack of limitations of the extent of violence, and of "laws" for its application.[79]

This fable was reshaped during the slavery crisis, in, for instance, the Illinois debates between Abraham Lincoln and Stephen Douglas in 1858, where, says Slotkin, Douglas "follows with fidelity the paradigm of race and cultural conflict articulated in the mythology of the Indian wars: where two unlike or antipathetic races or systems meet, war is inevitable and is fought to the extreme limits of extermination or enslavement."[80]

With its depiction of the allure and horror of violence and vengeance, *Uncle Tom's Cabin* is one key novel that *Emmanuel Appadocca* evokes for

78. For background, see Seymour Drescher, "Servile Insurrection and John Brown's Body in Europe," in *His Soul Goes Marching On: Responses to John Brown and the Harpers Ferry Raid,* ed. Paul Finkelman (Charlottesville: University of Virginia Press, 1995), 253–95.

79. Richard Slotkin, *The Fatal Environment: The Myth of the Frontier in the Age of Industrialization, 1800–1890* (1985; New York: HarperCollins, 1994), 53. In *Notes on the State of Virginia* (1787), Thomas Jefferson had warned that freed slaves could never be incorporated into the body politic; any attempt to do so, he explained, would "produce convulsions which will probably never end but in the extermination of the one or the other race." See Thomas Jefferson, *Writings* (New York: Library of America, 1984), 264. For further discussion: Richard Drinnon, *Facing West: The Metaphysics of Indian-Hating and Empire-Building* (New York: New American Library, 1980), 119–64. Also suggestive on the issues of race war and extermination are John W. Dower, *War without Mercy: Race and Power in the Pacific War* (New York: Pantheon, 1986); and Craig M. Cameron, *American Samurai: Myth, Imagination, and the Conduct of Battle in the First Marine Division, 1941–1951* (New York: Cambridge University Press, 1994).

80. Slotkin, *Fatal Environment,* 240.

contrast and comparison. *Moby-Dick* is another, and one that, in its rendering of retribution and anguished intellect and angered will, may be even more pointedly relevant today to an appraisal of Philip's book.

It is not known whether Philip read Melville's novel, which was published as *The Whale* in England in October 1851 where Philip was studying law. He may have read about it in the numerous reviews of *The Whale* that appeared in English journals and magazines. A recent study has shown that Melville's novel "received extraordinary attention in London." At least twenty-one reviews were published; many of them were "brilliant responses" written by respected critics "to what was plainly perceived as a remarkable book." British reviewers regarded *The Whale* "as a phenomenal literary work, a philosophical, metaphysical, and poetic romance," and it was "one of the notable works of the London publishing season in 1851."[81]

There are obvious differences between the two texts. *Moby-Dick* is a first-person narrative, told by the survivor Ishmael, while *Emmanuel Appadocca* is not. The objects of vengeance differ: Ahab focuses his hatred on the inscrutable white whale who tore away his leg, while Appadocca is obsessed with the father who betrayed his bond to his son. But there are, nonetheless, affinities everywhere. Both Melville's *Pequod* and Philip's *Black Schooner,* for example, are populated by an international crew of "meanest mariners, and renegades and castaways" who form a special society; both authors employ a host of epic similes; and both of them reflect ominously on the meanings of Nature.[82]

In a suggestive examination of *Moby-Dick* as a "mixed form" or "metaphysical" narrative, the critic Sheila Post-Lauria cites a discussion of "art and culture novels" by the eminent British man-of-letters, David Masson, which was published in 1859. For Masson, such novels (for example, Emily

81. See the Northwestern-Newberry edition of *Moby-Dick,* ed. Harrison Hayford, Hershel Parker, and G. Thomas Tanselle (Evanston, Ill.: Northwestern University Press, 1988), 700, 702, 709. On the significant differences between the English and American editions, see 667–89. British and American reviews of *Moby-Dick* can be found in *"Moby-Dick" as Doubloon: Essays and Extracts (1851–1970),* ed. Hershel Parker and Harrison Hayford (New York: Norton, 1970); and *Melville: The Critical Heritage,* ed. Watson G. Branch (London: Routledge and Kegan Paul, 1974), 251–91. See also Arnella K. Turner, *Victorian Criticism of American Writers* (San Bernadino, Calif.: Borgo Press, 1991), 198, 266, 307, 312–13.

82. Herman Melville, *Moby-Dick; or, The Whale,* ed. Harold Beaver (1851; New York: Penguin, 1983), 212. Subsequent quotations are from this edition. For a suggestive account of the close-knit work and language of men aboard sailing ships, see Greg Dening, *Mr. Bligh's Bad Language: Passion, Power, and Theatre on the "Bounty"* (New York: Cambridge University Press, 1992), 55–58. The ship was also a symbol for the State, for the American "Union," as in Henry Wadsworth Longfellow's "The Building of the Ship," in *The Seaside and the Fireside* (1850), a poem that reflects the tensions of the slavery crisis.

Brontë's *Wuthering Heights*) describe the individual's "progress through the very blackness of darkness, with only natural reason, or the revelation that can come through reason, as his guide." Masson continues:

> There is the mind preying on its own metaphysical roots; there is the parting, piece by piece, with the old hereditary faith, and yet all the remaining torture of the ceaseless interrogation which that faith satisfied. . . . There is the burden of sin and the alternate sulleness and madness of despair. . . . Sometimes the mind under probation is made to ascertain for itself that its perpetual metaphysical self-torture, its perpetual labour on questions which cannot be answered, is a misuse of its faculties, and so takes rest in the philosophic conclusion that "man was not born to solve the problem of the universe, but to find out where the problem begins, and then to restrain himself within the limits of the comprehensible."[83]

These terms characterize well the metaphysical questing that absorbs Ishmael, ravages Ahab, and obsesses Melville, and they are applicable to Philip's protagonist, who roams the ocean determined to find retribution for an injustice that is both personal and cosmic. As his willful but resolute, tenacious language bears witness, Appadocca's wrath and grief are focused in, and yet exceed, the crime that his father committed against him and his mother.

The sea is the turbulent setting for Melville's and Philip's novels, and, as the scholar Carl Pedersen has noted, it has a particular literary valence for African American writers. Referring to Douglass's depiction of slave revolt aboard ship in *The Heroic Slave* and Delany's account in *Blake* of black slaves rising against the crew of a slave ship, Pedersen states that "the sea functions as a trope marking the unruly space between the past memory of Africa and the present reality of slavery in terms of active resistance."[84]

83. David Masson, "British Novelists since Scott," in his *British Novelists and Their Styles: Being A Critical Sketch of the History of British Prose Fiction* (1859), cited in Sheila Post-Lauria, " 'Philosophy in Whales . . . Poetry in Blubber': Mixed Form in *Moby-Dick*," *Nineteenth-Century Literature* 45 (December 1990): 304-5. Masson's phrase "the very blackness of darkness" echoes Melville's description of Hawthorne's "mystical blackness," his "great power of blackness," in "Hawthorne and His Mosses" (1850). See *The Shock of Recognition*, ed. Edmund Wilson (New York: Modern Library, 1943), 192.

84. Carl Pedersen, "Sea Change: The Middle Passage and the Transatlantic Imagination," in *The Black Columbiad: Defining Moments in African American Literature and Culture*, ed. Werner Sollors and Maria Dietrich (Cambridge: Harvard University Press, 1994), 48. On Melville and the context of European resistance and the revolutions of 1848, see Michael Paul Rogin, "Herman Melville: State, Civil Society, and the American 1848," *Yale Review* 69 (1979): 72-88; Rogin, *Subversive Genealogy: The Politics and Art of Herman Melville* (New York: Knopf, 1983), 102-51; and Larry J. Reynolds, *European Revolutions and the American Literary Renaissance*, 97-124. On the American political scene, see Alan Heimert, "*Moby-Dick* and American Political Symbolism," *American Quarterly* 15 (1963): 498-534.

"Resistance" to the condition of slavery, and resistance to and revenge for its crimes, are major themes in *Emmanuel Appadocca,* and in a different sense, resistance looms large in *Moby-Dick,* in the sheer unmitigated opposition to the white whale that Ahab voices and acts upon. But the central relationship between these two texts is best indicated by the power of will that both Ahab and Appadocca display, and the command over others that they exercise as they prosecute their plans for revenge. Both captains often stay below in their cabins, always on the minds of, but not seen by, their men (*Moby-Dick* 198, 217; *Emmanuel Appadocca* 34); both brood heavily on their missions; and both vocalize their immense complaints against the universe and justify their determined conduct.

At one point in *Moby-Dick,* Melville describes Ahab on deck: "Captain Ahab stood erect, looking straight out beyond the ship's ever-pitching prow. There was an infinity of firmest fortitude, a determinate, unsurrenderable wilfulness, in the fixed and fearless, forward dedication of that glance" (220). Later, as he sits in his cabin at sunset, Ahab ponders: "'Twas not so hard a task. I thought to find one stubborn, at the least; but my one cogged circle fits into all their various wheels, and they revolve" (266). The chief mate Starbuck, by the mainmast at dusk, feels the intense hold of Ahab's will: "My soul is more than matched; she's overmanned; and by a madman! Insufferable sting, that sanity should ground arms on such a field! But he drilled deep down, and blasted all my reason out of me! I think I see his impious end; but feel that I must help him to it" (267). Ishmael does as well: "I, Ishmael, was one of that crew; my shouts had gone up with the rest; my oath had been welded with theirs; and stronger I shouted, and more did I hammer and clinch my oath, because of the dread in my soul. A wild, mystical, sympathetical feeling was in me; Ahab's quenchless feud seemed mine" (276).

In *Emmanuel Appadocca,* Philip, too, turns his protagonist toward assertions of "will" (for example, 14) and demands for obedience, and he exhibits Appadocca's concern for retaining the "veneration and awe" of his crew, "which seemed to crush their wills to an implicit and blind obedience to his" (34). Like Ahab, Appadocca *hates* passionately, expresses a maddened desire for revenge, and enjoins his crew to exact vengeance on the ships they attack (e.g., 37).[85]

Melville and Philip intend for their protagonists to captivate and terrify

---

85. Robert Alter has spoken of the ways in which the repetition of key words in texts—one could cite the repeated references to "will" in *Emmanuel Appadocca*—become "thematic ideas." See *The Art of Biblical Narrative* (New York: Basic, 1981), 92.

readers, particularly in their relentless cruelty. It is not clear, however, if this cruelty is meant to expose the character's evil, or, instead, if it is meant as yet another manifestation of a powerful will that transcends conventional moral categories. Writing of Napoleon in *Representative Men* (1850), Emerson counseled that Napoleon must not "be set down as cruel; but only as one who knew no impediment to his will; not bloodthirsty, not cruel,—but woe to what thing or person stood in his way! Not bloodthirsty, but not sparing of blood,—and pitiless."[86] The pitiless behavior of Appadocca and his men is evident, for instance, when Lorenzo orders the torture of the British officer, which Philip graphically describes, and in which he shows the crew taking enjoyment: "His executioners stood around immovable, calm, and fierce, as they always were, more like demons sucking in the pleasure of mortal's pains, than men" (156-57).

Appadocca himself is not present during this scene of torture, and hence Philip may seek to grant him a partial exemption from its demonic savagery. Earlier, there is a different, if related, effect, when Philip presents the response of the *Black Schooner*'s crew to Appadocca's indictment of his father's treachery: "Their usual ferocious character of mien was heightened, for the history which their chief had thus partly related, no doubt recalled to the greater part of those men who stood that morning on the deck of the *Black Schooner,* the injustice, *whether real or merely supposed,* with which they had been treated by others" (63; my italics). This point about their ferocity, constantly reiterated, is thereby linked to injustices which they may have suffered but perhaps did not suffer at all and have only imagined. Philip is here likely repeating an ambiguity in Milton's *Samson Agonistes:* are the vengeful actions that the hero performs the result of God's "motions" in him, the product of authentic heavenly inspiration, or are they only "supposed" to be so? The ambiguity makes all the more disconcerting Philip's references to the crew's "misanthropy" (64), the origins of which might be fantastical. This is tied as well to Philip's many references to the crew's and Appadocca's "cynicism," "disgust," and "distaste" (e.g., 64; 97).

These elements of moral critique and judgment, while present in the text, are less noteworthy than the main thrust of Philip's characterization of Appadocca, above all in the astonishing account of his life that Appadocca delivers to his student friend Charles Hamilton in chapters twelve and thir-

---

86. Ralph Waldo Emerson, "Napoleon; or, The Man of the World," *Representative Men: Seven Lectures* (1850), in *Essays and Lectures* (New York: Library of America, 1983), 732.

teen. The literary scholar William L. Andrews has made the important point that as American antislavery activity intensified in the 1840s, African American slave narratives grew more sophisticated and self-affirming, in contrast to the "self-effacement" that had marked earlier examples of the genre.[87] Yet the autobiographical "narrative"–Philip's term (98; 109)– that Appadocca articulates pushes self-assertion to extraordinary extremes, of the kind that Melville implants in Ahab or that, later in the century, Friedrich Nietzsche invests in the narrators of *Thus Spake Zarathustra* (1883-92) and *Beyond Good and Evil* (1886).[88]

Appadocca views himself as an agent of "retribution," an instrument of bloody "vengeance" appointed to make his father pay for the crime of abandoning his son. By taking his own revenge, Appadocca says he will discharge universal law and deter others from crimes like the one committed by his father and like the one, mirroring it, committed by the man who fathered the child of the "poor girl" whom Appadocca saves from death (101-4). To Charles Hamilton, Appadocca seems a blasphemer intent on "parricide" (111-12). But to Appadocca, when fathers violate their natural contract with their children, they are fathers no longer, and, thus, the child necessarily "undertakes the office of avenger." By killing the false father, the child "vindicates" law and serves the cause of justice. In line with the doctrine of higher law, Appadocca disobeys law in one sense only to act in accord with law in its most essential form, the law that requires obedience even if it means breaking human laws.

Appadocca's conception of law is, however, more embittered and brutal than that articulated by American abolitionists and higher-law foes of the Fugitive Slave Law. Appadocca scorns Hamilton's claim that he is a criminal; he is no more of a pirate than is the rest of mankind in a vicious, heartless world filled with schemers, killers, and fiends. Foreshadowing the English naturalist Charles Darwin's *Origin of Species,* published in 1859, and the English philosopher Herbert Spencer's writings on sociology, ethics, and government, Appadocca portrays existence as a struggle

87. William L. Andrews, *To Tell a Free Story: The First Century of Afro-American Autobiography, 1760-1865* (Urbana: University of Illinois Press, 1986), 100.

88. In the background here may lie the "runaway communities" that escaped slaves established throughout the New World. There were hundreds of them by the mid-seventeenth century, and, as Jon Thornton has noted, they were founded on strong leadership, strict military discipline, hierarchical authority, and inequality. See *Africa and Africans in the Making of the Atlantic World, 1400-1680* (New York: Cambridge University Press, 1992), 272-303. Appadocca is no democrat and is a revolutionary only in his ethical and philosophical positions.

and survival of the fittest: " 'The world can be compared to a vast marsh, abounding with monster alligators that devour the smaller creatures, and then each other' " (115).[89]

Appadocca's narrative attacks slavery and the slave trade (115-16), but embeds it within a broader, panoramic canvasing of the barbarism, materialism, and rapacious conduct that have dominated all phases of human history. Appadocca sounds not only like Ahab, a consciousness poisoned by the lust for revenge, but also like Shakespeare's Hamlet, Lear, and Timon, in their most sickened, hate-filled moments. Appadocca refuses to embrace Christianity as the means of redress and consolation: vengeance is his, not God's.[90]

Philip's Appadocca has something of Ahab's magnitude—the same outraged voice and vision—and this black Ahab belongs in the company of magnificent, monomaniacal heroes of epic and tragedy. Violent and vengeful, he is no Uncle Tom. Yet Emmanuel Appadocca is, finally, a tragic figure, a man of heroic frame but wasted gifts, consumed by the quest for justice and imprisoned by it. As the subtitle to the novel indicates, this is a story of a "blighted" life that is impaired and diseased, withered in its hopes, ambitions, and potentialities. "Blighted" is an action that slavery imposes on Appadocca and that, as a consequence, he then imposes, self-destructively, on himself.

Carlyle's observations on kingship in *On Heroes, Hero-Worship, and the Heroic in History* (1841) help to gloss Appadocca's character and fate. Carlyle speaks of "the Commander over Men . . . he to whose will our wills are to be subordinated, and loyally surrender themselves, and find their welfare in doing so, [and who] may be reckoned the most important of Great Men":

> It is a tragical position for a true man to work in revolutions. He seems an anarchist; and indeed a painful element of anarchy does encumber him at every step,—him to whose soul anarchy is hostile, hateful. His mission is Order; every man's is. He is here to make what was disorderly, chaotic, into a thing ruled, regular. He is the missionary of Order.[91]

---

89. For further discussion of this important point, see Selwyn R. Cudjoe's Afterword, below.

90. David Brion Davis, noting the crucial role that Christianity played in the British antislavery campaigns, states: "From Sharp and Wilberforce to Buxton and Joseph Sturge, religion was the central concern of all the British abolitionist leaders" (*Slavery and Human Progress* [New York: Oxford University Press, 1984], 139).

91. Thomas Carlyle, *On Heroes, Hero-Worship, and the Heroic in History* (1841; Lincoln: University of Nebraska Press, 1966), 196, 203.

Philip limns a figure of great intellect and imagination locked into a cycle of revenge; his cause is just but his conduct is wrong, and wrong because it cuts off any chance that he will fulfill his own highest potential. The "romance" as a genre "dares to posit a world of infinite possibility, a world in which cultural heroes and heroines come to grips with those negative forces, or villains, that interfere with the attainment of an ideal world,"[92] and *Emmanuel Appadocca* fits this definition. But this novel both glimpses these possibilities and forecloses them, for Appadocca is bound to a destiny that afflicts him, that he fights against, but that he cannot transcend except through murder and suicide. Philip wants readers to ask, what might Appadocca have achieved if he had been allowed a different narrative and place in history? The narrative that Appadocca delivers hence is measured by the conspicuous absence of another narrative that would have illustrated the person whom he should have become. This conjunction of written and unwritten life stories suggests Appadocca's personal tragedy and elicits for us the tragic tale of loss that Atlantic slavery endlessly repeated.

The historian Thomas C. Holt has commented on a "general pattern found in the autobiographies and memoirs of countless black men and women of diverse origins," such as the educator Anna J. Cooper, the black sharecropper Ned Cobb [Nate Shaw], the wide-ranging intellectual W. E. B. Du Bois, and the anti-imperialist theorist Frantz Fanon. In each case "there comes some traumatic confrontation with the Other that *fixes* the meaning of one's self before one even has had the opportunity to *live* and *make* a self more nearly of one's own choosing."[93] The narrative that Emmanuel Appadocca recounts shows a self riven between freedom and fate, a self whose imperious claims are made against the prescriptions that slavery and racism impose.

Emmanuel Appadocca is a compelling text that is sited within the networks of mid-nineteenth-century Atlantic culture, literature, and history. Yet in this text Philip also forecasts the protagonists and themes that would grip African American writers a century later, and hence, in its portrait of a burdened consciousness, it exceeds its historical moment and illuminates the modern and postmodern eras. This is a novel that in its most powerful moments not only belongs alongside *Uncle Tom's Cabin* and *Moby-Dick,* but that anticipates as well the alienation, revolt, baffled self-examination

---

92. Jane Campbell, *Mythic Black Fiction: The Transformation of History* (Knoxville: University of Tennessee Press, 1986), xi.

93. Thomas C. Holt, "Marking: Race, Race-Making, and the Writing of History," *American Historical Review* 100 (February 1995): 2.

and self-discovery that inform such novels as Richard Wright's *Native Son* (1940), Ralph Ellison's *Invisible Man* (1952), and James Baldwin's *Go Tell It on the Mountain* (1953), and such dramas as Langston Hughes's *Mulatto* (1935) and Imamu Amiri Baraka's *Dutchman* (1964), *The Slave* (1964), and *Slave Ship* (1967). Still another sign of *Emmanuel Appadocca*'s distinction is that the more one contextualizes it in its own era, the more it discloses its modernity.

EMMANUEL APPADOCCA;

OR,

BLIGHTED LIFE.

EMMANUEL APPADOCCA;

OR,

BLIGHTED LIFE.

A Tale of the Boucaneers

BY

MAXWELL PHILIP

φεῦ· ὦ μῆτερ, ἥτις ἐκ τυραννικῶν δόμων
δούλειον ἦμαρ εἶδες, ὦ πράςςεις κακῶς
ὅςονπερ εὖ ποτ'· ἀντιςηκώςας δέ ςε
φθείρει θεῶν τις τῆς πάροιθ' εὐπραξίας.
EURIPIDES

TITLE: *Emmanuel Appadocca; or Blighted Life. A Tale of the Boucaneers.*

Emmanuel or Immanuel means "God with us" (Isaiah 7:14; 8:8, 10). In the New Testament, referring to Isaiah and prophesying the virgin birth, the angel of the Lord applies this name to Jesus (Matthew 1:23).

"Appadocca" alludes to the Spanish Vice Admiral Don Sebastian Ruiz de Apodaca, who played an inglorious role in the Spanish surrender of Trinidad to British forces in February 1797. The British, at war with Spain and France, sent a military force of seventeen ships against the island. This fleet was under the command of Rear Admiral Henry Harvey (1737-

1810) and carried nearly eight thousand troops on board, led by Sir Ralph Abercromby (1734-1801). At the request of José Maria Chacon, the Spanish governor of the island, five ships, under Admiral Apodaca, had arrived in January 1797, to give the island protection. But Admiral Apodaca, fearing defeat and not wanting his ships to be seized, chose to set fire to them without attempting to do battle. This was considered so shameful that both he and Chacon (whose land forces offered minimal resistance) were made the subject of an inquiry by the Spanish crown.

See *Area Handbook for Trinidad and Tobago* (Washington, D.C.: U.S. Government Printing Office, 1976), 44-45; and P. G. L. Borde, "The Capitulation," in *The Book of Trinidad,* ed. Gerard Besson and Bridget Brereton, 2d ed. (Port of Spain: Paria Publishing, 1992), 68-75. For fuller discussion, see P. G. L. Borde, *Histoire de l'Isle de la Trinidad sous le Gouvernement Espagnol,* 2 vols. (1876-82).

In modern usage, "buccaneer" means "pirate," and refers to the roving bands of seamen who preyed on Spanish ships in the West Indies during the seventeenth century. Philip's term is somewhat different, however. "Boucaneers" derives from the French word "boucanier," which originally meant "one who hunts wild oxen." "Boucan" means "barbecue" (i.e., a barbecue frame), and "boucaner" means to smoke or dry meat on a barbecue. The "boucaneers"—the first appearance of the word is recorded in 1661—were a mix of English, French, and Dutch inhabitants of the islands of Tortuga and Hispaniola who hunted wild animals and cooked the meat on boucans. They were united in their hatred of Spain, because of the Spanish authorities' claims to exclusive rights in the Americas. In the 1630s, the Spanish began action to exterminate the boucaneers, who in revenge took to the sea as pirates, vowing eternal war against their Spanish foes.

For help with this term, I have consulted the *Oxford English Dictionary,* the *American Heritage Dictionary,* and Cyril Hamshere, *The British in the Caribbean* (Cambridge: Harvard University Press, 1972), 42-43. For historical context: A. O. Esquemeling, *The Buccaneers of America* (1684; London, 1951); and Charles Leslie, *A New History of Jamaica* (London, 1740-41).

For further discussion, see Selwyn R. Cudjoe's Afterword.

EPIGRAPHS:
The Greek epigraph on the title page is from the tragic playwright Euripides (c. 480-406 BC), *Hecuba* (c. 424 BC), lines 55-58. The speaker is the ghost of Polydorus, the son of Hecuba and Priam, king of Troy. Polydorus (as his mother does not yet know) has been murdered by the man who was keeping him safe from harm. Literally translated by Mary Lefkowitz (Wellesley College), the lines read: "O mother, you who come from the halls of kings have seen the day of slavery. Your fortune is now as bad as it once was good. One of the gods is restoring the balance from your previous happiness and has destroyed you." Here, for comparison, is a recent verse translation by William Arrowsmith:

> –O Mother,
> poor majesty, old fallen queen,
> shorn of greatness, pride, and everything but life,
> which leaves you slavery and bitterness
> and lonely age.
>
> Some god destroys you now,
> exacting in your suffering the cost
> for having once been happy in this life.

Hecuba, trans. William Arrowsmith, in *The Complete Greek Tragedies,* ed. David Grene and Richard Lattimore, 4 vols. (Chicago: University of Chicago Press, 1992), 3:501.

To HARRY DANIELS, Esq.,

4, ESSEX COURT,

TEMPLE.

DEAR FRIEND,

I DEDICATE TO YOU THE FIRST-BORN OF MY BRAINS. RECEIVE
THIS TRIFLING MARK OF ESTEEM IN THE SPIRIT IN WHICH IT IS MADE,
AND ACCEPT THE WILLING HOMAGE THAT I RENDER TO—OH, MOST
RARE POSSESSION!—A GOOD AND TRUE HEART.

MAXWELL PHILIP.

PREFACE

This work has been written at a moment when the feelings of the Author are roused up to a high pitch of indignant excitement, by a statement of the cruel manner in which the slave holders of America deal with their slave-children. Not being able to imagine that even that dissolver of natural bonds – slavery – can shade over the hideousness of begetting children for the purpose of turning them out into the fields to labour at the lash's sting, he has ventured to sketch out the line of conduct, which a high-spirited and sensitive person would probably follow, if he found himself picking cotton under the spurring encouragement of "Jimboes" or "Quimboes" on his own father's plantation.

The machinery, or ground-work of the story is based on truth – the known history of the Boucaneers. It is scarcely necessary to tell the reader that the other parts are fiction.

The scenes are laid principally in the Island of Trinidad. This is done entirely from natural predilection, for Trinidad is the Author's native isle, whose green woods, smiling sky, beautiful flowers, and romantic gulf, together with a thousand sweet and melting associations, eternally play on his willing memory, and make him cherish ever the fond hope, that when the spark of life shall have been extinguished, his bones may be deposited on the rising ground that looks over the sea, and that already contains the being who, in death, as well as she was in life, was the object of his deep love and high veneration.

4, ELM COURT,
TEMPLE
FEBRUARY, 1854.

MICHEL MAXWELL PHILIP

The author of "EMMANUEL APPADOCCA," the late Hon. MICHEL MAXWELL PHILIP, was born at Cooper Grange Estate, South Naparima, on the 12th October, 1829. From an early age he shewed a keen desire to learn, and made rapid progress in the little school at San Fernando, where he received the rudiments of his education. His great abilities and application were such that his friends decided he should have the benefit of a European training, and when he reached the age of fourteen, he was sent to St. Mary's Catholic College, Blairs, on the banks of the Scottish Dee, where his progress in his studies was rapid in the extreme. At the end of six years, however, he returned to Trinidad, and as a Clerk entered the office of Mr. HENRY HART ANDERSON, Solicitor. Here he did not remain more than a few months, leaving Mr. ANDERSON's office to read law with the Solicitor-General, the Hon. G. GARCIA, father of the present Attorney-General. Mr. PHILIP always entertained the highest respect for Mr. GARCIA whom in after years, when writing to him from England, he used to quaintly address as "Illustrious Preceptor." But MAXWELL PHILIP was not satisfied with the prospect of being merely a legal clerk or even reaching the *status* of solicitor, and in 1851 he again crossed the Atlantic and in London studied law with the earnestness which had characterized his collegiate career. It was during this period, though one of the busiest of a busy life, he found time to devote himself to literary work and in the year (1854) in which he was called to the Bar by the Society of the Middle Temple, he wrote and published "EMMANUEL APPADOCCA." Mr. PHILIP did not return to his native isle immediately but spent several months travelling through many of the principal historical portions of Europe.

In 1855 he returned to Trinidad and at once began to practice. His tall, commanding presence, his sonorous voice, deliberate well rounded sentences, his talents, evident knowledge and skill in argument, immediately attracted attention and his fame as a lawyer spread throughout the Island; his clients became numerous and it was not long before he became one of the most prominent members of a bar, which was distinguished throughout the West Indies for its talents and ability.

Mr. PHILIP's qualities soon attracted the notice of the Government and in consequence he was appointed to act for considerable periods as Inspector of Schools. Later, GOVERNOR SIR ARTHUR GORDON gave him a seat, as an unofficial member, in the Legislative Council. Then when the Hon. G. GARCIA retired from the Solicitor-Generalship Mr. PHILIP was appointed to act in his stead as the head of the office in which he had made his *début* as a law student. During Mr. LONGDEN's Governorship

Mr. PHILIP was permanently appointed Solicitor-General. As Attorney-General he acted on the following occasions: From 10th June 1873 to 20th July 1874; 9th July to 2nd Nov. 1886; 28th June to 21th Oct. 1878; 9th May 1881 to 2nd Jan. 1882; 2nd July to 2nd Nov. 1883; 1885 to January. 1886; February to May 1886.

Mr. PHILIP's aid was also requisitioned by the Government in other than legal matters. He was Chairman of the Road Commission appointed by SIR WILLIAM ROBINSON and he was a member of the old Board of Education, the College Council, the Board of Health, the Trade and Taxes Commission and the Franchise Commission of 1888.

It was always a matter of surprise that Mr. PHILIP should never have been promoted to a higher office in the Government, and at one time it was hoped that he would be the successor of Mr. JUSTICE COURT when he retired from the Bench, but Mr. PHILIP's claims, established by eighteen years' service were overlooked. Once, and once only, was promotion offered him, but the Chief Justiceship of the Gold Coast which waited his acceptance, offered no charms to Mr. PHILIP who preferred residence in his native land to the dignity of a seat on the Bench of another Colony.

With regard to Mr. PHILIP's career as a lawyer before he joined the ranks of the public service, it may be said that on all occasions he shewed himself an able advocate in both civil and criminal courts, but some of his greatest triumphs were obtained in the latter in most difficult cases on the side of the defence. For many years Mr. PHILIP was the only lawyer in the colony–having survived the others–intimately acquainted with the old Spanish laws of Trinidad, and he was consequently regarded as an authority upon all matters relating to Spanish jurisprudence.

In 1867, Mr. PHILIP was elected Mayor of Port-of-Spain and for three years occupied the office, during which he carried out some much needed reforms and initiated many improvements in the town. He took an active part at the public meeting which met for the purpose of calling upon the Government to restore the salary of Archbishop Spaccapietra, and also to induce the British Government to recognize that prelate as the Archbishop of Port-of-Spain. Although a staunch adherent of the Roman Catholic Church, it is pleasant to be able to record of Mr. PHILIP that he could also meet with cordiality the clergy of other churches. The late CHARLES KINGSLEY during his visit to the Island was invited by Mr. PHILIP to be present at a meeting of the Friends of Popular Education over which he was to preside. CANON KINGSLEY accepted the invitation and his letter is still preserved among the PHILIP family papers.

Mr. PHILIP's name is associated with a great number of Ordinances now standing on the Statute Book. The Arima Railway Ordinance was drawn up and passed by him and the Tramway Ordinance he drafted, advocated, and carried through the Legislature in the face of the almost fierce, certainly vigorous, opposition of the Chief Justice SIR JOSEPH NEEDHAM. He also proposed and carried the motion (in an extremely able speech) by which the projected annexation of the island of Tobago to Trinidad received the assent of the Trinidad Legislative Council.

In 1887, after thirty-two years of public life, Mr. PHILIP's once robust health showed symptoms of breaking down. He, however, refused to give up his duties even temporarily, but while on a visit to the Islands, which he described so exquisitely in the story here presented to the reader, he was suddenly overtaken by an illness from which he never recovered. He was conveyed to his residence at Maraval and there after some weeks he died on the 30th of June, 1888, aged 59 years.

In appearance Mr. MAXWELL PHILIP was of tall, commanding presence and carried himself with dignity; he was a highly accomplished man, the master of several languages; his eloquence was proverbial throughout the island and in many of the West Indian Colonies. He was exceptionally clever at *repartee* and some very good stories are told of him in this respect. On one occasion he was arguing a question before one of our local judges who was credited with being of a somewhat hasty temperament. The judge expressed himself as having formed his opinion upon the point Mr. PHILIP was laying before him and told him so. Mr. PHILIP still insisted upon his view when the judge hastily and abruptly asked him to pass on to the next point. The Barrister replied, it had been said: "Fools rush in where angels fear to tread"– "Come, come," interrupted the judge–"I never said that you were a fool, Mr. PHILIP." "Neither, your Honour," said Mr. PHILIP in his gravest and most sonorous tones, as he bowed towards the Bench, "Neither, your Honour, was I so imprudent as to in any way intimate that your Honour was an angel." Another good story is told of him which is so characteristic that it would be a pity to allow it to be lost. Some papers with reference to the disputed ownership of the bed of the Dry River–a problem which has waited a quarter of a century for solution–had been sent to him as Solicitor-General. A new Governor came to the colony and the question having cropped up again His Excellency sent for the papers. The Governor, in looking through them, found that Mr. PHILIP had had them three years and had apparently done nothing with them. Upon this the Head of the Executive wrote a sharp minute calling upon the Hon. the Solicitor-General to explain why he had been three years considering the question. Such a question would from the majority of Public Officers have elicited the minutest explanations of the why and wherefore, but Mr. PHILIP simply wrote in effect as follows: "I have no doubt His Excellency will agree with me that three years is not too long a period for the consideration of such an important question as the ownership of the Dry River." This answer completely silenced His Excellency.

In concluding this brief sketch of the life of the late Mr. MAXWELL PHILIP we cannot find a better tribute to pay his memory than that uttered by SIR WILLIAM ROBINSON at the meeting of the Legislative Council which followed Mr. PHILIP's demise. His Excellency said:

"GENTLEMEN,–Mr. GARCIA having taken his seat as Acting Solicitor General, I desire to ask you whether you concur with me in the propriety of placing on record some expression of our opinion as to the great loss which this Council has sustained in consequence of the death of the HON. MICHEL MAXWELL PHILIP. Mr. PHILIP was a man of whom Trinidad might well be proud. He was not only a remarkable man in Trinidad, but was a remarkable man in the West Indies, and would have been a remarkable man anywhere. Most of you Gentlemen, knew him for a far longer period than I did, and you, therefore will be more able than I am to speak in regard to his great gifts and to appreciate them. He certainly was possessed of a most wonderful memory, and he had to the full extent, what is called, "the Heaven born gift of Eloquence." In his well rounded periods and his well studied phrases we could always recognize great depth of knowledge on the matter of which he spoke, and in addition to that, he possessed special knowledge not only in regard to men and matters, but in regard to the history of this Colony, and the old standing customs and the laws that governed it. Now that Mr. PHILIP has left us, quite apart from the regret that I feel, I may say that I look back with a great deal of pleasure upon the intimate, I may say friendly relations which existed between us. He would come to me once every week, and he never left my room without my feeling that I had been interested, amused, and not unfrequently instructed, as the sweet singer says, with "the sweet food of sweetly uttered knowledge."

For two years and nine months Mr. PHILIP acted as Solicitor-General under me and on one occasion as Attorney-General, and as Her Majesty's representative, I say it without hesitation, and I say it with pride and with gratitude, that I found him not only a safe and wise Counsellor but trusty and loyal adviser. What I have said I feel Gentlemen, is quite insufficient and quite inadequate, but I trust you who hear it and all who read what I have said, will believe that my only desire is to pay a humble tribute to the memory of one of Trinidad's greatest sons. Stricken as he was a few months ago with a fatal illness, "death came" to him "with friendly care" and mercifully released him from what possibly might have been a prolonged illness of pain and suffering. Of Mr. PHILIP I think it may be said, although the phrase is very hackneyed, still it is nevertheless true, that "Take him for all in all, we shall never look upon his like again." I propose that, the Hon. Mr. FOWLER, Mr. GARCIA, Mr. FINLAYSON, and Mr. FITT, be a committee to prepare a resolution of condolence to be presented by this Council to Mr. PHILIP's nearest relations."

EMMANUEL APPADOCCA;

OR,

BLIGHTED LIFE.

A Tale of the Boucaneers

CHAPTER I

"Plots have I laid; inductions dangerous." *

RICHARD III

BETWEEN the north-west coast of Venezuela and the Island of Trinidad there lies an extensive expanse of water, known as the Gulf of Paria:—a name which it has derived from the neighbouring Spanish coast. At first sight this gulf presents to the eye the appearance of a vast lake. On the north, east, and south, it is bordered by the dark mountains of Trinidad: while, on the opposite side the cloud-capt Andes, which terminate in that direction, rear their towering heads, and present a lofty western boundary.

The gulf, thus narrowly surrounded on all sides, communicates with the great Atlantic ocean only by two narrow outlets, which are situated at its northern and southern extremities, and are respectively named "the Dragon's" and the "Serpent's Mouth." It is by these narrow straits, as the

---

*Philip begins each chapter with an epigraph from Shakespeare. To locate the passage in context, readers should consult: John Bartlett, *A New and Complete Concordance to Shakespeare* (1894); T. H. Howard-Hill, *Oxford [Old-Spelling] Shakespeare Concordances* (Oxford: Clarendon Press, 1969-72); Marvin Spevack, *A Complete and Systematic Concordance to the Works of Shakespeare,* 8 vols. (Hildesheim, Germany, 1968-70); and Spevack, *The Harvard Concordance to Shakespeare* (Cambridge: Harvard University Press, 1973).

reader will have already gathered, that Trinidad is separated from the main-land of South America. Shielded as they are by these elevated boundaries, the waters of the gulf are ever calm and placid. The hurricanes which periodically ravage the adjacent regions, never sweep their quiet surface: and ships from the ports of the neighbouring colonies usually avail them-selves of the protection afforded by this sheltered haven, and safely ride away the tempestuous months on its smooth expanse.

The scenery around this gulf is extremely picturesque and beautiful. Small green islands are dispersed here and there, and seem to float gaily on the bosom of the slumbering waters; the forest clothed mountains that beetle from above, cast their lengthy shadows far and wide, and the diving birds that continually ply the wing over the reflecting surface, throw into the scene some of the choicest features of romantic beauty.

It was here, that, on a lovely morning in the month of March, two skiffs might barely be seen floating quietly far, far away at sea.

It was as yet early: the gray mist of the tropical morning was just melting away before the rays of the rising sun, that was fast ascending from behind the mountains in the east; a thin haze, nevertheless, was still left surround-ing every object. Scarcely a ripple as yet marked the gulf, and in the quiet of the hour might be heard the waking haloos of the mariners on board their ships in the harbour of Port-of-Spain, as they summoned each other to the labours of the day.

The two skiffs were at a great distance from land. In the haze it was difficult on a hasty glance to distinguish them from the sea; but, on closer observation, they might be discovered to be a small fishing-boat, such as those which are generally seen on the gulf, and a curial, or Indian canoe.

There were three men in the fishing-boat: two who were rowers, and one that was sitting at its stern and was apparently the master. He was of mixed blood: of that degree known as that of mulatto, and seemingly of Spanish extraction, but his two men were blacks. The men were resting on their oars, the master was occupied in deep sea fishing, and the boat floated passively on the water. In the Indian canoe there seemed also but three men: one sat at the stern, the other two crouched in the centre, their paddles were carelessly rested on the sides of the light vessel, and the canoe, like the fishing-boat, was permitted to float unsteered on the gulf. The two skiffs were not far from each other, and as the haze cleared away, the master of the fishing-boat, in the musing calm attendant on quiet fishing, observed to his men, as he dreamingly looked on the canoe–

"Those fellows are Guaragons; I daresay they paddled from *home in* the canoe the whole of last night, and they are now taking their breakfast to get up to town before the breeze rises."

"Yes, sa," briskly rejoined one of the boatmen; "dey wok all night, all nakid as dey be dey; dey no 'fraid rain, dey no 'fraid sun, but when dey begin dey wok–wok so–night and day, you see paddle go phshah–phshah–phshah," here the speaker screwed up his little features to the utmost, in order to express the energy with which the Indians are supposed to paddle, while, at the same time, he endeavoured to imitate the sound of the paddle itself, as it dashes the water. "Awh!" he exclaimed, with emphasis, after this display, "dey no get dis Jack Jimmy," pointing to himself "foo do dat–no:– oohn–oohn," and he shook his head energetically.

The master smiled both at the humour of his man and the horror which he appeared to entertain for the work and exposure of the Indians.

"And den, wha dey eat," he continued, "ripe plaintin!* dey eat ripe plaintin fo brofost, ripe plantin fo dinna–awh! me no know how dey get fat, but dey always berry fat."

The strange little man continued in this vein to make his remarks about the Indians, and the master attended to his line until the morning was considerably advanced, and the sun had already risen to a great height.

"Now, my boys," said the last mentioned individual, "I think it is time for us to go, we have not had much luck to-day." With this he began leisurely to draw in his line, gazing listlessly on the Indian canoe while he did so,–"but these fellows are taking a long time to eat their ripe plaintains this morning, Jack Jimmy," he observed.

"Me tink so foo true, sa," replied the individual answering to that name.

"An da big Injan in de tern a de canoe da look pan awee berry hard–berry hard–hè bin da look pan awee all de mannin so," and then looking anxiously on the canoe, he continued, "an me no da see parrat, me no da see monkey, me no da see notting pan de side a de canoe, an you neber see Injan ya widout parrat an monkey."

Having delivered himself of this sage opinion, he looked at the canoe again, long and anxiously, shook his head, and moved restlessly on his thwart.†

"What is the matter with you, Jack Jimmy," inquired the master, "you seem to be displeased with these Indians?"

---

*plaintin [plaintains]: plants with broad leaves; a staple for food for Caribbean slaves. It was common for English writers to say in a derisive manner about slaves, "Let them eat pumpkins and plantains."

†thwart: seat across a boat.

Jack Jimmy made no answer, but gave expression to a sound like "hom!" Then began to look into the bottom of the boat, while he beat time apparently to his own ruminations with his chubby great toe.

"But what is the matter with you, man?" again inquired the master.

"Massa—massa—me—me-me-me no like close, close so to Injans pan big salt water, so, no."

The first part of the sentence Jack Jimmy pronounced moodily, but he shot out the latter part with such rapidity and earnestness, that the gravity of the master could hold out no longer, and he laughed heartily at his man.

"Bah! you fool," said he, when the fit was over: "what do you expect these Indians will do to us?"

Jack Jimmy, much piqued at being laughed at, raised his shoulders, and answered stoically—"Me no know; but me tink we better go."

"Yes: we are not doing anything here, and there does not seem much prospect of having better luck," said the master, "let us go." He then took up his paddle from the bottom of the boat, and put it over the stern to steer it.

The men began to row, and the little boat began to move through the water. The Indian canoe, which had remained all the time as passive on the water as the fishing-boat, was now also put in motion, by two paddles, and seemed to be steered in the same direction as the fishing boat. Jack Jimmy saw this, opened his eyes, and cried, in a voice that began to tremble,—"Dey da come, too." The master looked round, and saw in truth that the canoe was following in their wake.

The three persons now became somewhat uneasy, and anxious, about the intentions of their mysterious follower. After a time, however, when they saw it was not gaining ground upon them, nor seemed to be propelled with any intention of coming up to them, these feelings were considerably diminished, and they pulled calmly along, while the canoe followed at the same distance from the little boat.

When the fishing-boat had reached to within a mile of the ships which lay in the harbour of Port-of-Spain, the master was challenged by a brisk "Haloo" from the man at the stern of the canoe.

"Haloo, there!" cried the man in a commanding voice, "haloo, there—stop!"

The master paid no attention to this order, but pretended that he did not hear it, or did not consider it addressed to him, and he remained silent; but Jack Jimmy had not so much command over himself.

"Wha," cried he, "wha eber yierry Injan peak plain—plain so? hen!" and he shook his head mysteriously. "But wha," following out his reflections, "dey want we fo tap foo—tell dem we no da sell fish, ya; let dem come sho."

"Will you stop, there–ho?" again cried the man from the stern of the pursuing canoe.

"We cannot stop," replied the master, "if you wish to buy fish, come ashore. Pull boys," addressing himself to his men; "those seem to be strange customers." Jack Jimmy and the other boatman bent on their oars.

As soon as the little fishing-boat was put in a more rapid movement, ten Indians simultaneously sprung as if it were by magic from the bottom of the canoe, and ranged themselves at its sides, paddle in hand.

"Wha, look dey!" cried Jack Jimmy, pointing tremblingly to the canoe, "pull," addressing himself to his companion, "pull, me tell you:" and he himself drew his oar with all the energy and vigour which fear alone can impart. "Pull, me tell you," continued he, every moment, to exhort his companion; "pull, me tell you." Under these efforts the little shell boat skipped like a feather over the water: but it was no match for the canoe, propelled as it was by the vigorous paddles of twelve stout men. Like an arrow from an Indian bow, or like the noiseless course of a serpent, through the lake it drew on the little fishing-boat. Jack Jimmy and his companion exerted themselves to the utmost; the master too, plied his paddle strongly and continuously, but nearer and nearer the canoe approached. When at last it came opposite the pursued, the man at the stern dexterously threw his paddle on the other side, a rapid movement was made through the water, and the head of the canoe was at once athwart the little fishing-boat.

Jack Jimmy could bear it no longer; as soon as the boat was boarded, with a convulsive spring, he plunged into the gulf; while the syllables of his interjected "Garamighty" bubbled up after him as he disappeared. But the first impulse of the master was to draw his knife from the side of the boat, where it was stuck in a chink of the boards, and with a deep-mouthed "carajo"* was going to plunge it into the nearest Indian, but his arm was no sooner raised than it was paralyzed by a blow dealt him with his paddle by a man at the stern, and the knife fell from his grasp into the water.

"Fool," cried the man who had thus struck him, "what is the use of your resistance: do you not see we number more than you? Get into this canoe immediately, you and your man, and see if you can save that strange creature that is capering in the water there;" and he pointed to Jack Jimmy, who had now come again to the surface, and in the extremity of his fear, with his mouth wide open, and his white eye-balls glaring, was swimming most furiously out to sea. The sight was too ridiculous even for the occasion; the whole of the Indians burst into a fit of laughter at poor Jack Jimmy, who was

*carajo: an exclamation of anger or disgust.

fatiguing himself at such a rate that his strength would probably not have lasted more than two minutes.

"Paddle to that poor fellow," said the man at the stern, and the order was obeyed. But Jack Jimmy would not be taken; he dived several times to escape, to the no small amusement of the Indians: his strength however began to fail, and he was at last captured.

They took him into the canoe, when he was almost exhausted, and he was laid at the bottom of it, where he kept his eyes closed and stretched himself stiffly out, to pretend that he was dead. The Indians seemed highly amused by him. At last, however, he ventured to open his eyes, when, seeing some cutlasses and pikes that lay by his side at the bottom of the canoe, he closed them abruptly again and cried, "Oh La-a-r-rd, me dead!"

When Jack Jimmy had been saved from drowning, the master and the other rower were transhipped into the canoe. The master, shrewder than his men, thought he observed, in addition to the circumstance of speaking English, other marks in the Indians which resembled disguise. They seemed more assured and less savage than Indians generally are; besides, they had thick beards and mustachioes which the savages never wear; and, above all, their arms, instead of being rude bows and arrows, or at best rusty fowling pieces,* were beautiful rifles, cutlasses and pikes.

"But who are you?" he inquired after he had detected these appearances, and become justly alarmed by them. "Who are you, and what do you intend to do with us?"

"With regard to the first question," answered the man at the stern with stoical coolness, "that is not any business of yours;–in answer to the second, be assured that we mean you no harm. I hope you are satisfied. Now, my order to you is, that you ask no further questions."

"But, sir,–" the master was about to inquire again.

"Silence!" cried the man in a voice that carried authority.

He then took a small telescope that was concealed in a locker formed in the thwart on which he sat, and began to examine the ships and the harbour with seemingly great care and minuteness.

This examination continued for the best part of an hour, after which the man at the stern handed the telescope to the master fisherman and requested him to look also at the ships: "for," added he, "you will have to answer questions about them."

"I know them already," answered the master and returned the telescope.

* fowling pieces: light guns.

The latter instrument was carefully replaced, and a small marine compass was taken out of the same locker and placed before the man at the stern.

"To your paddles, it is now two o'clock, and will be late before we arrive."

The head of the canoe was immediately turned out to sea. The men plied their paddles, and the wind, which had just risen, wafted the light bark rapidly before it. Its destination, however, was incomprehensible to the fishermen, for they could not possibly conceive to what place a canoe that was thus turned out to open sea could be bound.

But whatever alarm they felt, they were obliged to conceal; for it would have been dangerous, they thought, to break the strict command of the man at the stern; and whatever they could have said or done, would have had no effect on men who seemed to be little accustomed to be crossed, and who, undoubtedly, had the power of enforcing their will.

They resigned themselves, therefore, passively to their fate: and did so with the greater readiness, as they had not, as yet, experienced, from those among whom they were so strangely thrown, any treatment which could lead them to apprehend anything horrible or atrocious.

CHAPTER II

"–Observe degree, priority, and place,
Insisture, course, proportion, season, form,
Office, and custom in all line of order–"
TROILUS AND CRESSIDA

THE canoe held a direct course out to sea the remaining part of the day. This was drawing fast to a close, when there might be perceived, straight over the bows of the canoe, and far, far away, a small dark object that seemed to rest lightly on the horizon, which was, at that moment, illumined by the red rays of the large round sun that was fast sinking behind it.

The head of the canoe was kept direct upon that speck, and the man at the stern seemed to make no more use of his compass.

Such was the rapidity with which the canoe went, borne away, as it was, by the breeze, as well as propelled by the paddles of twelve strong men, that within three hours after sunset, they were close to that which, a short time before, had appeared so small, so shadowy, and so distant.

The object proved to be a low, black, balahoo schooner,* whose model, as far as it could be observed by the starlight, was most beautiful. She was built as sharply as a sword, with her bows terminating in the shape of a Gar's lance,† while her stern slanted off in the most graceful proportions.

But the most remarkable part in her build, was her immense and almost disproportioned length, which, combined with her perfectly straight lines, low hull, and the slenderness of her make, gave her the appearance of a large serpent.

Her rigging was of the lightest fashion as two simple shrouds, which supported each mast, and the bow sprit and jibboom stays formed her principal cordage.

There was not a yard, a gaff, or piece of canvas aloft, so that the tall masts remained bare and graceful, shining under their polish. On these accounts, they could not be perceived at any distance, and a boat, discovering the vessel for the first time, would be at a loss to make out what floating object it was.

Her position also, and the manner in which she seemed moored—mast-less, as it would appear—was strange and peculiar. She was not swinging to the wind or current, but she rode under a bow and stern anchor, which kept her head directly towards the Dragon's Mouth, while the rippling waves, that still curled before the gentle night breeze, broke playfully on her side.

"What word?" sounded the hoarse and echoing voice of some one on the deck, as the canoe approached the schooner.

"Scorpion," the man replied in as sounding a voice, and the canoe boarded the vessel. The ladders were thrown out over the sides, and the man at the stern jumped nimbly on deck.

A sentinel stationed at the gangway lowered his weapon, and the man at the stern, for so we must still call him, passed.

The sentinel was a tall muscular man of a dark complexion; his face was almost entirely covered with hair, on his head he wore a red cap, he had on a red woollen shirt, his trowsers were black, and were secured round his waist by a thick red sash, in which were stuck a brace of pistols and a long poniard.‡

These and a cutlass, which he held in his hand, were his only weapons.

---

*balahoo schooner: the Spanish word "balahu" means schooner; the OED cites Smyth's *Sailor's Word-Book* (1867): ballahou, ballahoo, "a sharp-floored, fast-sailing schooner, with taunt fore-and-aft sails, and no topsails, common in Bermuda and the West Indies."

†Gar's lance: a spear with sharp point and keen cutting edges.

‡poniard: a dagger with a slender blade.

As soon as the man at the stern was on deck he was accosted by a tall, thin person with flowing mustachioes, and with marks of distinction from the sentinel, both in dress and in his appearance. He was richly and tastefully accoutred. He wore a jet black frock coat, which was richly but simply embroidered with gold; his trowsers were of unspotted white, and displayed neat and highly polished boots; round his waist he wore a richly fringed crimson sash, in which pistols and a poniard were also stuck; and a slender belt supported a handsome sword by his side. His head was covered by a red cap, and rich gold epaulets rested on his shoulders.

"Lorenzo," said this individual, addressing the new comer in a low and pleasant tone, "I am happy to see you back. Success, I hope."

"Success," answered Lorenzo briefly but courteously, "I have three strangers there in the boat, of whom, pray, order your watch to take care; the captain, I suppose is in his cabin, so I shall see him by the dawn of day. Good night, Sebastian, good watch."

"Farewell," answered the party addressed, and Lorenzo, our former man at the stern, disappeared.

This short dialogue carried on, as it was, in an under tone, scarcely broke the extraordinary silence which reigned on board the mysterious schooner.

After Lorenzo had disappeared, Sabastian ordered his men to take charge of the three prisoners in the canoe, who were accordingly brought on deck. Jack Jimmy, who after his fear had been lulled by the apparent harmless treatment of the Indians, had fallen fast asleep, was the most struck when awakening, with the extraordinary position in which he found himself suddenly placed. When he got on deck, he stood as if his limbs would not support him; he first looked aloft at the tapering masts of the schooner, then on the deck, and when his eyes fell on the men by whom he was surrounded, he opened his mouth for an instant in mute amazement, and succeeded at length to give expression to his terror in the words–"Garamighty! Way me be? Wha dish ya?"

"Softly, my little man," said the sentinel, in a voice that contrasted strangely with the weak shriek of the terror-stricken Jack Jimmy, "we don't speak so loud here."

"Massa, me hush," was the immediate answer of Jack Jimmy, and he closed his lips as firmly as he could, as an earnest of his determination to keep silence; but in the dark the white of his eyes may have been seen revolving from object to object with the rapidity of lightning.

"Follow this way," said a man, who had received instructions from the officer, to the prisoners; and he led them down a narrow stair-case to a small cabin in the foremost part of the vessel. "This is where you are to sleep to-night," said he to them, after they had been ushered in: "do you require anything?"

The captives answered in the negative.

"Well," continued the man, "make yourselves comfortable for the night, and be awake betimes to-morrow to see our captain—he gets up early."

He then posted himself at the door of the cabin, with his cutlass in his hand, like one who was to pass the whole night there. Not a sound more was heard on board the schooner that night.

When morning had arrived, the prisoners were brought on deck, and requested to be prepared to appear before the captain immediately.

The strange vessel on board of which they found themselves, could be better examined by daylight than by the dim star-gleam of the preceding night. The long level deck was scoured as white as snow; not a speck, not a nail-head, not the minutest particle of anything could be discovered upon it. The very seams were filled up in such a manner, that the material which made them impervious to water, imparted an appearance of general cleanliness. The halliards were all beautifully adjusted at the foot of each mast, and made up for the moment in the shape of mats, or other fanciful forms. The belaying pins, that were lined with brass, were beautifully polished, while the tapering masts were as clean and as smooth as ivory. The arrangement of the deck, also, was exceedingly neat: nothing but a few beautiful and simple machines for hoisting were to be seen, and in properly-disposed recesses in the bulwarks, glimpses might be caught of the rude instruments of destruction—of pikes that looked horrible even in their places of rest,—axes whose shining edges made the blood run chill, and grappling-irons, whose tortuous and crooked prongs made the nerves recoil with the thoughts of agony which they brought up. An awning, as white as the deck which it sheltered, was spread from the stem to the stern of the schooner.

Men dressed and armed, as the sentinel of the preceding evening, were leaning here and there, conversing together in a low tone of voice.

Of all these things, the one which particularly attracted the attention of the strangers was the extraordinary device that everything on board the schooner bore; namely, a death's head* placed on the crossing of two dead men's bones. This was imprinted on the rigging of the schooner, on its tackle, on the weapons which were arranged in the bulwarks, and the men wore it in front of their blood-red caps, and on their arms. This strange

---

*death's head: a human skull as the emblem of death.

circumstance had a powerful effect on the prisoners: Jack Jimmy opened his mouth and eyes, and seemed, on contemplating that sign, to devote himself to death already; and the master fisherman became still more anxious than he had been from the first. He recollected that in the various stories with which he and his fellows in the same pursuit had beguiled many a tedious hour, pirates were represented as always displaying a black flag, on which the same sad mementoes of mortality, as those which he saw everywhere on board the schooner, were imprinted.

The thought immediately broke in upon him that he might at that moment be among those lawless men, about whose horrible cruelties he had heard so much, and he shuddered at the reflection.

It is true he had not, up to that moment, experienced any personal outrage or even incivility; but might he not be reserved for those shocking tortures to which he had heard pirates were accustomed to resort, for the purpose of forcing their victims to the confession of what was alike improbable and impossible? His reflections now became gloomy and distressing; and thoughts that rush upon a man only at his last moments, or in situations of imminent danger, began now to force themselves upon him.

This train of thoughts was broken by Lorenzo, who suddenly emerged from the companion of the chief cabin and approached him.

Lorenzo presented quite a different appearance from what he did under his Indian disguise of the day before.

He was cleanly washed of the red ochre with which he had painted his skin; it now appeared fresh and clear, as it was by nature, although a little embronzed by a tropical sun. His features, which could now be properly read, expressed a character of manly firmness, softened by much humanity and tenderness. He wore the same dress as the officer whom he met on duty the previous night, with the slight exception that his red cap was more richly decorated. This seemed to be a badge of distinction, and it could be at once perceived from the manner in which he acted, that Lorenzo was in high command on board the strange schooner.

"The prisoners will not be wanted for half an hour," he said to the man on duty; "you may retire with them."

He then went back, and descended the stairs by which he had ascended.

These stairs led to a wide passage in the main-deck of the vessel, which extended from the stem to the door of the main cabin: he turned to the right, and proceeded to the part where that cabin was situated.

He passed by a number of doors and passages, but proceeded straight down the one in which he was, until he arrived at a certain door that stood immediately opposite him. He then touched a large skull of bronze that grinned hideously on it; it instantly flew open, and he stood before a tall, and full armed sentinel, who, immovable as a statue, looked him fiercely in the eyes.

The officer, without uttering a word, presented the index finger of his left hand, on which there was a large ring, the sentinel quietly stepped aside, and he passed.

He made a few steps, and from another niche in the passage another sentinel presented himself, he showed the ring again and passed; he went further forward, and was again met by another sentinel, he performed the same ceremony, and he was also permitted to pass. He went on and met several others, on whom the ring had the same effect; at last, he arrived at a sort of anti-chamber, where two black boys, in gorgeous attire, were waiting.

They immediately bent their bodies to Lorenzo as he advanced, and then stood ready to answer him any question he should ask.

"Is your master at leisure, Bembo?" asked Lorenzo.

"He is, senor," answered one of the boys.

"Say I am here, and desire audience."

The boy bent his body again and retired.

He immediately returned, and informed the officer that his master desired him to enter, and conducted him to a door.

The officer pressed a skull similar to that with which the reader has already been made acquainted; the door flew open, and he stood in a magnificent apartment, with a young man before him.

The apartment into which Lorenzo had entered, was vast and magnificent in its proportions; it was formed of the whole of the after part of the schooner, and of its entire width. It was richly though peculiarly decorated: the sides, unlike the plain wainscoting of ships in general, were made of the richest and most exquisitely polished mahogany, upon which were elaborately carved landscapes, in which nature was represented principally in her most terrible aspect,–with volcanoes belching forth their liquid fires; cataracts eating away in their angry mood the rugged granite, over whose uneven brows they were foamingly precipitated; inhospitable mountains frowning on the solitary waves below, that unheedingly lashed their base; chasms that yawned as terrific as the cataclysm that might be supposed to have formed them, and other subjects which blended the magnificent with the terribly sublime.

The precious metals were freely used to mark the shades and other

points in these highly wrought carvings, so that the fire which the volcanoes sent forth was cleverly represented by gold, the water by silver, and
so forth.

Large beads of gold surrounded each tableau, and separated it from the
next. On the skirting-boards at the lower parts were carved paleozoic creatures, that held between their extended jaws large richly bound volumes,
which were secured by springs against the rolling of the vessel.

The ceiling was decorated in the same peculiar manner: the two sides of
the celestial sphere were distinctly represented, with the signs of the zodiac
and the constellations finished in a perfect style, and scrupulously placed at
the correct distances from each other.

The furniture was in exact keeping with this rich, though strange style of
decoration. Soft and velvetty carpets covered the floor, or rather the deck;
fanciful ottomans, made in the shape of gigantic sea shells, covered with
crimson velvet, and decorated with pure and solid gold, were placed here
and there. Immense globes of the earth and the heavens, mathematical
instruments of the largest size were carefully arranged, and so effectually
secured in their position, that they could not be effected by the tossing of
the schooner. But what was particularly calculated to attract attention
among these various things was a gigantic telescope, whose principal parts
stood on a magnificent frame. More than ordinary care seemed to be devoted to this instrument, both to its construction and to its preservation, for
everything about it was exquisitely made and polished.

The young man who stood before Lorenzo, may have been about twenty-
five years of age: he was tall and slender, but infinitely well formed; his limbs
were beautifully proportioned and straight, and his hands were almost femininely delicate, notwithstanding the close construction of the bones, and
the hard, wiry sinews, which could be barely seen, now and then slightly
swelling the skin.

His complexion was of a very light olive, it showed a mixture of blood,
and proclaimed that the man was connected with some dark race, and in the
infinity of grades in the population of Spanish America, he may have been
said to be of that which is commonly designated Quadroon. *

But the features of this femininely formed man were in deep contrast with
his make; they were handsome to the extreme; but there was something in
his large tropical eyes that seemed to possess the power of the basilisk,† and

---

*Quadroon: a person having one-quarter black ancestry.
†basilisk: a legendary serpent or dragon.

made it difficult to be supposed that any man could meet their glance without feeling it.

This expression was increased by his lowering brows that overshadowed his eyes, and indicated, at once, an individual of much resolution; while his high aquiline nose, compressed lips, and set jaws, pointed clearly to a disposition that would undertake the most arduous and hazardous things, and execute them with firmness in spite of perils.

In brief, the most superficial observer might have read, in the face of that young man, the existence of something within, which was endowed with the power of controlling the most headstrong and refractory,–of quelling the most rebellious spirits.

It required not the discoveries of science to convince men, at a glance of his features, that there was a power in that mind which was reflected on his face, that wherever he was he would be by the necessity of his own mind– pre-eminent and uppermost; that men must, unknowingly to themselves, obey him, and act as he acted.

In addition to those animal attributes, the shape of his head was what the most fastidious could but admire; his forehead rose in the fullness of beautiful proportions, while, at the same time, those skilled in reading others' skulls would have declared that, with his high intellectual development, he did not lack those necessary moral accompaniments which the Creator, in his wisdom, has providently bestowed for the proper use and regulation of the former.

Withal, however, there might be discerned in the lofty bearing and haughty mien of the young man a stern and invincible pride.

The dress of our young hero was simple; he wore trowsers of the finest and whitest materials, and a Moorish jacket of crimson silk, large and ample sleeves; round his waist was folded a red silk sash, in which a gilded poniard and pistols mounted with gold, were stuck; his head was uncovered, and his black raven locks flowed over his shoulders in wild and unrestrained profusion.

When Lorenzo entered the cabin the young man was standing by a table, on which lay open a richly ornamented volume of "Bacon's Novum Organum," with the books of "Aristotle's Philosophy"* by its side.

It was evident that he was making his morning meditation on those learned tomes.

---

*"Bacon's Novum Organum"; "Aristotle's Philosophy": Francis Bacon (1561-1626), English statesman, essayist, and philosopher, whose works include *Novum Organum* ("new instrument," 1620); Aristotle, Greek philosopher (384-322, BC).

When Lorenzo entered the cabin he bowed profoundly.

"Good morning, Lorenzo," said the young man, still maintaining his high posture, and pointed an ottoman to the visitor.

"Well, how have you fared?" he inquired.

"Well, your excellency," answered the officer, "I have captured a fisherman with his two men, whom I have brought on board for your especial examination. I made my observations during the time that my men were resting, and have to report, that there are several deeply laden ships in the harbour, which, from all appearances, are ready for sea, and will sail within a few days. There seem to be prospects of a rich booty, with very little work for our men. There are no ships of war in the harbour. I have taken the marks and sizes of the vessels, which you will find on this paper, so that the fisherman may be accurately questioned. The ship, about which your excellency especially instructed me, is also in the harbour." Then, with a low bow, Lorenzo handed a paper to the young man.

"You have done well, Lorenzo," the latter said, and glanced over the paper for a short time, and, apparently, possessing himself of the information it contained, laid it by.

"Let your fisherman be brought, Lorenzo."

The officer left the apartment for a time and returned, shortly afterwards, with the fisherman.

The fisherman appeared bewildered by the grandeur of the place, and could scarcely restrain his eyes from wandering distractedly about.

The captain, after affording him some time to regain himself, requested him to dismiss his fears, and assured him that no harm should be done him if he spoke the truth, and began to interrogate him.

"You know the Harbour of Port-of-Spain, do you not?"

"I do, senor," replied the fisherman, "I fish in it every day."

"Do you know the ships that are there now?"

"Senor, I do not know their names, but I know they are nearly all English."

"Do you know the large ship that is anchored opposite the banks of the Caroni?"

"Senor, as I have said before, not its name; but I know that it belongs to a rich English merchant, and is laden with sugar for Bristol."

"Do you know when she is to sail?"

"Senor," answered the fisherman, "not positively, but, from her appearance, I should say she will sail in a day or two."

The young man proceeded in this manner and examined the fisherman about all the vessels which were reported in Lorenzo's paper to be in the harbour, but without, at the same time, receiving any more definite information.

After the questioning was ended, he requested the fisherman to be re-assured, and to fear nothing; he then pressed a spring at his feet, and one of the black boys appeared.

"Show this man on deck," said the captain. The fisherman was shown on deck, where the sentinel duly received him.

"Lorenzo," said the young man, "by the chart of this island, and, from my own experience, I know that there are only two outlets from this gulf–the Serpent's and the Dragon's Mouth. Ships but seldom go through the Serpent's Mouth, both, on account of its narrowness, and its distance out of the course of those that may be bound for England. It is, therefore, my opinion that the ships, which are now about to sail, will pass by the Dragon's Mouth; that passage is fifty miles to the north of this. It is my will that five men be sent with this fisherman of yours, to watch the sailing of the ships: go you, therefore, bear the token, and request the officer of the watch to attend to this order. When this is done, come you hither and let me know. It is my will to let the men have pleasure to-day as they may have work shortly."

Lorenzo bowed and retired: he shortly returned and informed the captain–as the reader must have already discovered him to be–that his order was executed. The captain asked no further questions, but, perhaps from the habit of being always strictly and implicitly obeyed, he never doubted but that things were done as he wished. Such, too, was the discipline that seemed to reign on board of the schooner, that scarcely five minutes elapsed before preparations were made, and a boat, with the fisherman, among others, was duly dispatched to do as the captain commanded.

When the captain was informed that his orders were executed, he pressed again the spring and the boy appeared.

"Sound the gong," he said: the boy bowed and retired.

CHAPTER III

> "See it be done, and feast our army, we have store to do it–
> And they have earned the waste."
>
> ANTHONY AND CLEOPATRA

No sooner had the captain given the order, than the whole schooner echoed with the deafening sounds of a huge gong, whose noise was sufficient to rouse the soundest sleeper in the lowest recesses of the schooner.

The sounds seemed to possess the power of transforming the vessel, where such quiet and silence a little before had reigned, to a scene of unbounded revelry. No sooner had they fallen on the ears of the grim and bearded sailors, than shouts of joy and mirth burst forth from the same men, who, but a short time before seemed pressed by a paralysing power into discipline, order, and the silence of death.

The deck then suddenly became a scene of the liveliest animation; small groups of men settled themselves here and there, some to sing, others to dance, and others again preferring less boisterous amusement, to listen to the long stories of some weather-beaten son of Neptune.*

The jolly songs of all nations, as sung by the different denizens† that formed the motley crew of the schooner, rose upon the bosom of the silent gulf. The Spaniard sang his animated oroco songs;‡ the Llanero, who had been seduced away from his native plains to seek as arduous an existence on the boisterous element, chanted the pastoral ditties with which he was accustomed to break the monotony of many a live-long night on the lonely Savanahs** of South America; the Frenchman rattled over his lively airs, and the jolly choruses of merry England, too, were not unheard on board of the Black Schooner.

The guitar here and there stimulated the Terpsichorean†† powers of some heavy sailor, and the schooner rang with the merry laugh of those who listened to the jokes of some funny old tar.‡‡ Nor were the joys of drinking unfelt. Every sailor had his drinking can by his side, and contentment might have been read on the rigid features of every one as he quaffed the stimulating liquor.

One of the chief subjects of attraction seemed to be an old sailor, whose features proclaimed him a son of distant England, while a deep scar on his forehead, and the brown-baked hue of his face, pointed him out as one who had seen service. He was entertaining those around him with some of his adventures, and was, at the same time, speaking in his native language, which was understood by his hearers. Few, indeed, were the tongues that

*Neptune: Roman god of the seas.

†denizens: inhabitants.

‡oroco songs: the derivation and meaning of "oroco" are unclear; perhaps suggests lively, pleasing type of song. The word may be connected to "rococo" which as a musical term refers to a style that is marked by light, gay ornamentation.

**Savanahs of South America: a savanna or savannah is a treeless plain or open, level grassland.

††Terpsichorean: from Terpsichore, the muse of choral dance and song.

‡‡old tar: "tar" (short for tarpaulin) is a slang term for seaman or sailor.

those men did not know; the wheel of fortune had turned them round and round in their day, and had cast them into many a different place, and there was scarcely a country in the world to which their pursuits had not taken them.

"Yes, by G–d," the old sailor was saying, "that ere Llononois was the very devil. I remember when he took Maracaybo;–a devil of a fight that was, and no mistake,–three nights in the swamps without bread or grog;* I remember when we took that place, there was a poor sinner that we suspected had some dibs. The commodore seized him–devil of a man he was–'Where have you buried your money? Says he–says he–the sinner, I mean, I have no money,' says he. Says the commodore, says he, 'you lie, you rascal, and I will make you show me the coffers!' He took the lubber†–by G–d I'll never forget that day–not I: he took the lubber and tied a line round his head, just as if he would season his head–as I would the main-shrouds–he tied the line round his head, and took a hitch in it with a marlin-spike, and twisted the line until you would ha' swore it would cut the lubber's head in two. The sinner sang out murder, but the commodore twisted the more, and asked him for the dibs. He said he hadn't any. 'Haven't any, you rascal?' cried the commodore, in a fury, and twisted the line tighter and tighter, until the eyeballs of the lubber swelled like a rat in a barrel of pork. Lord! I never seed the like–and Jim Splice has seen many things, too, I can tell you–but he still said he had no money. At last the commodore got angry–a terrible man he was when he was not, leave alone when he was–'Where is your money?' he cried, more like a devil than a man. 'I havn't any,' the poor man cried, but that wouldn't do: the commodore took his sword, opened the poor fellow's breast, tore out his heart, and bit it, telling the other Spaniards he would serve them just in the same way if they did not give him all the money they had. By G–d, I'll never forget that, anyhow! I never seed human flesh eaten afore that–Jim Splice never did–it was too much for me, hearch!" and the old sailor made a hideous grimace. "Yes: I wasn't much longer with that ere Llononois after that, I know. He was a brave man, though, after all, but nothing like our captain. There was a black day for him, however, ay, ay: that ere gentleman aloft keeps a good watch, I know, and he kept a sharp look out on that ere Llononois especially, and had the windward of him in no time. The unfortunate man was cast away afterwards among the same Spaniards, whose hearts he said he would eat, and had to skulk in the woods where he shortly afterwards died of starvation: by G–d, yes, of starvation."

---

*grog: a liquor cut with water and often served hot with sugar and lemon juice.
†lubber: clumsy person, worthless idler, unskilled seaman.

"And serve him right, too," the sailors unanimously cried, "what was the use of killing a poor brute when he could get nothing out of him?"

With such anecdotes as this Jim Splice diverted his companions. But there was on board of the schooner that day another subject, which contributed largely to the merriment of the sailors. This was no less a personage than Jack Jimmy. After the examination of the master fisherman, he, together with his companions, had been released from the custody under which they had at first been placed on their arrival on board of the schooner, and after having been admonished that if he threw himself overboard again, as he had once done from the fishing-boat, he would be quietly permitted to be drowned, he was left at full liberty to range the deck at large. When, however, the revelry began, still feeling strange, and fearing lest he should be in the way of the men, he had carefully rolled himself up at the foot of the mainmast, with his head supported by both his hands; and his eyes, the white parts of which could be seen at an extraordinary distance, eagerly fixed on the movements of the sailors. He had sat for a considerable time quiet and unobserved, merely giving vent now and then to his wonder, when that was heightened by any astonishing event in the day's amusement, by a laconic–"Awh! wha dish ya Baccra debble foo true–Garamighty! look pan dem!"

When, however, the other things which had afforded amusement to the sailors, began to pall; when the dancing had become fatiguing, the songs had been exhausted, and Jim Splice's stories had lost part of their attraction, the sailors began to look about for other excitement. It was at this moment, an unhappy one for him, that their eyes fell on the unfortunate Jack Jimmy: he was observed in his crouching position, where it was difficult to distinguish him from the ideal of a rolled up ouranoutan.‡

Struck with the peculiar comicality of the exhibition, the first sailor that remarked him burst out into an immoderate fit of laughter, and then touched his neighbour and pointed him out; the next did the same to his companion, until all eyes were fixed on Jack Jimmy.

"What have we here?" cried a maudlin young sailor, as he stood up and ran towards the object of attraction, the others immediately following.

"Let us see what is in that fellow, mates."

"Ho, the little prisoner!" rang among the merry men.

Three or four of them immediately tapped him on the head jocosely, and asked him to sing: Jack Jimmy trembling with fear, opened his eyes and mouth at once, "Massa, me no sabee sing," he replied.

‡ouranoutan: orangutan; ape

"Come, old boy! stand up–you must sing," said one of them, and they pulled up poor Jack Jimmy from his recumbent position.

If the appearance of the little man was calculated to raise laughter when he was crouching, it was much more so when he was standing up; and really there was something in him peculiarly comical. He was a little man of about four feet and a half, thickly set, and strong; his face was rounded at the mouth, and his long bony jaws projected to an extraordinary length in front. He seemed to have no brow, there was no distinction between his face and forehead; his huge large eyes looked like balls inserted into two large holes, bored on an even surface, while what was intended for a nose, was miserably abreviated and flat added the culminating point to an ugliness which was almost unique. To crown this extraordinary combination, a short crop of scattered hair grew on the top of his head, while the other parts were bare and shining, and now stained a dirty white with water.

Nature did not seem to have been generous enough to accord to him one single redeeming point; his head was joined by a short neck to square heavy shoulders, that rose about the ears of the little man; his legs were of the same shapeless proportions, and terminated at the base in large lumps of flesh, which seen unconnectedly with their appurtenant limbs, would scarcely have been taken for feet, if the short, chubby, and creasing toes, that were fixed to them, had not indicated their nature. To add more to this already ridiculous figure, the circumstance of dress was called in requisition. Jack Jimmy was clad in a dirty, ragged, checked shirt; with lower coverings that were once brown, but which were now of an obscure tawny color, acquired from the many incrustations* of dirt that had been permitted to be formed upon them. The sleeves of the shirt were tucked up in a roll which seemed to have become perpetual from the smooth waxing which friction had imparted to it. The tawny trousers were done up in like manner; and on the lower exposed parts of the limbs, might be traced on the black skin, the embedded salt which had settled there while the water trickled down after the plunge of the preceding day.

All these peculiarities, set forth in active prominence by the fear and excitement of the present moment, were quite sufficient to overcome the gravity of more serious men than those who happened, at that time, to be at the height of their merriment.

"Garamighty, massa! me tell you me no sabee sing."

"Well, you can dance, then;" and one of the sailors took a sword, and made so dexterously at the short legs of the little man, that, to protect those

---

*incrustations: an incrustation is a crust or hard coating.

members, he began to jump about like a dancing puppet–to the infinite gratification of the sailors, who roared with laughter. This sport, however, soon ended.

"Hark ye!" said a sailor: "Sambo, if you can't sing, you must submit to a penalty–bring up the old jib, Domingo," he added to one of his mates, "or a blanket."

"Yes, blanket him, ha! ha! ha!" cried all the men, "blanket him, ha! ha! ha!"

With the alacrity that sport alone can give, the sailors immediately brought a sail, into which they lifted the unfortunate Jack Jimmy, who, stupid with fear, all the while was crying–"Tap, massa–Garamighty!–you go kill me,–oh, Lard!–my mamee, oh,!"

They raised him on the sail, and began to balance him about, but Jack Jimmy, in the extremity of his fear, apprehending that they were going to do something dreadful to him, took a leap to get out of the sail, and in doing so, was pitched flat on the deck.

He stretched himself out two or three times, feigning the last convulsions of death, and lay at his length with his eyes tightly closed.

The sailors laughed; and, seeing clearly, from the heavings of his chest, that he was not so dead as he pretended to be, began to roll him violently about, as they said, in keeping with his own feint, to bring back life. But Jack Jimmy played his part well, and would neither open his eyes, nor show any other sign of existence.

At last one of the sailors said, aloud–"I know what will bring back the poor fellow: yes, it would be a pity to let him die so; Jack, lend me your cigar." Jack lent his cigar, and the sailor applied the lighted part to the thick great toe of the would-be defunct. He, however, would not move, but the sailor was persevering; Jack Jimmy remained quiet until the fire had fairly burnt through the thick skin, and had touched the more tender parts; when he felt it he was no longer dead; he sprang up briskly, on his resting part, and, catching hold of the toe, rubbed it with all his might, while he cried out–"Gad, Lard! me dead foo true;–wy–ee bun me foo true–Garamighty!"

The merriment of the sailors was extreme; the schooner rang with their protracted peals of laughter. But while they were thus at the height of their pleasure, the shrill sounds of a fife* pierced the vessel; and as if it were the death time of mirth and joviality, it was succeeded by a silence, which can be imagined only, where pestilence has ravaged a population, and has left its gloom, even on the sickly trees and rocks that lay in its devastating traces. It

*fife to arms: a fife is a small flute with a shrill tone.

settled itself like a fear-inspiring genius where, but a moment before, was naught but boisterous mirth; the hour of pleasure was passed, that of discipline and order had returned. One by one the sailors retired to their quarters, lifting bodily, along with them, such of their companions as had indulged too extravagantly in the delights of drinking.

To a stranger, the change was extraordinary. It would have been hard to believe, unless one had been convinced by the testimony of his own eyes, that there was a power so infinitely strong, as to control those, apparently lawless men, in the height of their self-willed pleasure; especially, when their spirits were heated with strong drinks, and the fierce propensities of their nature, were roused to a point when it was difficult to restrain them; but such there appeared to be. What was the spring, what the source, what the origin of that extraordinary power? What had the man done, young, as he seemed to be; and solitary, as he appeared, among so many stronger men, to enable him thus powerfully to impose the bonds of discipline, to recall and to sway a number of such men in the midst of their boisterous enjoyment? Was it the recollection of some dreadful deed of firmness, still fresh in the minds and hearts of those stern weather-beaten sailors, that sustained this fear of their youthful captain, or was it the mysterious influence of a curbing and omnipotent mind that chained them to its volition, it is not our part to enquire; suffice it to say, whatever the power, or however acquired, it existed, and that it was strong enough to drive back the sailors of the black schooner to the habitual discipline and order that reigned on its board.

The night was far advanced when the boat, which had been sent on the watching trip, returned.

Lorenzo was immediately informed that a large ship, deeply laden, had passed the "Boca del Drago."

"Well," said the officer, to the man who reported these tidings, "you have done your duty faithfully, but you have lost this day's pleasure; mark it down and the captain will not forget it. Get to your quarters, and to-morrow be early in my cabin—you may have to appear before his excellency."

The man made a bow and retired.

CHAPTER IV

"--Like lions wanting food,
Do rush upon us as their hungry prey."
HENRY VI

MORNING, beautiful and clear, such as it is only in the transparent regions of the tropics, had just come, when, in obedience to the order of the preceding night, the sailor returned to the cabin of Lorenzo. There he was subjected to a more particular examination than the leisure of the foregone night permitted, and he detailed, with accuracy, the various little incidents which had befallen him since he started from the schooner on his commission.

"The ship," he said, "is very large, and seems to be well manned. There were several persons on board, who appeared to be passengers. We pretended to be fishing, and we pulled backwards and forwards under her stern as she was sailing slowly before the light wind, so that we had an opportunity of observing her closely, and of seeing that on her stern was marked the 'Letitia' of Bristol."

"The 'Letitia,'" repeated Lorenzo, and a gloom passed over his countenance, as he remained for a minute or two absorbed by some devouring thought.

"Did she seem to sail well?" at length, he asked.

"Senor, the wind was light, and we could not judge of that; but, from her build, I think she would be a clipper," answered the man.

After Lorenzo had put some other questions to the sailor he dismissed him, and requested that the master-fisherman should be immediately brought. The latter was, in a short time, conducted to the officer's cabin, where he was interrogated in the same manner. The fisherman said it was the large ship which appertained to the rich English merchant, and of which he had already given information to the captain. The officer dismissed him also, and sought, at once, the captain's cabin. He communicated the report of the party, and in answer was ordered to go on deck, immediately, and get ready to set sail. When Lorenzo was detailing to his chief the report of the reconnoitring party, the deepest physiognomist* would not have been able to discover a wrinkle or a mark in the face of the young man, or to perceive the slightest change in his dark eyes that could indicate the existence of any particular feeling within. He sat like a statue, as silent and as still, with his piercing eyes fixed on the pupils of the narrator's, who, from time to time, was obliged to look down in order to relieve

---

*physiognomist: a person able to discern temperament and character from facial features.

himself of the torture in which he was kept by the eagle glance of his chief. But when Lorenzo arrived at the part of the report in which the description of the vessel was made, and the name "Letitia" was mentioned, there might be traced around his lips the rudiments of a sardonic smile of triumph— something like the flash of a ponderous cannon when a match is applied in the darkness of night, that dazzles for a moment, and then suddenly dies away in the thick enshrouding smoke that darkly typifies the terrible gloom of the destruction which springs from its midst.

Having heard the report of his officer, the captain ordered him to proceed, at once, on deck, and get ready to set sail. The officer bowed and retired.

When Lorenzo had quitted the cabin, the captain remained sitting in the same position in which he had received the report, and appeared occupied by some preying thought.

"Yes," he muttered, " 'Letitia,' that is the name: he goes in it. Speed well my purpose!"

The preparations on board the schooner did not require much time to be completed, and, in a few moments, the captain himself made his appearance on deck. It would appear, that except when the schooner was under weigh, he never showed himself to his crew. Like the priests of yore, who swayed mankind, he was no doubt apprehensive, that if he exhibited himself too frequently to vulgar view, the sailors, in getting familiar with his person, should lose much of the veneration and awe which they unquestionably entertained for him, and which seemed to crush their wills to an implicit and blind obedience to his.

When he appeared on deck, he was attired in quite a different fashion to the one in which he was seen in his cabin. He wore black trowsers, with broad stripes of gold on the sides, and a black frock coat, simply but richly ornamented with embroidery of the same precious metal. The red sash, as usual, was folded round his waist, and supported the pistols and poniard; his head was crowned with a flaming cap, in the front of which was wrought the death's head and dead men's bones; while, in addition to these things, a beautiful sword, with gold mountings, hung by his side.

"Weigh," he said, to the officer on duty, as his foot touched the deck; the vessel was immediately put under sail. The light breeze of the morning filled her well-trimmed canvas, and like a creature of life and grace the Black Schooner began to cut through the water. Scarcely a ripple marked where her sharp keel passed, as she moved gracefully over the quiet waters of the gulf.

The hills of the Bocas gradually arose more and more distinctly before her, as she quickly approached them. No scene perhaps in nature is more beautiful than the one which presents itself to the mariner as he sails through the narrow strait that affords a northern passage from the Gulf of Paria.

Standing in the midst of the clearest waters that bathe in graceful ripplings their luxuriant base, are clusters of small islands that are carpeted to the very beach with fresh and never fading verdure. Like a scene in a panorama, or like the trembling shadows which a tropical moon casts over the silent lake or placid stream, those islands seem balancing over a crystal surface, that shines and sends forth a thousand undulating reflections under the pure and clear rays of an undarkened tropical sun: or, as they recede to the eye, in proportion to the progress of the vessel, imagination might convert them into the terrestrial realities of those variegated* spots which the musing poet is fond to contemplate, to follow in their course, to speculate and dream upon, in the transparent and lulling pureness of a summer sky. Above these are seen the blossoming coral-trees with their scarlet flowers, that chequer the densely wooded hills, and stand amidst the dense foliage that surrounds them, marked and conspicuous like thousands of growing wreaths, that administering nymphs eternally offer to tropical nature in gratitude for her marvellous and beautiful works.

Over the shining waters themselves that lave these hills and fairy isles, are seen the long-necked pelican, in its shadowy flight, or its fierce headlong plunge after its watery prey; the spiry smoke, as it ascends from some reed-constructed cottage on the shore; the feathery canoe of some solitary fisherman, playing, like a child of the element, on the beautiful sea; the crooked creeks and receding bays that conjure up thoughts of lurking pirates; the sullen growling of the ocean, in long, high, and heaving swells, as it rolls on the ocean-side: all these mark the entrance of the Boca with the boldest and most beautiful features of natural beauty that fancy, in her wildest reveries, can draw and paint; while the gloomily ascending mountains of Paria, on the left side, with their precipitous falls, to be seen far, far away;–mountains, that stand dark and dismal like sulky lions on the crouch, and seem ready to fall–to fill up the narrow straits below, and to bury, far beneath their weight, the frail structure of fragile wood that intrudes with its rash and venturesome burdens into the very shadow of their black brow, tend to add to the scene a solemn and terrifying effect.

---

*variegated: marked with different tints or colors in streaks or spots.

The black schooner glided through the narrow outlet, and rose outside on the boisterous billows of the Atlantic.

The captain paced the deck in deep reflection. His dark eyebrows completely hid his eyes, which remained fixed on the deck. Their long and silken lashes swept the handsome young man's cheeks, his lips were compressed, and his black mustachioes imparted a still sterner, and more terrible appearance to his face. He wore the aspect of one whose resolution was taken to do a desperate deed, and whose nature still refused consent and revolted at the thought, like him who sacrifices to principle, and is doomed to drain a cup that makes humanity shudder.

He had directed the schooner to be steered in the course which the ships bound for England generally take, and men were stationed on her tall and raking masts to keep watch. The day passed: night came; still the schooner held her course, and silence reigned on board. Not a sound was heard, save when the shrill pipe called to duty, or told the hour. The next day came, and with it the order to prepare for fight, still there was no vessel in sight. But the captain was not one to give orders in vain. He knew his vessel, he knew the currents, and could tell the precise hour when he would overtake a vessel of whose departure he was apprized.

The sun was just sinking in the horizon, when the man aloft cried out—

"Sail, ho!—to leeward."

The captain stopped, and ordered his telescope; with that he discerned a speck in the distance, but far away.

"Keep her away," he cried, to the man who was steering:—"case your jib, foresail, and main-sail sheets, Gregoire;"—to the officer on duty; and the schooner edged off.

She sailed so fast that by midnight she was near the object that had appeared in the horizon, and which was now found to be a large ship gallantly careering over the ocean. Her white canvas shone in the moonlight, and the foam that gathered at her bows was brilliant with the phosphorescence of the Caribbean Sea.

"Take in the fore-sail," the captain cried; and that sail was immediately lowered.

The sailors were now all armed with pistols, poniards, and boarding pikes. As they stood grimly gazing on the ship before them, their black beards, red caps, and weapons, looked terribly dreadful, and the idea of some bloody deed could not but be suggested by their appearance.

The fife sounded a peculiar note, and all the sailors gathered at the foot of the schooner's mainmast. Here may have been heard the low whisperings of comrade to comrade: there may have been seen the fierce eyes of some, flashing as it were, in anticipation of something congenial. Some may have been observed to stroke their raven beards as if out of patience; others, leaned carelessly on their pikes. When they had properly formed, the captain stopped in his nervous walk, and, drawing himself up to the full height of his lofty and commanding person, said:–

"Associates, you have now another opportunity to revenge yourselves on the world. There," and he pointed to the ship, "there you have the wealth of some trader, that has neither capacity to enjoy it, nor heart to use it. Remember how frequently you have wanted the morsel which he could so easily have spared, but which you never found. Remember your wrongs and now redress them; take what the world would not afford you. By the dawn of the day we shall attack that ship. I expect nothing less than that which I have always found in you, give but your valour, and you shall have the booty–the reward of bravery. Go, rest yourselves until the morning."

This short speech, he spoke in a clear, deep, and sonorous voice; while the features of the speaker seemed more eloquent than his tongue. The bitterest hatred curled his lip, when he delivered the first part, and animation glowed on his countenance, when he spoke of the bravery of his men.

"Bravo! bravo!" broke out in loud and deep echoes from the assembled crew. The sailors, one by one, returned to the foremost part of the vessel, not without having first cast an inquiring glance at the ship before them. Some betook themselves to their hammocks, and others sat together smoking their cigars and conversing, in a low tone, on the probable events of the approaching morning.

The night waned: and, at last, morning came.

The captain, who, after he had addressed his men, had given orders to the officer of the watch to keep the ship always in sight, but by no means to approach her more closely, had descended into his cabin, now re-appeared on deck. He walked up to the helm, looked first at the compass, and then at the ship that was still a-head of the schooner. The ship appeared now in all her greatness. She was a large merchant-man, apparently, deeply laden, but by no means an indifferent sailer.

"Hoist the foresail," the captain said, and the sail was again put on the vessel, that seemed to feel it, for she now leaped over the waves like a snake on whose tail some passer-by had accidentally trodden.

"To your posts, my men," the captain again said, and the shrill fife re-echoed his command.

With the silence of death every man took his station, every gun was manned, every halliard was attended to, while the sides of the deck were immediately lined with men, who were armed with pikes and axes in addition to their pistols and poniards.

It is difficult to imagine the rapidity and calmness with which these preparations were made. We must call to the assistance of our memory the movements of beautifully adjusted machines as they perform their parts, to form an adequate idea of the promptness and ease with which the hundreds of men on board the Black Schooner, executed their captain's order.

The schooner now drew rapidly on the ship: she was light, and was a fast sailer, and fully felt the light breeze which was blowing at that early part of the morning. Not so with the ship pursued: deeply laden, and comparatively heavy, the light air had scarcely any effect upon her, and she was moving along but tardily. When the schooner had arrived within gun-shot from the ship, at the captain's order, a gun was fired, and the broad black ensign, with the frightful device of death, ran along the signal-line.

The shot boomed athwart the ship's bows, but she paid no attention to the signal; on the contrary, additional sails were immediately hoisted, and the vessel was kept freer from the wind. But the schooner still gained upon her.

The report of another cannon, from her side, echoed over the waters: still the ship kept her course. The captain spoke not a word, but looked with haughty calmness on the large vessel, as he stood lofty and erect on the deck, with his arms crossed over his breast. "Launch and man the boats," he said, after a long space of time had been permitted to escape; a loud cheer, which they could no longer suppress, burst forth from the men. More quickly than we can describe, the hatches were raised, and two boats were immediately hoisted out into the water; twenty men cheerfully jumped into each, and stood ready for the order to shove off.

The boats were towed at the sides until the captain's voice was heard— "Shove off and board," he cried, in the same composed and stern manner. A loud cheer from the sailors in the boats, and their comrades on deck, echoed the order. The boats leaped over the long waves under the vigorous efforts of the men. They approached the ship. They stood up, pike in hand, ready to climb its sides.

"Pull, my men," cried the officer in command, "we take her at once:" a flash was seen on the ship's deck, a loud report was heard, and, as the smoke ascended, the shattered remnants of the first boat were seen floating here and there, and those who had been in it, and, a moment before, had longed so eagerly for battle, were scattered about on the water dead and horribly mutilated.

The discharge from the ship told with a fatal exactness: the gun, it would appear, had been loaded with pieces of old iron, nails, and everything destructive that could be found; and the charge swept away men and boat with a dreadful crash.

"Lay on your oars, my mates," cried the officer of the second boat, fierce with anger at the destruction of his comrades: and in a few seconds she was alongside the ship.

"Board, board," – quicker than thought the assailants climbed the sides of the merchantman, but not to land on deck: a dreadful conflict ensued. The men of the ship resisted valiantly, like those who knew they were fighting for their lives: the foremost assailants were dashed into the deep. They slashed at each other – attacking and attacked. The assailants handled their pikes with fierce and unbreathing vigour, but they seemed to make but little head against the men of the ship. Here and there a boarder was to be seen, to hang to the ship for a moment in his death-grasp, while blood and brain gushed from his cloven head, to balance a moment in mid-air, and then fall heavily into the sea.

"Hurrah! hurrah!" – the cries of victory rose on board the British vessel, as assailant after assailant was precipitated into the deep, or sunk under the blows of the men on deck. Now the survivors rushed, for security, into the shrouds; now they clung to the ropes with teeth and feet, while, with their pikes, they kept at bay the opponents on deck. Like famished tigers, that would have their morsel or die, they fought, falling, dying, and almost dead: no shout, no word escaped them, but they did their work in terrible silence. On, on, the English sailors pressed. The shout of victory again rose; but three of the assailants remained – they were partly sheltered in the chains, and fierce as leopards at bay, they felled all that dared approach them; their companions were all cut down or driven overboard; perspiration ran down their brawny breasts; blood and foam bubbled from their mouths; and, with eyes as dry and lurid as the famished Panther, they slashed at their hard pressing opponents. Suddenly a loud cheer was heard; it rang over the ocean like the roar of a distant cataract; the still resisting three heard it: a hoarse cry came from their parched and husky throats.

"The 'Periagua,'" * one of them cried, and a long canoe-like boat was seen rapidly approaching from the schooner.

*The "Periagua" was a large boat made of the hollowed trunk of some huge tree, lined with boards to a very little height from the water.

The Boucaneers of the West Indies were accustomed to use such boats in attacks on vessels, both on account of their lowness, which prevented their being seen except when they were almost alongside of the vessel to be boarded, and on account of a means which they possessed, in such boats, for stimulating the fury of their men. This was a plug-hole: whenever the pirate captain imagined he perceived any coldness in his men he drew the plug and let in the water: to

The captain of the schooner himself stood in the stern, cool and collected, with determination marked on every feature. The boat approached nearer and nearer–two strokes more, and she was alongside.

"Now save yourselves or perish:" so saying, the captain drew a plug from the bottom–the water gushed in–the boat began to sink; with the courage of desperation, the pirates sprang on to the sides of the vessel. Their swords glittered in the air, their pikes were worked with the rapidity of lightning, the shouts of the attacked, the yells of the pirates, the splash of the killed, as they fell headlong into the deep, rose wild and appalling on the ear.

The men of the ship received this new attack with firmness: but they had already fought long; they began to yield; their blows fell less rapidly.

"On–on!" cried the captain, and in a moment he himself was on the deck. With a wild yell the pirates followed. The men of the ship now cried for mercy: but the slaughter went on. Revenge directed every blow–every stroke carried death. The voice of the chief was at last heard above the confusion and death-cries.

"Enough: spare and secure your prisoners."

The word arrested the sword that was raised to deal the last fatal blow, and stayed the pike that had destruction on its point. Every pirate gnashed his teeth because his vengeance was stopped–but who dared disobey?

"Cut the halliards:" 'twas done; and the masts of the ship in a moment stood bare, and she lay floating like a log on the waves.

The deck was crimson and slippery with blood; the sailors of the ship, that had defended her so bravely, lay in heaps, dead and dying.

The commander of the merchantman himself was stretched lifeless on the deck. He had rushed on the captain of the pirates as soon as the latter had gained the deck, and wielding with both hands a ponderous sword, made such a blow at him as would have cut him through; but by a slight movement the intended victim escaped the stroke, and before the commander could recover from the impetus of his own blow, the captain pierced him to the heart with his poniard. Without a groan he fell dead.

As soon as the ship was captured, the captain issued his orders to his men, that their wounded companions should be properly attended to; and the boat which, although it had been swamped, on account of its lightness, had not sunk, should be secured.

---

avoid drowning, his men madly made their way on the deck of the ship that was attacked, and almost in all instances took her. [Maxwell Philip's note]

These commands were immediately attended to. The pirates forthwith picked up their disabled companions, that still clung to the wrecks of the first boat: or those who, as yet, grasped, in a desperate effort for life, the lower riggings of the ship of which they had laid hold in their fall from the bulwarks or the deck.

The hatches were raised, and they began to examine the cargo.

The captain himself, with two sturdy sailors after him, descended the steps that led to the cabin.

Here were three persons apparently overcome with terror. A man of about middle age leant on the panelling of the cabin, with a long musket, surmounted with a rusty bayonet, in his hands, which trembled so much from extreme fear that they were utterly unable to raise the weapon which they sustained. On the floor lay a young lady in a swoon, while over her bent an aged priest, anxiously awaiting the appearance of returning animation.

"Mercy, mercy on us!" cried the first individual, as the captain entered the cabin; "take our money; I have gold there; yes, there is gold in my cabin: but, for God's sake, spare our lives: for the sake of my children and my family, spare an aged man, whose blood can avail you nothing," and the suppliant fell on his knees, still grasping the unavailing musket.

"Get up, man: kneel not to me," said the captain, indifferently. The voice struck the prostrate man like an electric shock; with a sudden start he raised his head, and gazed at the man before him.

"What voice was that?" he cried, and passed his trembling hands over his brow; and like him who labours, by one violent and forcible effort of the mind, to recall a thousand widely distant events; or like him on whom dawns the recollection of some long-passed, but horrible deed, he remained fixed to the spot, with staring eyes and fallen jaws. Again and again, he passed his hands over his brow, – "it was her voice! – what do I hear? – what do I see? – No, it cannot be – yet so like her: – no – yes – yes; – it is – my son. He started, like one in frenzy, from the cabin floor, and rushed on the pirate chief. The latter drew back.

"Keep away," he said: "I am, indeed, your son! – secure that man," turning to his men; and, while giving them this order, passed to the upper part of the cabin, at the same time casting a look of the bitterest scorn on him who had recognised him as his son.

So intent was the aged priest on watching the recovery of the young lady under his care, that he did not even raise his eyes from her face during the above unexpected recognition of father and son. But when the captain approached the object of his solicitude, he suddenly rose, and, throwing himself at his feet, implored him, in the most moving accents, to spare the innocence and honor of the young and helpless lady.

The captain, with what could be construed into a smile, bade him be re-assured.

"Fear not, old man," he said, "for the innocence and honor of any one on my account; I value my time much, and cannot spare a moment of it, either to blight the innocence or rob the honor of damsels;–continue your attention to the young lady." He then walked up to the seat at the top of the cabin table, and deliberately and coolly sitting down, ordered his men to search for the ship's papers and bring them to him.

There was not much difficulty in discovering these, for the steward, who had carefully concealed himself in his pantry during the attack, seeing that there was no longer any bloodshed, now crept out of his hiding-place, and offered his services to the searching pirates, on condition that his life should be spared. By means of his assistance, the papers of the captured vessel were immediately rummaged out, and handed to the pirate captain.

He glanced over them for a time, and at length musingly said, as if speaking to himself,–"The owners are rich, and they can afford to yield up this cargo to better men than themselves." He then delivered the papers to one of his men, and ordered the passengers' luggage to be searched. In the trunks of these were found large sums in doubloons and other gold coins,– money that had, no doubt, been destined to the buying of many a European luxury.

The search went on; and when the cabin had been completely rifled of every thing that was valuable, the captain proceeded on deck, and was followed by his men, and the passengers, who were now prisoners.

The pirates had, by this time, thoroughly examined the cargo of the vessel, and had found it to consist principally of the staple productions of the West Indies–sugar and rum–together with a small quantity of other minor commodities, such as tobacco and indigo.* A great portion of these light things was already collected on the deck, where the pirates were assembled, waiting for their chief.

"What has she?" inquired this personage, when he gained the deck.

"Sugar and rum, your excellency," one of the officers answered, and remained in silence before his superior, awaiting his orders.

The captain seemed to consider awhile, and then replied: "Stay here, and retain a man with you."

---

*indigo: a blue dye obtained from indigo plants.

The men were immediately ordered to get the boats ready to shove off to the schooner. Whatever light things the pirates could stow away were put into them. The wounded of their party were carefully lowered, from the decks of the captured ship, into the boats. The sailors of the ship, that had survived the action, were placed in the bows of the Periagua; and the prisoners, who, with the exception of the individual who had recognized the captain as his son, were without restraint, permitted to sit in the stern-sheets with the captain; and the young lady, who had now recovered from her fainting sickness, received all the attentions which the most perfect civility could offer, and which were evidently shown with the purpose of smoothing down the strange position in which she found herself. The boats were pushed off from the ship, that was left, sluggishly rolling on the waves, under the charge of the two men.

The pirates shortly gained the schooner, which during and after the action, continued to lie to the wind, at a short distance from the prize.

Lorenzo, he in whose command she was left, when the captain headed the party of the Periagua, stood ready at the gangway to receive his superior. No noise was heard on board of the captured ship or the schooner since the fight: the bonds of the same marvellous discipline seemed, unknowingly to themselves, to control the pirates, even at the moment of victory and exultation; but when the boats came alongside the schooner, human nature, it would appear, refused to contain itself any longer: and those fierce men, who had abandoned the entire world for the narrow space of their small vessel, and the inhabitants of the vast universe for the few kindred spirits who were their associates – that had separated themselves, by their deeds, from the world, the world's sympathy, and the world's good and bad, that had actually turned their hand against all men, and had expected, as they had probably frequently experienced, that the hand of all men should be turned against them, could not restrain their feelings of welcome, and three loud and prolonged cheers resounded, far and wide over the silent ocean, as they were wafted, in undying echoes, over the crests of the heavy and heaving billows. As comrade rejoined comrade, their grim and bearded faces appeared to relax from their wonted habit of ferocity, under the influence of a prevailing sense of joy: such a joy, those, alone, can experience who have seen every natural tie break asunder around them – who have felt the heavy hand of a crushing destiny, or have been hunted and driven, by the injustice and persecution of friend or relative, to seek shelter in that desperate solitude, which is relieved, but, by the presence, and cheered, but, by the sympathy of the few, who, like themselves, have been picked out by fate, to suffer, to be miserable, and to be finally, cast forth from the society of mankind.

The captain endeavoured not to restrain the joy of his men; but he sat stern, collected, and unaffected as ever, in the stern-sheets of the boat. No sign of pleasure or displeasure was written on his features: but if any change could be read, it was the passing shadow of a deep melancholy that rested, for a moment, on his resolute brow. Perhaps the reminiscences of some by-gone period were playing on his memory; perhaps the recollection of other days led him, in imagination, to some cherished spot, where he was wont to hear the joyful greetings of parent, friend, or lover. Perhaps the remembrances of that one moment, when, even the most unhappy, and the most perverse of men, feel for once, the soothing influence of those mysterious feelings of our nature, that melt, that soften, that gladden, and remain for ever in our recollection, the lonely stars of comfort in the heavy darkness of misfortunes. Perhaps the remembrance of such a moment, now flitted across the memory of the pirate captain.

Whatever was the feeling that cast its hue over his brow, like the passing shadow of a fleeting cloud, it came–in the twinkling of an eye, it passed away; and he remained, again, the inscrutable individual that he ever was.

The captain, on gaining the deck of the schooner, ordered that the prisoners should be properly treated: "Let, however, that man," pointing to the person who had recognized him as his son, "be kept in close custody."

Having said this, he looked around him on the schooner, where the same order reigned as before the attack, and went down into his cabin.

The day was now nearly spent, the sun was setting red, round, and fiery, as it sets only in the tropics.

The light goods, which the pirates had brought with them from the captured ship, and the prisoners, were transhipped into the schooner. The boats were hoisted into their places. The schooner herself lay in the same position–motionless, under its counteracting sails.

Some time had already elapsed since the captain went below, and no orders had, as yet, been given for the night. The officer, whose watch it was, walked the deck in anxious expectation of commands.

The captured ship rolled at some distance from the schooner, and it was apparent that it was necessary to provide for her safety during the night that was now setting in.

The short tropical twilight had nearly passed away, and darkness was gathering on the expanse of the waters, when one of the negro boys, whom the reader may recollect, sought the cabin of the chief officer, and delivered to him the same ring by which, it may be remembered, he, once before, gained admittance into the captain's cabin. As soon as Lorenzo received the ring, he proceeded to the after part of the vessel and gained admittance to his chief.

The latter was still in his dark uniform and was sitting by the large table that occupied the centre of the apartment. A chart was before him; by its side were, also, the papers which had been brought from the ship.

"Lorenzo," said the chief to the officer, after pointing to one of the ottomans, "it is my will that our prize be manned, and sailed to St. Thomas, where we shall sell the cargo. To-morrow, we shall deal with our prisoners, and divide the spoils already gathered. Let a sufficient number of men be sent on board the ship to-night, so that she may be properly manned, in case of any change of the weather. Let the schooner, in the meantime, be kept lying to, under her jib; and let the prize remain in the same position – a quarter of a mile from us. At dawn of day, let all the men assemble on the main deck, and wait for me.

The officer rose and bowed, to depart.

"Stop, Lorenzo," resumed the chief, "drink some wine:" a spring was pressed, and immediately one of the boys in attendance brought in a richly cut decanter and the necessary accompaniments. Lorenzo and the captain, respectively, filled themselves a goblet and quaffed it off in silence; after which the officer left the cabin.

CHAPTER V

"Come, my masters, let us share, – "
HENRY IV

OBEDIENT to the commands of his chief, Lorenzo drafted a number of men from the crew, and sent them on board the prize ship. The Black Schooner was kept in the position ordered by the captain; the proper watches for the night were set, and those on board the vessel retired to rest.

At the dawn of the next day, a peculiar sound of the fife summoned forth the whole crew of the schooner. In the space of a few moments, above three hundred men lined the long deck.

With the habit of continual discipline, they fell into order so quietly, that the space afforded by the deck of that comparatively small vessel, did not for a moment seem filled by the multitude which gathered on it. The pirates stood accoutred in, what might be called, their holiday dress. Their red woollen shirts and caps were worn with some care; their sashes seemed more symmetrically folded round their waists, and the weapons which were stuck in them, seemed adjusted with more than ordinary attention; while their black beards, faces, and hands, presented that clean, sun-burnt, half-sea, half-land appearance, which we easily discover in the aspect of a sailor while on shore.

The appearance of the crew, as it gathered that morning, contrasted in a striking manner with that which it wore before the attack.

Before the action, the pirates stood like men who were too much engrossed with one idea–one passion–to be capable of any thought which was unconnected with that. Their red caps were drawn carelessly over their heads; their dress was that of men who could not afford a moment's time to its adjustment, while the wildest ferocity sat on every line of their countenances. On that morning the absorption of mind had ceased; they seemed returned from the engrossing contemplation of the sanguinary and the terrible, to the softer feelings that lend to life those charms, which, empty though they be, still are sufficient to enliven its monotony, and sometimes even to smooth down its asperities. Their habitual fierceness, too, had yielded to the contentment by which they seemed animated, and their features were less rigid, and less ferocious.

The men had been assembled some time before the captain made his appearance: the change which was observed in their aspect, could not be read in his. He appeared the same, sternly collected, individual that he always was.

As soon as he appeared on deck, the officers respectfully bowed. The captain then seated himself on a deck-stool, which had been placed behind a small table for him. The boys, who always attended him, then deposited on the table several bags of money, and disappeared.

"My men," he said, when he had been seated, "our booty in gold has been small, but we shall, no doubt, find a sufficient recompense for our toil in the purchase-money of the ship's cargo, which it is my will to take to St. Thomas' to sell. Six thousand and five hundred dollars is the amount of what we have got. This I shall divide among you, and forego my own share until a day of better fortune. Let the wounded approach."

Those who had been but slightly wounded in the last engagement, and could bear the fatigue of walking, stepped forward. They received shares larger than those of their comrades in proportion to the injuries which they had sustained. Those who had lost a hand, an arm, a leg, or a foot, received four times the amount of booty; those who had lost an eye, a finger, or a toe, received twice the amount. When the wounded had duly been recompensed, the captain then addressed his men.

"Comrades," he said, "it was our misfortune to lose some of our brave associates in the fight, let those who were the friends of the dead come forward, as I call over their names, and receive their share:–Diego–who is Diego's friend?" One of the pirates stepped forward, and, raising his right hand, declared that he was Diego's friend. The share which should have been that of the dead, was then delivered to his friend.

"Martin," continued the chief, "who was Martin's friend?" Another pirate stepped forward, and, raising his right hand, in the same manner, declared that he was Martin's friend.

The captain went on in this manner, calling over the names of the lost comrades, and requiring to know their friends, until he came to the last of the men.

"Francis," he cried, "Francis's friend." Two men simultaneously stepped forward, and, raising their hands, each declared that he was Francis's friend. "How is this?" the captain asked, "it is not impossible to have more than one friend, but you know, my men, that it is the custom, on board this schooner, to have but one man to whom his friend may bequeath his share?"

The men then looked at each other: and each looked round at his comrades, as if appealing to them in testimony of his right to be considered the friend of the dead Francis.

"He was my friend," each said, and looked again at their comrades, in corroboration of his claim; but the pirates uttered not a word in answer to this silent appeal.

"My men," said the captain, "this has never happened here before: either Francis forgot his honour, when he charged both of you to be his friends, when dead, or one of you forgets his, when he asserts that he is Francis's friend. Now, Francis is no more, and cannot answer for this; the responsibility of this breach of honour, my men, rests, therefore, upon you: one of you must lie." The two men looked fierce when the chief coolly pronounced this word. "You know the law–choose your weapons–at six o'clock this evening you must fight: the survivor shall receive the share of Francis."

A low murmur of approbation rang along the line of the assembled sailors, and the two pretenders to the favour of the departed pirate stepped aside.

After the shares of the wounded had been duly allotted, and those of the dead scrupulously delivered into the hands of their friends; or, if there were no friends of the deceased, carefully set apart for the purpose of having masses said for them, the lots of the other pirates were shared out to them.

The officers of the schooner received theirs first, and those who might be called the common seamen, theirs afterwards. When the distribution was completed, the prisoners and strangers on board were ordered to appear. First came the surviving sailors of the prize ship. Out of the complement of thirty-five men, who had formed the crew of that vessel, five only had escaped death in the engagement. These came forth, pale and haggard, expecting, apparently, to hear every moment the dreadful command which, in some horrible way, should put an end to their existence. The five English sailors, with the exception of one, whose years might be more mature, were in the prime of life, and wore that hue of health which their calling imparts: howbeit the anxiety of the position in which they were placed had had its temporary effect on them.

They approached the captain with an air of uneasiness, turning their hats about in their brawny hands, while divers bumps might have been observed to rise now and then, and disappear immediately on their weather beaten cheeks: probably they were the various protrusions created by the quid,* while it went through the many revolutions in which it was then twisted.

"What were your wages, by the month, men?" inquired the captain, when the English sailors stood before him, bending on them, at the same time, one of his searching and stern looks.

The sailors looked at each other, then at the captain, and then at each other again, and could not, apparently, be bold enough to reply, lest the question might, eventually, prove to be some trap by which it was intended to ensnare them into some confession or other that would tend to aggravate their sufferings. The captain neither showed signs of impatience nor renewed his question, but remained still, looking steadfastly on the sailors, with the cool composure of one who does not wonder that others should feel embarrassed in his presence; but, on the contrary, expects a degree of confusion on the part of those who are addressed by him. The oldest man of the five, however, at last spoke and answered:

"Three pounds a month, your honor," raising his hand, at the same time, to the part of his head where the brim of his hat should have been, if that necessary cerebral protection had happened to be in its proper place at the time, and not in his hands.

"Have any of you received any advances on your wages?" again inquired the captain.

---

*quid: a piece of chewing tobacco.

"Half of a month's wages have been paid at home, your honor," answered the old tar, of which answer, when he had duly delivered himself, he looked anxiously round at his four companions respectively, and seemed to inquire, "what will this lead to?"

The captain drew from a purse several pieces of gold, which, when he had divided into several small sums, he gave to the sailors.

"There are your wages," he said, as he tendered the money to them, "for the five months that you have been on the voyage, we give, and do not take from such as you."

The sailors looked bewildered. They could scarcely believe their ears, and they cast glances of amazement at each other. Even the appearance of money, it would appear, could not re-assure them; they put out their hands to receive the tendered wages like men who were afraid to receive something that was given lest danger should be attached to it.

"We shall land you on the nearest head-land," continued the captain, "in the meantime, you may enjoy your liberty. If any of you wish to join my men, you can do so. The rules of the ship are few: I require but one thing— obedience. Death is the penalty of the least breach of discipline."

Having said this, the captain waved his hand, and the English sailors fell back behind the assembled crew.

The master fisherman and his men were next brought forward. They had by this time become perfectly at home in the schooner. The master fisherman found that the life, which he would be likely to lead on board would suit his Spanish blood, and Spanish character, well. Down to that time, also, he had been well treated.

It is true, the discipline of the schooner had appeared to him, accustomed as he was to the free and independent life of one of his calling, rather hard and unbearable; but the good companionship, and the profits of a pirate's life were sufficient, in his estimation, to outweigh that inconvenience. As for Jack Jimmy, and his other man, they, too, had familiarized themselves with their position: the latter seemed to care but for little, in this world, beside the luxury of eating, drinking, and sleeping. He found the schooner capable of furnishing him with those three things, and was not, therefore inclined, like the generality of mortals, to grumble about more, when he already enjoyed the three elements of his happiness.

The former, Jack Jimmy, it is true, was of a less contented, and more restless disposition; and the order and monotony of the schooner, to say nothing of the continual fear in which he had at first been kept, by the mystery of his novel position, tended to make him long for his own cabin; or, at best, for any other situation but the one in which he was then placed.

He became, however, by degrees more satisfied, the longer he remained in the schooner; for, he was not ill-treated in the first place, and the tricks which the men played upon him, the voyage, and the other things–except, perhaps, the fight–which had happened since his arrival on board, contributed, in the second place, to afford that excitement which, it would seem, his nature craved.

As the master fisherman appeared, the captain delivered to him a purse, and said:

"That will compensate you for the time you have lost: you will be landed soon, you, and your men."

Jack Jimmy had followed his master, or rather had been thrust forward with him, in a state of nervous trepidation. The movements of the little negro were as brisk and as rapid as those of a monkey. His head turned on his shoulders like a weather gauge in a storm, while his large white eyes were stretched open to their utmost width. His head seemed to be turned forwards, sideways, and backwards at the same time. One would have said that while he looked before him, he was afraid he should be struck backwards, or sideways; while he looked sideways, that he should be struck either from before or behind; and while he looked backwards, he was afraid that he should be struck from before or from the side.

He was going on thus, like an automaton in violent action, when the sound of the captain's voice fell upon his ear. He seemed, at that moment, struck motionless. He fixed his eyes on him, lowered what supplied the place of eyebrows, opened his mouth, threw his head and neck as far forward as he could, and remained rooted to the spot in deep examination of the young man before him.

This did not last long; for, with his usually rapid movements, he threw himself at the foot of the captain, before he had quite finished the few words which he had addressed to the master fisherman, clasped his knees franticly in his arms, and yelled out,–"Garamighty! da ee–da ee–da me young massa."

Jack Jimmy sobbed aloud, as he the more tightly clasped the knees of the captain. The latter looked down calmly and coolly on the little man, seemed to recognize him, but said not a word to him.

Pained by the apparent forgetfulness of his young master, he raised his head, and, looking imploringly up to the captain Jack Jimmy cried out, piteously:

"You no know me–you no know me, massa–you no know Jack Jimmy–you no 'member Jack Jimmy in de mule-pen–you–"

"Yes, I do recollect you, Jack Jimmy," interrupted the captain, "but you must neither make such a noise here, nor continue where you are." He made a sign with his hand, and two men stepped forward and led away the affectionate Jack Jimmy.

"Ah! my young massa," continued the affectionate negro as he was taken away, "ee bin da gie me cake – ee bin da gie me grog – an when dey bin want foo beat me ee bin da beg foo me."

When Jack Jimmy had been led away behind the assembled crew, and had been prevailed upon to become silent, which change did not take place in him until he had been threatened to be again rocked in the sail, the priest and the young lady were, in their turn, led forth. The former, although it was perceptible that he anticipated the gloomiest results, still had a resigned and serene air. He looked calmly on all that had taken place that day, and, perhaps, there might be read in his eyes a certain expression of surprise, that the pirates did not at once act with that blood-thirsty ruffianism which he had been accustomed, from his earliest school-boy readings, to attach to men of that abandoned life.

The young lady was, naturally, much more effected by the circumstances of her situation; kindness, however, had not been spared to reconcile her to it as much as possible.

Lorenzo had been strictly enjoined to show all marks of attention to her; and he seemed not to have required the positive command of his chief to do so: for she had at her command the chivalrous devotedness, which great beauty always draws from even the most stoical of men. She was exceedingly beautiful; such a species of beauty that we meet only in the tropics, – a beauty which we can compare to no known standard: something that belongs entirely to the warm clime by which it is produced; something that is more of the fanciful than of the real. She was of a middle age, slender, and of a perfect figure; her features were delicately and nicely chiselled; her complexion was of the clearest white, tinged with the slightest olive; her dark brown hair hung over a high and nicely moulded forehead, while her dark gazelle-like eyes imparted to her face a character of tenderness and softness.

The officer had exhibited the greatest solicitude on behalf of the fair captive from the moment she came on board the schooner; and now, when she stood on deck, weak and nervous, he might have been observed, from time to time, stealthily to give her as much assistance as the rules of the vessel permitted, and to pay her, perhaps, more attention than even the commands of his chief could have been intended to require of him.

When the priest and young lady stood before the captain, he spoke but very few words to them.

"You will be landed," he said, as he looked at the two persons, "with the others, on the nearest cape."

He waved his hand, and the captives were led away.

Lastly, the man who was found in the cabin of the captured ship, armed with a musket, and who had called the captain his son, was then led forward. Unlike the other prisoners, he was strictly guarded, and seemed to be treated with a severity that was the very opposite of that moderation which had been so generally and unexpectedly shown to the other prisoners that were in the same situation with himself.

The captain cast a stern and penetrating look on him, as he was brought before him, and said, in his stern indifferent manner:

"Prepare, to-morrow, for your trial; you know your crime." As he said this, he waved his hand.

The prisoner seemed tongue-tied for awhile, his countenance betrayed the most despondent fear; he seemed to become conscious, at once, of some great offence, under whose weighty recollection his whole faculties appeared overwhelmed.

He stood before him whom he called his son, and seemed to entertain for him more fear than any of the stranger prisoners who could claim no relationship or parentage to move his pity or secure his forbearance. He could not utter a word for the short moment that he stood before the captain, but when the pirates, who guarded him, laid their hands roughly upon him, to pull him away, the fear, the surprise, the consciousness which, till then, had deprived him of speech, lost their power under the influence of the terror that now seized him.

"But what–what is my offence? how dare you? My own son, to–" here one of the sailors, who guarded him, threw his sash over his head, and bound it so tightly behind, that not even a murmur of the unfortunate prisoner could be heard, as he was led away to the foremost part of the vessel.

The chief now rose and retired. The crew silently returned to their own quarters, and the Black Schooner which, a moment ago, was full of animation, was now left again quiet and apparently solitary, gracefully riding over the sparkling waves under her jib and half-mainsail.

CHAPTER VI

"Why, I will fight with him upon this theme,
Until my eye-lids no longer wag."

HAMLET

THE captain had retired from the deck of the schooner but a short time, when the sounds of the gong, which was the usual instrument for announcing a day of pleasure to the sailors, echoed over the vessel. The sounds were received with joy, and, in a short time, the deck of the schooner again presented the scene of life, which it had done but a few moments ago, but which had been momentarily succeeded by the contrasting stillness of death.

On this occasion, however, the sailors were not standing in the stiff restraint of discipline and duty, as then, but they delivered themselves up to enjoyment with all that impetuosity of pleasure, which strict constraint and proper separation of relaxation from labour necessarily produce. No boisterous mirth, nevertheless, obtained among them now, as on the other day. They were occupied in either speaking about the prize-ship, and the prospect of their booty, or in speculating upon the enjoyment which their share of the morning's division would procure them, when they should be allowed a day's sport in some friendly harbour. The liquors, which they had taken on board of the ship, circulated freely around, and the choice tobacco which had also fallen into their hands, contributed largely to their gratification.

The English sailors, who had been induced to make themselves easy by the forbearance with which they were treated, and had been invited by the pirates to mix in the merriment, joined freely in the carousals of the day. By that mysterious sympathy which instinctively exists between people of the same country, and children of the same soil, they had been drawn together around Jim Splice, and were now expressing their surprise at what they had seen, and experienced on board the Black Schooner.

"Ay, ay, shipmates," said Jim Splice, in answer to them, "you have come from a far country, hav'nt you? ha, ha! you thought you were done for, eh? when you saw our pikes, and our skull and bones; ha, ha! my hearties, you did'nt know us: and, when you came on board, you expected to be made to walk the plank, eh? We don't look for men's lives—what booty does that give? we look for something better; and if you, or that stupid skipper of yours wasn't foolish enough to fire upon us, why, we would have taken your money and your ship, to be sure, but those comrades of yours, that have now gone to their reckoning, would be here now, to take a glass of grog with old Jim Splice. But, by G–d, that was a reg'lar rattler that you gave the first boat–I never seed the like. It was foolish, though; what could your skipper gain by that?"

"Why," replied one of the sailors, "you see we had but one gun to fire salutes with, and our skipper had it loaded with all kind of material, and pointed it himself. He thought, you see, you would have cut away after the first discharge, you see."

"Then, by G–d," replied Jim Splice, "he counted without his host, my hearty; no one has ever seen the stern of this here Black Schooner," striking the deck on which he sat, with his hand, "as is commanded by that ere captain you spoke to this morning; and you may take my word for that, I know. That man that you saw this morning, I tell you, is the very devil, when his blood is up; he fights like a tiger–a reg'lar tiger."

"But, who is that old lubber that looked so miserable this morning–him who was guarded?"

"We don't know much of him," answered one of the sailors, "but I have heard our captain say that he was a rich old codger. I know he sent on board as many hens and sheep as would keep us on fresh provisions all the voyage if it had'nt so happened as we were taken. But why was he guarded that way?"

"Hum–no one knows," replied Splice, "I guess there is some misunderstanding between him and our captain; if so, God help him! for those who have misunderstandings with our fire-eater never get on well, I know; old Jim Splice would'nt be in that lubber's ducks for the richest West Indiaman that ever carried sugar, I know."

Here Jim Splice remained silent for a few moments, during which time he seemed to be wrapt in serious reflection.

"By G–d," he continued, "I was saying, yes–yes–I saw him once–ay, our captain, punish a shipmate that had'nt obeyed orders, and I sha'nt forget that, I know. Those that sail well with our captain are treated like his children, but God help those who cross him in his tack, all young and quiet as you see him!"

Splice became again silent, and looked absorbed, as if his memory was returning to some bygone scene in his chequered life.

"But, my hearties," he said, when he had been silent for a considerable time, "will you go ashore, or remain with us? This is the schooner for any man of spirit; by G–d! I should'nt leave this ere craft if they would give me the finest palace to-morrow. Here we lead the lives of men–ay, tough brave men–ay, no lubberly coxcomb* to make us jump about, or talk to us in

*coxcomb: vain, conceited fool.

oaths, by G–d, no. Every man here is a man; he has only to observe discipline, that's all, no mistake there, my boys; overboard with any one who dos'nt keep the rules–ay, this is the craft, my hearties. But what is the matter there?" as he said this, he pointed towards the bows of the vessel, where three men were standing, and seemed to be objects of attraction to all the other pirates, for the eyes of the whole crew were turned towards them. "Ah! I see," observed Jim Splice, "it is my two shipmates of this morning, that are going to fight it out. That's a bad business: we never see things of this sort on board this here craft; two men never claim the share of a dead comrade."

It was, as Splice had justly remarked, the two men, who had claimed the portion of the departed Francis, under the pretence of being his friends. The other person, who was standing by them, was the officer of the watch, whose duty it was to see the order, which the captain had given in the morning, carried into effect. As soon as it was six o'clock, he had proceeded forwards, and reminded the parties that the time for the duel had arrived. He found the two men, who were about to join in deadly fight, drinking with their comrades, apparently thoughtless of the bloody deed which they were now bound, by the order of the captain, to execute. One of them, however, did not seem as gay as usual, although he made strong efforts to conceal the thoughtfulness which now and then shewed itself in his dull and uneasy manner. It might be imagined that some serious thoughts of parent or child were forcing themselves on his unwilling memory; or, perhaps, remorse for some deed that was horrible even to his piratical conscience was at that moment haunting him.

When the officer had reminded the two men that the hour was come, they proceeded with him to the bows of the schooner.

The officer placed himself by the combatants with the evident purpose of being a witness, or, rather, the witness, to the deed.

The two men, who were to fight, proceeded in the meantime to prepare for the combat. They undid each his sash, and folded it carefully round his left arm, examined the edges of their poniards, and placed themselves in attitude, with the left arm raised, as if supporting a shield. This was done with the most astonishing coolness, not a word was spoken between the antagonists, not a malignant or malicious glance escaped from either the one or the other, but the features of the two men that faced each other were locked in that grave fierceness which is too deep to be expressed by changes of the countenance.

Having completed their preparations, the intended combatants stood for a time inactive, each apparently expecting the assault of the other, and displaying in their manly attitude the muscular fulness, bold glance, and resolute eye, which we admire in the statues of the ancient gladiators that art has bequeathed to our contemplation. They seemed by no means eager to assail each other; they evinced not the impetuosity of men who rush on each other in the out-burst of their rage: they seemed to be about to do something which they were, indeed, obliged to perform, but from which their natures revolted; their blood was too cold for the deed; the small portion of a dead comrade was too little to fire their spirits and spur them headlong on each other. Still they were obliged to fight. When both had stood, however, in this manner for a long time, the one who in the morning had first claimed to be Francis's friend, suddenly rushed on his antagonist, and raising his poniard on high made at his opponent.

By a sudden movement of the body the latter avoided the blow; as quick as thought the other drew himself up in his former position, and before his antagonist could regain the equilibrium which he had partly lost by bending his body to avoid the blow, he aimed a deadly stab, and the glistening poniard descended in sure destruction on the left breast of the stooping antagonist; but a dexterous parry with the muffled arm averted the blow, and the poniard passed harmlessly through the scarf. The apathy or indifference which existed at the beginning had now passed away, and the fight began to warm. The two fighters plunged with desperation at each other, but both seemed equally expert in the use of their weapons. With the agility and the pliability of serpents they avoided each other's blows by the rapid movements of their bodies, while their feet scarcely moved from the place in which they were at first planted. On–on they rushed at each other, but in vain: they were well matched. The fight now became still more animated; anger, rage, disappointment, could now be read in the grim faces of the combatants; their nostrils distended wide with fatigue, the perspiration poured down their dark faces, and their lips, curling high with rage and scorn, exhibited their clenched teeth, white and glistening beneath the shadow of their black mustachioes.

With a dreadful thrust, one at last buried his poniard deep into the neck of the other.

Exasperated by the cut, the wounded man made a desperate rush on his antagonist, who bent his body a little to the side and gave way to the assailant. Borne away by his own impetus, and already weakened by the wound, he staggered forward a little, and fell flat on his face. The victor waited for a moment for his antagonist to rise, but the unhappy man had received his death blow, and remained prostrate on the deck. The other, after this, did not seem to take the slightest notice of his opponent's fall, but proceeded with coolness to unfold his sash from around his arm and to wipe his bloody poniard. The officer on duty immediately went to the assistance of the fallen man, and summoning two of the men of his watch, ordered him to be removed from the deck. The two sailors bent over the wounded man to lift him, but they were sullenly repelled. He was the pirate that had claimed the share last.

"Leave me," he sullenly cried, "leave me, I say; let me die here." The sailors drew back.

"Come, comrade," said the officer, "you cannot expect us to let you remain here–remove him, my men."

The sailors endeavoured to lay hold of the man, but, with the impulsive strength of death, he brandished his poniard about him and kept them away.

"Let me die here, and be damned to me!" he exclaimed, "I was not Francis's friend, and I have deserved to be killed this way," and he churlishly dropped his head on the deck.

The sailors, who stood around the dying man, were surprised and shocked by his confession, for no instance of such base falsehood had ever been known before on board the Black Schooner. A strict sense of honor was maintained among the pirates. This was not only enforced by the stringent laws which existed, but was cheerfully cultivated by the men themselves, from motives not only of obedience, but self-preservation, for they were fully persuaded that the least breach of honesty among themselves, would be the end of their individual security, and the dissolution of their society.

Besides, to men of such dispositions, accustomed as they were to act openly and to hazard their lives boldly, such acts of calculating meanness were naturally disgusting.

It may be said that the very illegitimate pursuit in which they were engaged was itself dishonesty, but it is to be recollected that they considered piracy not in the shocking light in which better and more delicate minds justly view it; but they looked upon it more like adventures, in which men of spirit could engage with as much honour, as in fighting under the banners of stranger kings, for the purpose of conquering distant and unoffending peoples. They viewed, therefore, this act of meanness, on the part of the fallen man, with disgust, and the commiseration which was at first so spontaneously shown as to an unfortunate party in a duel, was immediately withdrawn when the dying man disclosed his crime.

The officer who witnessed the combat, upon hearing the confession, proceeded immediately to Lorenzo and reported the circumstance. That officer heard him with much concern: he knew the extreme penalty that was attached to such an offence, and his heart was sickened at the thought of an execution. He listened to the report of the officer until he had finished, and remained silent for a time, apparently meditating either intercession or some other means of avoiding the fatal punishment which he well knew the crime of the man would entail. Every hope, however, seemed to give way in succession, for, after he had remained silent for some time, he said, shaking his head:

"I wish to Heaven that man had never come on board the schooner, or that he should have died, at least, with his own secret. I shall communicate these things to the captain: but I pity the poor fellow."

Accordingly he left his cabin, and got access to that of the captain, when he repeated the report of the officer on duty. The captain heard him with the same grave and apparently apathetic coolness which characterised him, and then repeated, in his deep sonorous voice, the fatal sentence – "Let the punishment be executed upon him."

While Lorenzo was communicating the latter part of the intelligence, there might have been discovered a slight falter in his voice, and some embarrassment in his manner. He seemed to tremble at the consequence which such a short sentence would produce, while he himself was under the sad obligation of pronouncing the words which would bring about the fatal results that he seemed to dread so much. He, however, had managed to inform the captain of the poor man's crime, and he still hoped that the circumstance of his being already at the point of death, from the wound which he had received, would suspend the punishment which he but too well knew would follow that which, in the Black Schooner, was accounted the highest guilt.

Lorenzo, therefore, anxiously watched the countenance of his cold and stern commander, in the hope of being able to read in the expression which his report would produce, something that would lead him to believe that the unhappy culprit should be spared the horrors of an execution, when the hand of death seemed to be already laid so heavily upon him. But the features of the captain changed not: it is true, the minutest scrutiny may have detected a transitory alteration in the eyes, but that was more terrible than assuring. It lasted but for a moment, the face wore its own cold severity when the fatal "let the punishment be executed upon him" was pronounced.

Lorenzo silently rose, bowed, and retired. No man ever pretended to advise the chief; he seemed one who held counsel but with himself, he carried his discipline and his doctrine of expediency so far, that he never permitted either the suggestions of his officers, nor heard the prayers of mercy when once his commands were issued. Lorenzo knew that: more tender than his pursuit should have made him, he felt deeply for the wretched man who was doomed, that hour, to die for the satisfaction of the rigid laws of the schooner.

When Lorenzo left the cabin of the captain, he went on deck, where he gathered the men about him. These had continued in their places during the duel and the scene which ensued, apparently unaffected and unmoved by what was passing before them. During the most animated part of the combat, they had become as silent as if they were dumb, while their eyes were rivetted on the two who were fighting. But as soon as the duel was over, they fell again into the strain of mirth and revelry, which had been for a short time suspended, and the stabs and passes of the late combatants became the subjects of an animated conversation and of criticism.

But as soon as the wounded man had made known his crime, a general indignation seemed to seize the pirates.

They talked low and sullenly, and appeared to expect every moment something whose anticipation already had the effect of damping their hilarity.

Lorenzo repeated to them, for the sake of form, that which they already knew, and then repeated the sentence of the captain. The pirates spoke not a word, but a deep silence reigned among them. The officer of the watch was then requested to cast lots among his men for two who should execute the sentence. The two on whom the lot fell, preceded by the officer, shortly came up to the wounded man. They seemed very much dissatisfied with the duty that had devolved upon them.

The officer bent over the wounded man and reminded him that he had violated the most binding of their laws, and, at the same time, had exposed the life of a comrade to his own poniard, when he knew all the while that he had no right to contend for the portion which had been bequeathed by one dead comrade to another. He repeated the usual sentence passed in that case, and stated that the captain had also ordered its execution, and told him that within a few moments he should no longer live.

"Have you," he asked, in conclusion, "any request to make?"

"No," answered the wounded man, with the same sullenness as before.

The two men now raised the culprit on the bulwarks of the schooner. One of them supported him there, while the other proceeded to attach to his legs two cannon-balls, which were strongly tied up in pieces of old canvas. The culprit watched these preparations with the most unmoved indifference and most sullen cynicism. By this time he had lost a great quantity of blood, and his face was horribly pale and haggard, and wore under the shade of his malignant eyes an expression of deep malice, accompanied with a spiteful feeling against all men on account of the disappointment he had met, and the discomfiture which he had experienced in the fight. He spoke not a word; not a tender feeling seemed to warm his heart at that moment. The many years which he had, no doubt, passed among those from whom he was on the point of being cast away for ever, seemed not to recall to his gloomy recollection one single happy, or convivial moment which he might fondly contemplate; nor did the remembrance of some distant friend, of mother, or sister, or of wife, appear to force itself upon the man, whose moments were now numbered; but stolid, cold, and sullen, he lay on the bulwarks – on the brink of his existence.

The chest and other effects belonging to him were now brought and placed also on the rails. To them were also attached cannon balls, and they were supported in that position by one of the men who seemed to await the orders of the officer.

They had not to wait long: the officer made a sign, and the wretched man, with his effects, was precipitated into the deep. A few bubbles arose to the surface, and the ocean rolled on over the executed pirate. Not an eye followed the splash, not a pirate looked where the waters had settled for ever over their victim, but the crew seemed to erase, at once, from their recollection the existence of their late dishonest comrade. They still sat at their cans, but the elasticity of the revelry was broken, to those grim men themselves such a death was solemn; the recent execution damped their spirits, and their pleasure was no longer like pleasure. The men and the officer returned to the duties of their watch. The sun sank in the horizon, night came, silence resumed its wonted reign, and the Black Schooner rode in the stillness of the deep over the long lazy billows of the Caribbean Sea.

CHAPTER VII

"I stand for judgment: answer; shall I have it?"
Merchant of Venice

As soon as the sun had risen the next morning, the crew was again summoned to the main deck. They appeared, as on the day before, in their best costume, and fell into the same order.

The seamen, who belonged to the prize-ship, together with the master fisherman and his men, were placed by themselves, while the priest and the young lady were, as a mark of distinction, accommodated with deck-stools apart.

As soon as the men had assembled, the captain made his appearance on deck. He was apparelled in the uniform, which it would appear he always wore when he was out of his cabin: the deep red cap, with the skull and cross bones, also covered his head. The expression of his features, if possible, was that of even more gravity than usual, and the melancholy cast which stamped that gravity was, perhaps, somewhat more deepened. He seated himself immediately on a chair, which was ready there for him, and ordered the prisoner who, the day before, had been dragged away to close confinement, to be brought forward.

This individual was immediately escorted from the forward part of the vessel, and placed in the space reserved within the two lines of pirates, and face to face with the captain.

The prisoner was a man somewhat above the ordinary height, of a demeanour, which might have once been, to a great extent, commanding, but which seemed to have parted with whatever of native dignity it possessed, in proportion, as the spirit of excellence and elegance, which usually imparts character to the exterior, gave place to thoughts either of sordid pursuits, or to mean and selfish cares. He was now slightly bent, more, perhaps, from carelessness to his gait than with age: for his years could not have been very many. His hair, that still grew thick and bushy, was only just beginning to show a silvery tinge. His features were marked and manly, and must have been, at one time, very handsome, though now they were stamped with a disagreeable appearance of coldness and selfishness, which was calculated to arouse, at once, in a stranger's mind, a strong prejudice against the individual; while his sharp, twinkling, cozening eyes, in particular, that shone from under a veil of shaggy eyebrows, that flew from object to object, that rested on no man for a moment, nor dared meet the glances that they encountered, conveyed immediately an idea of the lack of that firm, unequivocating honor which is essentially necessary in the constitution of a proper character.

When the prisoner was placed before him, the captain fixed upon him a deep, penetrating, and earnest look, that made him cower, and then slowly and solemnly pronounced these words:–

"James Willmington, before God, and in the presence of these men, and in the name of Nature, I accuse you of having violated one of the most sacred and most binding of her laws; of having abandoned your offspring; of having neglected the being whose existence sprang from yours, and for whom you were bound by a holy obligation to care and provide."

The captain paused for a moment, and still kept his penetrating and unaltering eye fixed on the prisoner. The latter, on hearing this charge, raised his eyes in affrighted surprise, but quickly looked down as he met those of the pirate captain, while his color came and went.

"You shall be witness against yourself: because, although I lately took proper measures to make myself certain, that you were the individual who was indicated as the person that was my father; still, not having ever known you, and not possessing any tender instincts to guide me with regard to you, I should have always felt some slight doubt about your identity, if your fear, and miscalculating cunning had not, the day before yesterday, unwarily betrayed you into an avowal which, I must admit, I was not ready to hear from your lips. These men shall be your judges. You will be permitted full liberty to express yourself, at the proper time, as freely as you may think proper, omitting nothing that you may believe to be conducive to your safety. I shall reserve to myself the part of passing sentence upon you and of directing its execution; and I promise you, that whatever defence you may be able to make shall weigh as heavily as lead in your favour: for I should be loath to punish you if even you can contrive to justify yourself."

"But what is the meaning–?" the prisoner began to inquire.

The captain pressed his finger firmly on his lips, and Willmington was daunted into silence. The pirate captain then went on:

"I need not now call it to your recollection," he said, "that I am your son. Your memory, which all along was so unfaithful on that point, seems to have suddenly improved, when you saw me in the cabin of the ship which I had taken, and then you remembered well that I was your son. By your own confession, therefore, I am saved the trouble of proving for my satisfaction the natural connection which exists between us. It is, therefore, undoubted and settled, that I stand towards you in the relation of son to father, or, in other words, speaking more scientifically, I am your immediate progeny. This is clear. Now, by certain feelings which are implanted in us, and which are considered the laws of the Creator, written on the heart of man at his creation, we are admonished that the care of those who spring immediately from us, is one of our principal duties. But, as we are so apt to mistake habits for innate feelings, perhaps it will be better and safer, not to proceed on this one, however strong or indisputable it may appear. Let feeling, therefore, or instinct, be entirely eliminated, and let us appeal to Nature herself in her manifestations – to Nature that never errs. You admit that I am your son – your offspring; you owed me as such offspring, at least, protection until I was strong enough to provide for myself and to avoid injuries. Contrast now your conduct with your duty. You are aware, that from the hour of the birth of this, your son, up to this, you have never taken the trouble even to inquire what had become of the being of whose existence you were the secondary cause; whether the mother, of whom he was born, had survived to nurture him; whether he was exposed, in the helplessness of infancy, to the privations which overwhelm even maturer age; or worse still than all, whether he had fallen into stranger's hands, to be the humble object of capricious charity. You did not trouble yourself to learn whether the cold winds froze him in the very beginning of life; whether he was a prey to the beasts of the woods, or whether the vultures of the air had pecked or torn him, or had fed upon him; he was forsaken, and left unprotected by the person who had given him life – life, which with kindness is made happiness itself, but which by unkindness is rendered worse than the bitterest misery. The tiger will tear to pieces the bold intruder that menaces, nay, that approaches its cubs, and, fiercely fighting, will die for the protection of its young. The solitary bird of the desert will open its vein, and make its parched young one's drink of its life blood, then die; the venomous serpent will writhe and twist under the fiercest foe for its hatchling; but you, unlike the tiger, the bird, or the serpent, not resembling even the most ferocious brute, or the lowest reptile that crawls upon this earth, you cast away from you, and shut out from your mind and heart, until a cowardly consideration for your own safety made *you* remember it, the blood of your blood, and the flesh of your flesh, which even the common affection that you have for yourself – your very essential selfishness itself – should have made you love and cherish; or, at least, feed and water. I am your son; I charge you with having abandoned me from childhood; what defence can you make? I give you ten minutes to reflect and to answer."

The pirate captain then ceased: his eyes were fixed on the deck, his arms were crossed over his breast, and his features were locked in cold but firmest determination, and he had the air of one, who was resolved to go through a prescribed form with patience and precision. The men embraced the opportunity afforded by this pause to interchange looks one with the other. Their usual ferocious character of mien was heightened, for the history which their chief had just partly related, no doubt recalled to the greater part of those men who stood that morning on the deck of the Black Schooner, the injustice, whether real or merely supposed, with which they had been treated by others. Victims to wrongs and injuries which others had heaped upon them, they had permitted their feelings to become cankered. Accustomed for the most part to the circumstances of an easy, and as far as some of them were concerned, an estated position, they could not in the hour of adversity, bend to the petty pursuits of life, while their pride, at the same time, would not let them lead a different sort of existence among those who were either their companions or their inferiors in their better days.

Turning their backs on pretended friends and unkind kindred, they had fled to the protection of the sea, where they could enjoy the doubtful comfort of their misanthropy* to the full, and feed at pleasure on their own griefs; while their sword was ready to be used as well for pleasure as for booty, against the whole world to which they at the same time boldly and fearlessly gave defiance. The recollection of other days, however, fell upon their spirits, and how seared soever their sensibilities might be by a thousand scenes of blood, how hardened soever by long familiarity with misery, still those impressions to which in the day-dreams of their youth they had fondly bound their happiness, could not but be awakened by the tale that seemed to hold up to each of themselves the fleeting reflection of their own hopeful, but long since spoilt and blighted existence.

It was resentment, so strong as to have primarily germinated disgust in their hearts, and next a distaste for the society of their species, that had made them separate themselves from mankind and wander misanthropically about, until they eventually found themselves combined with others as unfortunate, as unenduring, and as proud as themselves; it was resentment of injustices of a similar nature to the instance to which their chief was a victim, that had changed their lot, and hating still the causes of their unhappiness, they were eager to wreak vengeance upon any individual to whom they could bring home any such offence. They interchanged fierce looks with each other, cast now and then dark and boding glances on the prisoner, and portentously stroked their dark and flowing beards. As for the prisoner himself, he appeared confounded; still there was not that vacant appearance of embarrassed simplicity about him which we generally observe in those that are innocent when unhappy circumstances put them at a loss. His was a distressing confusion—the confusion that conscious guilt, too clear to admit of even the shifts of equivocation and falsity had produced—a confusion that was doubled by the mortifying, degrading, and overwhelming fact, that his accuser, the witness, and the sufferer from his offence was his own son. The guilty father therefore stood dumb before the son—the judge.

---

*misanthropy: hatred of mankind.

The ten minutes had now elapsed, the captain raised his head, and said, "Do you then say nothing in your defence?"

"I–I–I do not understand what all this means," at last Willmington falteringly said.

"So much the worse," dryly observed the captain.

"You charge me with an offence," continued Willmington, "which you make worse than it is; you must remember men are not punished in society for such offences, and I do not see why I should be ill-treated on its account, when others are not."

An indistinct smile played about the lips of the captain, as he answered, "That is no defence."

"Beside," Willmington went on to say, "what right have you to constitute yourself my judge?"

"The right," answered the captain, "of an injured man, who avenges the wrong done to himself, and also to one who was his nearest and dearest blood, and whose memory demands justice."

"But, by the laws, a man cannot redress his own wrongs," said Willmington.

"By what laws?" inquired the captain.

"By the laws of the land," answered Willmington.

A sneer was to be traced on the rude lineaments of every pirate's face, when this answer was given.

"Look up there, man," said the captain, as he pointed to the black flag that was floating gracefully from the half lowered gaff, "while that flies there, there is no law on board this schooner save mine and great Nature's. Look around you, on the right and on the left, you see those who know no other laws but these two, and who are ready to enforce them. Look still farther around, you see but a waste of water, with no tribunals at hand, in which complaints may be heard, or by which grievances may be redressed. Place no hope, therefore, on 'the laws of the land.' Have you anything more pertinent to urge?"

"I have to request," replied Willmington, still more embarrassed, "to be landed with your other captives, that is all."

"Is that all?" coolly observed the captain; then turning to his men, he said, "my men, you have heard my accusation against this man. He seems unable to defend and justify himself. It is my intention to punish him by making him suffer that which I have had myself to undergo. Be you witnesses that I have given him a fair and open trial."

"Bravo, bravo!" ran in deep, but subdued tones along the ranks of the pirates.

"Listen to your sentence, James Willmington," continued the captain, "you are guilty, in my opinion, of the greatest crime which an individual, as a man and a father, can commit. You have prostituted the law of nature to your own selfish gratification, perjured yourself, and given that life for which you neglected to provide and care. I have afforded you an opportunity of showing yourself innocent–if you could–of this grave charge. You have not been able to do so. The punishment I design you is this: you will be cast adrift on the ocean; you will have an empty cask to rest upon; you refused me bread–I refuse you shelter on board of my schooner; you are guilty of what we all on board this vessel abhor; you are, therefore, no proper companion for us, and you must be thrust forth from among us. I shall, however, take care that you should survive as long as possible, that you may be the more able to realize the pangs of that famine which I endured by your heartlessness. In two hours' time the sentence shall be executed. Prepare to meet your Creator. Lead him hence."

"Good God," now cried the prisoner, his eyes seeming to be about to fall from their sockets with fear, as the full extent and reality of his danger, now clearly struck him, "good God, surely you do not mean to murder me: have mercy on me, I beseech you."

The captain did not raise his eyes from a paper which he had taken from the breast of his uniform, and which he was then reading. "But," continued the prisoner, as the pirates prepared to drag him away, "remember, I am your father, you owe me honour and respect–how dare you raise your hand against your parent?"

The captain at these words suddenly raised his head, and cast an angry and steadfast look on the prisoner, and after the lapse of a few seconds, during which he kept his eyes still rivetted on him, he said, with biting scorn–

"Remember that you are my father! you ought to ask me to forget it. It is because I remember you are my father that I shall now prepare for you your just measure of suffering. It is very probable you never expected to be called one day to account by the son who was the fruit of a delightful indulgence, but which was to be considered no longer than during the short space which it afforded you pleasure. Very little do you, and such as you think, when in the turpitude of your perjured souls, you delude the confiding and helpless things who sin from too great a confidence in your protestations of honor, or rather, are too innocent to detect your falsehoods, that the beings to whom you may give life are things who like yourselves may possess feelings, and who may one day seek to avenge the treachery practised on their mothers. Selfish man! your selfishness pursues you at the very moment when your existence is in all probability about to end. You crouched to me, and sought to propitiate me by a show of paternal sensibility, when you saw me enter with my friends the cabin where you stood writhing in your terror, and to-day you again remind me that I am your son. Now your paternal feelings are very strong, and your memory remarkably faithful when you expect to save your life by remembering me. But you, of course, recollected nothing of me, nor were you so feelingly sentimental when I once wrote to you for the mite, which you would never have missed from your treasures. Your selfish artifice shall avail you nothing here. In two hours, as I have said, you will be cast adrift on the ocean. Men, lead him away."

CHAPTER VIII

"O Lord—me thought what pain it was to drown!"
RICHARD III

WILLMINGTON was taken away and confined to the part of the schooner in which he had been kept since his arrival on board. The crew remained in profound silence, in the same order, and the captain was silently studying the paper which he had in his hand, and from the perusal of which he had a little before raised his head to address the prisoner.

After the lapse of a few moments, he handed it to Lorenzo, and requested him to have a machine made according to the plan set forth in it.

The chief officer bowed, and took it to the officer of the watch. The captain then slowly rose, cast a look around him on the ocean and at the prize-ship, then descended the cabin steps.

The men dispersed, and, in a short time, the deck remained in the occupation of those only whose duty it was to keep watch at that time.

At the bows of the schooner a carpenter was now to be seen busy at work. He was labouring in the greatest haste. Before him was a plan, and a young officer, the one in command, might be observed now and then to leave the sacred boards of the after-deck, and walk forward to inspect the thing that the man was constructing.

Two hours had now elapsed since the captain had passed sentence on the prisoner, and the time had now arrived to execute it.

The moments that completed the two hours had scarcely fled, before Lorenzo came on deck. He proceeded immediately to inspect the machine which he had ordered to be made, in obedience to the commands he had received.

The captain himself, a short time afterwards, made his appearance. The machine was ordered to be brought to the gangway, where he carefully examined it. It was made of an empty cask, to which something like the keel of a ship was attached. This appendage was covered with heavy sheets of lead, for the apparent purpose of being made to keep downwards, and so to prevent the machine from rolling over. The upper part was provided with a wooden seat, made in the shape of a Spanish saddle, the bows of which rose very high, and were crowned with a piece of flat board, which seemed intended to answer the purpose of a shelf.

When the captain had examined this machine, he ordered that a few biscuits should be secured on the shelf above mentioned, and, at the same time, commanded the prisoner to be led forth.

In the meantime, the deck had become again crowded, for every one knew what would take place at the end of the two hours, which had just expired. But the pirates were not now drawn up in the same order as before. They crowded in the foremost part of the vessel, some lounged on the bulwarks, others bent over the riggings, watching, in moody calmness, what was going on. No one dared assist in the preparations except those who formed the watch of the hour. The captive priest, also, with his beautiful ward, stood leaning on the taffrail of the schooner, isolated, as it were, amidst the many that were on board the vessel.

The prisoner was brought forward to the gangway. He was haggard and worn: the feelings of the two hours which intervened between him and that doom, which was worse than death, concentrated as they were into the intensest agony, preyed like gnawing worms upon his body.

"Hear my last prayer, for mercy's sake!" he cried, with passion, to the Captain, as he threw himself at his feet, "oh! spare me this dreadful death; give me but life, and I shall give you all I have. – Can you treat your father in this manner? Oh, my son – my good son – my beloved son! I shall give you all my property – if – "

"Bind his arms," said the captain.

The arms of the prisoner were immediately seized; he resisted madly and violently, and, in the strength of desperation, he shook off the first pirate that attempted to lay hands on him. But he was quickly mastered, and his arms were tightly tied with small cord behind his back. The machine was now supported perpendicularly, and it resembled, as it stood in that position, a horse ready saddled.

The prisoner became still more agitated and terror-stricken when his arms were bound, and his cries were more piteous and heart-rending.

"Oh! ask mercy for me, my men, he cried, imploringly, to the pirates around him, whose coolness seemed to mock his wretchedness, "I shall make you all rich; do not–do not throw me into the sea. Holy father, holy father," looking towards the priest, "you may succeed, you may move him, you may curse him; ask mercy for me–do not let me be drowned."

"Put him on," the captain said.

The wretched man was lifted bodily, and laid astride upon the cask.

"Curses on you! do not–do not, for your soul's sake, murder me," he cried, and struggled like those who alone can struggle who see death before them.

But it was of no avail. The pirates seized his legs, and tied them tightly underneath the cask, so that the miserable prisoner had not the power of making any other movements except that of inclining his body a little backwards and forwards.

"Fix the tackles." The tackles were adjusted.

"Fiends! hell hounds," he yelled out, as the first strain of the ropes was felt on the cask, and laid hold of the pirate that was next to him with his teeth–another strain, and he held between his teeth a shred of the man's woollen shirt.

The cask was hoisted up, to be let down overboard. The cries of the fated Willmington increased still more–he roared franticly. The cask with the prisoner balanced between the masts of the schooner for a moment, in cruel suspense, while not a sound was to be heard, except his hoarse, pitiful, and moving cries.

The pirates looked on with sullen calmness; the captain was the same imperturbable man. But the priest could not withstand this moving scene; he threw himself at the captain's feet, and earnestly begged him to show mercy:–"mercy," he added, "that was the most acceptable offering to heaven."

"Good priest," answered the captain, "if you can sooth the end of that wretched being, do so. But pray not to me, I never change."

Slowly–slowly–slowly–the cask, with its living rider, who was shrieking like the damned, was lowered: it reached the water: the tackles were unfastened, and away, away, it slowly floated on the long high waves that bore it rapidly from the schooner.

The roars and cries of the prisoner rang over the silent sea. Every eye was rivetted in awful intentness on the cask and its burthen. The captain's alone was turned away from the direction where his father lay pinioned on a cask at the mercy of the winds and waves. He cast but one glance on the cask as it was lowered into the sea, and never looked at it again.

Indifference–indifference, as cold and as icy as death, indifference, such as nature can admit but only when every fibre of feeling is burnt into hard callousness by the searing iron of some deep unpardonable offence, had wrapped its clammy folds around his heart.

Reader, have you ever felt the absorbing love that sank and merged your existence into that of a cherished object, and have you ever felt the gall of sneering ridicule from her? If you have, then you know the feeling that possessed the pirate captain. Have you ever demanded bread from a parent whom you may have loved to excess and received a stone, or have you ever asked water from the author of your existence and received poison? Then you can fancy the captain's sentiments, or have you ever, while straining your industry and energy to the utmost, been ground down to misery and despair by him from whom nature taught you to expect love and protection, while he himself was rioting in profuse abundance? if you have, and we trust heaven has always preserved you from such a bitter experience, you can then realize the feeling which existed in the bosom of the pirate captain.

"Make sail," the captain said to the officer of the watch, after he had cast a glance on the horizon.

The schooner which, during all this time, was lying to the wind under only a half of her mainsail and jib, was immediately put under the press of all her sails. She had shot a-head for some yards, when the captain gave orders to change the course.

"Ready about."

"Ready about," was echoed forwards in the firm disciplined tones of the sailors.

"Hard a-lee."

"Hard a-lee," the man at the helm answered.

The helm was put down, and the long snake-like schooner bore up gracefully to the wind, the sails fluttered for a moment, and she leaned smoothly on the other tack.

Like a dolphin she cut through the water; the spray played about her bows, and the waves barely touched her sides as she glided through them.

A signal had been made to the prize-ship, and she, too, was put under full sail.

Away–away–the schooner went, and left far, far behind, the wretched being who had been thrown overboard. He could scarcely now be seen, it was but when the cask rose and fell on the crest of the heaving billows that a glimpse could be had of him. But his cries still reached the flying schooner. They gradually grew fainter and fainter; then they came like the intermittent moans of agony, low, and few, and far between, and then they were heard no more.

The captain gave his orders to the officer on duty to steer a certain course and then left the deck.

The day had by this time passed, and the fleeting twilight of the tropics was yielding to the darkness of night. The crew of the schooner betook themselves to their respective quarters. But the priest and his ward still lingered on the deck. Their strained eyes were fixed in the direction where the cask and its load had disappeared, and fancied they saw, every moment, the unfortunate Willmington rise, now and then, in the dim crepuscule. But they watched in vain, and saw not what they imagined they did. Far, far out of sight was the cask already borne, and Heaven only knew where the living being, that rode upon it, still drew the breath of life.

Saddened by the event of the day, they at length, in melancholy silence, left the deck, when the darkness had increased and had deprived them of the power of continuing their useless watch. Night, then, closed over the Black Schooner; and the faint ripplings of the water as she glided through, were the only sounds that might fall on the listening ear.

CHAPTER IX

"Say that upon the altar of her beauty
You sacrifice your tears, your sighs, your heart."
TWO GENTLEMEN OF VERONA

SILENCE reigned over the schooner. The pirates had retired to their hammocks, and all, except the men of the watch, were wrapped in sleep.

In his cabin, in the centre of the vessel, Lorenzo sat alone and pensive. The hour when he ought to have betaken himself to his berth had already long passed, but he still sat in his chair at the head of the table that stood in the middle of his cabin. He was still dressed in his uniform, nor were his arms even removed from the sash that bore them.

He sat gazing silently on the lamp which burnt suspended from the deck. One would have imagined he was in deep contemplation of that vessel, if the vagueness observable in the fixed gaze of his eye, did not too plainly tell that the subject of his thoughts, the object of his contemplation was not the thing which was at that moment before him, but some other which was in his mind.

The flying hours passed: Lorenzo was still sitting in his chair in the same absorbed contemplation. Now a placid smile would play over his features, now they would be locked in the fiercest sternness. There seemed to be in him at that moment a conflict of emotions deep and violent.

At last, as if he had taken a final resolution, "I shall do it!" he exclaimed. He then drew from a desk materials for writing and penned a letter.

When this was done, he took off his boots, put on his slippers, and enveloped himself in his thick boat cloak.

He then cautiously opened the door of his cabin, in which the light was carefully extinguished, and went out.

He proceeded down the long passage which led to the captain's quarters, and in which opened a door that led to the cabins occupied by the priest and his beautiful ward.

Stealthily and quietly Lorenzo moved down the passage; a lamp faintly burnt at some distance from the entrance to the captain's cabin, and by its dim light might be seen the dark outlines of the men who, at intermediate distances, guarded the corridor.

Lorenzo could not but feel some alarm when his eyes fell upon those tall forms, for he was conscious that he was treading on forbidden ground, where, to be found without the ring–the usual passport–was instant death. Such was the rigour of the discipline in which alone suspicion could hope to find security.

It is true he was not within the circle of the captain's quarters, but, nevertheless, his being discovered in the passage at that time of night, and in such guise, would lead to consequences equally as fatal, as if he had trespassed on interdicted ground.

His careful concealment of his person, and the change of his boots, would have worn such an aspect of conspiracy in the eyes of his superior, that nothing could have been strong enough to blot out the distrust which the latter would ever afterwards entertain of him, if even the consideration of his services and old friendship should have proved strong enough to induce the captain to spare his life.

The thoughts rushed in an instant on the officer as he stood for a moment looking at the erect and steady sentinel at the end of the passage before him.

They fell on him with all the weight and dreadful truthfulness which they possessed. He remained for a moment irresolute, but at length the daring spirit which his mode of life had fostered, and that indescribable feeling people call love, but which is as incomprehensible as it is omnipotent in its influence, nerved him against the danger which he apprehended, and he took two or three steps forwards with the same caution with which he had come into the passage. But he had gone only a few steps when he saw that the attention of the sentinel was drawn in his direction. The latter hand changed his straightforward look and was seemingly endeavouring to discover some object which had attracted his notice up the passage.

Lorenzo stood—his worst fears he thought were about to be realised. He saw at once the certainty of his being detected, and the consequences of that pressed on his mind.

The thought, too, which always afflicts ingenuous minds, when they are conscious that they are not culpable of an offence from which they instinctively recoil with horror, but with which circumstances conspire to charge them, fell heavily and miserably upon him.

The most desperately situated always hope—there is a hope almost in despondency itself; Lorenzo still hoped, in spite of the peril before him, that he would escape discovery. He knew that he could not be seen by the sentinel in the darkness of the passage, and expected that the latter would turn away, when he found that nothing was to be seen. Lorenzo, therefore, remained quietly where he was. The sentinel continued to gaze earnestly up the passage, and at last came out of his niche, and began to walk straightway towards Lorenzo.

"I am lost," the officer said to himself, and at once made up his mind to stay where he was and surrender to the sentinel. The man came towards him, but there was such indecision in his walk, that the officer could not fail to perceive, at once, that the man on duty was only taking a walk to see if there really was any one in the passage, without being actually certain of his presence.

"There may be a chance of escape, yet," he said to himself, and drew himself closely up against the side of the passage.

As the sentinel approached, his anxiety increased. The sentinel drew nearer and nearer: the officer drew himself up closely—and more closely; the sentinel was now but a few steps from him, he pressed still more closely on the side. Gently it yielded, and Lorenzo caught himself as he was just falling in the inside of a cabin.

With wonderful presence of mind, he closed the little door that had admitted him, and heard the heavy footsteps of the sentinel as he passed it on the outside.

With breathless anxiety he listened to the steps; he heard them diminish until the sentinel had arrived at the extreme end of the passage, and heard them grow more and more distinct as he returned at the same leisurely pace.

Again and again the man on duty passed his door; it was, therefore, clear that he had not been discovered; but as his anxiety about the man outside diminished, new fears arose with regard to the place in which he found himself. How was it that the door of that cabin had been left open, when such regularity usually existed on board the schooner? Was there any one at the time in the cabin? if so, the same danger that threatened him outside would meet him within: for self-preservation had taught every officer, and every sailor of the Black Schooner, that their safety could consist only in the strict observance of its laws in their own persons, and the rigorous enforcement of them in others. Every one seemed to know, instinctively, that the chain which was so variously formed, could be preserved only by a careful protection of each particular link. Lorenzo knew if any one was in the cabin, and if he were there seen under such circumstances, the person would make it a point of duty to report it to the chief. His alarm, therefore, which had partly subsided, grew again upon him. He remained in the deepest silence and attention, listening to the steps of the sentinel outside, who was still patrolling the passage from his niche to its extreme end.

He endeavoured, also, to listen for the breathing of any one that might be in the cabin, for he wisely concluded, that if any person was there, he must assuredly be asleep, or else he should have heard him when he accidentally tumbled in. But he heard nothing.

His anxiety, however, was not satisfied. He crept softly by the bed, and listened again, but still he could hear nothing; he passed his hand over the narrow berth, but there was no one there.

"Ah! I see," the officer said to himself, "it is the cabin of José."

It was the cabin of the officer who was then on duty, and Lorenzo breathed more freely; but his anxiety was soothed down for a moment only, for he immediately recollected that the night was already much spent, and that the watch on deck would shortly be relieved; his difficulty was thus in no manner removed. He reflected for some time, and concluded, in a sort of despair, that fate was determined to ruin him, and he calmly yielded himself up to the unfortunate destiny which seemed to pursue him that luckless night.

He calculated that within half an hour's time the watch of José would have expired, and that he should surely be discovered when that officer came down to his cabin. There might be a chance–though a desperate one–of escaping the certain detection of the sentinel outside, although suspicion would inevitably be raised: but that was the less of the two evils that beset him. He resolved, accordingly, to wait until the watch on deck should be near expiration, and then to make a desperate effort to escape from his dangerous position.

He remained, then, standing by the door, on the outside of which the measured footsteps of the guard were still heard. The time passed away, and the sentinel still walked the passage. The watch was nearly expired and he was there still.

"All is lost," Lorenzo said to himself, and then he drew up his cloak around him in that resolute manner that indicates the determination which, from its extremeness, becomes the kindred of despair; as he drew his cloak around him, something fell from it: it was the letter which he had written. He felt about for it in the dark until it was found. It seemed to revive the feelings which had begun to slumber under the absorbing solicitude for his own safety.

"Shall I put myself in danger and still not succeed in sending this?" thought he, "what advantage do we derive from all our acquirements, our high and glorious reputations, our friendships, our exposures, and our perils?"–he hastily reasoned–"if we are driven by the necessity of preserving these to sacrifice the happiness which we fondly hope to realize from them? away vain and timid thoughts–I will hazard everything; but, happen what may, I shall send this."

Having come to this resolution, Lorenzo waited until the sentinel had arrived at the head of the passage, and had, on his return to his niche, passed the door of the cabin in which he was concealed: he then opened it softly, and stepped into the passage: and, gathering himself up closely under its side, began to retire with as much caution as he had come in. He kept his eyes all the while fixed on the sentinel or his shadow, so that he might easily anticipate his movements, in case he was discovered.

He had reached the top of the large passage, and was about to take the one which led to his own apartments, when the footsteps ceased, and the man drew himself up as before in his niche. It was evident that whatever suspicions he may have entertained at first had now entirely vanished, and that the greater part of the continued walk which he took, was intended more for his own recreation than for the interception of any one who he might have suspected was trespassing on the circle of his guard, for he seemed to be entirely given up to his own reflections. Lorenzo stopped when he saw this; he mused for a moment, but his resolution was not long in being taken. He bent himself on his knees and hands, and crept down the passage again; he stopped several times to study the movements of the sentinel, all which times he seemed to be the more assured of his safety; he crept in this manner until he reached a certain door, and was now but a few yards from the man on duty. The latter seemed still absorbed in his own thoughts; Lorenzo drew the letter from his breast, and pushed it under the door. As he supported himself on one hand, in doing so, the vessel lurched, and the hand holding the letter struck against the door. The sentinel raised his head for a moment, but, concluding that it was the inmate of the cabin who had struck by accident against the partition, he relapsed into his meditative state.

Lorenzo drew himself carefully back in the same manner as he had gone forwards. When he got to the head of the passage, he jumped on his feet and hastened to his own cabin.

He had scarcely shut the door, when he heard the heavy footsteps of the officer, who had now been relieved, on the companion stairs as he descended to his cabin.

CHAPTER X

"One half of me is yours, the other half yours—
Mine own I would say, but if mine then yours
And so all yours."
MERCHANT OF VENICE

ON the next morning when Agnes—by that name the priest called her—the fair captive, was going towards the door of the cabin which was given up to her use, she beheld a sealed letter at her feet. After her first surprise had somewhat lessened, she remained standing for a time in deep reflection over it, endeavouring to conjecture whose it might be, to whom addressed, and what could be its purport. At last, being unable to restrain her impulse of curiosity, she took it up and saw that it was for her. But the superscription was in the handwriting of a man—and not that of her guardian.

What mystery could that indicate? What could it portend?

Before opening the letter, the beautiful young lady remained for a long time gazing on it, while at the same time she was led away into a train of strange and complicated thoughts. Could that letter be, she inquired of herself, the forerunner of some attempt that the pirate captain contemplated against her safety and honor? She trembled at the thought: she recollected that among the outrages and ravaging descents of the Boucaneers, their cold-blooded cruelties upon the sex were not the least of their horrible deeds; and should this captain now design to add her to the multitude of those of her condition, who had been sacrificed to the profligacy of similarly lawless men? . . . It is true, up to that time, she had been treated with an amount of respect and kindness that could not be exceeded even by the fastidious solicitude of the most polite, or by the benevolence of the most virtuous; and this captain seemed to be somewhat different from the heartless freebooters of whom she had heard: but might he not carry under that stern, and apparently callous exterior, designs which would be the more to be feared as they should be the more premeditated. If so, what chance had she of resisting him? Words would not prevail with him; entreaties could have no effect on him; for she had seen him send his own father adrift on a cask on the wide ocean, and every thing, and every one on board of that schooner seemed to give way to him and sink under his will: what could move him, – what protect her?

A blush suffused her beautiful face. She was inclined to fancy that there might be one on board who would protect her. But yet they were both pirates, and why should she expect that they should incur one another's displeasure and enmity for her sake – an unfortunate captive. But although Agnes feared, still there was hope in her. Something told her, perhaps her own heart, that mysterious and unerring index of the truth, that he who had been so attentive to her from the moment when she set foot on board the schooner – that Lorenzo would defend her.

There is a mystery of mind, a language of thought, and a sympathy of soul, for which the greatest philosophers are still unable to account. There is that which conveys from the loving to the loved a mute and silent intelligence: there is that in us which converses without being heard, which communicates without being seen, and even while the tongue is tied and the eye is closed, tells to those we love of the sentiment that we foster and cherish in our breast. The mind of the young lady told her that Lorenzo would protect her innocence and honor, and she was somewhat calmed by this assurance, however slight and ungrounded, a more sceptical thinker would no doubt have considered it. Escaping in this manner from these unpleasant and dark thoughts that alarmed her, she was immediately recalled to herself, and proceeded to open the letter. She hastily and eagerly glanced over it, raised her head for a time, and then read, and read, and read again.

The letter was this: –

"Lady, though I am a pirate, recoil not from me. I am sensible to the feelings of honor, and need not be feared by any lady; in the uprightness of my soul I have dared to love you; deign to cast but one look on me, and let me believe I may hope.   Lorenzo."

Agnes read this over and over again in nervous trepidation, then folded it, and put it by.

She was a victim to strong contending emotions. She felt she knew not what for Lorenzo, but he was a pirate. She could not imagine that she loved: no, she did not; but she was grateful to the man as she had always seen him, gentle and kind, and apparently unstained by any crime: but she recoiled from the *pirate*. It would appear that even her gratitude could not succeed in mantling the hideousness of that name. Yet he was always so respectful to her! Could a pirate at heart be so? And if he were a pirate, such as she had heard those men were, could he write to her in that manner? No, it could not be. And joy glistened in her face as she seemed to congratulate herself on having come to a conclusion that was so favourable to Lorenzo.

Upon this she seemed to fall into an agreeable reverie: pleasure seemed to play on her face, as she thought she had successfully washed away the stain from the man on which her sentiments had already been anchored. Distressing thoughts, however, will force themselves on the happiest moments of our existence. At the height of her self-gratulation, the idea of the pirate again occurred.

"But who is he?" she inquiringly muttered, "what is he – a –? Oh! no, I cannot, I will not, I must not think of him," and she burst into a flood of tears. She wept and wept: now roused herself to extraordinary firmness, and resolutely dried her tears, but it was to let them flow in larger and fuller currents a moment after.

She was weeping over the ruined hopes of her own feelings: – of her first love.

Agnes had been born and brought up in the seclusion which necessarily surrounds a residence in the West Indies. She had seen but few persons besides the neighbours that had their plantations in the vicinity of her father's estate. She had never met any one on whom she could pour out the love that a tropical nature had lavished upon her. Her feelings at the moment when she got into the position which led to her meeting with Lorenzo were strong and fresh, and were in that state in which the mysterious law of human sociality required, that they should find an object on which they could alight and rest. They had alighted on Lorenzo – not by reasoning – not by calculation. They had alighted on Lorenzo, because they had alighted on him. Her feelings had flown and rested upon him, either independently of her volition, or so closely united with it, that it was not possible to say whether she loved, because she chose to love, or whether she loved because she found herself loving.

Such was the nature of her love: but if nature had implanted in her, feelings that were so strong, pure, and good, education had taught her that to control them was also necessary. She reflected that, above all instances, that was the one in which she required all the power that she might possess to restrain herself; for common prudence itself, unassisted by the imparted precepts of propriety, was sufficient to make her careful how she fostered the feelings, which had already risen in her breast.

Lorenzo was a stranger to her and hers, and the little that was known of him was disadvantageous to him, for it consisted of the certainty that he was a pirate–an outcast of human society. That was a sufficient consideration, and when the full force of it fell on the mind of the beautiful girl, she wept. She wept the tears that are the bitterest–the tears that flow when we are called away, by the dictatorial voice of principle and duty, from the pursuit of some fond object on which all the feelings of our nature are concentrated, and which we had complacently looked upon as the magnet of our happiness. On the one side she had her will and her affections; on the other she had the danger of an ignorance which was broken only by that which made it still more horrible. Like one, therefore, who is resigned to death, from the sheer insipidity of disappointed life, Agnes sat weeping in her cabin.

The tears fell not with the vigour of energetic sorrow, such as when the soul concentrates her strength to mourn away with one effort some heavy grief, but they dropped with the languor of over-settling despondency, such as when even the full tide of anguish cannot wash away the rooted sorrow.

She was in this condition, when the priest knocked at her door and entered.

"Was she ill?" the good father inquired, "she had remained so long in her cabin that morning?"

"No."

"Ah! but you are weeping: cheer up, child; come, come, dry those tears: you are, I see, thinking of home. Yes: there is a great difference between your good father's house and this vessel; but do not give way to sorrow, my child, we must be thankful to Providence for having delivered us from the death and dishonour which, it is likely, would have overtaken us if we had fallen into other hands, and we must not repine at its dispensations in any instance: cheer up. Besides, I have just been told to get ready to go ashore; they will put us on land soon, I suppose, although I cannot see it as yet myself."

Agnes saw very clearly that the good father had mistaken the cause of her grief, and was not a little glad to observe that he had so readily attributed it to the reminiscences of home. She remained silent. But the priest had only increased her embarrassment of mind, by the news which he brought, and which, he considered, as indeed he himself had felt them to be, the most joyful; for she learnt by his report that she was to leave the schooner: she was glad, and, at the same time, she was sorry.

She was naturally glad to be again restored to safety, and to revisit that home with its dear ones from which she was so nearly torn away for ever: and she was sorry to leave the schooner, because her heart had already begun to hover about it.

Which of the two feelings was the greater; judge for yourself reader.

Duty, however, and even safety called her away, and she must obey.

"When shall we go from this—when shall we be landed, I mean?" she inquired of the priest.

"I do not know exactly, child, but they told me to be prepared. But you have not, as yet, tasted food to-day; they have brought our morning meal: I have waited for you long,—come in and take some nourishment."

Agnes briefly excused herself from accepting the kind invitation of the priest.

"She was not absolutely ill," she said, "but certain thoughts had put her in a melancholy mood, and she felt no desire for food."

She insisted, at the same time, on his going to take his morning repast.

He hesitated for some time to leave her, but was, at length, prevailed upon to go, by her persisting assurances that she was not ill.

Left to herself, the innocent girl gave vent again to her tears; but she had not now any opportunity to indulge her feelings, for she was soon aroused from her sorrow by the re-appearance of the priest who invited her to go on deck.

They went up together.

The long schooner was now lying on the waves like some fish, that had concentrated its strength for a dart, waiting for its prey. She rose and sank with the waves, as she lay to the wind, like something that a more powerful hand than that of man had made to inhabit the element on which she so familiarly floated.

The usual silence reigned; every man of the watch stood mute and motionless at his station; the captain himself stood by the steersman with his arms folded across his breast.

The schooner had been thrown in the wind, to wait for the prize ship which was still at a considerable distance, but which was approaching fast under the press of her extensive sails.

She was, as we have said before, a fast sailer, but few vessels could keep up with the Black Schooner.

When the two vessels had set sail together from that part where they had remained since the fight and the capture, it was found necessary to reduce from time to time the sails of the schooner that the ship might be always kept within sight. Notwithstanding this, however, the former had imperceptibly outreached and distanced the latter, and it was now found necessary to put her in the wind, in order to allow time for the ship to come up.

Notwithstanding the information that they would be landed that day, the priest and Agnes could not see any preparations which might indicate such a thing. Far, however, to the east, land might be seen, high and blue, and like a passing cloud in the fleecy atmosphere of the tropics; still no boats were as yet got ready, and not an order was given. In course of time the ship drew nearer and nearer, until she had arrived within but a few yards of the schooner, when she was brought up heavily to the wind; her heavy canvas flapped, the waves broke on her huge bows, and she lay like a sluggish whale.

A boat was launched from the schooner and was despatched with a number of men on board the ship. After the lapse of a few moments, the cutter of the ship was launched, and was forthwith rigged out, and the sails were quickly bent. When this was done she was sailed up to the schooner, where provision to last for three days was put into her, and she stood ready for sea.

Orders were given for the strangers to come forward and embark.

Lorenzo, who had been in his cabin the whole of the morning, now came on deck. His appearance was not the same as it was wont to be. On his manly brow sat gloomy care and anxiety, and there was even something fierce in the expression of his lips. There was anxiety, deep anxiety, furrowed in his looks, but there were also marks of a deeper and sterner feeling.

When he came on deck, Agnes and her guardian were standing almost opposite the captain, on the starboard side of the vessel.

He saw them, but his eyes could not rest on them. Was he bashful?–was he afraid to meet the looks of a frail old man, and the timid glances of a helpless maiden?–he who had encountered enemies that every human passion had excited and embittered against him?–he whose daily life was a continuous challenge to man, to the powers that ruled the earth, and to the controlless element itself which he had made his home? No, he was afraid of himself: he was afraid of his pride. He had never placed himself before in a position to meet either slight or insult. He expected nothing from humanity, and he never placed himself in the way to be the object of its kindness or beneficence. But love–love–the leveller–had now overcome him: he had declared his feeling to a girl, he had, as he fancied, humbled himself, by putting himself in her power, and his pride was completely at her mercy. He therefore feared to look at her, lest in her looks he might read that which was–oh! more horrible than anything else to his nature–slight, indifference, or contempt. He had had a fierce struggle with himself at first to write the letter which he had put into the cabin of Agnes.

But he had no sooner done so than he repented of his act. The mastery that love had gained over pride was but temporary, it soon ceased, and he was left to be crushed under tyranny of that unrelenting feeling. How many conflicts such as Lorenzo experienced, are there not? How many hearts that nature formed but to be united and to swell and beat but in the community of each other, have shrunk, withered, and dried away in cold and comfortless solitude, because the love of another could not over-ride the fear of a risk, or an exposure of the love of one's self! How many a one has traversed this beautiful world, and moved on it as on the barren bareness of a desert land, with no congenial soul to enhance the pleasures of existence by its participation, or to diminish its miseries by its sympathy, because pride forbade him to disclose to some loving heart how much happiness it was in its power to administer.

These feelings, on the part of Lorenzo, did not arise from any low conceit that he entertained for himself: nor were they the emanation of that vulgar selfishness that concentrates existence, the capacity of possessing feelings, the desire of happiness, in one's single self, and there traces out their bournes* and limits; nor did they spring from the senseless and stupid vanity that bolsters itself up in all the "pomp and circumstance" of its fullfed ignorance. No: in the sturdy and the bold, such feelings do not, cannot exist. It was something better–nobler; something that could exist and thrive only in the community of exalted thoughts, and delicate sensibilities. It was a sensitive self-respect.

Lorenzo approached the pirate captain, and saluted him. The latter returned the salute, and, at the same time, fixed his keen eyes on his officer.

---

*bournes: a bourne is a terminal point or limit; goal, destination.

We have already said there was something peculiar in the eyes of the pirate captain: there was something that seemed to penetrate the inmost soul, and read the mind, and see what was passing there. This power he used on this occasion. The deep, earnest, steady look which he fixed on Lorenzo seemed to overcome the latter and his eyes bent before it. When the captain had looked long and steadfastly at his officer, he turned suddenly on one side, and seemed to contemplate in the same manner, the fair Agnes, that stood still leaning on the taffrail of the schooner, with her eyes fixed on the deck.

The captain had at once read in the manner of Lorenzo, that he was in love with the beautiful captive. His studious mind had long been exercised in connecting deductions and his deep knowledge of human actions and their springs, enabled him to trace, in one moment, the change which was perceptible in the appearance of his chief officer to its proper cause. He was at once convinced that Lorenzo loved Agnes, and he now looked on her with some interest. One would have said he was examining her in order to discover whether she was worthy of the affection of one whom he prized so highly.

The examination lasted long, and Agnes was justly alarmed concerning the meaning of this scrutiny on the part of the captain.

The persons to be landed were now assembled on the deck of the schooner.

The captain made a sign to the master fisherman to follow him, and he descended the cabin steps. When he had arrived into his apartment, he drew from a case a pair of pistols, and at the same time, took from his desk a purse of money.

"Listen to me," he said, to the master fisherman, "you have hitherto acquitted yourself well of that in which I have employed you, and I have rewarded you: now I require your further services. – I shall put you and the captives in a boat in a few moments. There is a young lady among them, together with an old priest: you must take care of her, and protect her. There are arms," pointing to the pistols, "for you, the others are unarmed. You, with these and the assistance of your men, can defend her against the sailors in the boat, in case any attempt be made by them to use the advantage of number which they possess. There is your reward," pointing to the purse. – "But, first swear by God and the Holy Virgin, that you will protect her at all risks."

"Senor, I swear."

"You shall be the master of the boat, and it shall be yours after you are all landed. Beat up to the land which you see before you from the deck. That is Grenada. In three days' time you will be there. Remember your oath. I never forget to punish."

"Senor, I shall," answered the master fisherman, who had all the gravity of the people to which he belonged, half by race and wholly by feelings.

The captain pointed towards the door, and the master fisherman was led away by one of the black boys who was in constant attendance there.

When the captain had disappeared from the deck with the master fisherman, Lorenzo was in a manner recalled to himself. He looked about him, his eyes met those of Agnes. His heart leapt. That look of kindness penetrated his soul; the gloomy conjurings of his pride vanished before it, and he seemed to be in the enjoyment of something to which, up to that moment, he had been quite a stranger. But, may he not have mistaken that expression of the eyes.

He looked again and again–their eyes met. Oh, no, he was not mistaken. He drew towards the young lady.

"Madam," he began.   , ...

"Lorenzo," sounded the deep voice of the captain, who had by this time come on deck again. He turned round and encountered the reproachful looks of his chief.

He went away from the side of Agnes, seemingly ashamed of having given so much license to his feelings, as to have neglected discipline for their sake.

The captives, the master fisherman, and his men were ordered into the cutter, and the captain himself assisted Agnes and the elderly priest into the boat.

The boat was ready to be cast off from the schooner, when the master fisherman remarked that one of his men was not in it. Jack Jimmy was missing.

"Ho! Jack Jimmy," went round the cry.

Jack Jimmy "heard it, but heeded it not." He was standing with his arms crossed over his chest.

"Jack Jimmy."

But he took not the slightest notice of the call. At last one of the sailors perceived him, and looking towards him, said,

"Jack Jimmy, will you come along?"

Jack Jimmy still remained silent where he stood.

"Will you come along?" and laying hold of him by the arm he attempted to drag him along.

"Massa, me no go–me no leave dis ya 'chooner as long as massa in ea," the little man said, with much determination.

"Will you come along sir?" and the sailor gave his ear a twitch–Jack Jimmy passively let himself fall on the deck, repeating–

"Me no go massa."

But another sailor came up at this moment, and the two of them dragged him along the deck to the gang-way.

"Oh! my young massa," he cried, as he approached the captain, "let me tap wid you, me no want foo go, me neber leafe dis 'chooner lang you ga–oh let me tap wid you," and he clasped the knees of the captain.

"Let him remain," said the latter to the men, who were approaching to drag him away again.

"Garamighty bless you, my young massa–me neber leabe you," and the tears trickled down the cheeks of the faithful little man.

The cutter was cast off from the schooner, her sails were set and she began to move through the water on her voyage towards land.

In the stern sheets sat Agnes, by the side of her guardian: her hand-kerchief was in her hands, and her head was bent over the side of the little vessel, and now and then she might be seen to apply the handkerchief to her face as if to brush away the spray of the sea.

CHAPTER XI

"I gained my freedom, and immediately
Ran hither to your grace whom I beseech
To give me ample satisfaction
For these deep shames and great indignities."
COMEDY OF ERRORS

WHEN the cutter was cast off, the sails of the schooner were filled, and she was again put on her course. Joy now seemed to beam on the fierce faces of the sailors, and if they had not been restrained by the discipline of the schooner, it was easy to perceive they would have vociferated their satis-faction in long and loud cheers; but, bound by the iron strength of her laws, they could only manifest the feelings which then animated them by a greater alacrity–if possible–in going through their duties.

The captain had retired and the command was left in hands of Lorenzo. That officer stood by himself at the taffrail of the schooner, engrossed by his thoughts, and anxiously watching the little cutter, that was now labouring over the heavy seas, as she sailed gradually away from the schooner, and was bearing from him, perhaps, for ever, that being who first called forth in him the power of that tyrannical sentiment to which Lorenzo, like other men of a less bold and hardy spirit, was subjected.

"She is gone from me for ever," thought the officer, "and has left me scarcely a hope. Perhaps, yes—no, she will try to forget the pirate."

Lorenzo strode gloomily away from the taffrail a victim to a multitude of different sentiments, among which the feelings of love, and those of pride in particular, fiercely contended for the ascendant. He could not contemplate a slight. To himself he was ever honorable, beyond the stigma which the world would cast upon him on account of his present condition, and even his love could scarcely move him to forgive one that he might imagine deemed him debased by the position which he occupied; he turned away, therefore, from the direction in which the cutter lay, and endeavoured to call forth different thoughts by the study of a chart which was lying on the binnacle.

The Black Schooner was kept in the same course for two days.

On the third morning, the island of St. Thomas' appeared. It lay far to leeward, and stretched under the thin clouds, like the blue outline of some great slate mountain. The schooner was again thrown in the wind. The captain, who had exchanged his uniform for a suit of plain clothes, now went on board the prize ship, and was attended by Jack Jimmy, who had been permitted to take his place with the two boys who usually waited on him. The greater part of the schooner's sails were taken in, and arrangements were made for keeping her to the wind, until the return of the captain. The ship was now steered for St. Thomas', and her large sails filled with the morning breeze. She rapidly approached the little island, which the policy and wisdom of the Danish government have made the Tyre* of the West Indies. The English ensign was hoisted, and the ship entered the little narrow harbour which affords a scanty shelter to the numerous vessels that traffic draws to the place. At that moment it was crowded with hundreds of vessels, as different in their appearance as the various parts the world from which they came. There might be seen the heavy Dutch galiotte,† with its crescent form and huge clumsy proportions; the sprightly Frenchman, with its light fantastic spars and long low hull; the Yankee clipper, with its tapering masts and snow-white sails; the Mediterranean faluchas, the sharp

*Tyre: Mediterranean port (southwest Lebanon), an important commercial center in ancient times.
†galiotte: a long, narrow merchant ship.

schooners from Curaçao, and the neighbouring Spanish coasts; all these seemed drawn together for the purpose of commerce, and numerous sailors were to be seen on board their respective ships, busily occupied in taking in or discharging the widely varying cargoes. A few other suspicious low-hulled crafts, were also to be seen in the offing, riding uneasy on short cables, and apparently ready for sea at a moment's requirement. The appearance of these vessels at once disclosed the business in which they were occupied. They were slavers, or otherwise engaged in some nefarious traffic, in which extraordinarily great fleetness alone could secure them profit, or protect them from certain destruction. At some distance from the town a majestic British ship of war was also riding at anchor.

The prize ship was boldly steered into the anchorage, and was shortly boarded by the officers of customs, who demanded, in the usual manner, to see the ship's papers. The officers were easily satisfied, for the easy and encouraging policy, which the Danes have been wise enough to adopt, for the purpose of drawing trade to their little island, did not require many forms in the clearance of the ships which might enter its port. To the apparent irregularities in the credentials it was easily answered, that the captain was the owner of the ship and cargo, that he had originally intended to take the latter to an English market, but he had changed his mind, and was desirous of selling it in order to undertake a voyage to some other part of the world.

The captain, after this formality had been completed, went ashore.

On landing, he was immediately accosted by the numerous merchants and others who may be always seen loitering, partly for pleasure and partly for business, in small coteries,* about the principal landing places of the West India islands. The quality of his goods, as well as their prices were eagerly inquired into, but no one seemed inclined to purchase. He wandered carelessly about the beach with the wide panama hat, with which he had disguised himself, drawn far over his head, expecting every moment an offer for his cargo; for it is in this manner, and in such places, that the cargoes of ships are frequently sold in the tropics. But no one made an offer; and, tired of sauntering about uselessly, he entered a neighbouring coffee house, and seated himself at the table of the principal room.

It was not long before he was followed in by a young merchant who had detached himself from one of the little groups above mentioned and had dogged him for a long time.

---

*coteries: a coterie is an intimate, exclusive group that shares a common purpose.

"I shall give you fifty dollars a hogshead* for your sugar, and take all," he said, as he accosted and bowed to the captain, at the same time presenting his cigar case.

"No," the captain briefly replied, returning the salute, while, at the same time, he accepted the usual West Indian courtesy, and took a cigar from the proffered case.

The merchant sat down at the table too, and requested the waiter, who brought the disguised captain a glass of sangaree, to serve him with the same. He then took out a cigar and began to smoke negligently, as if his mind was as little occupied by thoughts of business as that of a child.

They sat together for a considerable time without exchanging a word—a circumstance of rare occurrence in the talkative tropics, where men endeavour to find in conversation the relaxation which the places of amusement of other countries afford. But the disguised captain was one whose looks did not encourage access, nor was he one whom we would address by mere casualty or for the sake of a moment's pastime. Without being repulsive in appearance he was from a general manner that could not be easily understood, but which was at once felt, sufficiently uninviting as not to encourage any one to address him unless he himself was the first to speak. The merchant therefore did not feel quite assured and was by no means tempted to open a conversation with him. The disguised captain on his part was from natural disposition and taste, not inclined to exchange more words with the merchant or any other person in the island, than were absolutely necessary to the accomplishment of the object which brought him to St. Thomas—namely, the sale of the ship's cargo.

But, if looks are in a generality of instances justly accounted deceptive, they can always be considered so with perhaps much more truth in the merchant, whose business it is to assume the air of cold indifference, and to pretend to care but very little about the transaction in question, while perhaps his palm already itches over the bargain which he keenly meditates, and while he is perhaps already feasting in imagination on the princely returns which he anticipates from it.

"Come, I shall give you fifty-five," the merchant said, after a number of whiffs.

"No," the captain replied, in the same dry tone as before, looking straight before him, indifferently smoking his cigar.

*hogshead: a large cask or barrel; also used as an instrument of measurement, as in a hogshead of sugar.

The pursuits of his life time were so different from those of the generality of men, that besides the stern cynicism in which he had tutored himself, and the habit of contemplation that he had cultivated; he would not have been able to take interest in any intercourse with them. Perhaps, also there was not a little of pride intermixed with his silence. Accustomed to measure the stars, and to associate his thoughts with the sublimity of the heavenly regions, and raised to a proper estimation of himself by the given opinion of the many universities in which he had studied, and which had declared him a man of extraordinary talent, he almost scorned the intercourse of one who could speak to him only about the state of the market, the amount of money that certain individuals happened to possess, and the other things connected with the occupation of buying and selling.

Besides, he had long ceased to hold intercourse with living men – except, indeed, when it was necessary either to command them, to feed them, or to give them drink. He had found that too much evil was mixed up with the little good that he could derive from their society, and not considering that the mere endurance of the former was an object that was so worthy in itself as to command the exercise of his fortitude, he thought it prudent to refrain both from listening to the expressed thoughts of others and intruding his upon them. Books therefore, he made his companions – books, that could not deceive, could not betray, could not be mean, could not be penurious, could not make to suffer, could not disgust; but which contained the best of dead men's thoughts without much of their vileness.

It was not strange therefore that the two parties sat together silent.

Notwithstanding, however, the existence of this feeling on the part of the captain, his prudence suggested the necessity of saying something in order to enact with exactness the character of merchant-captain which he had for the time assumed.

"You seem to have much traffic in this island," he said to the young merchant, in compliance with this suggestion of his reason.

"A great deal," replied the young merchant, "we do business with all parts of the world. Never been here before? Not traded in these seas much I suppose? You do not seem to have been much exposed to the sun."

The captain made no answer to the last observation.

"We have lately suffered much," continued the merchant after a pause, "in our trade here from a rascally pirate that scours these seas. One vessel out of three is sure to fall into his hands. By the bye, you who are a stranger in this part of the world, have great reason to thank your stars that you have escaped him."

"No doubt," the captain coolly observed and drew a whiff of his cigar.

The merchant, also, drew two or three whiffs, and continued—

"It appears the captain of these pirates is a very remarkable fellow; he seems to care but little about the lives of those who fall into his hands, but contents himself with robbing them in a very gentlemanly and polite manner. Those that pass through his clutches, and put in here, tell such tales of him, that one would almost fancy they had been spell-bound during the time they were his captives."

"Indeed! interjected the captain."

"Yes: and the fellow is so remarkably skillful that he baffles all attempts to capture him, and always contrives to escape. They say he deals with the devil; that he knows his vessel, and his vessel knows him, for she does whatever he chooses. Sometimes she is seen in the rig of a schooner, at others in that of a brigantine, or brig, or barque,* or—God knows what else."

"How remarkable!" observed the captain.

"By Jove! that is not all," still continued the merchant, "he is bold enough to take his prizes into any harbour that may happen to be the nearest at the time—whatever it be."

"And has he never been discovered?" inquired the captain, as coolly as before.

"Bless me, no! If he does not actually deal with the devil, by Jove! the old boy always seems to help him, for he always manages to sell his booty, and get away before it is known that he had been there."

"A dangerous man, surely," again remarked the captain, "I must account myself fortunate, I perceive, that I have managed to bring my sugar safely into port."

"By jingo! yes—But, *apropos,*† those sugars, I shall give you sixty dollars," the merchant said.

The captain seemed to muse awhile and said—

"I shall take sixty, on condition that the money be paid this very moment, and also in gold."

"Agreed," cried the merchant, quickly: "wait here for me a short time; I shall bring you the money," and he went out of the room, with the air of one who was congratulating himself on having achieved an extraordinary feat.

In the course of half an hour the merchant returned, and was followed by

---

*brigantine, or brig, or barque: brigantine and brig, kinds of two-masted sailing ships; barque or bark, a three- to five-masted sailing ship, but can also mean any small vessel propelled by oars or sails.

†*apropos:* with respect to.

a servant, who seemed to be bending and groaning under a heavy bag of money which he was carrying.

"There," said the merchant, taking the bag from the servant, and laying it down on the table, "there are three thousand six hundred dollars in doubloons, verify them."

The captain spread the coins on the table, and begun to count them.

"It is quite correct–the sugar is yours," he said, when he had done so, and began to replace the doubloons. . . . . . The heavy footsteps of men were now heard on the stairs. They grew more and more distinct, and now they re-sounded within the extensive room.

"There is your man," exclaimed an individual, and the captain, on look-ing round, beheld his father, who was standing in front of a file of marines, under the command of a British officer, who was accompanied by an officer in the Danish civil uniform, that probably represented the local govern-ment in sanctioning the forcible capture of a British subject, by British authorities, on Danish ground.

The face of the young captain evinced neither astonishment, nor anger, nor scorn, as he stood looking with indifferent calmness on the warlike intruders.

"That is he–the pirate: seize him! seize him! cried Willmington, almost mad with excitement.

The officer remained undecided, and gave no orders. He seemed sur-prised, and inquired, after the lapse of a few moments–

"Is this the pirate?" and pointed towards the captain. "I fancy you are in some error: this gentleman does not appear to have ever left the land; besides, he seems too young to be what you say he is: you surely must have made a mistake."

Nor was it strange that the officer should thus have felt surprised at the appearance of the captain; for he had expected to find some villainous, yellow-blooded sinister-looking cut-throat, deformed, hacked with wounds, and disfigured with gibbet marks.* With this picture of a pirate still on his mind, he had pointed out to him a young man who seemed more calculated to pass his life in quiet contemplation and easy enjoyment, than to take part in the arduous and wearing pursuits of the world, much less to hold the position of a robber on the high seas. Besides, notwithstanding the hardy life which he was obliged to lead, the young man still so sedulously† culti-vated the refined habits in which he had been bred, and had so carefully kept

---

*gibbet marks: gibbet can mean either a gallows (for hanging criminals) or a post to which malefactors are tied for torture or public scorn.

†sedulously: diligently, carefully.

himself below deck, that he neither presented the rough cast of men of rough usage, nor lost, under a tropical sun, the natural paleness of his complexion.

"It is no mistake at all," exclaimed Willmington, "I know him well; I cannot be deceived. It is he who had me thrown overboard. Yes, he had me thrown overboard in the sea–to be drowned–to be drowned; but providence has now interfered to punish the perpetrator of the outrage committed upon me. And, and," he added, "you will now suffer for it," addressing the captain, while he took the precaution of clinging as closely as possible to the officer. For it would appear that even in the presence of the file of marines the recollection of the empty cask made him nervous.

"Nay, nay, good father," the captain said, with cauterising sarcasm, "the crime of throwing his kind and loving father overboard, would better suit the jargon that fills the mouths of such virtuous gentlemen as you." . . . A pause ensued.

"His father,"–"Are you then this old gentleman's son?" inquired the officer.

"He can tell you," answered the captain. "But I await your orders sir; lead me wherever it may be your instructions to do so."

The officer seemed more undecided than ever. He looked for an instant at James Willmington, who remained silent, and bent his eyes to the ground as they met those of the ingenious, gallant, young soldier.

"This is a strange and extraordinary business," he observed, "I am not aware that my commission obliges me to meddle with such apparently disagreeable affairs. However, young gentleman, for such you seem, and I can scarcely believe that you are what this old gentleman represents you to be, I have orders from my commanding officer, and sanction from the local authorities, to arrest you, provided you are the pirate who scours these seas?"

"It is he–it is he;–I am certain of it: he took our ship; he had me thrown overboard," vociferated James Willmington, scarcely affording the young officer time to complete his sentence, "I tell you, seize him, seize him!"

Disgusted with this uproarious outbreak, and somewhat stung by Willmington's imperative manner, the officer turned round to him and said, cuttingly–

"Perhaps, sir, you would have me take a rope and hang him at once: you must recollect, sir that I am not bound to regulate my conduct by any peculiar activity which may characterize your feeling against this person."

This language came the more readily from the young officer, inasmuch as he felt a prejudice in favor of the captain.

Free, frank, generous, and noble, as those of the order to which he belonged generally are, he could not but feel a certain interest in his prisoner, and he began to speculate on the extraordinary circumstance that a man, such as he seemed to be, should have found himself in a position of so equivocal a nature, as the one in which he was then placed. It appeared strange to him that one who seemed well educated, and who at the same time possessed such gracefulness of demeanour, and elegance of expression, could have freely chosen to herd with the wretched outcasts that usually crown their other numerous crimes with the horrible outrages of piracy: and should thus expose himself, not only to the danger of the horrid death with which such a crime was punished, but to run the risk of entailing upon himself the ignominy which the world, with one accord, unanimously casts upon the pirate. He justly imagined, that to drive an individual, such as he seemed to be, to such a life, there required very great causes, or, at any rate, unusual ones, which may have acted in a more than ordinary manner on a naturally too sensitive mind; and as great afflictions always call forth sympathy from the generous, the imagined misfortunes of the prisoner turned, in an instant, the heart of the officer in his favour. This was the impulsive judgment of the young man.

The noble and fresh-hearted, young officer, that feared not the prejudiced frown of any man, could afford, independently, to take the man as he found him.

"You will go with me," said he to the captain, "I trust you will see the absolute uselessness of any attempt to escape," and he significantly pointed to his men. "I shall not put you under restraint if you promise to walk with us."

"If you will take the word of a pirate," said the captain, bowing, "I promise to accompany you. If otherwise, I am willing to allow myself to be put under any constraint that you may think proper. I trust, however, that I am incapable of showing myself insensible to the indulgence of any gentleman, and least of all, to a British officer."

"That is sufficient," quickly replied the officer.

The party now left the room, and soon reached the boat that was waiting at the beach. They embarked: and, in a short time, arrived alongside the huge man-of-war, whose sides looked gloomy with the frowning guns as they peeped through the port-holes. As soon as the party gained the deck, the captain was immediately conducted before the commander of the vessel.

He was one of those venerable looking old gentlemen, who are now and then to be casually seen in the walks of the world, and who when once seen, forcibly draw from us respect and honor—with locks whose colour had long been worn away by the wind and washed away by the brine, and with one of those faces which tell by their rosy hue and frank openness, in the evening of existence, of a life so spent in duty and honour that not one single repentant wrinkle dared ruffle the brow where loyalty and truth had always sat. He was sitting in an elegant state cabin when the officer brought the prisoner before him. He raised his eyes from off the book which he was then reading, and began to examine him. He said nothing, but could not conceal the surprise which he seemed to feel at the appearance of the individual whom he was examining.

"You seem young to be engaged in such a lawless pursuit, prisoner," he said after a minute or two.

The captain bowed haughtily.

"You are aware," continued the commander, "that you are accused of a very heinous crime – that of piracy."

The captain bowed again in the same manner.

"You know that is an offence which is universally reprobated by all nations, and it is one which in its moral character is the blackest of crimes. It is my duty, therefore, to keep you on board this ship until I can put you in the hands of the authorities, whose business it is to deal with these matters. I shall sail for Trinidad in a few days, and you will remain in custody until my arrival in that island, where you will be delivered up to the civil tribunals."

The captain calmly bowed again.

"In the meantime," continued the commander, addressing the father and accuser, "you will be good enough to repeat, in the presence of the prisoner, the accusation which you made in his absence."

James Willmington, after a pause, then began, his voice trembling with excitement, and ill-concealed hatred.

"As I said before my lord, I, and two other persons, were passengers on board the ship 'Letitia,' which was bound for Bristol. We were two days' sail from Trinidad, when we were boarded by pirates, of whom this man, as we afterwards found, was the chief. After a brave resistance made by our crew, the ship was captured, and I and the others were taken on board the vessel of the pirates. The other captives were treated with much lenity, but I was kept in close confinement, and eventually, by the orders of this man, was even tied to an empty cask, and set adrift on the ocean, to meet there a lingering death, far more horrible than any sudden violence could have inflicted. To prolong my miseries, a few dried biscuits were tied to my cask. A whole day and night I was in this condition floating on the wild waves, and was worn out, and well nigh exhausted with suffering, when Providence came to my rescue. A sloop came sailing by, and with difficulty I made my cries to be heard. I was taken on board, and life, which was fast departing, was brought back by the kindness of the master and crew."

"I had overheard the pirates speak about St. Thomas' as the place whither they intended to sail for the disposal of the ship's cargo. I at once resolved to anticipate them if possible, to have the author of my cruel sufferings arrested, and to bring him to condign punishment. For this purpose I prevailed upon the master of the sloop, by offering him a large sum of money, to put in here, where fortunately we arrived before the pirates, and I had, by this happy accident, the opportunity of watching their arrival. This is the man who is the chief of the pirates, and who ordered me to be thrown overboard under circumstances of such refined cruelty."

After Willmington had spoken, the commander asked the prisoner if the accusation was true.

"True in all things," said the latter, "in all things, so far as they have been revealed. I admit everything that has been said, but my accuser," and here he fixed his piercing eyes on his father, "but my accuser has informed you only of the punishment; he has not told you why, when I treated my other captives with such lenity, I practised what he calls cruelties on himself. Perhaps, my lord," while his lip could be seen to curl with scorn, "perhaps he will tell you that I was only the executioner who inflicted the punishment which one of the most heinous crimes deserved."

"What do you mean?" inquired the commander.

"Simply ," replied the captain, "that this man is my father. He abandoned me at an age when I was too young to offend, and afterwards refused me bread when I was being famished. In vindication of the violated laws of nature, I, in my turn, abandoned him when he required my aid, and I cast him away from my vessel, when he required its use."

"Then you are this gentleman's son? and there are, therefore, family affairs connected with this business?" inquired the commander, with evident surprise, marked on his open and noble face; and, turning to Willmington, he inquired, also, whether he was really his father.

There was no answer.

"Young man," said the commander, "it was wrong, on your part, to treat your parent in this manner. If what you say is correct, he has treated you unnaturally, but there is One above us to punish such sins, and it is not yours to arrogate the right of taking vengeance, even when you consider yourself injured–recollect," he said solemnly, "recollect–'Vengeance is mine, saith the Lord.' "*

*'Vengeance is mine, saith the Lord': Romans 12:19.

"You speak, my lord," replied the captain, "as I should expect you to do; but you are scarcely a judge in this matter: you have not had to endure what I had. I can read in you, my lord,–pardon the personality–something which tells me that, if you had found yourself in my place, you would have acted in the same manner."

In the meantime, a young officer had silently descended the companion-steps, and, hearing the voice of the last speaker, he came quickly forward and gazed in his face, seeming to recognise him.

"Appadocca," he exclaimed and eagerly grasped the hand of the captain, "what brings you here? Why you are not the pirate, surely?–it cannot be!"

"Yes, I am the pirate," the captain calmly replied, while he pressed the hand that had grasped his.

"Good heavens! you deceive me–you–you–"

"Mr Charles," sounded the voice of the commander, "recollect, sir, you are in the presence of your commanding officer, and that you are speaking to a person who is under arrest."

The young officer retired a few steps, conscious that, although he was the commander's son, he was still subject to the rules of discipline.

Deep anxiety for the prisoner, however, was marked on his features, as his eyes wandered impatiently from the captain, whom we shall now call by his proper name, Appadocca–to his father, and from his father to Appadocca again.

The prisoner was now ordered away, and instructions were given to keep him in close custody. The officer in command, the sentinels, and the prisoner proceeded on deck. The young officer was about to follow, when he was requested by his father to stay.

"Do you know this man, Charles?" inquired the commander, when they were alone.

"If I know him, sir? every man who has studied in any university these seven years back, knows Emmanuel Appadocca. I studied mathematics with him in Paris, sir; and, if you remember, you will find I frequently spoke to you about him."

"Yes: I think, now, I recollect something of the name. But this seems a strange end for such a man as you always represented him to be."

"Yes; this does seem a very strange end," replied the young officer, "and I cannot but imagine that there is some error in all this."

"That old planter," observed the commander, "seems, however, to be very positive in his statements; and, in addition to this, appears determined to prosecute him to the utmost."

"It is to be hoped, sir," replied Mr. Charles, "that Appadocca will be able to establish his innocence."

"It is to be hoped, Charles—it is to be hoped," said the commander, and he took up his book.

CHAPTER XII

"Pity me not, but lend thy serious hearing
To what I shall unfold."

HAMLET

APPADOCCA was led to a narrow compartment in the gun-deck where he was locked up, and a sentinel was placed at the door.

The unexpected turn that his affairs had taken, seemed to have but little effect on his mind. The sad prospect of being tried like the meanest criminal, and condemned, perhaps, to an ignominious death appeared not to startle his settled cynicism.

When the door of the cabin was closed upon him, after having sat for a time in a deep meditation, he knocked from within and asked the man who kept guard without, for a piece of chalk, which, after some delay, was given to him. With it he began to draw algebraical figures on the boards that partitioned his cabin prison, and seemed engrossed in some deep calculation. In this manner the afternoon passed. When the short tropical twilight came and went, and he was no longer capable of seeing his figures, he seated himself down again and remained so until late in the night, when he stretched himself on the deck for the purpose of going to sleep.

He had not lain down long before the door of the cabin was silently opened, and an individual closely wrapped in a boat-cloak entered. The cloak was immediately thrown off, and, by the light of a small lantern which the stranger carried, Appadocca saw before him Charles Hamilton, his friend.

"Welcome, Charles!" said Appadocca, affecting more than usual lightsomeness, "welcome to my narrow quarters," at the same time, casting his eyes around the close cabin, which, for the time being, constituted his prison.

"Hush! Emmanuel," said the commander's son, "and, for G—d's sake, do not speak in such a trivial manner, when you are in such a dangerous position. Tell me," he continued, while the most impatient anxiety could be detected in his tone, "tell me how you could have brought yourself to this melancholy pass."

" 'Twere long to tell, and sad to trace," replied Appadocca. "as your own most noble and illustrious countryman has it . . . But you seem to be entirely cast down with anxiety–bah! banish that, and if you can accommodate yourself on this hard deck, sit down and we shall have a little conversation on 'the happy days gone by.' "

"Happy, indeed, they were Emmanuel, and little did I dream when we pursued our studies together, and when I, together with the others, almost worshipped the intellect with which heaven has blessed you, that I should ever have met you as a prisoner on board my father's ship, accused, too, of such a grave offence as piracy." This was spoken with such deep feeling, that Appadocca could scarcely continue his tone of assumed gaiety.

"But what is this Emmanuel?" asked Charles, as his eyes met the figures which Appadocca had traced. "Calculations? must I believe that your cynicism can have made you think so lightly of the sad doom which hangs over you as to permit you to work equations and solve problems at this moment?"

"Now, since you are bent upon being very serious," answered Appadocca, "pray accommodate yourself and I shall speak to you, and as to those calculations, they concern you more than you imagine. Let your ship be in a safe harbour within these two weeks to come: a comet will be visible in seven days' time, near the constellation of the Southern Cross;* the hurricane that will follow at its tail, will be more than many ships will be able to bear. Now sit down."

The young officer sat down.

"You ask me," began Appadocca, with his characteristic gravity, which had now returned, "first, how it has happened that I originally found myself a pirate, cruising in the Caribbean sea; and, secondly, a prisoner on board your father's ship. I regret much that even friendship should have interposed to elicit from me a narrative, which I have always desired to carry with me to the–scaffold now, I suppose. Nevertheless, now that I am on the brink of destruction, it may be well to let the world know the cause of my conduct towards the individual whom an unhappy accident made my father;–which conduct, I admit, may now look strange and criminal.

"You remember, when you left the university of Paris, that I was then preparing to compete in the *concours*† for the professorship of astronomy."

---

*Southern Cross: a constellation in the Southern Hemisphere.
†*concours:* public competition or contest.

"Which I always believed you would have undoubtedly won," interrupted the officer.

"Do not interrupt me. Within a short time after your departure, I received a letter from the faithful servant, who always attended her, acquainting me with my mother's death. You, who have known the more than ordinary fondness that my mother and I so strongly entertained for each other, can easily understand the overwhelming effect which such an announcement had upon me."

"I know, Emmanuel–pass over that quickly," said the young officer.

"Even my philosophy was not strong enough to bear up against it, and I fell into a fever, from the effects of which I did not rally for a considerable period.

"Well, with my mother's death, my means of support ceased; for she seems to have carefully concealed the fact from me, that all her little fortune had been devoted to my education, and had been expended for the purpose of keeping me, as much as possible, on a level with the station which her ancestors had occupied. I was consequently rendered incapable of continuing my preparations for the *concours,* and it became absolutely necessary for me to endeavour to gain my livelihood by my own exertions.

"When the whole of my lifetime, up to that period, had been passed in schools and colleges, you may easily imagine that I was not much adapted to friction against the world, and to fight in the scrambling battle, for bread.

"The only means I possessed was my pen,–precarious means! The only method of procuring food was by writing on those subjects, with which I had, more or less, filled my mind. Paris was overcrowded with individuals placed in a similar position to mine, who, however, possessed the superior advantage of being better able to thrust themselves forward; a thing which I sympathized too little with the world to be able to do. Besides, it was very problematical, whether success in Paris would bring me remuneration that would be sufficient to maintain me in the manner in which I had been brought up;–for you must know that literary men are badly paid in France. I felt, also, a certain disgust in remaining among those by whom I was known, when I fell into a condition which, at best, would be but precarious. For these reasons, I resolved to visit the British capital, where remuneration was reputed to be greater and more secure.

"I left Paris, after taking leave of but few of my friends, and went to London. When I arrived there, I found there were many subjects on which but little had been written; for the genius of the English people calls them a different way from the unprofitable consideration of abstruse subjects. I wrote about these things. I took my papers to the publications of the day. They did not refuse them:–'They would publish them,' they said, 'when there was room.' That, I found out by experience, was but an excuse. They were not inclined absolutely to refuse the articles, so they had recourse to that shuffling subterfuge, for they had their own friends to serve. I waited long–there still was no room; sometimes, at great intervals, a paper was published, but so sadly mutilated, that it became almost absurd.

"In the meantime, the small amount of money which I possessed became more and more diminished; still I hoped. Yes: I had that delusive, cheating, empty solace of the afflicted–hope. Hope, which mankind has complaisantly numbered among its cardinal virtues, because it holds out to each the lighted wisp that leads and leads him on until he finally stumbles into the grave that closes up his existence, All my valuables were disposed of, one after another, and I was at last left without a brass penny–without property, save my telescope. With that I would not–I could not part. I should have more easily yielded up my heart than dispossess myself of my old and only companion.

"Together with the letter which announced my mother's death, I received a casket which she requested, at her last moments, should be delivered into my hands. I had always been led to believe that my father had died when I was a child; but in the casket I found a letter informing me that he was not dead, and enjoining that I should ever study to cherish and respect him who was pointed out to me as my sire. My feelings told me at once that my good mother had been treated with injustice, and vengeance was my first impulse.

"I had always entertained peculiar opinions about women: I had been accustomed to consider her the superior of the two beings; nay, I had gone further: I had considered her one of those benignant spirits which the disciples of the theological system introduce in their allegories,–the ultimate link between this condition and a higher and more refined humanity. I had looked upon her as the embodiment of goodness, that sweetened existence with its smiles, and made sorrow shrink into insignificance by its sympathy; as a being in whom intellect and propensities were happily not made to preponderate over the loftiest attributes of human nature–the sentiments. Holding this belief, I had worshipped her in whatever condition I found her;–in gorgeous magnificence, or in sordid rags, as pure and spotless as the lily, or polluted or stained with foulest crimes. To me she ever was woman, and that was sufficient. On account of this peculiarity, I always looked with horror upon any man that could be base enough to take any advantage of her, or give her pain. Such an individual I considered unmanned and dishonored, and would shrink from him with disgust. Judge, then, of my state of mind, when I discovered that the crime which I abhorred so much was brought so personally under my reprobation.

"In a calmer mood, however, I thought that sorrow and restitution ought to suffice to obliterate crime; that, at least, I should give the offending party an opportunity of remedying the wrong he had done. Perhaps repentance might creep into his soul. I wrote, then, to the person who had been indicated as my father. He was a wealthy planter in Trinidad. I made it known to him that I was acquainted with the secret of my parentage. I described to him the utter distress in which I, his son, was then placed, and besought him to send me a pittance to sustain that life of which he was the cause.

"Months passed, and I received no answer. Certain feelings began to rankle in my bosom; I, however, took care not to be precipitate. Still hope sustained me. I was obliged to pass days together without food. On such occasion, I would stand by some thoroughfare and watch the over-fed passers, and meditate on that strange destiny which gave to some too much, and to others too little.

"One beautiful night, the stars were clearly visible, and I loitered towards one of the bridges that span the Thames, to enjoy the happiness of watching them. There, seating myself down on one of the stone benches, I forgot for a moment my distress, and felt as I was wont to feel in happier days. The night waned: –attracted by the lurid glimmer of Antares, * I fell into a reverie on the theory of the starry scintillation. It may have been one o'clock in the morning, –like the labourer whose thews and sinews were relaxed with the day's unremitting toil; the great metropolis was buried in that comparative repose which it enjoys only at that early hour of the morning. The rattling of numberless vehicles, the shuffling of thousands of bustling wayfarers had now ceased. Nothing was to be heard but the soon-ceasing rattle of some hurrying conveyance, the measured steps of the police officers, or, perhaps, the ringing laugh of some nightly merry-maker. My eyes were fixed on the stars, and I was dreaming on the orbs of space, when suddenly the low restrained sobs of intense agony fell on my ear. I suddenly turned my head, when I beheld a woman standing on the wall, apparently ready to throw herself headlong into the river. She had a child in her arms, and she pressed it to her bosom, while she loaded it with caresses, and bathed it with tears. Her sobs were those of despair. In an instant I comprehended her intention,

*Antares: a giant star, the brightest in the constellation Scorpio.

and creeping silently along the parapet, I suddenly stood up and seized her in my arms. She gave one convulsive shriek and swooned away.

"I had taught myself to look on misery as the actings of certain general laws: I had accustomed myself to look upon the most appalling phenomena of organic and inorganic life simply as the consummation to which they must necessarily come. I had studied to bring down to nothing the revolting aspect of misery, the bloody scenes of warriors weltering in their blood, or the ghastly hue of emaciating disease; but never before that night had there been presented to my eyes such a combination of utter misery, of gentleness, of innocence, of suffering, of goodness, and of despair, as I beheld blended in the woman whom I had thus rescued from perdition.

"She was young, as yet scarcely of the age capable to bear even the ordinary troubles of the world. Her auburn hair floated loose over her shoulders and her pale emaciated face, while the whiteness of her forehead was here and there to be seen between her dishevelled tresses. Her lack-lustre eyes were as sunken as if animation had already ceased; a tattered dress hung about her skeleton frame, and her fingers were more like those of a dead than of a living creature. The babe was as pale as the moon that shone upon it. Its sweet little features were locked in a calm lethargic sleep: its spirit seemed to sympathise with that of its mother; whilst neither her alarm and swoon, nor the bleakness of the night, could rouse it from its happy slumber, or draw a murmuring cry from its lips.

"I stood for a long time, supporting the unhappy girl in my arms, anxiously watching the return of animation. Her circulation was slow, for want had fed upon her strength.

" 'Oh, oh!–where, where–am I?–no–no–I am not there'–she wanderingly muttered, as she gradually recovered.

"Her head drooped in silence, as she became conscious of her position and exposure. I questioned her delicately on the circumstances that led to her taking so fatal a resolution as the one which I had, but accidentally, prevented her from carrying into effect. After much hesitation, she told me the story of her misfortune.

"She had been left fatherless and motherless. She had devoted herself to the man whom she had been taught, by his ardent professions, to look upon as her only stay, and whom she still loved; he had perjured himself, and abandoned her.

"She had hid her head in shame and misery from her friends, and by incessant toil had sometimes procured herself food: but she became a mother, and could no longer work. She had pined away with her babe in a hovel: at last to see her child daily droop under her eyes, maddened her; she could bear it no longer. There might be a happier lot, she thought, in another world, where at least there were no deceivers, and so resolved to flee from this.

" 'And is the father of your child rich, and able to provide food for it?' I inquired.

" 'He is,' she replied.

" 'Recollect,' I said, 'that however desperate your condition may be, still you have no right to take away the life of your child. The little innocent has been brought into the world by you, it is, therefore, your duty to devote your life to its care and preservation.'

"She wept.

"I had no money—my coat was scarcely good enough to protect me from the cold—I still had two buckles on my shoes, with which I had not parted because I knew their value would scarcely procure me a meal. I took them off and laid them on the babe. 'Those may serve to get your child some milk' I said. She refused them. I pressed her to accept them for the child, and after having obtained a promise that she would never again attempt to destroy herself I conducted her off the bridge.

"The history of the poor girl had made a deep impression on me; I was agitated, so I retraced my steps, and seated myself down again; but I could no longer study the stars: the mother and child were ever present to my mind. That girl was once happy, I thought. She may have shone in virtue and accomplishments. Now she is loaded with misery. And what has changed her condition thus? was it the visitation of Providence? was it sudden illness? was it her own crime? She had fallen a victim to her own virtues, her own confidence, her own fondness, her own gentleness. The angelic nature of her sex, was worked upon for her destruction, and after having been deceived, she was discarded,—she! nay,—not she alone—but the innocent child—too young to offend, too helpless to be criminal—was also thrown on the wide, unfeeling world. Has one human creature any right thus to load another with misery, to drive another to desperation, to convert the life of another—aye, and by a most villainous method—into a period of enduring suffering and anguish? The man, too, who has blasted her happiness, is rich, and perhaps, at this moment, when his victim and child are perishing of starvation, is surrounded by his merry minions and lemans, and is squandering away that wealth, of which the thousandth part would save his child from famine. I could no longer restrain myself. 'Great Ruler of the Universe,' I exclaimed, 'canst Thou permit these things? How is it, that

Thou, Who hast filled the space, That confounds human understanding, with such worlds of beautiful worlds; That hast so wisely adjusted their incomprehensible systems, that all revolve and move in perfect harmony, and submit implicitly to the great laws that Thou hast imposed upon them;– how is it that Thou hast given such license to one of Thy humble creatures, that he, apparently uncontrolled, can stride in wickedness over this fair world, and blast the life and happiness which Thou, also bestowed?–This, at least, is not wisdom! . . . '

"Hush! blasphemer, hush" a spirit seemed to whisper to me.

"Chide not Heaven foolishly! Thou sayest that He has ordained laws to which worlds that thou but faintly seest above, are subject:–that's true: carry thy reflections still farther. Thou beholdest above thee, with the naked eye, orbs, in regard to which thy powers of calculation are scarcely comprehensive enough to keep pace with thy vision. To thy sight, when assisted, these already uncountable worlds multiply themselves to numbers which thou canst attempt to speak of only in ratios; and, probably, when thy ingenuity shall have contrived to invent some instrument that will assist thy vision still more, thou shalt behold, open before thee, an immensity of orb-filled space, at the sight of which despair will well-nigh seize thee. Consider all these,–even the few that thou seest without unusual exertion,–they all exist, move, and revolve by the force of laws which are impressed upon them. Contemplate their mechanism and order. Take this one–it is the centre of a system, and stands the governor, amidst millions of other orbs that are subject and obedient to its guidance. It moves, and they move, too, with and around it; and it is itself subject to some other, from which it receives its motion and its law. Those others, too, that so humbly seem to follow it, are, each of them in its place, the rulers of others again, that are less powerful than themselves, and give their law to them. Each of these, apparently, disjointed parts, and these numerous groups of world-contained worlds, are united and cemented, under the all-powerful force of law, and form a whole that is more incomprehensible at the ratio of the unit of each, than its component parts. Still, notwithstanding this unrealizable immensity, behold the harmony and regularity with which they perform their revolutions. In these gyrations, that are as innumerable as themselves, not one clashes against the other; and when they diverge the distance of even a cubic inch, such divergence is ever exacted by the necessity of the self-same law, which so marvellously controls them. In the movements of these vast bodies time can be calculated to the utmost second; and in their inclination to a given point, towards which they have been verging for millions of your computed years, not a difference, except that which the known law seemed to require, can be traced, either in ratio, or in, what appears to your short-lived eyes, their remarkable slowness. Here mark law, and obedience to that law.

"From the sublime regions come now to earth. Thou mayest behold design and intelligence in the very inorganic matter that composes it, from the consolidated and hardened granite that resists and beats back the rushing ocean, to the minute particle that blinds thee by the roadside. Law is stamped upon them, and adherence to that law, composes their very existence. Again, the trees which shelter this beautiful globe tell, in their germination, their bloom, their blossom, and decay, of law and obedience.

"Proceed to organized things;—contemplate all living creatures, from the low and torpid lizard that creeps upon the tombstone, and turns its cold and clammy sides to the sunbeams, to the gigantic elephant—thou wilt find that every animal carries in itself a law and undergoes the pains of retribution whenever it violates that law. Thus the browsing sheep that forgets its instinct, and feeds on poisonous herbs, dies. The scorpion, that turns his sting upon itself, also dies. The antelope, if it throws itself down on a rock must necessarily be dashed to pieces. In all these things you see law, and its safeguard—retribution. Man, as well as all other beings, is subject to it, and the penalty which its violation entails. If you establish false systems among yourselves, and consent to postpone to an imaginary period, this penalty, which ought to be made to follow closely upon every violation of the law, surely Heaven is not to be blamed. Duty is poised between the reward of virtue and retribution:—man has the license to choose, between either meriting the former, or bringing down the latter, upon himself. The great error of your social physics is, that you remit this penalty to a period of time, which if it were even unimagined, would fail to afford the principal and best effect of retribution,—the deterring from crimes.

"Like those who dwelt on the banks of the Nile of old, who built cities for dead men, and gave them kings, and made laws for them, and established vast prisons and instituted judges, and sketched out places which the most fevered imagination cannot realize, and surrounded them with pleasures, or filled them with horrors, either as happy regions where virtues were to be rewarded, or frightful holes in which crimes were to be punished, you permit the evil-doer to live his wicked years, and sink amidst the weeping sorrow of friends or bribed strangers into the quiet grave, then read the lessons to mystified listeners—that evil deeds are punished. If the wretch, who poisoned the life of that miserable creature whom thou but now didst rescue, were made to suffer the one-hundredth part of that misery which he has caused: his mates in vile wickedness, appalled by the example, would shrink in trembling fear from the perpetration of like crimes. You forget, in your social system, the wisdom of the race which you affect to despise, while you cherish the theological philosophy which you were eager to borrow from them, and tie the hand of the avenger, and blunt the double-edged sword of retribution. You punish the man who takes away the life of another; who consigns another to the oblivion on which neither misery nor pleasure intrudes, and him who makes the life of the living worse than death, you permit to roam, in his foulness, this beautiful earth, and only hope that the retribution which you yourselves ought to bring about, will be wrought by the very hand of the Being who operates here but by his created agents. And then, thou short-sighted, impulse-ridden, and reason-limited mortal, complainest in loud and senseless terms against Heaven, while at thy own door lies the wrong. Know that man himself, by law, is the avenger, the retributionist on himself or others.

" 'Ah! is it so?' I said. I reflected, and found that it must be so.–The scales fell from my eyes.–'True, true,' I cried.–Heaven forgive the impulse of a short-sighted mortal.

"Then this man, who may now be rolling in profusion while his child is dying of hunger, ought to be made to bear the stings of famine, too, and suffer the same misery which he has inflicted on others.–And–oh! a fearful light broke in upon me–and the man from whose hands I demanded not existence, but who has given me life, and abandoned me in my misery, ought likewise to feel some part of the sufferings which I undergo. Yes: the only prevention of crime is to make its punishment follow immediately in its course.

" 'Then, hear ye powers above,' I exclaimed, 'this miserable life I devote to vindicate the law of nature which has been violated in me, and in your child; and I swear, by the Great Being who gave me reason, that I shall not rest until I have taught my father, that the creature to whom he has given life possesses feelings and sensibility, and is capable of taking vengeance.'

"I resolved, at once, to start for the West Indies, and to go to the docks, as soon as it was light, to procure a ship. So, on the impulse of the thought, I proceeded to the place where I had my lowly lodging to fetch my telescope. But, although I knocked loud enough to awake the soundest sleepers, the door was not opened; I, therefore, sat on the steps until daylight came. When morning had dawned I again knocked, but was refused admittance. 'Then give me my telescope,' I prayed. The telescope had been sold the night before for my rent, I was told. I was overwhelmed. It was natural enough the master of the house should require his money, but I never could have contemplated that my telescope would have been taken from me. Rallying from the shock that I had received, I begged to see the master. After some time he came to the door. He was a fat heavy little man, whose voice came wheezingly from his encumbered chest. I implored him to restore me my telescope, telling him that it was my only companion and solace in life, and I offered to work for him in whatever capacity, how mean soever it might be, for the few shillings that were due to him, provided he would give me back my telescope. 'Go along with you,' he answered, 'do you take me for a fool?' and shut the door violently in my face. I turned away, and was so dejected in mind and wasted in body, that I could not walk. The morning advanced, and the street began to present the busy scene by which it was every day animated. My musings imperceptibly turned on the motley crowd before me. I contemplated the scene in which there might be observed the shrewd cabman driving to death his jaded horse, the affluent man of business, hurrying with inclining head to the pursuit of greater wealth, the afflicted widow, moving along in modest grief; the age-stricken and poor cripple crawling in his sordid rags, and the man of fortune with his air of self-satisfaction, his dangling jewels and his gaudy equipage. I remarked that these different persons passed each other as if no kindly word or salutation had ever rested on their heavy tongues–like gruff animals that hurry in silence to their separate lairs. Each seemed intent on his own pursuit. The driver did not withdraw his attention from his horse's head, nor did the lordling stop to succour the decaying wretch; the man of business did not raise his eyes from the ground, on which he seemed to count his gains, to notice the sorrowful widow: yet these men possess wealth enough to render thousands happy without injuring themselves.

"They have wealth enough to have my telescope restored to me, and cause my happiness; still, yon wretched being may–nay, will probably sink into his grave for the want of a brass penny from any of these, and I–I should probably be handed over to the police officer, were I to make one more effort for my telescope. 'Mankind, farewell!' I exclaimed, from the force of my disgust, 'I may pity you, but never can love you.'

"I then walked down to the London Docks where, after some inquiry, I found a ship prepared for a voyage to Jamaica. I offered myself to the commander as a seaman. He began to depreciate my capabilities, and said that I should, probably, encumber others rather than be of any service.

"I told him that I could steer a ship, and take observations; I did not mention my competency to do the other parts of navigation, for I was afraid to prejudice him against me; for individuals of that class pride themselves on the idea that the great secret of managing a ship, is in their hands alone, and that other men are, or ought to be–entirely ignorant of it.

"Finally, I asked him to examine me, on the mariner's compass, and on navigation.

"He readily did so, and the ignorant creature put me some miserable questions, about the sun's altitude at noon, and some such matter which he had been mechanically taught. I answered them, and encouraged all the while the important and patronizing air which he had assumed. When we have no money, and desire the accomplishment of any purpose, we must learn to use towards men, a passport that is equivalent–a sympathy with their vanity. The result was, that I was immediately granted a passage to Jamaica, on condition that I should work it.

"As I sailed down the Thames and gazed on the banks of the river, I became a prey to the saddest reflections. Fancy had often whispered to me thoughts of a brilliant and happy career. The lightness of heart with which I began and prosecuted my studies: the happiness which I derived from them, and my total unacquaintance with the world, had never permitted me to speculate a moment on the possibility of misfortune or of distress. I had fondly cherished the hope, that in Europe, the centre of the highest human civilization, I should have been able one day to bring down some truth from the stars to mankind, and should have crowned the labours of a life-time, with banishing away some of the ignorance in which the human species was enveloped. But when I experienced the prostration of want–the prostration that arises not from an enfeebling of the body, or from a decay of mind, but simply from not possessing the conventional medium of exchange; when I saw that our most glorious enterprises are subject, on account of a necessary evil of civilization, and the iniquitous habits of mankind, to be blasted; I became persuaded that, without money, no man can hope to propagate truth; and the difficulty of carrying my projects into execution was forced upon me. This, however, could partly be overcome. But as I left Europe, I felt that all hopes of realizing my designs were gone.

"The ardour which had, however, inflamed me in one pursuit, fired me also in another, and to it was added the force of unswerving necessity;–that of visiting on the individual who was the primary source of my sufferings, the same amount of them as I was enduring.

"But I find I am becoming prolix. It is now late–you and I require rest; come again to-morrow night and I shall let you hear the other part of the adventures, which have ended in leaving me a prisoner on board your father's ship, and a narrator to you of my history."

The young officer rose up, and, shaking hands with Appadocca, bade him good night with that melancholy sympathy which only true and disinterested friendship can inspire.

CHAPTER XIII

"No, no: 'tis all men's office to speak patience
To those that wring under the load of sorrow
But no man's virtue nor sufficiency
To be so moral when he shall endure
The like himself. Therefore give me no counsel
My griefs cry louder than advertisement."
MUCH ADO ABOUT NOTHING

THE next night, about the same hour, Charles Hamilton again betook himself to the cabin prison of Appadocca, who resumed his narrative as he had promised.

"When I arrived at Jamaica, I proceeded at once," he continued, "to San Domingo,* where I knew there were many at that time to whom the world was as disgusting as it was to myself, and who, I judged, would be the proper instruments to aid me in my schemes. The French revolution had torn up whole families together, from the soil on which they had been rooted for generations, and had driven them to distant countries for protection and subsistence. They had carried with them, to their new homes, a strong hatred for their then democratic country, in particular, and for the whole world in general. For suffering tends not to soften the feelings or expand the heart. Pain, either mental or bodily, sours the sweetest nature, and it requires the strongest fortitude to endure it without anger.—Even Zeno†️ strangled himself when he had known pain.

"Among such men only who hated the world from having, like myself,

---

*San Domingo . . . the French Revolution: the French Revolution began in spring 1789 and continued, often with terrible violence, throughout the 1790s. The French colony of Saint Domingue (the western part of what is now Haiti) was the scene of the first major slave revolution in the New World, 1791–1802. See C. L. R. James, *The Black Jacobins,* 2d ed. (1963); and Robin Blackburn, *The Overthrow of Colonial Slavery, 1776–1848* (1988).

†Zeno: Greek philosopher (c.336–c.265 BC), founder of the Stoic school of philosophy (see below, p. 160).

experienced injustice, I thought I could live. When I arrived at San Domingo, I found that even my anticipations were exceeded. I found the exiles existing in a state of cynical philosophy, in the midst of the virgin forests that covered the island. They lived in rude huts, erected apart from each other, which they called boucans. There they passed their lives in the society only of their dogs, and of their apprentices or servants, that jointly aided them in the chase by which they subsisted.

"The instinct of active pleasure seemed entirely eradicated from their hearts; for after the day's work was done, and they had killed the animal which promised them food for a few days, they usually stretched themselves on their bed of reeds, and sullenly smoked away their waking hours.

"This life was so congenial to one who had suffered much, that I should have settled myself with the others, amidst the solitude of the wilderness, and would have there prosecuted the studies with which my existence was so strongly wrapped, if I had not a vow to fulfil.

"How seductive soever I thought those boucans to be, I was obliged to abandon the idea of enjoying the calm quiet which they promised, and to form a scheme to carry into effect the resolution which I had taken.

"I was not long in San Domingo, before I met some of my fellow students of the French University, who, as belonging to the old aristocracy, were banished from France. I found them disgusted with the arduous life which they were obliged to lead, and fretting over the destiny which had, with so little justice, deprived them of so much at home, to allow them so little in their new country. I availed myself of their impatience, and proposed to them a life which was by far less monotonous than that which they then followed, and which, beside, was attended with greater gain–to say nothing of the opportunity which it would afford of avenging themselves on men, and not on harmless brutes. They received my proposal with acclamation.

"On the spur of the moment we procured a vessel. I was elected captain, and we went in search of adventures on the high seas. I led my followers on recklessly in action, and at other times, I kept them under an iron discipline. The success of my enterprizes gave greater weight to my position, to which I had been elevated, only from a great respect with which it seemed they regarded my character. I was consequently enabled to develope my original plan more and more. The time at last arrived–I sailed to Trinidad.

"By going ashore in disguise, and by a variety of other means, I learnt that my father was about to take passage in a ship for England. I watched the sailing of the vessel, and captured her some days after her departure. Then I effected that which I had designed, and attempted to make him undergo the same miseries, to which he had subjected me. Chance, however, seems to have rescued him; and, as you see, through his instrumentality I am now a prisoner."

"And I hope, Emmanuel," said the young officer, "you will now consider your vow as performed, and will cease to follow up this course of unnatural enmity to him who gave you life."

"Cease!" exclaimed Appadocca, "cease! men of my caste never 'cease!' What I do, I do from reason: and as long as I am under the domination of that power, you need not fear that I shall ever 'cease.' I have long buried impulse, and I endeavour to act up to the dictates of the mind. Do not imagine that I could have sacrificed my life—by the ordinary standard of existence but only half spent—and devoted it to the attainment of an end, and then stop, and fold my arms because a slight accident has happened to cross me in my schemes. No—no. Be it again recorded that I now renew the vow which I made twelve months ago. I again devote my life to the vindication of that natural law which has been violated in . . . "

"Stop! Emmanuel," cried the young officer, with warmth, as he stood quickly up, and grasped the uplifted arm of Appadocca, "do not—for G—d's sake—for my sake—for your own sake, make another diabolical vow. Emmanuel, you must know you cannot but afflict your friends by choosing to remain in this unfortunate mesh in which you have entangled the intellect and the heart that God has granted to you. I curse the day that the name of this father of yours was ever made known to you; it has led you to the perversion of your natural faculties, to the branding of yourself with the stigma of parricide—against which all nature revolts—and to your flying in the very face of Heaven."

And the officer seemed deeply afflicted.

The captain still maintained his calm indifference, and, after the lapse of a few seconds, said—

"Parricide—hum! and what would you have called, perchance, the act of the father if the child had actually died of starvation? what if life had ebbed from sheer inanition? You look only on the right of the parent and not on that of the child, who, be it said, has a double claim—a claim that nature gives him, and one which he inherits from the measure of kindness and protection that his grandfather manifested to his immediate progenitor when he himself was the child. You say, too, that all nature revolts against the parricide—as you call it: error,—nature revolts only against injustice. All things are entitled to a certain measure of justice; and the natural contract between parent and child is based on the condition that, as the former has loved the latter, and protected its infancy, the latter, will yield obedience, honor, and respect, and gratitude to him. Where the condition be not fulfilled, the contract, by necessity, ceases, the child becomes absolved from his obligation; and if he resents more than ordinary wrongs that may have been done to him, he can assume, with all approbation of moral philosophy–nay, nature calls upon him to undertake the office of avenger, and to vindicate her law. I am no parricide!

"You need not fear that I shall prostitute the faculties with which you are pleased to say God has gifted me; and, as for my flying in the face of Heaven, in that respect you deceive yourself.

"I war not against God. On the contrary: recognise in me but the mere tool of His justice. To believe that the Almighty could thus look on, on crimes, and tie the hand of the avenger, is to suppose no just God. No–no, the only difference between your sentiments and mine are, that you imagine He reserves His rewards and punishments to be meted out in Heavens and in hells–and I, on my part, can demonstrate, and consequently must, and do believe that he uses a less cumbrous machinery, and makes law–law which he instituted and impressed on things,–the regulator of his creation, and the vindicator of itself. No: as long as I live, I shall make it the end of my existence to prosecute the unworthy author of my days, until the world shall learn by a dire deed that it is contrary to justice to give life to a sentient being, then abandon it; and that all organised creatures are endowed with sensibility to make them feel, and spirit to make them resent injuries."

"You have sunk yourself," replied the officer, who seemed more inclined to follow out his own opinions, than to give ear to the arguments of Appadocca, "sufficiently deep in crimes, Emmanuel, without taking any additional vows to load yourself more heavily with them. You may have suffered grievous injuries, I do not gainsay, but why should privations have led you to the vile course of robbing and thieving?"

"Robbery and thieving?"

"Yes, robbery and thieving: for how otherwise can I designate piracy?"

"Ha! I see," replied Appadocca, controlling himself, "I see you have either not gone far enough into philosophy, or that you blind yourself to its lights. If I am guilty of piracy, you, too–the whole of mankind is guilty of the very same sort of crime."

"What do you mean by this?" asked Hamilton.

"Simply, that which my words convey," replied Appadocca.

"Perhaps you will explain yourself more amply?" suggested Hamilton.

"Well," rejoined Appadocca, "what I mean is plain enough, and it is this, that the whole of the civilized world turns, exists, and grows enormous on the licensed system of robbing and thieving, which you seem to criminate so much. The barbarous hordes, whose fathers, either choice or some unlucky accident, originally drove to some cold, frozen, cheerless, and fruitless waste, increasing in numbers, wincing under the inclemency of their clime and the poverty of their land, and longing after the richer, and more fertile, and teeming soil of some other country, desert their wretched regions, and with all the machinery of war, melt down on the unprovoking nations, whose only crime is their being more fortunate and blest, and wrench from their enervated sway the prosperous fields that first provoked their famished cupidity. The people which a convenient position, either on a neck of land, or the elbow of some large river, first consolidated, developed, and enriched, after having appropriated, through the medium of commerce, the wealth of its immediate neighbours, sends forth its numerous and powerful ships to scour the seas, to penetrate into hitherto unknown regions, where discovering new and rich countries, they, in the name of civilization, first open an intercourse with the peaceful and contented inhabitants, next contrive to provoke a quarrel, which always terminates in a war that leaves them the conquerors and possessors of the land. As for the original inhabitants themselves, they are driven after the destruction of their cities, to roam the woods, and to perish and disappear on the advance of their greedy supplanters. Nations that are different only in the language with which they vent their thoughts, inhabiting the same portions of the globe, and separated but by a narrow stream, eagerly watch the slightest inclination of accident in their respective favours, and on the plea, either of religion – that fertile theme, and ready instigator – or on the still more extensive and uncertain ground of politics, use the chance that circumstances throw into their hands, make incursions and fight battles, whose fruits are only misery and wretchedness. A fashion springs up at a certain time to have others to labour for our benefit, and to bear 'the heat and burthen of the day'* in our stead: straightway, the map of the world is opened, and the straggling and weakest portions of a certain race, whose power of bodily and mental endurance, renders them the likely objects to answer this end, are chosen. The coasts of the country on which nature has placed them, are immediately lined with ships of acquisitive voyagers, who kidnap and tear

---

*'the heat and burthen of the day': from Christ's parable of the laborers in the vineyard (Matthew 20:12).

them away from the scenes that teem with the associations of their own and their fathers' happiness, load them with irons, throw them into the cruel ordeal of the 'middle passage,' to test whether they are sufficiently iron-constituted as to survive the starvation, stench, and pestilential contagion which decide the extent of the African's endurance, and fix his value. This my dear friend is an abstracted idea of the manner in which the world turns. But, as we used to say when we were younger, and happier, *in generalibus latet fraus,* * allow me to descend to particulars, and to bring my observations more closely home to society as now constituted. In all the various parts which form its whole, you will be able to trace the same spirit to which I impliedly referred in viewing the conduct of congregated individuals,–nations. You find those whom fortune has called to the first place in the state, instead of exerting their intellect to the utmost stretch, and expanding their heart to its greatest width, for the wise and virtuous government, and for the development of the happiness of those who are subjected to their rule, wasting their time in the pursuit of the most shadowy gewgaws,† squandering, in empty vanities, the tax-extorted treasures of their subjects–treasures that could have preserved the flame of many a light of humanity, whose doom it has been to flicker for a moment in a garret, and be for ever extinguished; or pampering their already over-fed bodies to the point that sensitive reason refuses to longer hold together with such masses of matter. Those again in secondary spheres, use the authority with which they are invested, not with the keen discernment of delicate justice, but on the spur and press of passion. Is there some conquered people to be governed?–they send their weak-minded, afflicted, and helpless friends or relatives to govern those whose ancestors gave philosophy, religion, and government to the world, but who must now themselves stoop, to cut wood, and to carry water, when, by the common rules of justice, they should be permitted to enjoy the land from which they have sprung, and to participate in its dignities.

"What villainous case is there, that with the ready fee, does not find the well-turned and silvery measures of the orator to palm it forth. The widow's mite,‡ or the prince's prerogative, may depend upon the issue,–'tis all the same. Poverty and utter want may follow the words of the cunning speaker, and rascality and villainy may rise triumphant,–what matters it?

---

* *in generalibus latet fraus:* Latin, falsification lies hidden in generalizations.

†gewgaws: things of no account or worth.

‡the widow's mite: a small coin or portion; alludes to Christ's story of the widow who gives generously of the little she possesses (Mark 12:42).

"At the side of suffering humanity stands the willing doctor, and plies, and plies the rich patient with make-show drugs.

"From the pulpit invectives flow, for the voice of religion; charity yields to controversy; the denunciation of others' condemned and re-condemned errors supply the place of the practice of benevolence; and in the name of that Christ, who came with 'peace and good will to man,' evil passions are roused, daggers whetted, and massacres sanctified; while he, who, with spectacles on nose, and twang in voice, moves the ready machine, grins in his closet over the glittering gold that his lectures, invectives, panegyrics, and homilies, bring in.

"This is not all. Are you hungry? the baker sends you bread compounded with pestilential stuffs, grows rich, visits the church, sympathises with heathen savages, and sends delegates to call them within the bosom of his sweet civilization. Are you thirsty? the herb that nature furnishes you for your refreshment is taken and turned, and painted, and fried till it becomes poison, and then given you with balmy smiles.

"The world can be compared to a vast marsh, abounding with monster alligators that devour the smaller creatures, and then each other."

"Apply your argument, Appadocca," said Hamilton. "for I do not properly feel its force."

"The application follows, naturally, my dear Charles," replied Appadocca. "It is this: If I take away from the merchant whose property very likely consists of the accumulation of exorbitant and excessive profits, the sugar which by the vice of mortgages he wrings at a nominal price from the debt-ridden planter, who, in his turn, robs the unfortunate slave of his labour, I take what is ethically not his property, therefore, I commit no robbery. For, it is clear, he who wrenches away from the hands of another, that which the holder is not entitled to, does no wrong."

"Hum," groaned Hamilton, "nice distinction."

"To myself I am unstained," continued Appadocca, "notwithstanding the necessity that made me require the aid of expediency. No man can say that Emmanuel Appadocca ever fed his pirates with the lawful property of any one."

A considerable pause ensued.

"But it strikes me, Emmanuel," said Hamilton, resuming the conversation, "you forget, in your observations, that commerce, and the voyages which you seem to censure so much by implication, are the proper stimulants to civilization and human cultivation."

"A very vulgar error, my dear Charles, and quite unworthy of your father's son," replied Appadocca. "The human mind does not require to be pioneered by Gog and Magog* in order to improve. It is not in the busy mart, not at the tinkling of gold, that it grows and becomes strong; nor is it on the shaft of the steam-engine which propels your huge fabrics to rich though savage shores that it increases." No: there it degenerates and falls into the mere thing whose beginning is knack, whose end is knack. The mind can thrive only in the silence that courts contemplation. It was in such silence that among a race, which is now despised and oppressed, speculation took wing, and the mind burst forth, and, scorning things of earth, scaled the heavens, read the stars, and elaborated systems of philosophy, religion, and government: while the other parts of the world were either enveloped in darkness, or following in eager and uncontemplative haste the luring genii of riches. Commerce makes steam engines and money—it assists not the philosophical progress of the mind."

"I cannot admire this strange and extraordinary theory, Emmanuel," answered the young officer, evidently disposed to terminate this startling conversation.

"You may call it strange and extraordinary, if you please," answered Appadocca; "but it is not the less true on account of its novelty: it is scarcely to be expected to commend itself to the world I know, because, forsooth, it is new and strange: although the systems and notions which are now as familiar as household terms, were, once upon a time, quite as new, strange, and extraordinary. Mankind is doomed to draw its venerative and uninquiring self along. Science cannot accelerate its unwilling movements. For my part, I shall cling to my own doctrine, and shall give an account of my actions to a Supreme Being, when the time arrives to do so."

"Well, well, I shall not discuss such points with you," replied the officer, "I cannot congratulate myself on possessing wits sharp enough to cut through your strings of subtilities, I give up, therefore, these unprofitable points: my instincts, I must declare, are against piracy."

"Instincts, indeed!" partly interjected Appadocca, "another stumbling block, and obstacle to science. There are no such things as instincts in man: he alone is distinguished from the rest of organic beings by the indefiniteness of his mind and sensibilities. The habits in which men are brought up, the notions of ignorance which they have compounded and adopted they call instincts, and thus saddle wise and good Nature with an amount of

*Gog and Magog: the Book of Revelation refers to a Satanic invasion by "Gog and Magog" (20:7-10; see also Ezechiel 38-39).

absurdities that would make her blush, if she were conscious of the faults which she is made to bear on the ground of having implanted, in the human breast, feelings which are as ridiculous as they are false. As for you, Charles, I am somewhat surprised at you. It is clear you have not improved since you left the university. The time that you had for contemplation during your student's life, ought to have produced better fruits than an unconditional adoption of the vague notions of the unreflecting, as soon as you found yourself among them.

"Pardon the freedom with which I speak–our friendship alone has made me depart from the usual silence which I invariably maintain."

"No–no apology is necessary, my dear Emmanuel–I know you–I know you! Besides, we have always observed, that those who are endowed with a certain amount of intellect, like the pendulum of a clock, are liable to go as far from a given centre, in one direction as in the other. But let us drop this topic, and think of your safety. I have heard your story, and really I am not surprised that such a sensitive individual as you should have been driven by so much injustice to a course which, with all my sympathy towards you, I cannot but denounce. Appadocca, we have seen happy and innocent days together, before either injury had driven you into–into–crime, or the business of the world had thrown part of its cares upon me: I could not stand with my arms folded and see you tried like a malefactor, and, perhaps, end your life under the hands of a vile hangman: I have formed a plan to facilitate your escape."

"A plan to facilitate my escape?"

"Yes, I am in high command on board this ship, and I have men who are devoted to me. This very night you will be put on shore."

A pause ensued,–in which Appadocca seemed buried in deep reflection; while Charles Hamilton, quite surprised by the coldness manifested on the announcement of what he considered the happiest news to a prisoner,–the prospects of escape–grew gradually pale, and paler as the truth began to break upon him that his friend, from some strange doctrine of his own, might obstinately refuse to consult his safety, and to avail himself of the means of escape, which Hamilton could lay in his power.

After the lapse of a few minutes, Appadocca grasped the hand of the young officer.

"No, no," he said, "Charles, I esteem you too much, and venerate the law of nature too much, to avail myself of this kindness. Recollect that confidence is placed in you; you are bound to use it scrupulously, else retribution will surely follow any breach of it. I thank you from the bottom of my heart for your good intention, but I cannot,–I will not accept your offer. If I escape, I shall do so without compromising any person, least of all, one of my oldest, and most esteemed friends."

"I was not aware," replied the young officer, somewhat piqued, "that I required to be reminded of the confidence which is here placed in me: be not, however, so foolish as to refuse my offer, let me entreat you."

"Do not press me."

"I stake my friendship in your acceptance," said the officer with some determination. "He who refuses the good offices of a friend when he re-quires them, especially in a case of life and death, can have no proper feeling for him who proffers them, and he is to boot–a fool. Good night, Emmanuel," continued the officer, getting up, somewhat angry, "I give you until to-morrow to think of what I have offered.–Good night."

The officer went out of the cabin, and Appadocca was left by himself.

CHAPTER XIV

–"I'll serve his mind with my best will."
TIMON OF ATHENS

A short time after the capture of Emmanuel Appadocca, there might be observed a narrow canoe, with a single individual in it, far out at sea, apparently going still farther out,–for it was lustily paddled against the long sweeping waves that seemed at every moment to be about to bury the frail bark under their heavy volumes.

The trade wind, which still blew, seemed to impede the progress of the canoe, and it was evident that the solitary person, who sat in its stern, found it necessary to exert all his strength in order to make any headway.

But whither away such a frail vessel in the immensity of the ocean, and still going farther out to sea? and what could be the design of the individual who seemed to brave so recklessly the fury of the waves?

Upon closer observation it might have been perceived, that the person who sat alone at the stern of the canoe was our old acquaintance, Jack Jimmy.

As soon as his master was captured, he had taken to flight, but not with the design of abandoning the interest of his young master, as he still called Appadocca. He had managed to insinuate himself among the coteries of boatmen and porters that skulked about the beach, and unobserved among them, he had been able to watch what befell his master. Effectually he saw Appadocca, when he was marched down a prisoner to the boat, and witnessed his embarkation. He discovered by his inquiries, that the boat belonged to the British man-of-war, that was then lying off the harbour, and heard the tale which had by that time become a nine day's wonder of the place, "of a man who was taken by a pirate, thrown overboard, picked up by a vessel, and had come to St. Thomas' after the pirate, and had had him taken."

Jack Jimmy had now gained sufficient intelligence; his own sagacity developed to him the whole extent of his master's position.

"Good bye, buddee," he cried, as soon as he had heard the last word of the story, and set off, at the height of the speed at which his short legs would carry him, and left his wondering story-tellers in convulsive laughter at his apparent eccentricity.

Jack Jimmy kept running in this manner for nearly two hours, without any abatement of the speed with which he had started. Perspiration flowed in torrents over his cheeks, and those who met him, stopped to stare at the individual who was so eccentrically giving himself such violent exercise while exposed to the scorching rays of a vertical sun.

Jack Jimmy did not stop until he reached a secluded spot by the sea-shore, where, at the foot of two opposing hills, the sea had eaten away a deep recess, and had left as in exchange for the land which it had robbed, numbers of strange and beautiful shells, that paved the place. Within this natural shelter, some fishermen's canoes were drawn up. Jack Jimmy looked around him carefully, and seeing no one at hand, he walked up to one of the canoes, and with two stones managed to grind asunder the small rope with which it was fastened to a stake, and then concentrating his powers, endeavoured to launch it. But his strength was not equal to the task: vainly he repeated his efforts—still no success—he gave up the task for the moment, in despair, and sat on the ground and wept from vexation.

His despair soon gave way to a fiercer feeling.

"You must go in de water," he cried, addressing the canoe, and rising in desperation, he applied his strength to it again;—it began to move a little. "Tenk Gad," Jack Jimmy cried. Again another strain:—it moved again, and by little and little, Jack Jimmy got it nearer and nearer to the water's edge: by one long and straining effort he finally succeeded in launching it.

He sprang into it as soon as it was afloat, tore up one of the thwarts, and paddled with it vigorously out to sea.

When he had got at a considerable distance from land he stopped.

The sun was then sinking, shedding soft and sweet brilliancy over the evening hour. "Yes, me 'member," said Jack Jimmy, "wen we lef de 'chooner, you bin behind a wee"; and after having thus spoken to that luminary, and probably made his calculations, in his own original way, he steered the canoe towards the east, and continued the powerful use of his paddle until he arrived at the spot where the reader has discovered him.

Jack Jimmy held his lonely course on the great ocean until next morning, when he discovered the pirate vessel at a distance. He redoubled his strokes, and made for her. In a short time he had gained her side.

Arriving alongside, he nimbly jumped on board, and threw himself flat on the deck, with his face downwards, and at the foot of Lorenzo, who was standing with a spy-glass in his hand at the gangway.

The officer had perceived the small canoe, and on using his glass, he had discovered that the lonely individual in it was Jack Jimmy. His mind at once misgave him. "The captain is taken" was his first thought.

It was with impatient anxiety, therefore, that he inquired of Jack Jimmy, when he got on deck, what had become of his master.

The little negro shook his head convulsively at the question, and interjected, "Massa!" but seemed incapable of saying anything else. Lorenzo waited a few moments, but Jack Jimmy could say nothing more.

"Speak, fellow," cried he with vehemence, "where is the captain? Is–is–is he taken?"

"Ah! Garamighty," answered Jack Jimmy.

"Will you speak, sir," cried Lorenzo with fury. "Is your master taken?"

Jack Jimmy shook his head violently again, and cried, "Yes, yes, Garamighty, massa, massa!" he continued, "big, big English ship, take massa."

"And where is the ship?"

"In St. Thomas', massa," answered Jack Jimmy.

"Make sail," was Lorenzo's immediate command; "keep her way."

The schooner immediately sheered off to the wind, and in an instant was bounding over the waves for St. Thomas'.

When she neared the island, Lorenzo prudently cast her in the wind, and remained lying-to until it was dark, at which time he drew nearer the harbour, and making use of a boat, reconnoitred the "big English ship," as Jack Jimmy had described it.

After the officer had properly examined the large ship-of-war which held his chief captive, and had managed to elicit further and more explicit information from Jack Jimmy, whose excitement of nerves had now a little subsided, he began to think of the measures which he ought to take to effect the liberation of his friend and superior. His first impulse was to fife to arms, to attack the huge fabric, whose very sides seemed to frown destruction on the light schooner. Prudence, on reflection, however, forbade such a step. There was too great disproportion between the large ship and the small craft of the pirates, and between the armament and complement of the one and of the other; and even if, by a fierce and sudden assault, the pirates should carry the man-of-war, what chance was there of rescuing the chief? Probably he was secured in some deep recess below decks, whither, perhaps, even the roar of the ship's guns could scarcely echo; and if even the comparatively few men that composed the crew of the schooner, could gain any advantage over the four-times more numerous complement of the ship, it could only amount to a mere temporary possession of the upper deck. Besides, the whole harbour, on the event of a combat, would be alarmed, and it was probable that the pirates, even if victors, would be entirely unable to contend against the multitudes which would be dispatched against them from the shore. "No, I must try other means," thought the officer. After much deliberation, he at last resolved on the plan of watching the ship-of-war, and of discovering, by every possible means, in what part of the vessel Appadocca was confined, so that he might attempt a surreptitious entry on board, and carry away the prisoner.

For that purpose he sent three men ashore in disguise, that they might procure as much information as possible. These were not long at a loss in devising means for doing so.

The pirate schooner was manned by individuals who had been of a superior class in society, before they exiled themselves from it. Chiefly men of education, they were doubly dangerous in their illicit pursuits, inasmuch as they could bring to bear upon their purposes, the assistance of art, and the power of inventing.

They easily disguised themselves when they were ashore, as vendors of fruit, and as the other small dealers that may be seen of a-morning, in their little canoes around the ships at anchor, in the ports of the tropics.

In their assumed course of bartering, they managed to elicit from the sailors of the man-of-war, intelligence about Appadocca, and the part of the vessel in which he was confined.

As soon as they became possessed of as much information as they possibly could procure, they returned on board the schooner, and carefully narrated the sum of their observation to Lorenzo.

Return we now to Appadocca himself.

CHAPTER XV

"What noise is this? Give me my long sword, ho!"
ROMEO AND JULIET

THE period accorded by the friendship of Charles Hamilton to the prisoner, for the acceptance or rejection of his offer to become the means of his escape, had now expired, and the two young friends were sitting together in the cabin-prison in which Appadocca was confined.

"So you will not consent to put aside your insane notions and escape, when I place it in your power to do so?" said Charles Hamilton, dejectedly, and, at the same time, somewhat scornfully, twisting his whiskers.

"No!" replied Appadocca with much decision.

"Then," replied the officer, "I shall have nothing farther to do with you; they may hang you, quarter you, and do, G–d knows what else to you."

"As for that matter," answered Appadocca, affecting something like the same satire as his friend had used, "you may exercise your own discretion; but is it not a little absurd that, because I am not willing to sanction the mis-use of the authority which you possess on board your father's ship, in your allowing me, who have been brought here a prisoner, to escape, that I, on that account, should lose your favor, and cease to be deemed worthy of your notice, even if I should happen to be hanged, quartered, and done G–d knows what else to?" and Appadocca smiled good-naturedly.

"This is the second time, Emmanuel, that you have adverted to my authority on board this ship, and reflected on my conduct in endeavouring to befriend you: I hope it may be the last. You must recollect that I am an Englishman, and an English officer, and I consider that I possess as delicate a sense of honor and as great a knowledge of duty as any gentleman whosoever."

"And I," replied Appadocca, "I am an animal, – sub-kingdom, *vertebrata,* genus *homo,* and species, – 'tropical American'; naturalists lay my habitat all over the world, and declare me omnivorous. I do not pride myself on possessing merely such an indefinite thing as sense of honor, or great knowledge of duty; but observation has made me acquainted with the universal laws which nature has imposed upon us in order to secure to us contentment and happiness; and your wishing to make your station on board this vessel subservient to my escape is in opposition to one of those laws, the certain precursor of your own unhappiness, I shall not consent to it. Speak to me no more on this subject."

"If, Emmanuel, I had considered that my good faith was concerned in making an offer of escape to you, you may rely upon it, I should neither have attempted to lower myself in my own estimation, nor should I have subjected myself to the animadversion of your nice and exquisite philosophy. I shall use the same liberty of speech as you have done, and assume the right of telling you, that His Majesty's ship, which my father has the honour to command, was built, fitted out, and sent to sea, for the purpose of fighting the enemies of England, and not for the purpose of scavenging for pirates and freebooters: my commission was granted for the same purpose. I consider, therefore, that this vessel ought not to be made the lock-up of accused individuals; nor ought my father be obliged to abet and to assist the malice of hard-hearted planters, or interfere in the actions of strangely arguing sons–I therefore consider myself bound by no honour in this affair; and I am, consequently, free to act as I please. I recognize in you my ancient and respected friend, and I offer you my assistance to escape. You may accept it or not–this is Saxon."*

Charles Hamilton spoke this with considerable warmth and seriousness.

"Bravely spoken, Charles," said Appadocca, "and, although part of your speech may have sounded harsh to ears more unwilling than mine to hear the truth, still I admire you for it. Why did you not speak out in this manner before. You may depend upon it, man, it is always better to express one's self boldly, throw aside expediency, and bring out the truth, which, though harsh and unpleasant, is, nevertheless, the truth, and must be told. What is there to be feared? A proper man has nothing worth keeping, which he should apprehend to lose, save his honour and his spirit of rectitude. What though interest-seekers quake in their coats lest their smoothly-varnished opinions should not draw the approbation of their fastidious patrons: a man, worthy of the name, must follow out the spirit of his manliness, and that is all. Take the furious bull–society, by the horns, and though its lurid eyes shine fire upon you, nay, though it gore you, shout out your truths still higher than its bellowings; and when its madness-fit is over, your truths shall live, nay, ride it even as a broken-spirited ass.

"Men of such boldness there have been, who, Lycurgus-like,† have exiled themselves from all to throw their truths into the world. Society may have branded them, starved them, cursed them, and driven them into hovels, there to perish and to rot, but they have ever re-risen in their thoughts, and now their names receive, on the bended knee, the unbounded veneration of mankind.

*this is Saxon: the Germanic language or any dialect of the Saxon peoples; here, implies a direct, plainspoken statement.

†Lycurgus-like: Lycurgus was an Athenian orator and statesman (390–325 BC).

"Still I will not accept your proposal."

"But for G–d's sake, Emmanuel, speak seriously," said Hamilton, hastily, "you surely do not intend to let this obstinacy of yours prevent your escape;" and the young officer looked anxiously in Appadocca's face.

It would appear that, notwithstanding the previous refusal of his friend, he never contemplated but that at the last moment he would avail himself of his assistance and escape.

"Call me obstinate, as you may," replied Appadocca, "I shall not accept your offer."

"Then is it possible that you seriously refuse to save your life?"

"Not I, by Heaven," replied Appadocca.

"Then why not adopt my proposal at once?"

"Because my doing so will not only involve a breach of discipline, but will also compromise your honour,–two sacrifices which we must pronounce disproportioned, when we consider the very small necessity that demands them."

"Do you recollect that death will be your sentence?" eagerly demanded Charles.

"I do recollect it," answered Appadocca. "And pray, what is death?"

The latter part of the question was put with such cynical coldness, that Charles Hamilton found himself unwittingly silenced.

He remained tongue-tied for a few moments, and with the greatest embarrassment repeated the question of Appadocca. "What is death, you ask?"

"Ay, what is death, I ask? let your embarrassment repeat the question," remarked Appadocca.

"Why, death," replied the young officer, "death is–is–is the–the highest of all–of all human punishments–and sufferings."

"Remarkably fine," replied Appadocca, with some satire, "remarkably fine, I once entertained better hopes of you, Charles Hamilton, when you were at College; but now I find, that like all other persons, you have thought, that it was necessary to cultivate the intellect, only during the time when you were at college,–that you were to live in mind, or rather, according to the dictates of your reason, as long as you were there; but that as soon as you became emancipated from your scholastic thraldom, throwing aside convictions, you were to live entirely in body, merely copying the bad habits of most men, which they self-deludingly style 'instincts.' You speak and think absolutely like those animals that are driven above decks there by your orders, and who turn their tobacco in their checks, bellow forth their strange and meaningless oaths, and pull the ropes, by precisely the same moving power as one of your guns sends forth its iron and brimstone charge, when fire is applied to the touch-hole. That distinguishing essential which we, with so much complaisance, place on ourselves, to divide us from quadrupeds and our other fellow habitants of this earth—reason, is as much consulted as the stars. You observe the whole of organized life clinging to the idea of preservation, that they may continue for a brief period the state in which they happen to find themselves, and permitting this idea, in sympathy with the herd of men, to grow unreasoned in you, you fancy that I, also, should start from death with the same fear, and consent to depart from the course of conduct which my intellect prescribes to me, for the mere purpose of avoiding it. You do not consider what really is life, and less, perhaps, what is death. If millions of men are content to cultivate a sluggish existence, and shrink from ennobling enterprizes, in order that they may avoid this bugbear with which they ignorantly frighten themselves; nay, if they can be worked upon by this terror to compromise the only imperishable part of our nature—the idea of self-respect or honour—you must not fancy that I, my dear Charles, am willing to do so, too!"

"If you are not, I can only say your instincts are ajar," observed the young officer, who felt himself again unable to answer Appadocca.

"There, you speak of instincts again: I have no instincts. If you mean certain ideas which are the necessary fruits of my organization, I shall observe, that far from their being ajar, they, on the contrary, are the only ones which are in harmony with whatever we know of nature and of its Author."

"Hold, Emmanuel, do not go any further, you will be guilty of irreverence."

"Irreverence! it is not I who can be guilty of irreverence, it is you, and the rest of the ignorant world, that are 'guilty of irreverence;' for, by surrounding death with the terror you do, and by considering it the greatest of earth's afflictions, you effectually depreciate the goodness and consistency of the Maker of all things."

"In what manner?" inquired the officer.

"Listen to me, and you shall hear. The whole of this globe, you are aware, is animated. Every object here, from the fibrous and silken down that flies about, carrying the seed of some gigantic tree, to the mountains of consolidated rock, is the theatre of life; and that theatre itself possesses a peculiar animation of its own, or laws of self-development. The various forms and shapes which people these things, vary in their periods of existence from centuries to the incalculable and indivisible points of time which human ingenuity has hitherto deemed it idle to note. You have the birds of the desert; the huge animals whose years are to be counted but by the hundred; you have again the infinitesimal insect, which comes into existence this moment to depart the next; so that in the shortest space of time that man can calculate, nature ushers into life millions of millions of sentient beings, to sweep them away again with the same rapidity with which they are made. This earth on which this process takes place has existed, as far as we can discover with certainty, for several thousands of years, so that millions of millions of beings have continually perished during every short moment into which the numberless days of those thousands of years can possibly be divided. To consider that death is so dreadful as it is supposed to be, when we find it on such an amazingly extensive scale, and principally, also, among creatures whose only apparent happiness is the mere possession of life itself, is to call the Ordainer of these things cruel–which is untrue, or, as we used to say long ago, *reductio ad absurdum.* * What you choose to convert into the horrible and dreadful, is only the working of a wise and general law–that of transition: we live here to-day in one shape, to live to-morrow in a different one. Man has stupidly shut his eyes to this fact as he has done to many other things, and pitifully mourns over the action of a universal and useful law."

"Emmanuel, I am a plain sailor, and do not pretend to deal in niceties of logical distinction," replied Charles, "and although it is not my purpose to continue this very peculiar conversation, still I must ask, if our death is merely a transition from one state to another, how is it, that when we have entered into our new condition, we do not retain any consciousness of our previous existence."

"The answer is plain enough," answered Appadocca, "when the harp is unstrung the sounds depart: when we change from one condition to an-other, we necessarily cease to be of the first, else there would be no change at all: and as our consciousness of that condition was merely a natural consequence or effect of it, it follows, that when the cause ceases, the effect must necessarily cease also."

Appadocca remained silent for a while.

"And as for the ignominy," he continued, "of a death on the scaffold, for

---

reductio ad absurdum: Latin, taking an argument or principle to impractical or absurd lengths.

such a crime as the one which is imputed to me, it is purely ridiculous. It is not because mankind may be eager to alter, by their vote, the nature of things, that these things become intrinsically changed."

Appadocca stopped, apparently expecting Charles Hamilton to speak; but he, however, was anxiously gazing on the side of the ship, and was apparently intent on listening to some sound that it seemed he heard.

"Did you hear that?" he at last asked, in a low tone.

"What?"

"Hush!–do you not hear that sound?"

"Hum! Perhaps–I think I do; I think–I–I–hum! I–know it," answered Appadocca, while his face brightened up a little.

The officer drew nearer to the side of the ship to listen–Appadocca remained where he was.

The dull sounds of muffled instruments could now be distinctly heard. From its direction, it could be easily discovered that these instruments were applied to the dead light,† which had been carefully battened in for greater security against the prisoner's escape. The sounds continued, and the sharp point of a large chisel, with which some individual from the outside was endeavouring to wrench away part of the cover, was now seen through the dead light of the ship.

The young officer looked round inquiringly at Appadocca, but met, in the gaze of that individual, only the coldness that characterized him.

"An attack, an attack!" he cried, and rushed out of the cabin. His instincts, as he called them, at once belying the ingenious arguments with which he had lulled his spirit of honor, when his friendship for Appadocca interposed.

He arrived on deck in time to hear the sharp challenge of the marine on duty.

"Who is there?" no answer was made to the challenge.

The guard was called out. The marine fired. In return only a derisive shout arose from a boat that was now moving away in the darkness. One, two, three volleys were fired in succession, when the angry voice of a man was heard from the boat.

"Cowards!" he cried, "come after us, and do not expend your ammunition foolishly."

It was the voice of Lorenzo.

On hearing the reports of the spies that he had sent on shore, that faithful

†dead light: thick window or shutter.

officer had formed the plan of carrying Appadocca silently away from the cabin in which he was confined. For that purpose, he had waited until the night was far spent, and with a few trusty men had cautiously approached the man-of-war.

The pirate party came in a boat that was greased all over on the outside, and which was propelled by muffled oars.

The men were all dressed in black, and wore for the occasion, dark woollen caps, which were drawn over their heads so as perfectly to conceal their faces. They had boarded the ship for about half an hour, and two men were working away vigorously; the blows of the covered mallet drove their muffled chisels more and more deeply into the chinks of the dead light.

"Have you nearly got through, Gustave?" inquired Lorenzo, the enterprising officer of Appadocca.

"Nearly, senor," answered the man.

"Thanks to Providence," muttered Lorenzo, "Appadocca will be rescued."

O disappointment wherefore dost thou exist? The words had scarcely escaped Lorenzo when a splashing noise was heard near the man-of-war.

The sailors, as is customary with them, when their ship is at anchor, in order to improve their opportunities, had hung out a fishing line. As adverse fate would have it, at the very moment when the party of Lorenzo was about completing a breach in the cabin in which their captain was confined, a large shark happened to take the bait. Pricked by the hook, the fish began to swim furiously around the ship, beating about with its huge tail. The water immediately became covered with foam, and the noise increased more and more.

"Jump up, Domingo," said Lorenzo, when he perceived the imminent danger of discovery which they ran from the noise that the creature was making in the water, "jump up and cut away that cursed thing."

But it was too late: attracted by the splashes made by the shark, the sentinel looked over the bulwarks, and perceived the man that was just sliding himself down the chains of the man-of-war, after having dexterously cut away the line by which the fish was caught.

The pirates had no alternative but flight, and they were quickly making away when the young officer got on deck.

Part of the crew of the large vessel was called out, the boats were manned, and sent after the mysterious visitors. But it was of no avail: those who had gone in chase shortly afterwards returned, and reported that they could discover nothing of the boat.

The circumstance was duly reported to the commander. After much consideration on such a mysterious adventure, the latter wisely concluded that the party of the pirate captain were in those waters, and that their approach to the ship was for the purpose of attempting his rescue.

Further, on examination, marks of the tools were made out on the deadlight of Appadocca's cabin. He himself was narrowly questioned, but he stated with perfect truth, that he knew nothing of the matter.

Orders were then given to weigh anchor at the dawn of the next day.

END OF VOL. I.

SECOND BOOK

CHAPTER XVI

"O conspiracy!
Shamest thou to show thy dangerous brow by night
When evils are most free?"

JULIUS CAESAR

THE small cutter that was carrying Agnes and the other captives held her course towards the land.

It could not but occur to the priest and to his ward, unaccustomed as they were to encounter dangers, that their position was one which was in itself highly, if not imminently perilous. There they were, thrown in an open vessel on the ocean, and sent on a voyage which was to consist of three days' or more beating up against the wind and the waves, while their little vessel was every moment subjected to the accidents of a very tedious and difficult navigation.

These thoughts were the more forcibly thrust upon the priest, when after the lapse of a day, and on the approach of night, it was to be perceived that no progress towards the land had been made. the little cutter had tossed about on high billows, had tacked and re-tacked, still at the close of the day she was not much nearer the end of her voyage than when she was thrown off by the schooner. Under the influence of these thoughts, the priest lost much of his cheerful equanimity. He looked concerned, and his conversation did not flow so freely as it was wont to do. Perhaps this was a happy accident for Agnes; for that young lady, apparently disinclined to speak or to listen, still leaned over the side of the cutter, and, from time to time, cast a side-long look at the schooner that was sailing away in another direction.

The first night of the voyage came, and augmented still more the alarm of the priest. He felt his isolation among the other men whose pursuits and habits were different from his, and now freely allowed his mind to conjure up fears of assassination and robbery. To add to his suspicions, the sailors of the captured ship seemed to herd closely together, and to sympathise but little with their fellow passengers. The master fisherman, true to his promise, paid the greatest attention both to the sailing of his little vessel, and to the safety and comparative comfort of those who had been placed under his especial care.

When the sun, that true and never disordered time-keeper of the tropics, had on the next morning illumined the ocean, the first thought and first action of Agnes, was to cast her eyes around and survey the horizon. Nothing was to be seen; the Black Schooner had disappeared. Scarcely believing her eyes, she looked and looked again; it was as the eyes made it out, and not as the wish would have it; there was no vessel to be seen. Dejected, wretched, sad, and disappointed, she suspended her further survey, and began again to contemplate the blue waters that were rushing past the jumping cutter. A sad feeling was that of Agnes, the feeling which arises when we lose the last memento of some dear and cherished creature: the memento which, in the absence of the object that it recalls to our memory, receives, perhaps, the same amount of worship as the being itself which it represents. Whatever be the nature of such a token, it is all the same: a golden toy, a lock of hair, a favourite pin, a prayer-book, these are amply sufficient to strike up within us the active feelings of grief-clothed happiness, and to awake anew the recollections of periods whose real and unbroken felicity never permitted us to contemplate or fear a change. To lose one of these imaging toys, is the breaking away of the last link that binds us, in one way at least, to the objects which they symbolized. On such sad occasions the heart is striken with a prophetic fear, which like the canker-worm ever afterwards eats deeply, and more deeply into our spirits, until there is nothing more to eat away.

Agnes felt this when she could no longer see the Black Schooner. As long as she could gaze on the vessel, there was still a little consolation, or, perhaps her grief was still subdued, but when that vessel disappeared from her view, it reached its height and preyed upon her without mitigation. Who has not stood on the sea-washed strand and watched the careering ship that was bearing away father, lover, or child, and felt his tears restrained as long as a waving handkerchief could convey the ardour of a last "farewell," but who, a few moments after, experienced the bitter misery that followed, when the ship had disappeared from the view, when an unsympathizing horizon had veiled in silence and in obscurity his lost and lonely friends, and his damp spirits were left free to recoil upon themselves? What person is there, who in the hey-day of existence, at the age when the heart is fresh, and the spirits are high, when necessity intervened to drive him away from among friends and relatives, has not felt the pang of separation more and more as every familiar object was, one by one left behind, and gradually disappeared from his view.

"Agnes, you are sad," said the priest, who notwithstanding his own anxiety, and disquiet of mind, could not but mark the unsettled and unhappy state of his ward.

"Not very, sir," the young lady replied, "though our present condition is not the most pleasant."

"Truly not," answered the priest, "still we must hope that we shall soon arrive on land. Recollect, that, although we are not now very comfortable, we are still on a voyage towards home, and that thought ought to support us under greater inconveniences than the present."

"Yes," replied Agnes, "we are returning home, and that is a comfort. . . . How beautiful this water is," she continued, falling naturally into that romantic train which was necessarily called forth by the present state of her sentiments, "how remarkably beautiful are those blue waters, and how pure and transparent is that thin foam which now fringes yon crystal wave!"

"All the works of the Creator are beautiful, my child," answered the priest.

"Yes," continued Agnes, "and the ocean is so still and quiet: who could ever imagine that it contained so many terrible monsters."

"True;" remarked the priest, "surfaces, my child, are, alas! too frequently deceptive. For instance, take the appearance of the ocean this beautiful and blessed morning; it looks as pure and unspotted as when the sun first dawned upon it on the fourth day of creation; still, how many murderous deeds have there not been done upon it since that time, and over how many wrecks of human fabrics has it not rolled? If we could penetrate its depth, and see its bed, we should probably behold the skeletons of the fierce Caraibs* that first inhabited this part of the world, and their rude instruments of war, blended confusedly together with the bones and elaborate weapons of their more polished conquerors; while the large fishes that still hold possession of their medium of existence, now peer with meaningless eyes into the naked skulls, or rummage for their food the rotting wrecks of the bristling war-vessels that once rode these seas."

Agnes felt thankful for this long and solemn observation, which gave her time to think on one of the vessels that had not as yet become a wreck beneath the ocean.

After a pause, the priest continued:

"This basin over which we are now sailing, my dear Agnes, may have once been high and dry land, and the islands which are scattered about in this horse-shoe fashion, may have been—"

*Caraibs: Caraibs or Caribs refers to Indian people of north Southern and Central America and parts of the Caribbean. The Caribs and the Arawaks were the two major Amerindian groups of Trinidad and the eastern Caribbean.

"Stop, sare," interrupted the master fisherman, who the reader may recollect was constituted the captain and proprietor of the cutter when it was dispatched from the schooner, and who was now sitting between Agnes and the priest, steering the boat, "stop, sare," he said, endeavouring to make himself understood in English, "me wees hear something they say there," and he made an almost imperceptible sign towards the bows of the cutter, where the sailors of the captured ship were sitting together, and speaking among themselves in a sort of half whisper. The master fisherman's attention had been attracted towards them by a few words which he had overheard, and being suspicious lest they should presume upon their numerical strength, and make an attempt to take possession of the cutter, he was anxious to make himself acquainted with their plans in order to anticipate them.

"We will never get ashore at this rate, Bill," said one sailor to another.

"I'll be d–n–d, if we will," answered the other, "what the devil does that d–n–d jack Spaniole know about steering a boat."

"Don't speak so loud," whispered another.

"He don't understand English, and I don't care if he did," answered the other.

"Yes, I think it is a devilish hard case," joined in another, "that we should be obliged to sit here and let that fellow, who don't know a jib from a paddle-box, steer the boat."

"What do you say if we take the management, my hearties?" inquired a lean, long-featured individual.

"Hum," groaned one.

"Suppose we do?" inquired another.

They whispered still lower among themselves for a moment.

"I say, you sir–you sir, keep her off, will you, don't you see the wind is right ahead?" shouted one to the master fisherman, in a tone of derision.

"Keep her head up, Mr. Spaniole, d'ye hear? don't you see the wind is turning her round?" cried another.

These insults seemed lost on the master fisherman, for he took them with marvellous fortitude.

"My good men," said the priest, "forbear: consider where we are, and under what circumstances we are placed; pray, do not endeavour to cause any quarrel."

"Mind your own business, parson, will you?" shouted a bolder sailor than the others, "it is you who already prevents us going any faster; so, if you don't wish to be sent to Davy Jones, hold your tongue."

The priest became now quite alarmed:

"Do not answer them," he whispered to the fisherman.

"Hollo! there; ready about," continued one of the sailors, apparently bent on provoking a quarrel, "ready about," and he proceeded to let go the jib-sheet.

The master fisherman now quickly stood up, with the marks of anger already becoming visible in his eyes.

"Stop, or me kill you," he cried, while he levelled one of the pistols, with which he was armed, at the audacious sailor.

"Kill him, will you," simultaneously shouted two of the sailors, and rushed together towards the stern of the cutter, "kill him, will you, you cutthroat Spaniard?"

The master fisherman stood firm where he was. He now held both of the pistols, which Appadocca had given him, and raising them to a small distance before him, awaited the two men.

Undeterred by the weapons, they rushed on.

"Stop for your life!" cried the master fisherman, highly excited.

"Be reasonable men," cried the priest, as he also stood up to defend himself.

The men came on; – flash, – a report – and the bullet pierced the foremost one. He fell into the bottom of the cutter, and rolled over the master fisherman's other man, who had been wrapped in sleep in that part from the very moment that he had got into the cutter.

"Hon!" he groaned and awoke, as the sailor that was shot rolled heavily upon him, when, seeing the blood, he jumped up.

The shrieks of Agnes, the fierce and deep Spanish oaths of the master fisherman at once told him how matters stood. He grasped the first of the sailors that came within his reach, and wrestled with him. Both fell into the bottom of the cutter, and rolled about on the ballast.

The quarrel had now assumed a serious aspect; furious at the death of their comrade, the other sailors rushed to the stern of the cutter. The master fisherman discharged the other pistol: it told, another sailor fell. But the shot was no sooner fired, than one of the two other sailors, closed with the master fisherman. They wrestled: each pressed successively his adversary on the side of the cutter, endeavouring to throw him overboard; but they were well matched: their strength was equal: now, the master fisherman was down, and seemed to be about to be thrown overboard; now he had the sailor down in the same position. Both fought with desperation, and clung with the pertinacity of iron to the side of the vessel. The cutter, having no one to steer it, had flown into the wind, its sails were flapping, and its boom was swinging violently, from one side to the other. The master fisherman was now down; over, over, the sailor was gradually pressing him; his grasp began to relax: he was bending farther towards the water; the sailor raised himself a little, so that he might have a better purchase to strike the final blow: as he did so, the boom swung violently, and struck him on the temple, with a great splash, he fell a yard or two into the water. The master fisherman quickly rose, and went to the assistance of the priest, who had met the attack of the remaining sailor, and was now holding him down in the bottom of the cutter. The master fisherman clutched a stone, and in his passion, was going to dash out the brains of the prostrate sailor.

"Hold!" cried the priest, "no more violence: bring a rope, and let us tie him."

The master fisherman drew back his arm, and let fall the stone. Even in his fury he felt the force of his natural veneration. He brought a rope, and tied the sailor down.

"Do the same to the other," said the priest, now almost exhausted by his effort, "tie him too."

The remaining sailor, who was still languidly rolling at the bottom of the cutter, with the fisherman, was next pinioned.

"See now to the wounded," said the priest, who now, when his first terror was over, displayed great presence of mind.

The two men who had been shot were examined. They still breathed, although their wounds were very serious.

The attention of the priest was now turned towards Agnes, who sat almost petrified with fear in the place where she was.

"Thank God, this danger is also past," said the priest to her, "I must be guilty of some grievous sin, indeed," continued the good father, "to have thus drawn down upon us the chastisement of Providence. Twice have we passed through bloodshed and death, and who knows what new perils we may still have to encounter before we reach Trinidad."

"Yes: and when shall we reach it? It looks as if we were never to get back," and Agnes was overwhelmed by a multiplicity of different feelings.

"Let me see," said the priest, "I think it would be easier to proceed straight towards it, than to be beating about on these seas."

"Have you any object to go to Grenada in preference to any other place?" he enquired of the master fisherman, who had now adjusted the sails of the cutter, and resumed the tiller.

"No, he had not," was the reply: "he was endeavouring to make that island because it was the nearest land indicated to him by the pirate captain."

"Would it not be easier to sail at once to Trinidad?" again asked the priest.

"Most decidedly," was the answer; "the distance was greater, it was true," added the master fisherman, but that was overbalanced by the fairness of the wind, because they would then be able to sail with a free sheet and should gain Trinidad within an infinitely shorter space of time than it would take to make Grenada, by beating up against the wind from the position in which they then were.

"Then let us steer to Trinidad," said the priest.

"Very well," replied the master fisherman.

The cutter was kept off, the sheets and tacks were slackened, and the little vessel, now feeling the full force of the wind began to tear through the water.

Away, away, it went. During day and during night the master fisherman sat gravely at the tiller; neither fatigue nor want of sleep could induce him to entrust for a moment the command of the little vessel to his man; "He had taken an oath," he said to the priest, when he requested him to take some rest.

It was on a beautiful morning when the priest and Agnes, on awaking from their uncomfortable slumbers, beheld themselves within the Gulf of Paria.

They looked with highly-pleased astonishment at the master fisherman, who wearied and worn, still sat at the rudder. He returned the glance with the same visible contentment and pleasure.

"We are indebted to you, my good fisherman, for your incomparable conduct towards us. We shall scarcely be ever able to show you sufficient gratitude," he said.

"Not at all: we must deal well towards those who conduct themselves in a proper manner to us," said the fisherman, in the best manner he could; "now I am at home again; I am on my own gulf,—where do you wish to be landed, sir?"

"Land us wherever you please: we will be always able to make our way to Cedros," answered the priest.

"To Cedros? I shall take you there at once," answered the master fisherman, and then turned the cutter's head to that part of the island.

"Agnes," whispered the priest, "I have always found much that is to be admired in the humbler classes; they require but proper treatment, as all other men do."

"This seems to be a very worthy man," replied Agnes, more in respect to the priest than from any desire to converse, for Agnes had ceased to be over communicative since the capture of the vessel in which she had been a passenger.

The sugar-cane fields arose more conspicuous and beautiful to the view as the vessel drew nearer and nearer to the land; and within a few hours Agnes arrived on the plantation and was locked in the affectionate embrace of her aged father.

CHAPTER XVII

"And winds of all the corners kissed your sails
To make your vessel nimble."
CYMBELINE

"Had not their bark been very slow of sail."
COMEDY OF ERRORS

THE grey dawn of the morning found the crew of the man-of-war busily at work. The unwieldy machines clanked and reclanked as the sturdy sailors heartily threw their whole strength upon them, in raising the heavy sails and weighty anchor.

As soon as there was sufficient light to see, watches, who were provided with the most powerful telescopes, were sent up to the very top of the tall masts to survey the horizon, in order to discover, if possible, the pirate vessel, which was supposed to be hovering about at no great distance.

After a careful survey, the report was made, that far out to leeward there was a sail – that it was apparently a vessel which was lying-to.

"Look again," shouted out the officer of the watch, "what is she like? is she square-rigged?"

"No, your honor."

"What sort of a thing is she?"

"She looks to be a fore-and-aft, your honor."

Willmington was called, and, on being required to do so, gave the best description he could of the pirate vessel.

"It is likely the same vessel," the officer remarked, after he had heard Willmington.

"Cheerily, men, look active."

The sailors scarcely required any exhortation. They went through their work with more than ordinary good-will. In the first place, the idea of something like active service excited them, for they felt oppressed under the ennui of leisurely sailing from one port to another; and they longed to chastise the rash temerity of those degraded wretches who had the insolence to make an attempt of rescuing a prisoner from their lordly ship.

The majestic structure, therefore, was soon put in motion, and was now to be seen sailing magnificently before the wind. Gradually it gained on what was at first distant and obscure. As the ship drew nearer and nearer to it, the vessel grew more and more distinct, and could now be clearly made out as a long, low, rakish schooner. It was, in fact, the Black Schooner.

The huge vessel-of-war approached nearer and still nearer, but the schooner remained still stationary where she was. The sailors of the man-of-war prepared for action with enthusiasm. They could easily judge, from the shape of the schooner, and its peculiar rig, that she was the vessel of a pirate, if not of the pirate of whom they had so often heard. They saw their prize before them. The schooner, they thought, must yield to the superior strength of the man-of-war, and her conquest would be the easiest thing in the world. Besides, the little vessel could not but perceive their approach, and as she did not sail away, they argued there must needs be some cause, either mutiny or some other disagreement on board, which neutralized the authority of those in power, and which, consequently, would make her a still easier prize. They prepared their guns, on this account, with the keenest alacrity and lightness of heart, for men are always the more enthusiastic and brave when they are pretty well assured that they can command success.

The large vessel sailed down on the small schooner, that was still lying-to, the standard of England was already waving from the spanker, the men were standing at their several stations, and the commander himself, who had now come on deck, was anxiously waiting until he came within gun-shot of the schooner, to signal her to surrender. The ship drew still closer, the order was given to make ready to fire, when . . . . like the shadowy fleetness of a dream, the masts of the Black Schooner at once became clothed in canvas, the black ensign with the cross bones and skull ran up the line on her gaff in chilling solemnity, while on the top of her raking masts floated two long pendant flags as red as blood, and the sharp vessel began to glide like a serpent silently over the waters.

Fearful of losing his prize, which was well-nigh within his reach, the commander of the ship-of-war observing the movements of the little vessel, quickly gave the order to fire. A loud and rending report of several guns at once echoed over the waves, and the shots dipped, and dipped, and dipped again, and fell harmless within a short distance of the schooner. The flag of the pirate schooner was lowered and hoisted, lowered and hoisted, lowered and hoisted again, in derision, as she steadily held her course. Another discharge . . . and the shots sank as harmless as before: again the pirates lowered and hoisted their flags.

Every sail was set on the unwieldy ship, and her enormous studding-sails covered her yards and booms. Her hull could scarcely be seen, under the vast sheets that shaded her. The waves boiled up on each side of her bows, and like a whale, furious with a wound, she left behind her a wake of foam.

The Black Schooner glided along like a slender gar. Confident of the fleetness of their vessel, the pirates seemed inclined to mock the large and threatening fabric that was pursuing them. Ever and anon they changed their tack, and the vessel itself, which seemed to anticipate their wishes, played gracefully on the blue surface.

When all the ship's studding-sails were set, and she was sailing rapidly before the wind, they would suddenly change their course, and draw their obedient vessel as close as possible up to the wind. As soon again as the man-of-war went through the labour of taking in her superfluous sails, again they would change their course. Now they shortened their sails, and then, as the ship gained on them, they had them up again as if by magic. Now they sailed away to a great distance, and then tacked and returned as if to meet and brave the pursuers; all the time, however, they kept out of the reach of the man-of-war's guns with astonishing precision.

The chase continued thus the whole day, until night came and veiled pursuer and pursued.

Vexed with disappointment, and irritated by the taunts of the pirates, the commander of the man-of-war ordered the sails to be taken in, and the vessel to be luffed up* into the wind. The order was immediately obeyed, and the crew, in thorough disgust, went away from the station to which they had that morning rushed with so much buoyancy.

It was, indeed, sufficient, to try the moral fortitude of the most philosophical. On one side there was a large heavy vessel, of size sufficiently huge to have crushed two such vessels as the pirate-schooner, from mere contact: on the other was that small and light vessel, which could be so easily destroyed, but which, notwithstanding the most eager desire on the part of the commander and crew to capture her, had so tantalizingly escaped them. After the continued chase of a whole day, the large vessel had proved as impotent and as incapable of carrying out their wishes, as a piece of floating

*luffed up: with the head of a ship turned toward the wind.

timber; and what was still more galling, they had, in addition, been exposed to the most annoying derision of the pirates. Worse again, there was no probability of her being able, at any time, to overtake the schooner; for it was too clear that their vessel could not sail so fast as she. The only chance of their capturing her was, in their taking her by surprise, an event which could not be reasonably calculated upon, when the pirates exhibited so much prudence and precision. The sailors, therefore, doggedly retired to their respective cots, muttering all the while, strong and complicated oaths against the individual who built the fast-sailing schooner.

As for the commander himself, he bore the disappointment with the less dumb patience, as the discipline of the ship did not bind him down to so much silence, as it did the crew. He fumed only as seamen can fume, and vowed, in the extremity of his anger, that he would perpetrate, Heaven only knew, what extent of cruelty,–which he never meant,–upon the insolent pirates, if he once had them in his power.

When calmer moments, however, succeeded to his wrathful feelings of disappointment, he began to think deeply on the course which it was prudent to adopt, in order to have a probable chance of capturing or destroying the schooner. The batteries and the crew of the ship, he rightly concluded, were of no use against an enemy that was sufficiently wise and experienced always to keep beyond the range of his guns; and, as for overtaking the schooner, it was a matter of absolute impossibility. He could decide on no clear plan. He, therefore, resolved, in that conjuncture, to sail about in those parts under little canvas, and trust to accident for a means of capturing the pirate vessel. The ship was, therefore, kept under only a part of her sails that whole night, and she moved almost imperceptibly.

At the first dawn of the next morning, watches were sent up the masts, and the horizon was carefully surveyed in search of the enemy which night had shrouded. Nothing was to be seen. The watch was, nevertheless, continued.

About four hours after sunrise, a vessel could be barely distinguished on the horizon. It was steering in the direction of the man-of-war. It rapidly approached, and as it drew nearer and nearer, it was discovered to be a long, low, sharp-built brig, with white port-holes, apparently a Mediterranean trader. She sailed so fast, that within three hours from the time when she was first discovered, she was opposite the large ship. She passed her at a short distance, but beyond the range of her guns.

The man-of-war immediately hoisted her ensign as a signal to the brig to show her colours; in answer to this signal, the strange vessel hoisted the Mexican flag.

The extraordinary speed of the strange brig, her low hull, the more than ordinary symmetry of her make and rigging, could not pass unobserved. They at once attracted the notice, and called forth the admiration of the sailors on board of the man-of-war; and leaning carelessly on the bulwarks, they were studying the beautiful brig before them, and were viewing her with the delight that seamen experience when they see a fine vessel.

"If that ain't that ere identical pirate customer as we chased yesterday," said an old grey-headed sailor, gravely, as he stood looking at her, "it's one of the same sort, I know."

"What are you saying, now," asked a young man next to him. "Why, the vessel we chased yesterday was a fore-and-aft schooner, and this one is a brig: where are your eyes?"

"Is this all you know?" inquired the old tar, indifferently, with a slight satirical smile. "Well, let me tell you, younker, that them ere customers change their skins, just like snakes, by G–d; and these eyes of mine that you inquire of, winked at a sou-wester long before you knowed what was what, my boy," and the old seaman walked away to attend to some passing occupation, while, from time to time, he cast a stealthy look from under his spreading straw hat, at the vessel he seemed to hold in suspicion.

This feeling towards the Mexican brig was not confined to the common sailors alone: all seamen have an eye for the beautiful in ships. The commander himself was struck by the remarkably fine proportions of the vessel. He interrupted his habitual walk to gaze at her.

"A fine craft that is, Charles," said he to his son.

"Yes, sir," replied the latter, "a very beautiful model."

"Look at her run, what a beautiful stern, and how sharp at the bows!" continued the old gentleman, with enthusiasm.

"And how remarkably fast she sails, too," rejoined Charles.

"Hum!" remarked the old gentleman, "she seems very light to be a trader."

"It strikes me so, too," replied Charles.

"The merchant who could have built that vessel to carry cocoa and coffee, must have been a very great fool, Charles," continued the commander, still looking at the tidy brig that was sailing away magnificently before them.

"Yes, sir."

"I begin to have my suspicions, Charles," resumed the commander, after a pause, "that Mexican flag protects many a rascal: I shall make the fellow heave to."

So saying, he ordered a gun to be fired, as a signal to the brig to lie to. The report of the huge machine of destruction rang over the waters, and the shot skipped the waves and sank. The suspicious brig paid no attention to it, but held her course, and, in four hours' time, went out of sight, leaving the commander in now stronger suspicion with regard to her nature and character, and, in a furious rage into which he was thrown by the cool contempt with which his command was treated. He looked at the brig that was leaving his vessel behind, as if the latter was at anchor, and fretted, when he considered that his large ship was unable to enforce his order on account of its comparative slowness. With greater impatience than reason he looked only at what was, for the moment, a defect in the large man-of-war, and forgot, at the time, that if the two small vessels which had so mortified him, those two consecutive days, had over his ship the accident of speed, she, in her turn, possessed the infinitely more serviceable advantage of greater strength and more heavy metal.

"Well, younker," said the same old sailor of the morning, to the same young man who had doubted his penetration, "well, younker, what do you think of that ere customer now, eh? He has the wind in his maintopsail, has'nt he? and seems to have plenty of pride of his own, and won't speak to nobody. Ay, ay, them customers, never throw away words or shots, I know. Come, younker, I'll give you a another wrinkle," continued the old tar.

"Well, let's have it?"

"Mark my word," continued the old sailor, in a low and mysterious tone, "if you don't see that ere customer again, before long, my name is not what it is, I know," and winking impressively on his hearers, he rolled away chuckling with self-satisfaction.

The man-of-war continued there the remaining portion of that day and the night which ensued: nothing happened, during that period of time, to relieve the longing anxiety of the man-of-war's people.

The next morning the usual watches were again sent up the masts. About noon, a vessel came in sight. It was steering, like the one of the previous day, directly towards the man-of-war; and seemed to approach her with an equal degree of speed. As she drew nearer and nearer, she was made out to be a light brigantine, such as those that are to be seen on the Mediterranean. Strange, however, the hull and make seemed to be the same as those of the vessel spoken the day before: but the new comer, instead of painted port-holes, had but a plain white streak.

The men evinced the same admiration for this "craft," to use their own term, as they did for the one of the day before. There was, however, such a striking similarity in the hulls of the two vessels, that their admiration soon gave place to a feeling of mixed surprise and suspicion.

"What can those two crafts be?" they mutually asked each other.

"They are men-of-war," some answered: "but where are the port-holes of this customer?"

"By jingo! I think they are pleasure boats," said one.

"Oh, no, they look to me like Malaga boats," said another.

"But they are of the same make," observed a third.

"Ay, ay, don't you see they are sister-vessels, fools, and are on the same voyage?" said another, gravely, who, up to that time, had maintained unbroken silence, and had, with the aid of a serious aspect, looked wisdom itself.

"Ay, that's it, that's it," they all cried, at this suggestion, "they belong to the same owner, and are on the same voyage."

All seemed to concur in this opinion, except the same old sailor, who, on the previous day, regarded the Mexican brig with so much suspicion. He seemed to entertain doubts about this new vessel, as he did with regard to the other.

"Well, younker, what do you think of this fresh gentleman, now?" he said, satirically, to the unfortunate young man who had offended his self-esteem, and who seemed now to be entirely devoted to the revengeful ridicule of that elder son of Neptune.

"Don't know," was the crabbed reply.

"Don't know, eh? you will know, perhaps, when them young eyes of yours have squinted oftner at the sun, my hearty, hi, hi, hi!"

The brigantine drew nearer and nearer, and seemed carefully to measure the same distance at which the brig of the day before had passed. She came with her sails filled with the fresh breeze, and was passing the man-of-war, when one of the heavy guns of the large vessel was fired. The shot fell across the brigantine's bows, but at some distance from her.

Her sails still bellied with the wind; she still skipped along, and the beautiful and pure white wavelets of foam still swelled on each of her sides.

"Who the devil you may be, I shall have you to-day," said the commander, looking intently fierce at the brigantine. "Give him another shot."

Another deafening report was heard, and the grey smoke shrouded for a moment the dark riggings of the war-vessel, and then grew thinner and thinner, and rose above her masts.

A moment after, four flags ran up the peak of the brigantine.

"Ho! read what the fellow says, Mr. Cypher," cried the commander, with no small degree of excitement, "he hears what we can say, I see."

Mr. Cypher took the telescope.

"Y," he said, "O," he continued, "U,"–"YOU," he proclaimed, with a loud voice.

"Hoist the answering pendant:" it was done.

The first four flags of the brigantine were now lowered, and four others hoisted in their place.

"A," proceeded Mr. Cypher, deciphering the new signal, "R," "E,"– "ARE,"–"you are."

"Hoist the answering pendant:" it was done again.

The four flags were again lowered on board the brigantine, and four new ones were again hoisted. They were read, and were found to signify 'too.'

"What can the fellow want to say?" inquired the commander, vaguely: "answer his signal."

The signal was answered, and other flags were again hoisted on board the brigantine. When all the signals were taken together, they read–

"You are too far, your guns don't carry."

While at the conclusion of the process of exchanging signals, the broad black flag, with its head and bones, was spread over the mainsail.

"The rascals," muttered the old commander, as he moved away from the bulwarks, with indignant disgust, "it is the same set, may the devil take them!"

"Ha, younker, what d'you see now, eh? You will believe old Jack Gangway another time, I know," said the same old sailor, who all along had been so knowing and so suspicious.

"Crack on, crack on," cried the old commander, "and haul your wind, we may edge up to her on a close bowline, and let her feel our metal."

All the sails of the large vessel were now set. She was drawn closely to the wind, and leaned under the fresh breeze.

No sooner was this manœuvre completed, than the brigantine's sails were also trimmed, her long yards were braced sharp; her vast mainsail was pulled in almost on a line with her rudder, and her head was put almost into the point of the wind itself, or, as seamen would designate it, into the "eye of the wind," her stern was turned to the ship-of-war, and as she gradually left the latter behind, other four flags ran along the signal line. When read they said–

"Au revoir."

And the black flag rose and fell, rose and fell again, at the mocking ceremony, that was intended to accompany this salutation.

This chase continued the rest of the day. The hours quickly fleeted by, and when gauzy twilight had shed its soothing and dreamy haze around, a few waves of the pirate's flag, might still be dimly perceived, like the trembling of the phantom—leaves of dream; and then darkness spread its shrouding mantle over the ocean.

The sun had risen, the man-of-war was lying-to under one or two sails, the others had been taken in during the night; at some distance in the direction, in which the brigantine had disappeared, a vessel, apparently a wreck, was to be seen. She was a barque: portions of her masts were broken away; her rigging was slack, loose, and dry; her racketty yards waved from one direction to the other, as she clumsily rolled into the trough of the sea, or rose heavily on its crest. Their braces dangled loosely and neglectedly about, and either dragged overboard, or swung with a spring from one part of the deck to the other. In keeping with her disordered gear, her hull itself exhibited the greatest neglect and uncleanliness: the barnacles grew unmolested, to a considerable height, and the marks of the lee-water from the scuppers, stained her sides. The few sails which still remained on the unsteady yards were tattered and worn, and tied up in the oddest manner imaginable. The vessel had her English ensign tied upside down, in token of distress, on the little that remained of the main-mast's rigging: an indication, which was not by any means required, inasmuch as the miserable manner in which she rolled about, was quite sufficient in itself, to tell that she was in a wretched condition.

As soon as the distressed vessel was perceived, signals were made to her to launch her boats, and to send alongside; but they seemed to be either not understood, or the people of the barque had no means of answering them.

But one solitary individual was to be seen standing on its deck, at the gangway, and wistfully looking towards the man-of-war.

The commander was not willing to launch any of his boats, he had, during the three or four days that had lately expired been so much cheated by pirates, that he was now made more than ordinarily cautious, and he repeated his signals, and waited many hours, either to have them answered, or to force the people of the distressed ship to launch their boat and come alongside his vessel: but neither the one thing or the other was done.

"These fellows can't be cheats," he said, "else they would have sailed away, though, it strikes me, it would be difficult for them to spread a sail on those yards of theirs," said the commander, as his good feelings began to press upon him.

"They may be starved to death, or ill, have a boat launched, sir," said he to the officer, after this short soliloquy, "and let them pull to those poor fellows. Tell the officer he must not let any of the men go on board, he may do so himself, if he thinks it necessary."

Joyfully the true-hearted sailors, eager to succour their suffering brothers, lowered a boat, which a moment afterwards was bounding away in the direction of the distressed vessel.

They soon approached near enough to admit of speaking, and at his order, the men rested on their oars to allow the midshipman in command to hail the barque.

"What ship is that?" asked the midshipman.

"The Sting," answered the solitary individual, who was standing at the gangway.

"Where from, and whither bound?"

"From Pernambuco to Liverpool," answered the individual.

"What cargo?" demanded the midshipman.

"Cayenne pepper," answered the individual.

"What is the matter with you?" asked the midshipman.

"Have been boarded by pirates—by a Black Schooner—men cut down in defending the vessel—the pirates left but me and another man, who is now ill below—they took away every thing," answered the individual.

"It must be those same devils of pirates," whispered the boatmen one to the other, "who have raked that cove; what fellows they seem to be, we will singe them some of those days though—be damn'd if we don't."

"If you would only let one of your men come on board for a moment to help me trim the yards, I should be all right," added the individual at the gangway.

"Hum!" muttered the young midshipman; "that's not much, but I fancy, old boy, you will do yourself no good in setting your sails, unless you wish the wind to help you take them in. Pull alongside, men," he said, after a second or two, "I shall go on deck and help him."

The boat soon boarded the vessel.

"Keep the boat off," said the officer, as he grasped the ropes of the steps.

"Ay, ay, sir," said the boatswain, and the boat was shoved off from the vessel.

A shrill sound was heard, the apparent sides of the distressed barque opened, the stern fell heavily into the water, the racketty yards and old ropes went over the side, and from amidst the wreck of the skeleton ship, the Black Schooner sprang forth as she felt the power of her snow-white sails, which, with the rapidity of lightning, had now clothed her tall masts.

This metamorphosis was so sudden, that the schooner had already begun to move before the boatmen comprehended the change. They quickly pulled alongside, and fastened their hooks, but no hand of man could hold them. They were all torn away by the speed with which the schooner went. Every man in his turn let go his hold, and the boat, with its angry crew, was left floating far behind in the wake of the flying schooner.

CHAPTER XVIII

"Demand me nothing; what you know you know;
From this time forth I never will speak word."
                                          OTHELLO

"Torments will ope your lips."
                                          IBID

AFTER he had been defeated by the untoward accident of the shark in his attempt to rescue his captive chief, Lorenzo betook himself on board the schooner, a victim of disappointment and disgust.

He felt irresistibly inclined to break out in the most violent terms, and hurried down into his cabin as soon as he got on the deck of the schooner. He then partially gave vent to his feelings by speaking almost aloud.

"It would have been bearable," he said, "bearable, if we had fought, and had been driven back; but to be foiled at the very moment when we were completing a breach, by a brute of a shark: confound it, and all other sharks, the brutes!" and thrusting his hand deeply into the bosom of his coat, he paced rapidly up and down his narrow cabin, while, from time to time, his lips moved violently as if he were repeating his anathemas against the particular shark and all the others.

This fit, however, did not continue long.

Schooled under the continual insecurity and danger which attended the life that he led, in which safety itself demanded the exercise of the greatest foresight and calmness, he speedily curbed his instinctive impulses of rage, and immediately began to deliberate with coolness and precision on the next measures which it was requisite for him to take.

He did not deliberate long. Accustomed to act in the face of danger, and to oppose his ready resources to sudden contingencies, he never required much time to debate with himself on the best and most prudent course to be adopted under unforeseen circumstances of danger. At this conjuncture, he resolved to watch the man-of-war closely, and to embrace the very first opportunity either to steal away Appadocca, or to rescue him at a calculated sacrifice of some of his men. For that purpose, the schooner was kept in the same position in which she was, until, as we have seen, the man-of-war made the descent upon her. Lorenzo purposely awaited the approach of the large vessel, so that he might have the opportunity of keeping, as he intended, close to the man-of-war. Nothing ever escaped the disciplined vigilance of the pirates, and although they seemed to be taken by surprise, still they had their eyes all the time on the movements of the pursuing vessel; and, as the reader has seen, disappointed so signally the encouraged expectations of its crew and commander.

When night had put an end to the chase of that day, Lorenzo put his men busily at work.

In a few moments, the ordinary sails of the Black Schooner were symmetrically folded within the smallest imaginable size, and carefully covered up at the foot of each of the masts, and from under the deck, yards, cordage, and sails for a square-rigged vessel were brought up, and, in as short a time, the thin tapering masts were seen garnished with the numerous ropes, yards, and sails of a full-rigged brig; while to complete the metamorphosis, strips of new canvas were carefully cut in the shape of the imitation portholes, which are generally painted on the sides of merchant vessels, and were closely fastened to the sides of the Black Schooner, and adjusted in such a careful manner as to conceal completely the guns of the disguised vessel.

It was in this guise that the Black Schooner passed before the man-of-war, and showed Mexican colors.

After Lorenzo had closely reconnoitred his pursuer, and had raised the suspicion which procured him the salute of a gun, he again sailed away out of sight, and with the same expedition as of the night before, the mainmast of the apparent brig was immediately divested of its yards, and, in their places, the sharp sails of a schooner were again set. In the rig of a brigantine, the Black Schooner again passed before the man-of-war.

But these distant surveys, for caution prevented him from going within the range of the ship's guns, were not sufficient to satisfy Lorenzo, who now began to suffer under the most impatient anxiety with regard to the safety of his chief and friend.

The brave officer feared, that annoyed by his inability to overtake the schooner, the commander of the ship might, perhaps, have immediately ordered the execution of his prisoner; that Appadocca might, by that time, have been dealt with in the summary manner in which pirates were usually treated, and had been hanged on the yard-arm without accusation, hearing, or judgment.

"If so," cried Lorenzo, as this fear grew more and more upon him, "if so, I swear, by the living G–d, that I shall burn that large vessel to the very keel, and shall not spare one, not a single one of its numerous crew to tell the tale–cost what it may, by G–d, I'll do it."

To procure information, therefore, about the fate of one whom he loved as a brother: and in order to satisfy his doubts, he resolved at once on taking one or two of the man-of-war's men, and settled on the expedient of the distressed barque, with which the reader has just been made acquainted.

The young midshipman had no sooner laid his foot on the deck of the disguised schooner, before he was strongly grasped by the powerful arm of a man who had been carefully concealed behind the false bulwarks of the skeleton barque, while the voice of Jim Splice–he was the man–whispered in his ear,–

"Don't resist, young countryman, all right."

But as soon as the first impulse of the young officer had passed away, and he discovered that he was left on board a vessel which presented an un-mistakeable appearance of being engaged in some forbidden trade, and when he saw before him numbers of fierce-looking, armed men, he strug-gled for a moment, and succeeded in drawing his sword. But Lorenzo, the formerly solitary man on the deck of the distressed vessel, calmly stepped up to him, and said,–

"Young gentleman, be not alarmed, no violence will be done to you: sheath your sword," and casting his eyes around on the men, continued, "you see, it will not be of much service to you against such odds."

"Who are you?" peevishly inquired the young officer, "what do you in-tend to do with me?"

"I shall soon tell you," replied Lorenzo, "if you will be good enough to accompany me to my cabin."

"What cabin? and what to do? You may cut my throat here," said the midshipman, angrily.

"Perhaps you would not be so unreasonable," remarked Lorenzo, softly, "if you were to hear the little that I have to inquire of you: pray, come with me."

"I shall not go with you," angrily rejoined the midshipman, "I am in the hands of pirates, I know. You may murder me, where I am, but I shall not go down with you to any cabin."

"Then stay where you are," coolly answered Lorenzo, and he walked away to the after part of the schooner, and ordered Jim Splice to let go the young man.

The older sailor relaxed his grasp, but availed himself of the opportunity which he now had, to whisper in the ears of the midshipman –

"Don't attempt to crow too high here, shipmate, else you will get the worst of it, d'ye hear?"

And the old tar winked his eye to the young midshipman. The familiar sign of knowingness contrasted strangely with the terrible moustachios and beard with which Jim Splice had deemed it characteristic to ornament his homely and good-natured old face.

In the meantime all sail was set, and the man-of-war was left far behind. The sailors had now again posted themselves at their regular stations, and the ordinary quiet had now succeeded to the short excitement of making sail. The midshipman was still standing in the same spot where Lorenzo had left him. His anger, however, had evaporated to a considerable extent, under the wise prescription of leaving the angry man to himself, which Lorenzo was wise enough to make, and like all men who are not absolutely fools, the midshipman had thrown off as much as possible of that wasting and useless attendant – rage, as soon as his first impulses had somewhat subsided.

Instead of continuing in that dogged sulkiness, in which he had been left by Lorenzo, he was now examining, with an interested eye, the make, rigging, and equipment of the strange schooner.

It was at this moment that a steward approached him, and inquired if he was then at leisure to attend his master in his cabin, and led the way to the part of the vessel in which that was situated. The midshipman, without answering, followed. Lorenzo was already there, waiting for him. The officer politely stood, bowed to the stranger, pointed to a cabin chair: the midshipman seated himself.

"Before mentioning the business for which I have entrapped you, young gentleman," said Lorenzo, "I must tell you, that you need be under no apprehension as long as you are on board this schooner, and that you shall receive the proper treatment that one gentleman owes to another, unless, it is understood, you force us, by your own conduct, to act otherwise than we usually do."

"Gentleman! how dare you compare yourself to me, and call yourself a gentleman?" said the midshipman, with more of impulse than of reason.

Like one who has disciplined his mind to pursue his purposes, with a steadfast straightness which is not to be diverted by any accident, though not, perhaps, without some disdain for the immoderation of the young man, the pirate officer heeded not his last remark, but proceeded as if he had not heard it.

"My purpose for enticing you on board this vessel, is to procure information about my chief, who is now a prisoner on board the ship to which you belong. You will be good enough to give clear and categorical answers to the questions which I shall put to you."

This was said in a firm, although cool tone.

"What? do you imagine," inquired the young officer, with scorn, "I am going to tell to a pirate what takes place on board a vessel in which I have the honour to serve? By Jove, no!—it is hard enough to be kidnapped by a set of rascals, without being asked to play traitor and spy, to boot. But—"

"Cease this nonsense," interposed Lorenzo, "you waste time, answer me first, is Appadocca alive?"

"I shall not give you any information," peevishly replied the young officer.

"I do not see," remarked Lorenzo, mildly, and almost paternally, "I do not see that it can possibly affect your honour if you give me a very simple answer to a very simple question. I ask, if Emmanuel Appadocca is alive?"

"I shall answer you nothing," said the midshipman, insultingly.

"Shall answer me nothing," calmly echoed Lorenzo, while, like the still and steady terrors of an earthquake, the signs of anger were now fast gathering on his brow. He reflected a moment.

"Young man," he said firmly, men do not usually speak with negatives to me, or such as I am. You seem disposed to run great risks—risks, of the nature of which you are not, perhaps, aware. Let me caution you again; I put my former question,—is the captain of this schooner, who is now a prisoner on board the ship to which you belong, alive and safe?"

"I have said I shall answer none of your questions," replied the midshipman, "trouble me no more."

The pirate officer rose, and drew forth a massive gold watch.

"You see," said he, pointing to the time-piece, "that the minute-hand is now on twelve, when it reaches the spot which marks the quarter-of-an-hour, I shall expect an answer. In the meantime make your reflections. If you wish for any refreshment speak to the man outside, and you shall have whatever you desire." So saying, the officer rose, made a slight bow, and left the cabin.

The young officer being left alone, seemed by no means inclined to trouble himself about the last speech of the pirate officer. He moved about the cabin restlessly. Sometimes he stopped to examine one object, and then another.

No further thought than that of the moment seemed to intrude on his mind; and the consequence of his persistence in refusing to answer the questions of the pirate officer never seemed to break in upon him. The levity of youth was, perhaps, one of the principal causes of this strange carelessness. He was also highly swayed by the notions which he had gathered from among those in whose society he lived. These led him to entertain an extravagant idea of his own importance, which, among other things, could not admit of accepting terms from the officer of any nation that was lower than his own, and, least of all, from a villainous pirate. He, therefore, affected to treat the pirate officer with a contempt, which it was as inexpedient to show, as it was silly to entertain.

He was moving about in the temper which we have described, when the door of the cabin opened, and Lorenzo entered. He moved up to the upper part of the cabin, and seated himself.

"Will you now answer my question?" he demanded, "the hand is on the quarter."

"I have already told you, no," replied the youth.

Lorenzo called – an attendant appeared.

"Let the officer of the watch send down four men," he said.

The attendant retired. In a few moments four men, under the command of a junior officer, entered the cabin. Lorenzo stood – pointed to the midshipman –

"Torture him until he speaks," he said, and abruptly left the cabin.

The pirates silently advanced on their victim.

"The first man that dares approach me, shall die under this sword," shrieked the midshipman, furiously, and brandished his sword, madly. Still the pirates advanced more closely to him. They beat down his guard, surrounded him, and, in the twinkling of an eye, he was bound hand and foot. Lifting him bodily, the pirates carried him on their shoulders out of the cabin.

He was then taken to a narrow compartment at the very bows of the vessel, that was, it seemed, the torture-room.

The appearance of the room was sufficient to strike one at once with an idea of the bloody and cruel deeds that might be perpetrated there. It was a narrow cabin into which the light could never penetrate; for there was no opening either for that or for fresh air. The small door which led into it was narrow and low: it turned on a spring, and seemed so difficult to be opened, that one was forced to imagine that it was either loth to let out those that had once got in, or that it was eager to close in for ever upon those that might enter through it.

The deck was scoured as white as chalk, and, like the shops of cleanly butchers in the morning, was scattered over with sand. The sides of the cabin, as if to augment the darkness that already reigned, were painted a dark, sombre, and gloomy colour, which was here and there stained by the damp.

In contrast to this prevalent hue of frightful black, hung a variety of exquisitely-polished torturing instruments. Cruelty, or expediency, or necessity, seems to have exhausted its power of invention in designing them, so different were they in form, and so horridly suited to the purpose of giving pain.

These seemed to frown malignantly on those who entered that narrow place; and the imagination might even trace, in their burnished hue, and high efficient condition, a morbid desire, or longing, to be used.

To make the "darkness visible,"* and to reveal the horror of the place, an old bronzed lamp hung from the beams of the upper deck, and threw a faint and sickly light around.

In the centre of this cabin lay a long, narrow, and deep box, which was garnished within with millions of sharp-pointed spikes. The torture which the victim suffered in this machine, was a continued pricking from the spikes, against which he was every moment suddenly and violently driven by the lurching of the vessel.

In this the midshipman was immediately thrown, and he shrieked the shriek of the dying when he was roughly thrown on the sharp instruments.

"Hell! hell! the torments of hell," he yelled out, as the sharp spikes pierced him to the quick.

As he made an effort to turn, he increased his agony, and as the vessel heaved, the points went deeper and deeper into his flesh.

Already the suffering of the young man was at its height, and by the livid light of the glimmering lamp, large drops of death-like sweat, could now be seen flowing over his pallid face, which was locked in excruciating pain.

"Oh, God!" he cried, frantic with suffering, "Heaven save me."

His executioners stood around immovable, calm, and fierce, as they al-

---

*"darkness visible": one of the characteristics of Hell in John Milton's epic poem, *Paradise Lost* (1667). See 1:63.

ways were, more like demons sucking in the pleasure of mortal's pains, than men.

The young man seemed maddened with pain, his shrieks pierced through even the close sides of the torture-room.

"Will you speak?" inquired the officer.

"Yes–no. Oh, good God! No–yes: curse you all–you devils; you demons–d–n you," were the frenzied replies.

An hour passed; his pains and shrieks continued; albeit the latter now grew fainter and fewer. Nature could endure no more: his nervous system sank under pain and exhaustion, and he swooned.

The pirates removed him, and plied him with restoratives, and he gradually revived.

The suffering of the midshipman had produced a weakening effect upon him, such as disease produces on the strongest minds; it had destroyed his hot and fierce spirit. Yes, the pain of the body had conquered the resolution of the mind, and after the first torturing, the young officer was less spirited, less boisterous, and less impatient.

Animation had scarcely returned, when the wretched victim was again thrown on the spikes which, piercing through his fresh wounds, added still more to the agony which he had before endured. The pain this time was not bearable.

"Oh! save me from this," the young man cried, convulsively, "kill me at once."

"We want not your life, what good is that to us?" replied the junior officer in command of the pirates, "we wish only to hear about our captain, who may be at this moment undergoing the same pains as you."

"Then remove me, and I shall speak. No, yes, no, yes."

"You will then cease to play the fool at your own cost," was the laconic and unsympathizing reply of the above-mentioned officer, who, at the same time, dispatched one of his men to report that the prisoner was willing to speak.

Lorenzo, in a few moments, crept into the narrow room.

"Will you now answer my question?" he inquired of the victim.

"Yes."

"Is the captain alive and safe?"

"Yes."

"What are the intentions of your captain about him?"

"To–oh! take me away from these spikes: oh! these cursed spikes."

"Speak."

"To take him to Trinidad, to be tried."

"When is your ship to direct her course to that place?–Take him out, men."

The victim was taken out.

"She was–oh! what happiness–she was to do so, to-day."

"That's enough. Young man, I admire your spirit: it might be developed into something useful under proper discipline; as you are, at present, you are only a slave of impulses, that are as wild as your original self. Take him to the surgeon's room."

Giving this order to his men, Lorenzo left the cabin of torture.

CHAPTER XIX

"If I do lose thee, I do lose a thing
That none but fools would keep; a breath thou art,
Servile to all the skyey influences,
That dost this habitation where thou keepest
Hourly afflict:"
                                        MEASURE FOR MEASURE

WHEN the men of the man-of-war pulled on board, after their young officer had been entrapped into the schooner, and reported the occurrence to the commander, notwithstanding the great command which, considering his life and avocation, he had over himself, he flew into a violent passion. The success which had, up to that time, attended the pirates, either in flying from him, or in outwitting him, had already tried his patience to the utmost. To have met an enemy equally armed, to have tried the fortune of a fight with him, and to have been beaten would not, perhaps, have had such a mortifying effect on the mind of the old commander as to have been subjected to the tantalizing deceptions and mocking cunning of the pirates.

He walked the deck as furiously as his gouty old limbs would carry him, and spoke to himself in a voice that was hoarse with passion.

"First," said he, "the blackguards waited until I was just about to give the order to fire, and then sprang out of my reach. Then their d–n–d schooner sailed so fast, and this tub of a thing was so slow, that by G–d, by making the masts creak again, I could not force her to move faster; while all the time those d–n–d villains were playing about me, and amusing themselves at my expense: the devil take them. Then the rascals went and took down their own sails, and rigged themselves up in a brig's canvas, and passed by me—fool as I was. I showed the blackguards bunting, instead of sending a broadside into them at once, d–n them; and now, at noon-day, when the sun is high in the heavens, when every man can see fifty miles before him, I have let those rascals come almost alongside, and kidnap one of my officers. D–n them, d–n them.

"I tell you what it is, Charles," continued the old gentleman, red in the face with rage, "the weight of a feather in my mind would make me hang—by G–d, yes–hang at once that astronomical friend of yours; hang, I say, on one yard-arm, and that d–n–d rascally looking father of his on the other: for it is these fellows, d–n them, that have been the cause of my being insulted and duped by a set of ruffianly cut-throats," and the old man walked the deck even still more violently than before.

His son, who had listened to this explosion, was too prudent to interrupt it or to reply to it.

He knew his father: he knew that, like the generality of persons of a warm, generous, frank and open disposition, his outbreaks were as furious and unmeaning, while they lasted, as they were short-lived; he, therefore, remained silent, and permitted the fit to exhaust itself.

"Hark you," continued the commander in a tone that indicated a subsiding of the paroxysm, "let the course of the vessel be changed immediately, and let us go to Trinidad. I shall not be lumbered with rascally pirates, and villainous planters, on board my ship. My vessel was made to fight better foes than these scurvy sea-thieves. Crowd on canvas, crowd on canvas, and let us steer for Trinidad at once, and deliver these foul fellows into the hands of the lawyers. But first, call up that friend of yours: a fine companion for a British officer, Mr. Charles–a very fine companion!"

"You forget, sir," meekly remarked his son, "that when I knew Appadocca he was not a pirate."

"Well, well, that will do, let the man be brought before me."

In a short time Appadocca, under the charge of two marines, was led into the presence of the commander.

Imprisonment and anxiety, if he was still capable of feeling the latter, seemed to have had no effect upon him. His calmness, his cynicism was the same. Solitude, which to other men is at best but dreary, and is ordinarily but the provocative of reflections which may, perhaps, be embittered by the events and scenes which they recall–solitude which, to Appadocca in particular, one might suppose could have been only an encouragement to musings, which were likely to be attended if not with sorrow, at least with but little happiness, appeared to have had no effect on him. He seemed, if we can use the expression, but to enjoy his own misanthropic seclusion, and as for the circumstance that he was a prisoner, that made no change in him. He looked upon every position with the eye of fatalism, ay, and of that fatalism which does not arise from the obligation of any religious creed, but which is the tasteless fruit of a long series of disappointments and calamities – the fatalism of despondent resignation.

Such a feeling has influenced more than one mortal in his earthly career. Full many a warrior, whose praises are now chimed through an admiring world, has gone forth to achieve wonders, to conquer, and to be great, with such a sentiment rooted in his heart. Full many a conqueror has let loose the eaglet of his ambition, without seeing the rock or prominence on which the still young and strengthless master of the far skies could rest, save, indeed, the shadowy foot-hold that hope could fancy to discover in the sombre workings of inscrutable fate.

Such was the feeling of Emmanuel Appadocca, the pirate captain: such was the strengthening thought which buoyed and supported him in the unnatural career into which cruelty and unkindness had drawn him, and that idea imparted to him equanimity under all adversities, courage and valour in the fight, unscrupulousness in according judgment, boldness in working retribution, and stoicism* in imprisonment.

"Tell me, sir," said the commander, endeavouring to resume as much of his native dignity as his heated blood would permit him; "tell me, sir, in what bay those lawless men – the pirates who follow you – hide themselves, and where I can surprise them. I expect the truth from you, sir, although you may denounce your associates by speaking it."

The lips of Appadocca curled a little.

"My lord," he answered, "as long as I was on board my schooner, we sought no other shelter than that which was afforded us by the high and wide seas."

The commander looked at Appadocca fiercely in the eyes.

"I should be sorry," he said, "to suspect you of falsehood or prevarication, since you have been the fellow-student of my son: but your answer is vague and unsatisfactory. Do you mean to say that you have no harbour, no creek whither you were accustomed to resort, after your piratical cruizes?"

"None, my lord: after our 'piratical cruizes,' as you, I daresay justly, call

---

*stoicism: philosophical doctrine or school, emphasizes that persons should be indifferent to both pleasure and pain, should conform to natural law, cultivate virtue as the highest good, and not allow themselves to be ruled by passion.

them, we were in the habit of taking our booty for sale to the nearest port and of depending upon our own skill and watchfulness for safety."

"Hum!" muttered the commander, after a pause, "you are aware, sir, that one of my officers has been kidnapped by your rascally associates, as I presume them to be," continued the commander, with his temper evidently breaking through the composed dignity which he endeavoured to retain. "Now, sir, the punishment that I should feel justified in inflicting upon you, would be to have you hanged, at once, on that yard," and he pointed to the main yard.

"My lord," calmly replied Appadocca, "I am in your power, the yard is before you, you have men at your command, do whatever you may choose with me."

The commander looked at him steadfastly for a moment or two.

"D—n him!" he muttered, and turned away.

The frankness and generosity of his nature were again gaining ground upon his temper.

"I should not like to have anything to do with the death of this fellow, after all. It is a pity that his bravery is thrown away among those rascally devils," he whispered to his son. Then, addressing the two men who guarded Appadocca, "take the prisoner away. See that canvas be put on the ship, and steer for the Island of Trinidad, Mr. Charles."

"If you will allow me the liberty, my lord," said Appadocca, as the marines were about to lead him away, "I would tell your lordship that you need be under no apprehension on account of your officer: we are not in the habit of using violence, or of ill-treating our captives when there is no occasion for doing so."

"Hum!" groaned the commander somewhat incredulously.

"And, if you allow me, my lord, I shall request my officer to be especially careful of putting any restraint whatever upon your midshipman," continued Appadocca.

"What the devil do you mean, sir?" briskly inquired the commander, "do you wish to insult me?"

"By no means, my lord," answered Appadocca.

"And how do you tell me, then," continued the commander, "that you will 'request your officer,' when there is no officer to be requested?"

"Although there is no officer to be seen, my lord," answered Appadocca, "still I can request him: all things can be done by a variety of ways, my lord."

"How am I to understand you, sir?" inquired the commander.

"Simply in this manner," replied Appadocca, "that if you allow me, I shall communicate with my chief officer, and request him to take care of your officer."

"And how do you propose to do so," asked the commander, after a considerable pause.

"Only with four flags," answered Appadocca.

"What will you do with those?"

"I shall make signals with them."

"But there is no vessel in sight."

"No, my lord."

"How, then, can your signals be of service?" inquired the commander.

"Pardon me, my Lord, if I decline to answer this question. The sparrow by caution flies the heavens with the hawk."

"I should suppose, sir, when you have now no prospect of 'flying the heavens' again," said the commander, "you could have no objection to give us a piece of information, which cannot but be serviceable to us. However, make the signals, sir. Bring four flags there."

Appadocca took the flags and adjusted them in a particular manner on the line.

"Stop!" cried the commander, when they were about to be hoisted. "What warrant have I that you will not say more than is necessary?" he inquired of Appadocca.

"None, my lord, except my word," coolly replied Appadocca, "if you consider this of any value, take it, if not, reject it. But recollect, my lord, if I had been inclined to be a deceiver, I should have remained in the society of mankind, and should have prospered by coating over my rascality with the varnish either of mock benevolence or of sanctimony; I should not have openly braved the strength and ordinary notions of the world."

"Very well, sir, proceed," said the commander.

"Within a few minutes after the completion of the signals, you will hear the answer—the report of many guns fired at the same time," said Appadocca, and made a sign to hoist.

"What is the fellow going to do?" inquired the sailors one of the other.

"He is going to speak to the 'old boy,' I suppose," answered one.

"He won't do him much good, I fancy," remarked the other.

"No, he will leave him in the hands of the landsharks, I guess," said another.

In the meantime, continuing to make the signals, Appadocca adjusted and re-adjusted the four flags in a great variety of ways, and, at last, said to the commander:—

"Now, my lord, listen."

In a few moments the report of distant guns fell on the ear.

"Magic, by G–d!" each sailor exclaimed.

"How very strange," the commander remarked.

"Bring up all the glasses, there," he said, "and send up there Charles, and see where that firing comes from."

Men immediately climbed the masts, and surveyed the horizon. No telescope of the man-of-war could discover whence came the report of the guns.

After this Appadocca was led back to his cabin, and sails were put on the huge vessel that now began to move majestically through the water.

There is a soft and sweet pleasure in sailing among the West India Islands. He who has not sailed in the Caribbean sea, he who has not stood on the deck of his gliding vessel, and felt the cooling freshness of the trade winds,* and seen the white winged birds plunge and rise in silent gracefulness, he who has not marked the shining dolphin in its playing course, and seen the transparent foam rise and melt before the scattering breeze, with the blue waters below, a high smiling sky above, and the rich uninterrupted beams of a fierce and powerful sun, gilding the scene, can scarcely say that he knows what nature is. For, he who has not seen the tropics has not seen her as she is in her most perfect form.

The ship held her course through the waters which, reflecting the rays of the sun, undulated like a sheet of molten silver, in which she seemed but the gathered dross floating on its surface. As she moved and broke that shining surface, the waters frothed for a time about her and then closed in smoothness again; while the sea birds playfully gathered in the silvery wake, the weeds which shone, like golden drops, in the pebbly bed of some clear and limpid stream.

With nature smiling thus around him, with the silence which brings not gloom surrounding him, with the balmy breeze rising fresh and sweet from the bosom of the waters, fanning him into contemplation, the hardest-natured man must feel if only for a moment, the chastening quietude, which only nature, and he who is mirrored in nature, can impart and bestow.

The bosom in which the snakes of envy or hatred have long nestled and brooded, may feel itself relieved of half its oppression and suffering whilst gazing at nature's beautiful works, as manifested among the islands of the tropics, and beholding in its embodiment of splendour the omnipotence of the Creator. How many a heart whose life-blood has been frozen under the

*trade winds: winds that blow almost constantly in one direction.

influence of ingratitude, cruelty, revenge, and pride, or, perhaps, of the sad consciousness of a country's thankfulness – a country in whose cause youth, energy, wealth, and talents – may all have been spent, has not been soothed into mild quiescence by scenes like these?

There are countries around which the works of man have thrown a veil of enchantment; there are climes that are sacred, because some Heaven-born poet sang there; there are spots about which the memory of mankind has clung, and will for ever cling: such countries and such places are made famous, great and enchanting by man alone. Their beauties sprang from his hand. The idea which plants on them the ever-enduring standard of veneration arose from his valour, his heroism, or perhaps his benevolence, but whatever charm or interest the tropics possess they derive from nature, and from nature only.

For three days together, the ship continued her course, amidst the horseshoe formed islands of the West Indian Archipelago, which, at a distance at sea, appear merely like heavy clouds where nothing is real, nothing is animated, resting on the surface of the waters.

On the morning of the fourth, the towering mountain-peaks of Trinidad which inspired in the devout Columbus,* the name which the island now bears, appeared in sight.

Gradually the bold and rocky coast which girds the island on the north, grew more and more distinct and as the day waned, the ship entered the channel that separates the small island of Tobago from Trinidad, and bears the name of the latter.

The old commander, with necessary caution, ordered the greater part of the sails to be taken in; the vessel moved along slowly, and was borne down principally by the strength of the current.

The commander stood on the quarter-deck admiring the romantic scenery which presented itself on the left to his view. There the overhanging rocks rose perpendicularly from the heaving ocean, whose long lasting and lashing billows broke on their rugged base, and shrouded them in one constant sheet of white bubbling foam, and as they towered and seemed to lose themselves in the clouds, they bore on their hoary heads forests of gigantic trees, whose many colored blossoms appeared far out at sea; while down their furrowed sides torrents of the purest water fell foaming in angry precipitance. Here some cave hollowed by no hand of man – the home of the

---

*Columbus: Christopher Columbus (1451-1506), Italian explorer whose first voyage to the "New World" (he landed at San Salvador in the Bahamas) occurred in 1492. He made three later voyages to the Caribbean.

untiring pelicans that ply the wing the live-long day, would send forth its hollow murmurs, as it regurgitated some heaving rolling wave that had intrusively swept into its inmost recess. There some rock from whose side time had torn away its fellows, stood naked and bare, sullen in its solitude, and resisting the powerless waves that dashed themselves into a thousand far-flying sprays upon its jagged front; and here again some secluded creek, eaten deeply into the heart of the frowning highlands, in which the waters lay smooth and quiet, like tired soldiers after the toil and strife of battle.

Such scenes might well make an impression on those who looked on; and even the rough weather-beaten sailors, to whose eyes nature may have long grown familiar, stood leaning on spar or anchor viewing the awe-inspiring scene.

Among those on deck stood also James Willmington: and what were his feelings, he whose memory had been so recently recalled to deeds which could not render him an easier-minded man, if they had not had the effect of making him a better one? Nature is itself an accuser! To the bosom where all is not right, she speaks in terror. The trembling of a leaf, the sudden flight of a startled insect, the gliding of a lizard appals the guilty conscience. Could the man on whose head the crime of huge injustice pressed heavily– the man whose cruelty had blasted the life which he gave, and who was at that moment conducting to the gallows the child whom he had begotten– could such a man mingle the stirred sentiments of his soul with the sublime grandeur of nature, and send them forth with the voice of the mighty proclaimer, in mute veneration to the throne of God? No! nature is not cruel, nature deserts not its humblest offspring, she, therefore, could receive no sympathy from the heart of such a man.

Let us now go to the cabin of Appadocca. He was sitting on the rude accommodation which had been afforded him, with his arms crossed over his breast, and his earnest eyes fixed on the mountains of Paria, which he could see on the right, through the port-hole that admitted air and light into his cabin, and which had now been opened, inasmuch as it was considered a matter of impossibility for him to escape, while the ship was under sail on the high seas.

He was absorbed in deep thought; and he watched the neighbouring mountains with more and more earnestness, as they rose higher and higher to the view, on the gradual approach of the vessel. Twilight came, and threw its mellow hue around. It soon departed, and the scene, which was but a short time before enlivened by the powerful sun, was left in gloomy silence.

As the ship approached the little islands of the Bocas, nothing could be heard but the roars of the lashing surges, as they broke at regular intervals on the rocks.

Night came, dark and dreary. The ship approached the largest of the three small outlets. Every one on board was fixed in silent attention to his duty. The senior officer stood at the shrouds, trumpet in hand, with the aged commander by his side. Every man was at his post, awaiting in anxiety the command to trim sails, in order to enter the difficult passage.

That was always a moment of anxiety in every vessel going through it; for such was its narrowness, and the strength of the current that swept down the channel along the Venezuelan coast, that if a ship once went but a yard further down than where she ought to trim her sails, and luff up through the passage, it became a labour of many weeks to beat up against the wind and current to the proper place.

The critical moment came; the ship was within the Dragon's Mouth; she trembled as if she had been lashed by the tail of some sea-monster, ten times larger than herself, as she mounted the cross chopping seas, which always run high and heavy at that entrance to the Gulf of Paria.

"Lee braces all," the commanding officer trumpeted forth.

"Luff."

The ropes glided through a thousand pullies, and the heavy chains of the tacks clanked through their iron blocks as they were eased away. The sailors moved in disciplined order from rope to rope, and the deck sounded with their rolling foot-falls. The serious marine intermitted his monotonous and limited march for a moment, and leaned in a corner to give room to the busy mariners.

Appadocca had continued to sit in the same position as we have mentioned a few lines back, from the fading of the short twilight up to that time, which was now near mid ight.

Although he could not see, nevertheless he seemed during the whole time to use his ears for the same earnest purpose as he had done his eyes; and as soon as he felt the heaving labours of the vessel, and heard the noise that was made by the falling of the blocks on the deck, he sprang from his seat like a young horse when it is goaded.

"Ha! this is the time at last," he exclaimed, in a subdued tone, and springing towards the port-hole with one effort of impulsive strength, he tore down its frame work: next, he grasped the stool on which he had sat.

"Confusion," he cried, "it will not yield:" the stool was tied to a ring on the deck.

When Appadocca discovered this, he seemed slightly alarmed: he stood for a moment thinking how he could unfasten the stool. To undo it with his hands was a labour of hours, and he had nothing with which he could cut it. His eyes quickly surveyed the cabin; he rushed towards a basin which had been allowed him, he placed it on the deck, and jumped upon it. With the pieces of the brittle ware, he began to saw at the lashing of the stool.

It was a tedious labour, one which required an unconquerable perseverance to overcome.

Full ten minutes – minutes that on such occasions are more precious than years – had expired, and he had made scarcely any progress. As he sawed through one fold of twine, another appeared, but still he persevered, and blunted every piece of the broken basin in succession.

The stout heart and persevering hand will conquer immensities of obstacles.

At last, at last, the folds were sawn through. Appadocca seized the stool with both hands.

"Now for life again, and the accomplishment of my design," he said, and endeavoured to pitch it through the hole, but ill-fortune stepped in again to baulk him. The stool was too large to pass through the opening, he tried it various ways, but with no success.

"Destiny," he calmly muttered, as he put it down with the fortitude of Diogenes. *

He cast his eyes around him; there was a large Spanish pitcher of clay, such as are used in the tropics, in which water was brought to him: a drowning man, they say, will grasp at a straw: he laid hold of it, he tried it, it passed the opening.

"Now, farewell, good ship," he said, and leaned over the side of the vessel. He allowed the pitcher to fall quietly into the water, and he himself, plunged after it into the unfathomable waste.

"A man overboard!" some one cried on deck.

"No, no:" said another, "it's only the slack of the main-brace."

"Are you sure of that?"

"Quite sure."

"All right."

---

*Diogenes: Greek philosopher (c.410-320 BC), founded the Cynic school, favoring austere self-sufficiency. It is said that he once wandered with a lantern through the streets of Athens, in search of an honest man.

CHAPTER XX

"The torrent roar'd; and we did buffet it
With lusty sinews; throwing it aside
And stemming it with hearts of controversy."
                              JULIUS CAESAR

ON jumping into the sea, Appadocca swam dexterously after the pitcher, which he had thrown before him; then resting one hand upon it, and moving the other easily through the water, he paused a moment to gaze at the large ship that was now looming in the darkness, and was rapidly leaving him far behind.

The vessel continued her course. It was evident no one on board of her had seen his escape. He was left alone on the sea. He now began to swim in the direction in which long habit had taught him the coast of Venezuela was situated. As he progressed through the water he pushed the pitcher before him. Now and then he paused, and rested as before, with one hand on the pitcher, while he lightly floated himself with the other. Hours passed, and every succeeding one found the indefatigable Appadocca buffeting the waves with a heart of resolution, and an eye of determination. The thick darkness of the night was fast passing away, the gray dawn of morning was appearing, and the dark mountains of Venezuela began to rise to the view with that cheating delusion which mountains at that early hour of the morning present, and by their apparent nearness, one moment seduce the weary oarsman into the grateful belief that he is fast approaching the end of his irksome labour, only to irritate him the next by their constant and still greater recession.

The swimming fugitive felt encouragement and support from these two happy circumstances. More and more vigorously he stretched out his arms. Only three miles now seemed to separate him from the land. The currents and the sweep of the waves were in his favour.

On, on he pushed his befriending pitcher, and swam and rested alternately. The desperate hazard which he had incurred in throwing himself overboard in a boiling sea in a part where all the sharks of the neighbouring waters assemble to feed upon the refuse that is borne down by the gulf-current, seemed about to terminate happily and prosperously, and the act which at first may have borne the appearance of a voluntary seeking of death on his part, was about to result in deliverance and safety.

Perhaps even the seared, stoical heart of the cynical Appadocca, under these happy forebodings, throbbed a little more highly than usual.

But the grounds on which pleasure and hope are built, are too often sandy: our highest subjects of joy and congratulation are, alas! too liable to be converted, in the imperceptible space of a second, into those of misery and woe. So it proved with Emmanuel Appadocca.

When, as we have remarked, these prospects dawned in reality upon him, his strokes were made with more vigour; he became, consequently, the sooner tired, and was obliged to pause for rest more frequently.

After one of these intervals, after having "screwed up his courage to the sticking point," he gave his pitcher a push before him. The vessel floated to a considerable distance in front, then suddenly melted to pieces and sank for ever.

The soft clay of which it was made was dissolved by the water, and could no longer hold together.

If Appadocca had, a moment before, permitted his cynicism to incline beyond its medium point towards joy, so now he could not prevent it from verging to an equal distance on the opposite side. He had, but a few minutes ago, been induced to hope that he should be able to reach the land. Prospects of once more heading his faithful followers warmed his heart; and the prospect, too, of still being able to execute his design upon the man whose heart was too bad to open to repentance and justice from the lessons of his victim-judge, and from the perils out of which only the sheerest hazard had delivered him: but now, with the assisting pitcher his hopes also sank. It was now next to impossible that he could reach the shore; for although like the pedestrian who, with certain intervals of rest, may walk the whole globe, he could swim a considerably greater distance than seven miles – the distance which now intervened between him and the land – by now and then holding to something which could assist him in floating until he had rested, still it was impossible now for him to accomplish, much fatigued as he already was, at the utmost more than a mile; and the shore was still three miles away. Despair, utter despair would have seized a mind that was more susceptible of ungovernable influences, but Appadocca made up his mind not to be drowned, and continued to swim. He had not swum to any great distance, when he began to experience the want of his pitcher; his limbs began to feel exhaustion, he muttered something to himself, and went on still; his limbs became more tired; sensibility began to diminish; his arms grew stiffer and stiffer; on, on, still he went; his features manifested exhaustion, his respiration grew shorter and shorter; already nature could bear no more; his eyeballs glared like those of one in the last agony in drowning; his strokes became weaker and still weaker; already he swam more heavily; his chest sank deeper and deeper into the water; the mountains before him began to wheel, and pass, and vanish like clouds floating over a mist; his vision was indistinct, and nature drooped, exhausted with one long breathing; he was sinking, sinking, sinking . . . . when ... ... something met his feet, and Appadocca stood on a sunken rock with the water to his chin.

Surprised to a certain extent by such an unexpected occurrence, he at once remained where he was, fearful less the first step he would take should lead him again into the danger which he had, at least temporarily, escaped.

He stood there for a considerable time; but although the position was one, which on the point of drowning, might be very advantageous, still it ceased to be so when the immediate danger had passed; and now, on the contrary, presented another peril; for Appadocca was now exposed, in his motionless state, to become the prey of the very first hungry shark that might happen to swim in that direction, and what was still worse, he felt that the sea was every moment rising higher and higher. It was therefore clear that he could not stay much longer where he was. He began to resolve, but before he could determine on any definite resolution, a large wave broke over him; for mere safety, he was again obliged to swim. He had not gone far, when in spite of his strong will, his limbs would not move. Thus with his resolution still strong, and his volition still active, Appadocca, nevertheless, found himself rapidly sinking.

"Oh! destiny," he bubbled out, as the water now almost choked him, "is there such a thing as destiny?" He was sinking, sinking, sinking, when something, something again met his feet.

Appadocca quickly planted his nerveless feet as firmly as he could, upon the support which it would appear that destiny, which he had well nigh invoked for the last time, had again placed under them. He concluded at once, that he had fortunately alighted on a layer of rocks, which ran far out to sea, and of which the one that first received him, was about the beginning. To ascertain the correctness of his judgment he ventured, after he had rested a little, to put one foot forward, it rested also on the rock; the other, it rested too.

Appadocca now waded along towards the shore, swimming now and then, when a larger chasm than usual intervened. As he approached the land, however, the rocks began to sink lower and lower, until at last he was left without a footing. There was yet a considerable distance between where he was, and the shore, and in his condition, the prospect of being saved, even after the succession of unexpected auxiliary accidents was but slight and precarious. Nevertheless, he was obliged to hazard all; so he began to swim again. His arms after the rest they had had, were more powerful. On–on, he went–closer, and closer–he drew to the land; still the distance was immense to a well-nigh exhausted man. His strength began again to fail; but a few strokes Appadocca, and you are on land. His strength diminished more and more, shadows again began to flit across his vision, his senses reeled; he was sinking, no befriending rock now met his feet; he disappeared. . . . . In a moment he rose again, in the second stage of drowning, with his features locked in despairing agony. As he came to the surface the rolling volume of a sweeping billow met him, carried him roughly to the shore, and threw him high and dry on the white sandy beach, that was glimmering under the scorching rays of a fiery sun.

The tide ebbed away and left Appadocca on that which was now dry land. Nature was overwhelmed, and he seemed scarcely strong enough to rally from the swoon. There he lay, far from human succour, with the land rising perpendicularly from the beach, for a great distance away along the shore, and thus shutting out to those who might inhabit that part of the country, any immediate view of the sea, or the shore below. The fugitive might have lain in this state until nature, by an effort scarcely to be expected in his condition, might have suddenly revived, or what was the more probable, life might have quietly departed from the miserable man, had not the same fortune which seemed all along to befriend him, again interposed to foster still the spark of life which now scarcely lived in him.

A wild bull, maddened with fury, came bounding over the heights. The animal was so headlong in its race, that rushing to the ridge of the precipitous highlands, ere it could abate its speed, it was borne away by its own impetus over the ledge, and with a tremendous bound, it rolled dead at the foot of the still insensible Appadocca.

In a few moments two horsemen appeared above, and reining up their horses carefully at the edge, looked down on the late object of their chase. They were children of the Savannahs–the Bedouins of South America.* They were two Llaneros, their lassos were coiled in wide circles round one arm, while with the other, they clutched a short spear and the powerful reins with which they governed their still unbroken horses. They looked carefully at the now motionless animal, which but a second before careered so proudly over the plain, and was so formidable to them, shrugged their shoulders, and were turning their horses' heads to return, when the atten-

---

*the Bedouins of South America: members of nomadic tribes.

tion of one of them, seemed attracted by an object at the foot of which the body of the dead bull lay.

"*Es un hombre*–'Tis a man," both of them said, with great excitement. " 'Tis a man, go you and look at him, Juancito."

One dismounted, and, leaving his horse in charge of the other, scrambled down the rocks to the beach. He examined the body and cried out to his companion above, that life was still in it.

"*Esta un hombre de cualidad,*"–"he is a great man," he added.

Moved by their spirit of native hospitality, and partly influenced by the not unselfish motive of saving the life of a great man, the two Llaneros began to devise the means of getting Appadocca on the dry land above, and of conveying him to the house of the Ranchero, whose oxen they tended. But it was next to impossible to carry him up those rocks on which only the most steady-footed could manage to move; besides, it was necessary for one to remain above to hold the horses which, unguarded and unrestrained, would have obeyed their strong instinct and scampered off to their native wilds.

In this difficulty the natural recourse of the Llaneros was to their lassos. But those could scarcely be used, as the projections of the rocks would have shattered in a thousand pieces the person whom they designed to save, if they undertook to hoist him up along their rugged surface. They, therefore, had to think of some other expedient: but no other occurred to them, and they were obliged to recur to their lassos, in the use of which they were so long and perfectly practiced. They thought, however, in conjunction with the resolution of adopting this expedient, of removing Appadocca to another part of the beach, from which the rocks did not rise so roughly. This was easily done, and having fastened their lassos together, they secured one end to Appadocca, and the other to one of the horses; one of the Llaneros spurred the animal forward, while the other remained at the edge to guide the rope as much as it was in his power to do.

By this means the still insensible Appadocca, was brought safely on the table land. After the violent shaking he had received, he seemed to come to himself a little; he opened his eyes, but it was only for a moment. He was no longer insensible, but he was totally prostrated, and sank again into an inactive condition. He was then placed on the saddle before one of the Llaneros, and they rode off towards the house, whose roof could be barely discerned from amidst the clustering branches of the trees by which it was surrounded.

The Llaneros soon alighted at the door, where they were met by the Ranchero, and the insensible stranger was carried in.

Like all the houses of the Ranchas of South America, this was an extensive wooden building, built of only one story–a necessary measure against
the ravages of the frequent earthquakes which shake so terribly those tropical regions.

The large and shady fronds of the beautiful palms that decorate the level
and grassy Savannahs, were cleverly sewn together to form a covering,
which was as effectual in excluding the dews and rains, as it was in itself
romantic. No ceiling concealed the beams and rafters which supported this
primitive roof; but from the exigences of the climate, and probably from the
unwillingness to raise highly finished structures in the wilds, where the
inhabitant scarcely ever saw the face of any one beside those of the Llaneros
who tended his numerous and half-wild herds, the space between the low
flooring and the roof was entirely unoccupied. The apartments were extensive, and as airy as such a climate required. Windows opened in all directions, and the winds of heaven swept freely through every crevice of the
house. The furniture seemed to be as simple and as primitive as the building
that contained it. A few heavy chairs, made of the hides of the oxen, that
formed the wealth of the Ranchero, were placed about, here and there,
more for the service of the few individuals who occupied the place, than for
the accommodation of visitors or strangers, both of whom were exceedingly
rare, if ever seen in those solitary wilds. Indian hammocks hung in several
places, and moved to and fro, before the power of the wind that blew into
the apartment; and on supports from the walls, rested beautiful Spanish
saddles, whose bows and stirrups of massive silver, attracted immediate
attention. Around the house stood some magnificent trees, under the shady
boughs of which, herds of oxen, which were partially reclaimed from the
wild state in which they had been bred, now quietly chewed their cud, not
without, however, casting from time to time, a wistful look on the strong
palisades that fenced them in. Wild looking undressed horses, restively
cropped the short grass that grew around the house, and now and then
tugged with evident impatience, the tethers of cowskin, that restrained
their liberty.

Away, at a short distance from the inhabited house itself, stood also pens
for cattle, and apparently a slaughter-house, on whose roof the large heavy
vultures of South America, pressed and fought and nibbled each other for a
footing, while around it were strewed a thousand horns, the spoils of the
fierce natives of the plains, that had fallen there under the Picador's knife.
To complete the peculiarity of the scene a few half naked and fierce looking
individuals, loitered here and there, carelessly smoking their cigars; or
leaned against the fences, and criticised the ruminating oxen within, as

objects among which their entire life had been spent, and with such apparent skill and earnestness, as to leave one to fancy that the world contained nothing that deserved so much interest in their estimation as the animals which formed the tissue of their associations, and of their fathers' before them. The horses that were tied in their rude accoutrements, to the posts of the fences, and the huge spurs of solid silver, which were tightly thonged to the naked heels of those men, showed that they belonged entirely to the plains, and were probably there, only for the purpose of receiving the orders of the master.

"Feliciana," cried the Ranchero, as Appadocca was carried into the large chamber that formed, what in Europe, would be called the withdrawing room—"*Feliciana ben aca,*—Feliciana, come hither."

At this call, a beautiful young lady appeared, and started back as she beheld the pallid, wasted, and haggard, but still beautiful face of Appadocca, while, at the same time, the low interjection of "Jesu!" escaped her lips.

"*Que se haga todo neccessario por esc infeliz,*" "Let every thing be done for this unhappy man," said the Ranchero, who even in the half barbarous life that he led, did not entirely lose the distinguishing politeness of his people.

CHAPTER XXI

"O, thou didst then ne'er love so heartily:
If thou remember'st not the slightest folly
That ever love did make thee run into,
Thous hast not loved:"

As You Like It

APPADOCCA, under the care of the fair Venezuelan, was carried into an extensive chamber, which was much more comfortable than any one would have imagined any part of the house could be. He was laid on a couch that was unornamented, but that was as white as the flock of the cotton-tree. It was not to rest, however, that he was thus accommodated. His fatigues and privations overpowered the strength which his peculiar philosophy had tended to maintain, and the movement and exercise of the hoisting, and transporting on horseback, had completed what they had begun. He was seized with a violent fever, which now terribly manifested itself in the wildest ravings.

Alarmed at the state of the stranger, Feliciana called every one into service. Peons* flew here and there and everywhere, for herbs and weeds, while she herself remained by the bedside of the delirious sick man, watching every movement that he made, and listening to every word that he uttered.

Nature overcame even this passing madness, and Appadocca fell into a light slumber. Feliciana, with looks even more serious than when she went to attend her unknown patient, left the apartment.

Feliciana was a little above the middle size, exceedingly well formed, and majestic in her appearance. Her face was in itself a study, on account of the many different expressions which it wore at one and the same time. Her forehead was large and expansive, indicative of a large amount of intellect. Her nose was slightly elevated at the centre, and at the same time full and rounded at its termination; her lips were full and well formed, while the compression which marked the slight pout that they possessed, pointed to much firmness of character. To heighten all these separate individual expressions, nature had bestowed upon her large melting eyes, that swam like the gazelle's, in a bed of transparent moisture, and in which, it would be difficult to say, whether sentiment, or the serious contemplation of the Spanish character prevailed the most.

Upon the whole, a student of physiognomy would have pronounced, on seeing the beautiful Venezuelan, that Heaven had bestowed on her a high degree of intellect, a high degree of sentiment, and a high degree of firmness. She would have been at once pronounced one who was capable of great discernment, of forming high designs, and of overcoming every obstacle that might oppose their execution; while, at the same time, the sentiment which was clearly perceptible in her eyes, could be very accurately predicated as that, which, from its decided prevalence and preponderance, would always act as the leader of her mental and more solid endowments.

Her dress, in addition, was calculated to make these striking features, and her handsome person still more conspicuous. It was of dark materials, and adjusted in a manner that attracted from the general idea of simplicity that prevailed in it, while, at the same time, it displayed to advantage the gracefulness of the wearer. As a head-dress, a dark veil or mantilla, hung loosely from a high and valuable comb, down along the side of her face over her shoulders, and enhanced by the contrast her beautiful and clear complexion.

---

*Peons: peasants, menial workers. Usually refers to the Spaniards who came to Trinidad from Venezuela during the nineteenth and early twentieth centuries.

Nature in youth, especially when such youth has been weakened by no unphilosophical propensities, ever inclines to amendment. In Appadocca, especially, whose lifetime had, up to that period, been spent in the practice of that strengthening discipline which consists in the happy combination of exercise for mind and body, it turned towards health with extraordinary vigour; so that the stranger, who but a few days ago had been as near death as mortal man could be, and during whose feverish paroxysms one would have imagined that the reason which regulated the form that still writhed in its madness, was about to take a last farewell of the machinery which it had up to that time animated and guided, now presented the clear eye, the earnest look, and the same stern resolution that usually compressed his lips. The only remaining indication of the fatigue which he had undergone, and of the subsequent illness, was the increased pallor of his complexion, and the slight attenuation of his body; in a word, it was in body and not in mind that Appadocca now showed signs of illness.

It was a day or two after this gratifying change had shown itself, when Appadocca and the beautiful daughter of the house were seated together in the large apartment which we have before described.

The stranger was sitting in one of the peculiar but luxurious chairs of cow-hide at one side of the wide window, and Feliciana at the other.

Politeness and gratitude, independently of a sense of duty, called forth the gallantry of Appadocca in entertaining the lady. He discoursed on a life in the wilds, on the marvels that nature can there continually display to the eyes of the wondering spectator, of the free and independent life of those who inhabited the "Llanos;" and from this high and general theme he descended to the particular beauties that surrounded the romantic abode of his host himself.

He spoke on. But his greatest and most graceful eloquence could not draw a word from his beautiful auditor, or even secure a silent nod. She sat with her head turned away towards the window, her eyes fixed on the ground, and wore an air of more than ordinary seriousness. She seemed entirely wrapped in a web of her own reflections.

Appadocca could not but remark this reverie. After having yielded several times to his habit of silence, and given way to his own abstracted moods, he would awake himself suddenly, and seeming to feel the embarrassment of the situation, would address the young lady again on some new and interesting topic. But it was in vain.

"Senora, I hope, is not ill?" he at last inquiringly observed.

"No, senor," was the laconic reply.

"Then senora is a little melancholy," rejoined Appadocca, after a moment or two.

No answer.

"Banish, senora, that pernicious feeling. Life is itself sufficiently insipid and sour, and does not require to be made more bitter by melancholy. Look out, see how nature softly smiles before you. The birds fly from branch to branch, and chirp, and are happy; the insects—listen to the hoarse cicada—seem enjoying their insect happiness; even the very grass, as the breeze turns its blades to the beams of the beautiful sun, reflect on our minds an idea of felicity. How can you be melancholy when you look out?"

Feliciana turned and bent her large eyes fully on Appadocca, looked at him intently for a few moments, and then turned away again.

Struck by the action, and not feeling himself as indifferent as he usually was, Appadocca said nothing.

A long interval ensued.

Feliciana kept her head in the same direction: at the sides of her eyes two drops began to gather; they grew larger and larger, and in a few moments stood like two crystal beads ready to burst. Not a muscle, however, not a fibre of the beautiful weeper, seemed to sympathize, or quiver in unison with this silent grief. Like a statue of alabaster she remained rooted where she sat, and one could judge of the emotions which might affect her, only by the two transparent drops which balanced heavily at the corners of her eyes.

Appadocca saw this, and remained silent from respect to the sorrow of Feliciana. He thought of leaving the room, and giving the young lady freedom to indulge in that grief which seemed so deep and overpowering. Although prompted to do so by his sense of propriety, still he found himself detained by he knew not what, and seemed half to suspect that the sorrow had some sort of connexion with himself,—"Else," he reasonably argued, "the young lady would have concealed her grief in the privacy of her own apartment."

Appadocca, therefore, remained where he was, in deep silence, watching the tear drops that now again grew gradually smaller and smaller.

"Can one who owes, senora, a large amount of gratitude," he at last said, in a mild, subdued tone, "be of any service to her?"

She was still silent.

"Can I do anything to dry these tears?" Appadocca again inquired.

Feliciana suddenly turned her head, and fixed her expressive eyes steadily on the inquirer. She maintained her earnest look for some time, then rising, said, with great excitement,—

"Yes, you can dry these tears. Shun the wicked pursuit in which you are engaged, and then these tears may never again escape to betray me. Nature could never have intended you for a pirate."

At this sudden action, and unexpected language of Feliciana, Appadocca required all his self-command to conceal the surprise which he felt.

"I a pirate, senora!" he said, "may I ask how it is you have been induced to suppose me one?"

"Put no idle questions," she quickly replied, "I feel that you have sacrificed yourself to such a life. You, too, have confessed it. Why was it, that in your ravings, you called on your men to board, to cut down, to make prisoners? that you spoke of blood, of booty, and still worse, of revenge; and revenge, too, it would seem, on your own father? Do you think, to persons as I am, in my position, the least word of those–of those–of those–" she contended with herself for the expression, "those whom we wish well, can fail of its meaning. I am a stranger to you: but let me not prevail the less on that account; let me pray and beseech you, in the name of God and the saints," she continued, clasping her hands, "to promise me to abandon a life that is hateful both to Heaven and earth, and to think no more of those terrible projects of slaughter and revenge, about which you spoke so much in your sleep."

"Pray, senora, sit down," said Appadocca, as he rose quickly from his seat to conduct her to hers.

"No, leave me," she exclaimed, more excited, "I shall not sit down till you pass your word. Remember the dear person whose picture you now wear on your heart, and which you so affectionately pressed to your bosom, when the fever was on you. Can you suppose that she can look down from heaven, with joy or pleasure, on the son that she nourished, when he has abandoned himself to a course that God and man alike reprobate and condemn? Picture her in the society of the saints and angels looking down upon you, at the head of your lawless and cruel men, red with the blood of your murdered victims, and rushing forward to plunder, and to spread misery around as you go. Do you think that the sight of her child–her son, in this position, can impart to her either happiness or pleasure? Think of that: and, when ever you press her picture to your heart, recollect you only go through a cheating mockery, that the life you lead takes away from her happiness, from the happiness even of heaven. Remember the tears that she may have shed for you while here: remember the cares and anxieties she may have suffered for you; those, surely, were enough: and, if death ended her miseries on earth, do not you spoil the joy which she may now enjoy in heaven?"

"Enough–enough," cried Appadocca, with more warmth than was his habit, "stop, stop, I implore you."

"Then promise me."

"My vow is recorded in heaven, I cannot promise," answered Appadocca, drily.

Feliciana staggered stupefied to her seat, while she gazed, without the power of utterance, on the person before her.

"You will not promise!" she said, recovering herself, "you will not promise! Well, I shall promise,–I now vow,–that I shall follow you to the end of the world, until you consent to renounce for ever this wicked life."

So saying, she sprang violently from her chair, and rushed out of the room.

Appadocca, after the disappearance of the agitated Feliciana, sank back into the cow-hide chair, almost confounded by the scene which had just been enacted, and well-nigh distracted by the thousand reflections which it made to rush upon him. The first thought was of his safety.

"Suppose," he quickly reasoned, "others beside Feliciana, should have heard his disclosures during the fever; what could he expect under such circumstances, but to see the kindness with which he had been treated, suddenly changed into a most ferocious spirit of revenge." For he knew, too well, what cruelties the pirates of the West-Indian sea had, under Llononois and other captains, practised on the unfortunate inhabitants of those coasts.

Those atrocities could not be blotted out from the memory for centuries, and it was likely, that at the very name of pirate, the revenge of the Spaniards would break out as uncontrollably as fire in its favourite food.

And it was probable, that not stopping to consider whether he was actually what he was supposed to be, they would at once immolate him, to the memory of their slaughtered and plundered countrymen. This thought, however, soon gave way to those of a different nature,–to those which in his own manner of thinking, affected the most important accident of existence, and was, in his estimation, higher in value than life itself–namely, his honour.

It had not escaped him from the very moment that his convalescence had permitted him to exercise his discernment, that his beautiful and kind nurse, was in love with him. That could not but strike him; and though his stoicism balanced violently on the contemplation of the handsome form, and on appreciating the character of the mind which was as pure, as simple, and as artless, as the flourishing wilds which had reared and still surrounded it, still it required no great restraint over himself–himself, who had long banished from his heart the sentiment, that lends to life a charm, and who was now well exercised in choking to instant death any fresh feeling as it began to spring–to renounce for ever every desire to encourage or foster the affection that showed itself to him as clear as the sun at noonday. It would have been dishonor to steal away the heart of the innocent creature that watched over him with a mother's fondness and anxiety. He resolved, therefore, to be always on his guard, and to maintain more than ordinary restraint in conversing with her, in the hopes that the feeling which evidently animated her, might perish from the absence of sympathy.

It was, consequently, with alarm that he beheld the violence of feelings which Feliciana exhibited during the scene which we have depicted. "No ordinary interest," thought Appadocca, "could call forth such an impassioned remonstrance as Feliciana had made, and make her surmount all maidenly timidity, and speak to him as she did. For in what could it interest a stranger? whether an unhappy man, whom she had accidentally succoured was a pirate or not: and those tears; persons of her race, he thought, weep only on deep subjects. And, finally, the desperate resolution of following him all over the world, professedly to hold back his hand from crime, was a thought that only one great feeling could inspire."

Such were the reflections of Appadocca, they were made in a moment: and they immediately produced a resolution as firm as it was sudden. "I must leave the house of this good Ranchero," said Appadocca to himself, with much energy of mind. "God knows, I am already pledged to the causing of sufficient misery. I shall not stay here to add any more to the necessary amount. Not in this place particularly, where I have met with so much hospitality and kindness."

These reflections had scarcely been ended, and Appadocca's brow was still knit in the energy of his own thoughts, and his eyes still glimmered forth the fire of his excited mind, when soft footsteps were heard within the room, and on turning his head, he beheld Feliciana, who had again entered the room, and was now advancing towards him.

She was, by this time, comparatively calm; the paroxysm of her feeling had passed, but she appeared still determined on one purpose. Feliciana walked to the window as she entered, and said to Appadocca, who stood up to receive her:

"Pray forgive me, sir, for the lengths to which I, a mere stranger, was bold enough to proceed just now."

"There needs no forgiveness, senora," quickly rejoined Appadocca, as he led her to the other cow-hide chair at the window, "where no offence has been given: on the contrary, might I speak so freely, I should say, that the warmth you have so lately manifested, can be taken only as the indication of a high degree of feeling."

Appadocca spoke in a calm and serious strain. The young lady coloured slightly at the end of this speech.

"Among different persons, senora," continued Appadocca, with the apparent purpose of bringing about an intended end, "it would, perhaps, be a breach of civilized politeness to speak with the same latitude that I now intend to do. But, I think as we understand each other, it would be well nigh folly to keep back a few necessary words, simply from the circumstance that the laws of polished social intercourse may tend to render their plainness awkward. It is very clear, senora, that I have been fortunate enough to enlist in my favour, your most friendly sympathy, perhaps I should be justified in mentioning a much stronger feeling."

Feliciana coloured deeply.

"For my part, I cannot but express myself sensible to the existence of such a sentiment, and can only say, that from a self-same affection, I am capable of appreciating and responding to yours. But, senora, there are but few instances of real happiness under the sun. The beautiful sky that frequently enlivens our spirit, and cheers us up for a moment, is, alas! but too frequently, suddenly darkened and obscured by the dark clouds that bring tempests in their course. The innocent and snowy lily that gladdens our sight to-day, decays and falls away to-morrow. The days and years on which we may have been counting, during a long life-time, for the realization of a few moments of joy, may arrive at last, loaded with bitterness. The thoughts and sentiments which oft gladden us in our waking dreams, wean us away for a time from care, and foster in us the hope of undecaying felicity, then pass like the flashes of the lightning away, to leave only gloom and desolation behind.

"For my own part senora, I have long sacrificed myself to one object. I have long banished away Emmanuel Appadocca, from Emmanuel Appadocca: it boots not to tell the reason why. The world to me, it is true, is the world; the stars, the stars; but the halo that once surrounded them is gone – the feeling with which I may have regarded them is gone from them, and has centred itself in the now single end of my existence. For a long time mental anguish and I have been companions, and from its constant proximity it has chased away the softer feelings, whose aspect is too cheerful to bear the approaching shadow of that demon. My heart is wasted and its tenderness gone; gratitude for you, senora, is all that I dare encourage in my bosom. Let me exhort you, for your own sake, to forget the unfortunate man whom accident and distress brought into your presence. Forget him, and by doing so, avoid much suffering on your part, and, at the same time, confer much happiness on him. For if at the hour when this existence of mine will be about to terminate, there should linger in my fading memory some object that I could not look upon with cold indifference; if when the breath of life shall be on the point of passing I should not be able to shut my eyes and say, 'mankind, you have among you nothing that is dear to me,' the pains of succumbing nature would be tenfold heavier than they might."

In speaking thus, Appadocca had unwittingly to himself risen from his seat, and approached Feliciana, who, deeply affected, hung down her *head*.

Warming more than usual, Appadocca caught her hand as he spoke.

"To throw away a thought on a person of this temper, Feliciana," he proceeded, "I need not tell you, is doing an injustice to yourself, but fear not that I am insensible to your kindness. I feel it as much as I am now permitted to feel such things, and may destiny," continued he, with more warmth, "be ever propitious to you;" so saying, he abruptly let fall her hand, and walked towards the door.

"Stay," cried Feliciana, as she rose to keep him back: but Appadocca rushed out of the room.

The young lady resumed her seat; her high temper had now yielded to a more tender feeling: one that buoys not up, nor supports so much, for there is a spirit of pride in high wrought vexation, that imparts strength to the other faculties and to the body. Like the last convulsion of the dying madman, it derives from its very extremity and excess, uncontrollable strength; but when that is broken—when it is softened down by tenderness or pity, the mind which was but now strong under a fierce influence is left weak, impressible, and like the vision of a man rising from a swoon, when that influence is removed. Thus the feelings of Feliciana instead now of following the course of her stronger and more predominant powers, yielded entirely to the softer endowments of her nature, and her affection vented itself in a more seductive, more natural, more overcoming way. She no longer endeavoured to disguise to herself the extent to which her affection had already gone. She perceived at once that the sorrow which the involuntary revelations of Appadocca had cost her, had a different source from that which she would fain have believed at first; and that her apparently chivalrous denunciation of his course of life, and her resolution to follow him, and like a good angel, to stay his piratical hand, did not spring from a mere instinct of abstract right and wrong, but rose from a more interesting and personal feeling.

This great point being laid bare, she at once considered the circumstances, and the recollection of the last speech of Appadocca fell upon her heart, like the chilling hand of death. She sat in silent sorrow, and the evening had long yielded to night, when her father returned from the Savannahs to interrupt her grief, and to divert for a few moments the dark and troubled currents of her thoughts.

CHAPTER XXII

"This week he hath been heavy, sour, sad,
And much, much different from the man he was;
But till this afternoon, his passion
Ne'er brake into extremity of rage."
COMEDY OF ERRORS

THE night was far advanced, when Appadocca undertook to carry into execution, the design which he had formed of leaving the Rancha. He cautiously went out of the apartment which he occupied, and found no difficulty in opening the carelessly fastened door of the house. He went out softly, and when he had got outside, he had to stand still for a moment, in order to have recourse to his memory to help him to form some sort of idea of the position in which he found himself: such was the excessive darkness. Had he previously petitioned nature for a night, which might effectually shroud him from any one that might pursue him, she could not have sent one that was more dark or dismal. The blackness of the wilds, heightened a thousand-fold that of the night, which itself required no augmentation. Objects seemed heaped together in one pitchy chaos, and nature seemed to sleep heavily under a canopy of gloom. The fire-flies that flew low and lonely on the level Savannahs, seemed to show their light, merely to point out the surrounding darkness. In the same proportion with this thick gloom was the silence of the hour, which permitted the faintest sounds to be heard. At long intervals the brief but sonorous cry of the owl, as it signalled to its mate, would fall upon the ear; or there might be heard the hoarse and unearthly shriek of the night raven, as it vented its rage at the falling of some fruit, which it carried in its beak; or, perhaps, the low sound of some tethered and invisible horse that cropped the short grass hard by.

Incapable of seeing one foot before him, Appadocca could not proceed. He remembered well where he was, but the darkness confounded his calculation, and he knew not in what direction to move.

"The pen lies there," he said, "no there – no there," and vainly pointed where he could not see his own hand before him.

In this dilemma he bethought him of the stars: full of hope he quickly looked up: the heavens were as dark as the earth, not a star was to be seen.

"Shall I stay where I am," he inquired of himself, "until the morning star shows itself? this gloom will not, it cannot last!" No there might be a chance of his being discovered, and who knew the inconveniences, that such a circumstance would bring.

"The wind – there is no wind."

Appadocca wet the tip of his index finger with his saliva and turned it round.

"Ha! there is a breath," he said, as he felt the chill, on the tip of the moistened finger. "The wind," he argued, "blows at this hour in these regions, at a point varying from north-east to east. Following such a course, I shall assuredly open on the ocean: good."

Appadocca now began to move along, keeping his index finger straight before him, and taking care to moisten it from time to time. He proceeded under the pilotage of his sense of feeling, and heard the drowsy dialogue of some Llaneros, as they lazily turned in their hammocks, in some neighbouring pen, and asked each other, if he did not hear some one walking.

The soft breeze still gently blew, and afforded the same means of directing himself. He tumbled here and there into the deep furrows which the heavy rains had made. The severe shocks and bruises which he received, as he fell into those holes, were quite sufficient to try the endurance of a strong man, much less that of one who was but just recovering from illness. Fortunately the point to be attained was not far off, and Appadocca, after having groped his way for an hour, heard the low moaning of the ocean before him. He approached as much as he thought he could with prudence, for he conjectured that the ground would be the more broken and torn, as it verged nearer toward the sea; and, finally, sat down on the grass to await the approach of morning.

The gray light which temporarily chases away darkness immediately before the advent of morning, to leave a moment afterward the gloom which it dispelled for a time, came. Careful not to lose one favourable moment, Appadocca immediately got up, and advanced in the direction in which the sea was rolling. Again, however, he was obliged to suspend his progress, for darkness again returned.

At the approach of the real light Appadocca felt his sensibility deeply moved by the view which opened before him. The great Atlantic rolled heavily below, and it was only where the horizon, limited vision that its silently rising mountains would appear as if they were at last levelled into easy quietness. Its moving volumes were as yet undisturbed by the wind, and the transparent haze that still floated over its surface, imparted an air of repose that well befitted the hour. The mountain-peaks of the little islands that lined the shore, rose forth to contrast the wild waste of waters, and then came the high land on which he stood, that verged to the north-west into capacious bays and havens, and pointed out towards the east, and advanced high and lofty like a battalion of fearless soldiers, against the billows that lashed them, and that had likely lashed them long long before they bore the adventurous Columbus to its foot. At his back, also, lay the level and wide-spreading Savannahs, where, too, only the horizon bourned the sight.

Solitary and alone in such a situation, Appadocca could not refuse to his heart the pleasure of admiring such a scene; and, although prudence, not to say safety, pressed him to hie away from the Rancha, he could not resist the temptation of resting and feasting his eyes upon that which was before and around him.

Rousing himself, however, from the influence of this feeling, he endeavoured, and succeeded in descending the cliffs, and resolved to wait until fortune, or, to use his own expression, destiny, should send in his way, one of the numerous little vessels that trade along that coast.

That day passed, and destiny—the broken reed—was not kind enough to send a vessel his way. Worn out with anxiety, and weakened by the want of food, he drew himself up in the chasm of a rock, with the intention of resting himself there in the best way that his unbroken fast, and the uninviting accommodation would permit.

Despite these two unfavourable circumstances, he fell into a deep sleep, and had been under its influences for some hours, when he was startled by a most terrifying noise. It seemed that numbers of savage animals were assembled immediately above his head, and were designedly giving vent in one unbroken roar to their dismal and fearful howlings, that rose above the measured breakings of the billows below.

"What can this be," said Appadocca to himself, as he awoke; "what now comes to break this slumber that weans me from the sense of hunger?" So saying, he jumped up and walked a little way from the foot of the cave, across the beach, and looked up. He perceived the dark outlines of some large animals, that were moving about restlessly on the ridge, and were howling in the manner we have described.

"Ha!" he exclaimed, "shall I have escaped from the scaffold, the waves of the Atlantic ocean, and from the jaws of the sharks that fill the Bocas, to be, at last, ignominiously devoured by wild beasts; by Heaven, then, whatsoever you be, if you attack me, I warn you, you will attack one that is prepared for you, and one who is ready, at this moment, to make any one, or any thing, bear a heavy amount of chastisement."

This was spoken in a resolute and even fierce and over-confident tone. The speaker seemed impatient.

There has not been, perhaps, a single philosopher since the human race began, to ruminate on rules and plans of human excellence, who can be said to have entirely controlled the emotion of anger. All our other feelings seem to give way, and yield to the discipline of a well-watched life, and to the strong volition of our reason, but that passion alone still remains uncontrollable; smothered it may be for a time, it is true, but it is liable on the very first occasion, to be fiercely kindled. It seems to be so intimately connected, although negatively with the pleasures of the mind and body, and consequently with the gratification of the actual cultivation of philosophy itself, that any derangement of any of these things acts in producing the feeling which human perfection is too weak to avoid.

Notwithstanding his cynicism, Appadocca was irritated by the numberless difficulties that fell to his lot to surmount.

'But a feather breaks the loaded camel's back': he had undergone privations, borne sufferings, staked life, happiness—all that was dear and solacing to man—on the accomplishment of a design; after exerting himself to an extent that such as he, only, could exert themselves; after sacrificing the happiness that a lovely and angelic being was willing to confer, he was, at the eleventh hour, of his suffering, when hope began to beam again, now exposed to be devoured by vile unreasonable creatures.

These reflections might have been made on another occasion, without endangering the temper of the person who made them. But Appadocca was now almost maddened by fatigue and hunger. Famine makes the most steady violent, and human nature has already a sufficiently hard duty to contain itself, even when starvation is not present to gall it into rage.

In this mood he stood boldly on the shore, looking up at the wild beasts, with his chest heaving highly and quickly, and apparently desiring that they should rush upon him at once, and afford a butt to his fury, and put an end to his unsweetened existence. His wishes were partly fulfilled.

The animals rushed to and fro and seemed to be looking for a footing to descend the crag; but their instinct apparently did not deem it sufficiently secure for that purpose, for they drew back and howled as if disappointed of their prey.

"Fools," cried Appadocca, addressing them with more rage than reason, "go further down the ridge if you would have me to feast upon."

One of the animals, bolder than the others, went as far forward as possible, and seemed to have found a means of descending, but as the creature endeavoured to rest the weight of its body on the projection, on which it had laid one of its paws, it gave way. Its balance was lost and headlong it tumbled down the precipice. It had no sooner reached the ground, than Appadocca, wild as the animals themselves, threw himself upon it and buried his thumb and finger into its neck.

"Now you must either kill me, or I shall kill you, vile creature that assails me, as if mankind could not inflict sufficient injury without your coming from your native wilds and forests to aid them. Die, by Heaven! or I shall" – saying this, he contracted his muscles as tightly as the sinews of a convulsive man.

The animal lay for awhile stunned by the fall; but as soon as the blood commenced to circulate again, it felt the pressure on its windpipe, and began to kick violently.

"Kick your spirit away, vile brute, I shall not budge," cried Appadocca, now half mad with fury.

On its legs the creature stood, and shook its head and plunged, and away it went with Appadocca still clutching its wind-pipe with the grasp of the dying crocodile. The animal staggered a few paces and fell heavily to the ground, strangled to death.

Appadocca got up from the ground to which he had been borne by the beast in its fall, and walked round his prey in triumph.

"Whatever you are," said he, "provided you are flesh and blood, I shall have a meal of you."

He groped about among the small stones that strewed the upper part of the beach, and found what he seemed to have been searching for, a flint. He dashed it against a larger one and with the sharp pieces of it he began to cut through the hide of the animal that he had killed. He then succeeded in cutting a large portion of the still quivering flesh, and eat it.

What will not famine relish? Oh! hunger, that eternally tells us of our lowliness. Hunger levels. Hunger brings down the highest and proudest individuals to the standard of the meanest creature, whose instinct is to eat, whose life is concentrated in devouring, and whose death comes by over-feeding.

After Appadocca had fed upon the reeking flesh of his victim, he seemed recalled to himself: the madness of famine was past. He now looked upon the carcass before him with the indifference that formed the greater part of his nature, and the faint glimmerings of the fact that he had defied that beast which was now before him, and had engaged it in mortal combat, disgusted him: he contemned himself, too, when he recollected a little, the vain boastful and undignified language that he had held, and bent his steps in much sadness towards the same crevice where he had slept away the first part of the night. The other animals had fled after the fall of the one we have mentioned, and the stillness of the night was, as before, broken upon only by the moans of the ocean.

The next morning revealed to Appadocca the extent of the danger that he had escaped the night before. The animal was discovered to be one of those American tigers or jaguars, which pervade the plains of South America, and whose hunger has not unfrequently surmounted their instinctive cowardice so far as to bring them to the very houses of the Rancheros. The huge and powerful jaws of the animal, in which his bones could have been ground to pieces, attracted the attention of Appadocca; and when he observed the wound on the animal–the rude incision that he had made with the flint, and recollected the bloody meal that he had made of its flesh, he shuddered in disgust.

It was now that, withdrawing his eyes from the jaguar, he perceived at a distance a small craft tossing about on the heavy billows. He nimbly climbed the eminence to have a better view of what he feared his fancy might have too flatteringly pictured to him. It was in reality a small *fallucha* that was labouring on the heavy seas. Her course was under the land, but on the reach she was edging sea-ward. Alarmed at this appearance, he came down the cliff and ran along the beach towards the little vessel. Having got nearly opposite, he hallooed as loudly as he could. He was not heard; again he cried, but with as little success as before.

"Am I destined again to meet with other misfortunes?" he muttered, calmly. "Am I destined to be left to perish on this unfrequented shore? Oh, my father! how many events seem to arise to befriend you. Were I not sufficiently grounded in my belief, I would be almost tempted to believe that destiny, or Providence, or something else, exerted itself to shield you from your merited chastisement. But avaunt, vain, and stupid thought, the fatalities that have befallen thee, Emmanuel Appadocca, are only the acting of one of the grand laws by which yon sun stands where it is, while the earth wheels around it; or by which thou thyself throttled the huge beast last night. Dost thou not see that the distance is too far for thy voice to reach? Providence has instruments enough among his creatures, He does not interfere with our little concerns."

Muttering this, Appadocca climbed the heights, took off the jacket with which the hospitable Ranchero had provided him, and waved it in the air.

The mariners on board the *fallucha* held their oars in mid-air.

"They have seen me," said Appadocca, and waved the jacket again.

The *fallucha* had discovered the signal.

Casting away the jacket, Appadocca threw himself at once from an overhanging rock into the sea, and began to swim boldly out to meet the vessel that was now slowly approaching him.

His eagerness however, was now well nigh proving his death; for miscalculating the distance as well as his strength, he had ventured farther than his fatigues could justify. He was just sinking from exhaustion, when the powerful arm of a sailor from on board the *fallucha* grasped him.

He was laid on one of the rowers' benches, where he lay insensible. The sailors gravely bent over him, and tried every means for producing reanimation, which was not easily attained, for the Spaniards had no effectual restoratives, and Appadocca was now so overwhelmed, that the healthy elasticity of nature was almost destroyed.

Appadocca proffered his thanks to the four men who formed the crew of that little vessel for their kindness, as soon as he had come to himself.

"Who are you?" asked the captain, after receiving the thanks, "and where do you come from, you do not seem to me to be a seaman?"

"No," readily answered Appadocca, "I went out from Trinidad in my pleasure boat, together with some friends; we were taken through the Bocas by the force of the currents, and having inadvertently approached too near a whirlpool, we were capsized. My friends have been drowned. I am the only one who have survived: I managed to swim ashore, and had to encounter a number of accidents, and a large amount of suffering, I at last saw your vessel."

"And where are you going," he demanded in his turn, anxious to divert further inquiry.

"To Trinidad."

"To which port," again demanded Appadocca.

"To any one where I may be able to sell my cargo," answered the captain of the *fallucha.*

Appadocca yielded himself up to his reflections.

The captain could not withdraw his eyes from the stranger. He looked at him with the peculiar expression of the face, which indicates the absence of entire mental satisfaction, with regard to the reality of the object gazed upon. Still there was nothing in the appearance of Appadocca that could warrant any definite suspicion; but there was a combination in it, nevertheless, which forcibly attracted attention, and inspired a peculiar sort of feeling that probably was akin to awe.

The morning gradually passed. When the strong trade-wind sprang up about eleven o'clock, the rowers pulled in their sweeps; the feather-like sails of the *fallucha* were hoisted; her head was pointed towards the Bocas, and the little vessel began to mount over the waves under her closely boarded sheets. The sailors now carelessly threw themselves at full length on the rowers' benches; the captain kept his eye on the bows of the little vessel; and Appadocca gazed pensively on the ocean before him. Had any of those who were on board the *fallucha* cast his eyes towards the land that lay on the lee, he would probably have made out the dim outlines of a female form that was waving a white handkerchief in the air.

At night-fall, the *fallucha* was in the chops of the outlets.

Appadocca thus saw himself, by a strange coincidence, in the same place and about the same time that he had jumped from the man-of-war. He gazed on the rolling waves which nature had surrounded with the terrors both of the animated and unanimated portions of creation. For the rocks beneath the impending mountains, together with the waves that looked merciless and unrelenting, raised at first sight the idea of sure destruction: while the huge repulsive sharks that are there to be seen in thousands reminded one of a still more painful and frightful death.

"*Nil arduum,*"* muttered Appadocca, as he gazed on the scene of his daring adventure, "said the Roman poet, and no mortal ever enunciated a greater truth. Here are these overwhelming waves that seem to carry sure destruction on their frowning crest, that roll over an abyss, which if it were dry, would be difficult for man to fathom, that contain within themselves all sorts of huge and destructive monsters, in comparison to the smallest fins of which, man, enterprizing, achieving man, dwindles to the insignificance of the rose twig by the side of the towering magnolia: still the human race subjugates them even in their fiercest mood, and from their frail fabric of boards and pitch, men make war on their dangerous denizens. Not only that, but I, my very self, at the hour of midnight, when man and beast retire

---

*"*nil arduum*" . . . the Roman poet: Latin, nothing is hard. An inexact quotation from the Roman poet Horace (65-8 BC), who, in one of his odes, writes, "nil mortalibus ardui est" (Odes 1.3.37), which means "nothing is too difficult for mortals."

to their habitations, and sleep away darkness and its horrors, I plunged into the terrific waters with only a clay-pot to help me through, and here I am, principally by dint of perseverance, safe and sound. Oh, human race, you know not your power; you know not what you could do if you would only throw away the superstitious fears in which you have enthralled yourselves, and venture to assume a position, which the indefiniteness of your intellect assuredly intends you for. But you must study the law of nature: until you do that, you cannot be fit to achieve great things; as you are, you are living merely like brutes, with this aggravation, that the resources of your reason give you a greater facility of corrupting yourselves, and of becoming cowardly and base, the natural effect of corruption.

"Had I permitted myself," continued Appadocca, "to be nursed in the lap of an enervating luxury, either mental or bodily, to be surrounded with numbers of base menials, whose care was to prevent even the dew of heaven from falling too heavily upon me, who were to prepare the couches of indolence for me, who were to pamper my body, beyond the power of endurance, and at last transform me into an animal lacking thews and muscles? if I had been tutored to look upon the falling of a picture as a calamity, or been taught to tremble at the ramblings of a mouse; and more, had I permitted my mind to be enslaved by the ignorant notions of fiends, of horrors after death, and of all those things by which the world is made to quake in utter fear, should I have undertaken the execution of a design that would have been made to appear, even more terrible than that death in which its entire failure could have resulted? No, decidedly not.

"And, my good father," a sardonic smile might have been marked about his lips, "rejoice while you can, amidst vain pomps and ceremonies, surrounded as you are again by smiling and sympathizing sycophants, for your time of merry-making will be but short."

Such were the half-muttered reflections of Appadocca as the *fallucha* crossed the Bocas.

Having once cleared the straits, the little vessel drew closely under the land on the left side with her sails filled by the cool and gentle land breeze. She was sailing up to Port-of-Spain, among the beautiful little islands with which the reader was made acquainted at the beginning of this narrative. The curling wavelets of the smooth gulf broke on the sharp prow of the fast-sailing *fallucha,* and kept up a soothing music that invited to repose. The rustling of the trees that grew to the water's edge, charmed the ear of the mariner; the land breeze wafted far out to sea the sweet perfumes of the wild flowers, which nature *is* known to create only in the tropics.

The little vessel was doubling a small promontory, and entering the beautiful bay which indents the coast about that part, and is known as "Chaguaradmas Bay," when the hasty splashes of several oars were suddenly heard, while, from the darkness of the night, the approaching boat was still unseen.

The splashes every moment grew more and more loud and distinct, they sounded more and more near, and suddenly a large boat, pulled by ten armed men, appeared, and the next instant the *fallucha* was boarded; as nimbly as antelopes the men jumped into the little craft.

"*Que es ese?*" the Spaniards simultaneously cried, and each drew his knife.

"Lorenzo," exclaimed Appadocca, with more warmth than his cynicism could justify, and, in a moment, that officer–for it was he–was affectionately shaking his chief by the hand: they were both much affected.

How sweet it is when loving relatives have died away, one by one, when lover has been inconstant, and has shot the arrow–coldness–through the loving heart; when the ingratitude of professed friends has frozen the limpid currents of our feelings, when the world has heaped upon us miseries on miseries, and then has cast us forth; when father shews the front of enmity to filial deservedness, when we are isolated in ourselves in this great world of numbers, of movements, and of alacrity; how sweet it is to meet, after separation, the friend whose heart-strings throb in sympathy with ours, and about whose head the shadows of suspicion could never play.

At the sound of the captain's well-known voice, a loud and prolonged cheer from the men in the boat, echoed in the silence of the night far and wide over the gulf, and was repeated long and loudly by the ringing dales on the shore,

"Thanks, thanks," exclaimed Lorenzo, in his joy, "to the chance that sent us after this vessel."

"Where is the schooner?" inquired Appadocca.

"Behind that promontory, that you barely see: she is there safely hidden."

"Then take the helm," said Appadocca, "and steer to her."

Lorenzo attempted to take the tiller out of the hands of the captain, but met with strong resistance.

The captain of the *fallucha* brandished his knife, and called on his men to assist.

"Stop," coolly said Appadocca, "do not resist: I shall give you five hundred dollars for your little vessel and its cargo. Submit, I am Appadocca, the young pirate."

"Jesu!" cried the captain of the *fallucha,* "whom did I receive on board my vessel?" and he resignedly gave up the tiller.

The command of the *fallucha* was now taken by the pirate party. She was immediately put about. On making two or three tacks she headed the small promonotory, and discovered the long Black Schooner that lay enshrouded, in the silence of night, on the smooth and deepening bay.

CHAPTER XXIII

"There are more things in heaven and earth, Horatio,
Than are dreamt of in your philosophy."

HAMLET

AFTER Lorenzo had been satisfactorily informed, by the confessions of the midshipman, with regard to the safety of his chief, deeming it no longer necessary to hazard any nearer approach to the man-of-war, he kept the schooner where she was: while, at the same *time,* he continued to keep the ship-of-war still within sight. He was enabled to do so by an instrument of a very peculiar and strange device. From the tall masts of the schooner, there were reared to an immense height into the air long poles of steel that were joined and joined again to each other, and were, at the same time, carefully secured on all sides; at the top of these were adjusted large globe-shaped metallic mirrors, that were filled with a thick white liquid, which was continuously agitated by a small electric engine, which received its power from a battery on deck. These mirrors, when the sun was at a certain height, were made, by a trigonometrical principle, to receive impressions of objects that were beyond the scope of the human eye, and by conveying those impressions to other mirrors, that were fixed in a thousand different ways, to the several parts of the vessel, gave the power to an individual on deck to see every movement of any vessel which would otherwise be invisible, while his own remained unseen.

Thus, by the force of the same genius with which he might have shone among men on the side of good, Appadocca was enabled to excel, to be unapproachable and irresistible in his career of crime and evil. The firmness of mind which enabled him to curb the natures of even pirates, and to establish a discipline on board the Black Schooner that made his men simultaneously act as if they were but the individual members of only one single body moved but by one spirit, might, perhaps, have procured for him the reputation of a wise and great leader; the powers of invention, which supplied even the deficiences of human nature, and permitted him to make almost every element his servant, could again have handed down his name to posterity as that of a profound philosopher, if his talents had been turned to a proper object. But the combination of circumstances–destiny, decided otherwise, and instead of finding himself in the high position of good, Appadocca, found himself, by the very necessity of those self-same talents, in the high position of evil.

It is not Emmanuel Appadocca alone that has been thus doomed to bury a high intellect in obscurity, or been impelled by circumstances to expend its force in guilt. No: the world seems scarcely as yet prepared for genius, a higher humanity is required and must exist, before the man who possesses it can find a congenial place of existence on this planet. Mere chance now moves the balance in which he is weighed; circumstances either hazardously call him forth, or he is left to feed upon his own disgust, until his rough sands are run, then earth covers over the fire that ought to burn only in the skies. From among one hundred men of genius scarcely one ever goes beyond the boundary of the desert on which so many flowers are destined to "blush unseen." *

It was two hours after noon, on the day which we have above mentioned, that Lorenzo was standing by the helmsman of the schooner, eagerly reading the reflections of the mirrors, when the signals of Appadocca from the man-of-war fell upon his eyes.

"What is this?" involuntarily exclaimed the officer, as he read the well-known symbols of his chief.

"Too late, too late! his stupidity has already made him undergo the torture," he exclaimed, as he deciphered,–

"Treat well the officer, for they treat me well. – SCORPION."

Lorenzo gave an order to the officer on duty; a piercing sound was then heard; in a moment or two, the sides of the schooner became peopled with men, whose brawny arms were bared up to the shoulders. Not a word was spoken. The polished and shining guns of the schooner were immediately pointed, they seemed to thrust their muzzles through the port-holes, as if they worked by one impulse, by their own choice and their own action, for the slightest difference could not be traced either in the time or in the manner in which each separate piece was moved to its proper place.

Another piercing sound: each gun was fired at the precise moment. The

*"blush unseen": Philip here quotes from Thomas Gray's "Elegy in a Country Churchyard" (1750): "Full many a flower is born to blush unseen / and waste its sweetness on the desert air."

schooner shook under the deafening explosion that followed, and the ocean rang, and rang again with the echo.

This was Lorenzo's reply to the request of Appadocca.

By the aid of the same machine, that officer perceived when the man-of-war set all her sails, and began her voyage to Trinidad, as he concluded, both from the revelation of the young officer, and the direction in which she was steering. He rejoiced when he observed this, for he was persuaded that, in the event of the man-of-war entering the Gulf of Paria, he would be able triumphantly to rescue his chief. For the thousand bays and creeks which diversify the shore, the distance at which large vessels are obliged to remain on account of the harbour's shallowness, and the lukewarmness of the inhabitants of the town with regard to pirates, for they have seldom or never been subjected to the ravages of those people, he calculated, would afford him all assistance, while they should, on the contrary, tend to perplex, hinder, and embarrass the enemy.

He immediately ordered a certain quantity of sails to be put on the schooner, and began to follow the man-of-war. He kept always out of sight, and at noon on each day, the sails were lowered, the same machine was erected, and he made his observations on the ship of-war, which sailed away majestically, its commander little knowing that he was followed by a cunning, vigilant, and determined enemy.

Four hours had not elapsed since the man-of-war had crossed the Bocas, before the Black Schooner also passed them, and thus left in the water behind her the person to whose rescue she was going.

Lorenzo kept her head still towards the centre of the gulf, then went about, and, with one tack, gained the headland, behind which the schooner now lay concealed.

In that position, Lorenzo quickly disguised himself, and taking possession of one of the many little vessels that sail along the shore from the Spanish main, went up to Port-of-Sapin, and heard the confused intelligence that Appadocca had committed suicide.

His cargo was sold, and he could remain no longer in the harbour for fear of detection, so he resolved upon the plan of taking another *fallucha,* and of returning to Port-of-Spain as a different captain. He lay in watch for the first vessel which might pass, and destiny willed that the one which he should board should carry Appadocca.

As soon as Appadocca had arrived on board of the schooner, after having bowed to the officer and men, who saluted him, he descended the companion-steps and requested Lorenzo to follow.

They arrived at the Captain's cabin: and Jack Jimmy, who met Appadocca at the door, stood on tiptoe, threw his head forward, opened his eyes, and was just on the point of venting some exclamation, when Appadocca made a sign to him to be silent. The little man, almost bursting with the internal ebullition* of the greeting which he was obliged to restrain, retreated into an angle, and Appadocca passed on.

"Sit down," said he to Lorenzo, when they had arrived into the cabin, "and allow me to express my approval of the brave and wise manner in which you have discharged your duty during my absence."

The officer bowed modestly.

"Has the crew always acted up to its office?" Appadocca demanded.

"Yes, your Excellency," replied Lorenzo.

"The unfortunate accident," proceeded Appadocca, "which happened, deprived us of our last booty: but, in two days' time I shall let the men have as much as they can desire. I shall let them have pleasure to-morrow. Lorenzo, let us drink together."

Appadocca pressed a spring, and one of his attendants appeared and laid on a table wine and drinking-cups. Appadocca filled a goblet and passed the decanter to Lorenzo.

"Thanks to you, Lorenzo," said Appadocca, and drank.

"To the joy of your return, your Excellency," said Lorenzo, and did the same.

In a few moments after the officer left the cabin.

CHAPTER XXIV

"For valour, is not love a Hercules,
Still climbing trees in the Hesperides?"
LOVE'S LABOUR LOST

AT early dawn on the morning that followed the departure of Appadocca, Feliciana was sitting in the principal apartment of the Rancha. She was occupying her favourite chair by the window, and with her cheek resting upon her hand, was gazing listlessly and absently on the green grass without, on which the dew still sparkled in the silvery rays of the rising sun.

She seemed occupied by her own thoughts, although the beautiful pic-

---

*ebullition: sudden outburst or display, as of emotion.

ture of waking nature–a scene always enchanting in the tropics–was before her, and every moment, as she heard the rustling of the *carat* that roofed the house, or the creaking of the cedar windows as they became heated with the sun, or any other sound which might resemble a footfall, she turned her head eagerly to look, and turned away again, evidently disappointed when she saw nothing.

The morning merged more and more towards noon, she more and more frequently turned round to look, but seemed every time disappointed as before, for Appadocca, whom she was expecting, did not appear.

"Can he be ill," thought Feliciana, "Maria, Maria!" she cried, as she became more and more alarmed by the idea.

An old servant appeared, and was immediately sent to see if the stranger was well.

She soon returned, and said that there was no one in the room.

Feliciana jumped up and rushed into the apartment which Appadocca had occupied. No one had slept on the bed.

The truth now broke in upon the young lady. Her countenance fell; she walked back dejectedly to her chair, and looked out as before.

"What shall I do?" asked the old domestic, who had now a long time waited in vain for the orders of her absent mistress.

Feliciana started: "Tell my papa," she said, and turned away her head.

The old domestic went slowly and in a sidelong manner out of the apartment, gazing at the young lady the whole time, and muttering "what is the matter with the child?"

Feliciana remained where she was the greater part of the day, closed her ears to the repeated exhortations of her old servant to take food, and declared, in answer to her pressing questions, that she had had a disagreeable dream the night before, which had thrown a feeling of melancholy over her the whole of that day. When she retired to her apartment in the evening, the young lady hastily gathered her valuables, and wrote a letter, which she addressed to her father, and sat quietly and pensively until the night was half spent. She then rose, and carefully let herself out of the house, and walked slowly and cautiously away, until she got to a considerable distance from the Rancha. Once in the open field, the bold Feliciana began to run, for it was only by running that she could keep pace with the rapidity and activity of her thoughts. The next day she was by the sea shore, and was just in time to catch a glimpse of the little *fallucha* which had received Appadocca on board, as she was sailing away. She waved her handkerchief, but no one on board saw her, and the *fallucha* left her behind.

Undaunted by this accident, the young lady continued her journey along the shore, moving, however, in an easterly direction.

Oppressed with fatigue, she sat for a moment, in the evening, on the grass, to rest herself.

The dull sounds of horses' hoofs in a short time were distinctly heard.

"I am undone," Feliciana exclaimed, and turned to look.

Two horsemen were seen rapidly approaching in the direction by which she herself had come.

"They are my father's men," she said to herself, and looked about for some tree, or other object, behind which she might conceal herself: but there was not a thing at hand.

The horsemen drew closer and closer again; she looked round once more: at a short distance, the grass seemed to grow richer and thicker. She crept along towards this point, and threw herself flat into the tuft: but she was barely concealed, and durst not hope to escape being seen.

"I cannot avoid being taken," she said to herself, and seemed unnerved by the thought. The horsemen approached nearer and nearer. The thoughts of Appadocca crowded on her; the conflict of undefined feelings which had taken place in her mind, had ended in leaving her a being that was devoted to that mysterious man, and one who could now form no idea of life in which he was not the beginning and the end. Her fears now yielded to a stronger feeling; she drew from her bosom a gilded poniard, and vowed that she would not be deterred from fulfilling her vow as long as she lived. The horsemen had almost arrived to where she was, they came opposite to her, they looked neither on one side nor on the other, but seemed entirely absorbed by the subject on which they were conversing in a loud tone of voice.

From her hiding place Feliciana could see them distinctly. Joy, joy! they were not her father's men. But may they not be other persons that were sent after her in one direction, while her father's own Llaneros went in another? She remained quiet and listened.

"No, I shall not take less than seven piastres* each for my oxen; and, as for my jack-asses, I shall not let them go for less than four piastres a-head," said one of the horsemen.

"You are quite right," replied the other; "those people in Trinidad can afford to pay a good price for their bullocks. By-the-bye, have you remarked what a number more of beasts we sell since the English took that island. I

*piastres: or piasters, Spanish coins.

understand these fellows live entirely on beef, and that is the reason why they are such good soldiers."

"Good or bad soldiers," answered the other, "if they eat beef, and make us sell our cattle, that is all we care about."

"They are merchants," said Feliciana to herself, and resolved at once to speak to them.

"Yes, continued the first speaker, "I shall not–"

"Ho!" cried Feliciana, springing from the ground, "senores, senores, ho!"

The horsemen looked round, and crossed themselves, and at the same time, cried, "Jesu!"

"Stop, stop, I wish to speak to you," Feliciana continued.

The horsemen reined up their horses, and remained apparently under the effect of some powerful fear.

"What may she be?"

"Who knows what she may be! that's just the reason why we should obey her," replied the other.

In the mean time Feliciana came up.

"Shall we speak to her?" one inquired of the other.

"Where are you riding to, senores?" she inquired.

They looked inquiringly at each other, and then asked each other in a whisper, "Shall I answer?"

"Where are you going to, senores?" she repeated.

"To Guiria, beautiful lady," one at last answered.

"Be good enough to take me with you," said Feliciana.

The horsemen looked amazed at each other.

"I shall give you two hundred piastres."

The two horsemen opened their eyes.

"Two hundred piastres?" they repeated inquiringly.

"Yes."

"And who are you, beautiful lady, that are thus solitary in the Savannahs? are you one of us or some blessed spirit that is permitted to walk the earth. We are good and true catholics, do not harm us, we beseech you." The two horsemen here devoutly crossed themselves respectively.

"I am no spirit," answered Feliciana, "but an unfortunate lady, who is flying to the rescue of–of–her–husband: pray take me on with you, and I shall reward you, as I have said."

The horsemen mused, and whispered to each other for a moment. Then one of them dismounted.

"Senora," he said, "Heaven forbid that we should ever commit the crime of leaving a lady in the wilds without shelter or protection. Allow me to assist you in mounting my horse."

Feliciana was supported on the saddle. The three persons then proceeded on their journey. The horsemen changed places alternately at the various stages of the journey; and while one walked at the side of Feliciana's horse, the other rode by turns, until they arrived in the environs of the town of Guiria, where Feliciana found a number of opportunities to continue her wanderings in search of Appadocca.

CHAPTER XXV

"How would you be,
If He, who is the top of judgment, should
But judge you as you are? O, think on that;
And mercy then will breathe between your lips,
Like men new made."
MEASURE FOR MEASURE

AFTER Appadocca had jumped overboard, the large ship passed the Bocas safely, entered upon the still waters of the gulf, and within a few hours afterwards her large anchor was cast off the harbour of Port-of-Spain.

As the vessel approached nearer to her port of *destination,* Charles Hamilton had become more and more anxious, and uneasy about the fated doom which he saw every moment hanging lower and lower over his friend. He reasonably argued that, with such a willing witness as James Willmington, and with such a stoical disposition as his friend had formed to himself, there would not be the slightest chance of Appadocca's acquittal when he should be tried. For Willmington, it was to be supposed, would not attenuate the least feature of the case nor would Appadocca descend from his high notions of philosophy to conceal or deny the charges that would be brought against him.

In this state of mind, Charles Hamilton considered a long time, and endeavoured to think of some means of still saving his friend. It was, however, a difficult and perplexing matter, for the only available measures that he could adopt, were doggedly repudiated by Appadocca himself.

"Confound his obstinacy," the young officer muttered, when he thought of his friend's infatuation; "he might have been saved long ago if it were not for that."

Among a number of expedients and plans, Hamilton at last adopted the one of having an interview with James Willmington, of endeavouring to soften down his persecuting feeling, and of establishing, if not terms of kindness and affection, at least those of neutrality and indifference between him and Appadocca.

It was in this disposition, that long before the sun had risen on the morning after the man-of-war had come to an anchor, Charles Hamilton requested a servant to ask James Willmington to be good enough to attend him in his cabin. Willmington, whose excitement had kept him awake the whole night, shortly appeared.

"Be good enough to sit down, sir," said Hamilton.

Willmington sat down.

"I have taken the liberty, sir, of asking you to my cabin, to speak to you on a subject that I am aware must be very delicate; but my great anxiety for my friend, and the just apprehension that I entertain with regard to his life itself, have led me to put aside whatever reluctance I should otherwise feel, and to speak to you on that head."

Willmington looked stolidly and vaguely at Hamilton, and said not a word.

"You are aware, sir," continued Hamilton, "that Appadocca runs, at this moment, the risk of his life."

"I am aware, sir," replied Willmington, briefly.

"Well, sir, shutting my eyes to all family quarrels–"

"There are no quarrels in my family that I know of, sir," interrupted Willmington.

"Perhaps you will hear me out," remarked Hamilton.

Willmington exhibited the rudiments of a bow.

"Shutting my eyes to all private quarrels between you, I say, I cannot but consider it a misfortune that a young man, like Appadocca, should be brought to a disgraceful death on a scaffold at such an early age. You will be the only prosecutor in this case, and, to a certain extent, you hold his life in your hands; will you suspend–suspend your animosity, and give Appadocca a chance of escape?"

"I do not understand you, sir," said Willmington.

"I do not think there is much obscurity about what I said," remarked Hamilton, in his turn.

"Do you mean sir, to ask me to connive at a felony, and to permit a criminal to escape?"

"Call it what you choose, sir; I ask you to save Appadocca from an ignoble and untimely death," answered Hamilton.

"Then, sir, I must tell you at once, I cannot. The law must take its course. Beside, sir, I feel called upon by public justice and morality, to bring to punishment the individual in whose favour you are making these representations."

"Hum," groaned Hamilton – "you forget one great point," he said after a short pause.

"What is that, sir?" inquired Willmington.

"That by bringing Appadocca to the scaffold, you will disgrace your own blood," answered Hamilton.

"I do not much care for that, sir," answered Willmington.

"But you might show some consideration, at least, to your own son," said Hamilton.

"He did not show any to me," sullenly replied Willmington.

"That is no reason why you should not: and you must recollect, he justified his harshness to you precisely on the same grounds as you now do yours. Besides, he may again, one day, justify any vengeance that he may be inclined to wreak upon you by your conduct to-day."

"There will not be much chance left of his doing so, I warrant you," replied Willmington, with a sardonic smile.

"There is many a slip between the cup and the lip," said Hamilton.

A pause ensued.

"Beside," continued Willmington, re-opening the dialogue – "besides, he is my son only of a sort."

"What do you mean," inquired Hamilton.

"That his mother was not Mrs. Willmington," answered Willmington.

"Do you mean to say, then, that you do not consider you owe any duty to your children that may not have been born in wedlock?" inquired Hamilton.

"Scarcely," answered Willmington.

"You consider, therefore, that where the word of a priest has not been pronounced on your union, you are absolved from your honour, and from natural obligations?" inquired Hamilton.

"I do," answered Willmington.

The lips of the young officer curled up with scorn, as he stood up and said, with ill-concealed disgust:

"Leave my cabin, sir; leave my cabin. By G–d you are not made worse than you are. If I were Appadocca, I should have hanged you outright, and not sent you with a philosophical scheme to float on a cask and to be picked up.

"Hark you, sir," continued Hamilton, in a suffocating temper, "if you have a son that resembles you more than Appadocca does, born of Mrs.

Willmington, under*stand*–send him to me, sir, and, by his own appointment, I shall give him satisfaction for ordering you out of my cabin."

Willmington turned to leave, but met face to face a servant that came rushing in.

"Your honour, your honour," the man cried with much excitement, "the pirate prisoner has drowned himself."

"What?" exclaimed Hamilton, and fell back into his chair.

"The pirate prisoner, your honour, has jumped overboard. When the steward went into his cabin this morning, he was not to be found: on examination, the skylight was discovered to be open."

The officer leaned his forehead on his hand.

"There, sir," he said, "your vengeance is satisfied: public justice and morality are vindicated."

"Scarcely," muttered Willmington between his teeth, and left the cabin.

Charles Hamilton was deeply affected by the supposed suicide of his friend; recollections of bygone days crowded on his mind. He recalled vividly to himself the happy hours which he and his friend Appadocca had spent together in the lightheartedness and warm fellowship which only students can feel, when strong and mutual sympathy links them, and carries them together through study and through recreation: he pictured to his mind, the ardent and aspiring youth, such as his friend then was, with a mind that was stored with learning, and a heart that was overflowing with abundant benevolence, and then contrasted him with the cold, soured, cynical man, whose mind was now entirely engrossed with schemes of death and revenge, and whose heart now beat but in cold indifference, or throbbed with a more active feeling, only when retribution and punishment quickened its action. He then thought of the career which hope would have foretold on the one picture–a career, that like the stars themselves which Appadocca measured, was to be ever bright and brilliant, that might have shed its light on humanity, and might, perhaps, have signalized an epoch of philosophy and certain truth; and he thought, on the other hand, of the actual reality of a life spent in the degrading society of the reputed scum of mankind, with its energies and powers exercised and lost in devising methods for robbing others, and closed at last in immorality and crime.

Such thoughts weighed heavily on Charles Hamilton, and when he proceeded on deck, his step might be observed to be less light, and his eye less quick than they were wont to be.

As for James Willmington he walked on one side of the deck restlessly, and bit his nails.

"The fellow," he interjected to himself, "to go and drown himself, when I expected to have made him feel the consequences of his insolence, in having me put on a cask and set adrift. The villain! to go and drown himself, when the gallows and the hangman's hand ought to have sent him to his account. Never mind, he is out of the world, and one way is as good as another, there is no fear now of being judged again in the name of nature."

Willmington smiled satanically.

"He is gone, and that is one blessing, at least, and he will, no doubt, meet those in the other world who will be better able to answer his philosophy than I."

And a diabolical smile played on the lips of that heartless and selfish man.

"Have that man landed at once, Charles?" said the commander dryly, who was attentively watching Willmington, from the quarterdeck.

His attention had been at first attracted by the restless and impatient movements of Willmington. He had remarked the workings of his lips, and had noticed the bitter sneer that settled upon them at the end. The dislike which he had always entertained for that man, was worked up to its height by this exhibition.

"He could not have been uttering a prayer for his son," he justly thought; "prayers do not end so. No–no–he must be truly a vile individual. Death ought to suspend, at least, the enmity of the bitterest foes. It is a strange father that can curse the memory of his own son, however great a reprobate he may have been. Have that gentleman landed immediately, Charles," he again said to his son.

In a few moments, James Willmington was made acquainted with this order, and was told that a boat was ready to take him ashore.

"Thank God, thank God!" he cried, almost aloud, and quickly ascended the steps of the quarter-deck, to take leave of the commander.

"My lord, I have to bid you, good morning," said he, as he approached the commander.

"Good morning,–good morning," quickly replied the person addressed, apparently desiring to have as little as possible to say to the individual, who was taking his leave.

"I am much obliged to you," continued Willmington, "for the protection and assistance, and–"

"Not at all, sir," dryly rejoined the commander, "I have only discharged the duty which I owe to all His Majesty's subjects on these seas."

"Yes, my lord," pursued Willmington, "and I trust my lord, when you land, you will condescend to remember your former guest."

"I thank you, sir," replied the commander, as dryly, as before.

"Good morning, my lord."

"A very good morning, sir."

The boat, soon bore Willmington away from the ship.

"If the world possessed many more like that man," said the commander to his son, while he pointed to Willmington, who was now on his little voyage toward the shore, "it would indeed be worse than a den of thieves."

"I am afraid there are many more of this sort, sir, than you imagine," replied Charles, "and that the world is not even as good as a den of thieves, for they say, those individuals recognize a certain code of honor."

"Things were not so in my time," replied the commander "when I was young, Charles, we feared God, honored the king, and dealt justly and honorably by all men."

"The times, then, are changed, sir," said Charles, "and the greatest misfortune is, that such characters as that Willmington, unluckily for humanity, make as many Appadoccas."

"True," observed the commander, "it is a misfortune. I always thought I perceived much to be admired in that unfortunate Appadocca. I am rather glad, I must say, that he has drowned himself rather than permit himself to be dealt with by the executioner."

On landing, Willmington hurried up the magnificent walk of almond-trees, which lead from King's-wharf, into Port-of-Spain. He pursued his way through the city, and scarcely recognized the many wondering friends and acquaintances, who proceeded forward to congratulate him on his return, for they had heard of the accident which had befallen the ship in which he had taken passage; and also of the manner in which he, in particular, was treated.

When he had arrived at the beautiful Savannah which lies at the Northern-end of the city, he diverged into a footpath that led to the beautiful villas with which Saint Ann's-road is ornamented. He quickly walked up the road a little way, and immediately stopped at the gate of a magnificent and romantic suburban house that stood in solitary grandeur, amidst the beautiful trees that belted it.

He rang at the gate-bell, and was immediately admitted by the servant, who started back, and almost went into hysterics at seeing his master back again.

"Gad bless me, massa, da you, or you 'pirit?" inquired that official, as he opened the gate and let his master in, who, without noticing the wonderment of the man, rushed into the house.

"Ah! is it you, Mr. Willmington?" said his wife, with fear, surprise, and joy, all confusedly pictured on her face.

"Heavens be praised, and thanked," and she embraced him affectionately.

"Tell me, tell me all about the accident that befell you," she asked.

"Not to-day, dear," answered Willmington; "not to-day, dear. Only thank Providence that I am again safe. I shall relate everything when I am more composed."

CHAPTER XXVI

"Avaunt! and quit my sight! let the earth
Hide thee!
Thy bones are marrowless, thy blood is cold!
Thou hast no speculation in those eyes
Which thou dost glare with."

MACBETH

IT was with the greatest difficulty that James Willmington succeeded in restraining the curiosity of his wife until the period which he himself had appointed to tell her the particulars of the capture of the ship, and also the singular circumstance of his trial, punishment and rescue.

The period had now arrived.

In a beautiful and fantastic pavilion, into which the soft evening breeze wafted the sweet perfume of a thousand delicate flowers which bloomed around, sat James Willmington. He was seated at the head of a vast, spreading table that was loaded with the choicest and most delicious fruits that the tropics produce. Opposite to him sat Mrs. Willmington, on whose side two very beautiful infant daughters were respectively placed. On the right hand of Willmington was his son, a youth of about eighteen, who was dressed in the uniform of an officer.

The pure wax tapers that burnt in chaste and elegant candlesticks of solid silver, shed a cheerful and soft light around. The faint music of a small fountain that played hard by, fell soothingly on the ear, as it grew louder and louder, or fell fainter and still fainter, according to the direction and strength of the lulling breeze that seemed to sport with its jets. The old family pictures that hung on the walls looked down fiercely and frowningly, or smiled upon the happy and quiet group, according to the stern and warlike disposition or the benignant characters of each.

The servants had all retired for the time to their own apartments; and Willmington sat quietly smoking an exquisite cigar, and sipping from time to time the crystal iced water that stood in a tumbler by his side.

"I shall now tell you," he said, "the succession of accidents which has brought me back to Trinidad," and he began to relate the particulars of the capture of the merchant vessel, the distribution of the shares, his trial, his being thrown overboard, the agony that he suffered on the cask, and finally his providential rescue, the capture of the pirate captain and his supposed suicide. He narrated circumstance on circumstance, quickly passed over the alleged causes of his sufferings, and mentioned Appadocca as one who claimed to be his son.

"Confound his impudence," cried the youth of eighteen, "I wish I had been there, I should have caned his insolence out of him. The idea! to call my father, his father, vile cut-throat as he was. I wish I had him now. But do you know anything at all of him? How came he to claim you as his father, sir?" he inquired, after a time.

"Do not interrupt me;–do not interrupt me," was the only answer Willmington made to this home and embarrassing question.

Time had flown during his long narrative. The clock had already struck eleven–a late hour in the tropics–when he was concluding.

"Yes, my children," he said at the end, with great solemnity, endeavouring to make the contemplated impression, "there is one above to punish evil doers."

"Ay, and he never slumbers," replied a deep sonorous voice from without, and in a moment afterwards the pirate captain stood before James Willmington.

The cigar fell from his jaws, that palsied with terror, now gaped asunder. His hand trembled, and threw over the glass of iced water towards which it was being stretched, his silvery hair seemed to stand on end, and with a sudden bound, Willmington started from his seat and reeled over his chair towards a corner of the apartment.

"Get out of my sight, get out of my sight, accursed, damned spirit; in the name of Christ, I conjure you!" he cried, while his eyeballs glared, and large drops of sweat trickled down his forehead that was almost green with fear.

Appadocca calmly raised the chair from the floor, drew it to the head of the table, folded his thin cloak around him and sat down.

"I did not design to deliver you up to the authorities," shrieked Willmington, almost inarticulately. "No, no! I had only intended to frighten you, I would have allowed you to escape. Oh, yes, I would have protected you; yes, yes, I would have protected you like a father. Forgive, forgive me, and scare me no more."

Appadocca looked round upon the miserable Willmington, who, contracted with terror within the smallest possible heap, crouched in a corner.

"Do not look at me," cried Willmington still more terrified, "vanish, vanish, in the name of Heaven and all the saints. If you come from Hell–to-to haunt me,–return, return. It was not I that wronged you. Forgetfulness, forgetfulness–I intended–I intended always–always to find you out. Your mother, aye, your–your mother loved me. Have mercy–mercy–on me,–the vessel–the vessel took me by–by chance to St. Thomas. I did not–I did ask him: no–no–I was sorry–sorry, when–when–you were drowned. Mercy–mercy."

"Come here and make your will," said Appadocca, authoritatively, without paying the slightest attention to the cries of the wretched and almost distracted man.

"Make my will? will!" recommenced Willmington, "do you intend to murder me? Hence, hence, I am a Christian, you have no power on me. No, no,–do not–do not–out, out of my sight, damned, reprobate spirit."

"I am no spirit. Speak not to me so sillily. Make your will, I say," said Appadocca, with more authority, "and do not let these children suffer from your loss. The minutes that you can remain with them are counted."

"Will, will!" exclaimed Willmington, as if already staggering in his intellect.

"Will? I have no will to make. My will is made already. Do not speak to me of wills–do not speak to me of wills, I do not wish to die–I will not die. Leave my sight–leave my sight–leave my sight."

"Then settle your other affairs," said Appadocca with the same authority as before. "I allow you five minutes; at the end of that time you must go with me."

"No–no, I will not go with you," shrieked Willmington, "I did you no harm–I intended you no harm. Let me live a little longer–give me but seven years to live–five–two;–half a year;–a month–a week, a day;–do not take me away so soon. Let me live, let me live. Do not take me with you. It was not I that drowned you."

"It would be prudent on your part to fill the five minutes, which are accorded you, more profitably than by these vain petitions. I–"

"Vain petitions! Let them not be vain; look at the children that I have to maintain and protect: do not take me away from them," cried Willmington, interrupting Appadocca.

"I am no ghost," continued Appadocca, "but something worse."

"Was he not drowned?" Willmington began to mutter. "Did he not jump into the sea–at the Bocas–or farther out?–Can he–could he have been saved? no, no, delusion–delusion. His face is as pale as death. He is still and quiet as the grave;" continued Willmington, as he gazed intently on Appadocca, who was still sitting calmly at the table.

The period had elapsed, the moment of doom had now arrived.

"The period is past, your time is come," said Appadocca, "rise and go with me."

"No–no," shrieked Willmington, madly,–"no–no–no."

And with a sudden spring he jumped from the corner to one of the doors: he was roughly thrown back by some person who was outside: he then rushed to another, and was again repelled–to another, and he was once more forced back. He sprang on to the jalousies, and as he succeeded in opening one, he was quickly shoved back by some powerful arm from the outside, into the room again.

Like one who endeavours to flee from devouring flames, that rush in merciless fury to close him in, and finds every passage, every outlet, or crevice for escape barred against him, the unhappy man reeled back into the room in the madness of despair.

"Murder–murder," he shouted, "John!–Charles!–James!–Edward!–Murder!–Murder!–pirates!–fiends, pirates, robbers, police, police."

"Ho! there! Domingo,–Gregoire!–Alphonso!–José!" called Appadocca, with his habitual calmness.

Four men on the call entered the room. Their flashing eyes shone from beneath their overhanging red caps, and their long beards and mustachios exhibited a peculiar appearance under the silvery light of the tapers, which tended to display to the full their dark and dry complexions.

"Secure him," said Appadocca pointing to Willmington, as the men entered.

"Do not touch him for your lives," cried the young officer, the son of James Willmington, that sat on his right.

He, like his father, had been under the power of a supernatural terror from the moment that Appadocca entered, and had been addressed as a visitant from another world; but when he became awake to the fact that the intruder was a being of flesh and blood, he grasped his sword that lay on a table, and rushed at Appadocca.

"Do not touch him for your lives," he cried, while he made a lunge at the breast of the pirate-captain who still retained his seat. The point was already touching the cloak of Appadocca, when the heavy weapons of some unseen individuals from without, shattered the slender sword into a thousand pieces.

"Secure you the young man, Baptiste," said Appadocca, unmoved by the danger which he had so narrowly escaped.

A man immediately stepped into the room and threw his arm round the unresisting young officer.

The four men had rushed upon Willmington. Despair had maddened him into a sort of courage: he met the foremost one of them half way, and grasped him around the throat, with the clutch of death. The pirate also seized him, and the two men, animated with passions which though different in their natures were equally fierce in themselves, grappled like madmen, and staggered violently to and fro. The strong effort of the pirate, could not throw off Willmington, who clung to him with the tenacity of the serpent that tightens its refolded coils around the triumphant tiger that still presses its paw on its bruised head.

Lashed into rage, the pirate drew his knife: it gleamed for a moment overhead, and was descending, with certain death upon its point, when—

"Hold!" cried Appadocca, "no blood;" help him Gregoire, José, help him, there."

The voice of the captain arrested the disciplined arm.

Spurred by the immediate commands of their chief, the other pirates closed in upon Willmington, and by the exercise of violent force tore him away from their comrade, who stood for a moment with his eyes fiery and glaring from anger, and with his chest heaving heavily and quickly.

The prisoner kicked and shouted until the words rattled hoarsely in his throat; but he was now in no soft or gentle hands. Sooner than we can write it, he was tied hand and foot; his cries, nevertheless, still resounded through the place.

"Gag him," was the immediate order.

The prisoner's neckcloth was roughly undone, and violently thrust into his mouth.

"Away with him."

The pirates stretched out two pikes: the prisoner was laid across them, they raised him on their shoulders, and walked silently out of the apartment.

"Now unhand your prisoner, Baptiste," said Appadocca, to the man who held young Willmington. Baptiste let go his hold.

"My father, my father," shouted young Willmington and rushed first to one door, and then to the other, all of which he found guarded on the outside.

"Sir, you cannot go out," said Appadocca.

"I will go out—I will go after my father," ejaculated young Willmington.

"You cannot, and shall not," answered Appadocca.

The young officer rushed to all the doors in succession, and was rudely pushed back at each.

"You see you cannot go out," observed Appadocca.

"Who are you? what do you wish to do with my father?" inquired the young Willmington, as he turned disappointedly from the door.

"I shall tell you, by-and-bye," answered Appadocca.

"Tell me at once, and let me out," cried young Willmington.

"That cannot be."

"That must be: I must rescue my father," rejoined young Willmington.

"Banish the idea: you will never be able to do so," replied Appadocca.

"Why not?"

"Because you will be prevented," answered Appadocca.

"Prevented?—prevented? Hell, itself, with all its legions, shall not prevent me," shouted young Willmington. "I will rescue my father."

"Do so," answered Appadocca.

The young man rushed to the doors again, and was thrust back as before. After a series of vain attempts, he staggered, almost exhausted, into the centre of the room.

"You see, sir, I make no ungrounded assertions. It is impossible for you to follow your father," said Appadocca.

"Why impossible? Confound you as a cut-throat—murderer," asked young Willmington.

"Because," answered Appadocca, without noticing the harsh epithets, "because he is implicated in a vow that must be fulfilled."

"I understand no such vow," said young Willmington, "and if I had a sword, I should force my way in spite of you."

"Ha! we shall now understand each other, sir," said Appadocca, then threw aside his cloak, unbelted his richly-ornamented sword, and laid it on the table. "You can use that, sir," he said to young Willmington, while he pointed to it, and stepping towards the door—

"Lend me your sword," he said to one of the men.

The person gave up his sword at once to Appadocca, who went round the room, and carefully bolted every door, one after the other. After that, he said to his men:

"Retire into the high road, and remain there until I call."

The men retired from the doors, and Appadocca closed with the same care the one by which he had entered.

He was now left in the apartment only with young Willmington, Mrs. Willmington, who lay insensible on the floor, where she had fallen at the appearance of Appadocca, and her two infant daughters, who stared on in a state of absolute stupefaction.

"Now, sir," said Appadocca to young Willmington, standing by the table, and leaning on the sword which he had borrowed, "allow me to speak to you. I am your father's son."

"You are not," indignantly remarked young Willmington.

"It is an honor," said Appadocca with a smile, while he bowed to the young man, "which I have never prized, I believe your stock is stamped with a peculiar mark: behold it!" and Appadocca opened his little finger as widely apart as possible from the other, and pointed to something between the two fingers,

Young Willmington looked, stared, and started back in astonishment, but spoke not a word.

"He," continued Appadocca, after this disclosure, "treated me with harshness, injustice, and cruelty, and wronged, in addition, one whose place I now supply, and in whose name I seek vengeance. I owe him nothing except punishment. I am, therefore, your father's sworn persecutor, and retributioner. You, he has always treated with kindness and affection; the bonds of natural obligation have been drawn the tighter on you by good deeds. You are, therefore, by the principles of justice, his natural defender. Now he is named in a vow that I have made, and I cannot let you rescue him. I have the power to prevent you from making any attempt to that effect, and I shall do it. But there is yet a satisfaction which I can give you, and I shall do so. With my life, the persecution which is now carried on against your father will cease; for I shall leave none behind me to take up my cause. I am willing, therefore, to throw life and death on a hazard, and to afford you as fair a chance as possible of purchasing your father's deliverance by your valour and bravery. My sword, which I offer you, is of the finest metal, you may rely upon its fidelity. I challenge you to mortal combat."

Appadocca put himself in an attitude of defence, bent his left arm over his back, raised his head proudly, and held his sword straight before him.

Young Willmington was undecided: he seemed to be under the power of a thousand different and conflicting feelings. There was no possibility of denying the well-known family mark with which Appadocca was stamped; he saw, consequently, before him his brother, by the laws which nature had made, whatever he might be by those which man had framed, and was forced to recognize in that brother the prosecutor, enemy, and almost murderer of his father. He was divided between two duties, the duty which he owed to a father, and that which he owed to a brother.

"I shall not fight with you," he said after a long pause. "If you grudge us any of his property, take as much as you please, but render us back our father."

"Will not fight!" exclaimed Appadocca, "I had imagined that your father was the only selfish coward in an old race of reputedly brave men."

"Coward do you call me?" inquired young Willmington, with a frown.

"Ay, coward," answered Appadocca. "First you made a thrust at me when my attention was directed otherwise, and now you seek to wound my feelings by supposing the possibility that I could grudge you your father's wealth. Grudge, indeed! his most precious jewels would disgrace me. My men, however–the friends that received me, shall enjoy it. Coward, ay, thrice four times coward; again, and again, I proclaim you as such."

"No more, defend yourself," cried young Willmington, and he clutched the sword which Appadocca had laid on the table.

Young Willmington warmly pressed on Appadocca who still stood on the defensive. Thrust after thrust, lunge after lunge came in rapid succession from young Willmington. Respiration came short and quickly. He made a desperate thrust at Appadocca, who with a slight but quick movement of the wrist at once disarmed his adversary.

Young Willmington bowed haughtily, while his face grew crimson with vexation.

Appadocca quickly picked up the sword and presented it again to the young officer.

"No, no, I am satisfied," said the last-mentioned person, and refused it.

"You ought scarcely to be so, sir. Recollect this is the only chance that will probably be afforded you," replied Appadocca, "to recover your father. Try it again."

"Have you any object in pressing me to fight longer? By the law of arms you are not justified in thus asking me again when I am defeated," said young Willmington.

"Perhaps not," answered Appadocca, "but you must recollect this is a very particular case. To be frank, I must confess I am scarcely satisfied with the chance that I have afforded you, I like to satisfy justice, sir. Pray try it again."

"Strange man, I shall," answered young Willmington, and then began to prepare himself more deliberately for this second combat.

The swords were again crossed. Willmington no longer thrust so *wildly* as he did–he fenced more cautiously. Appadocca still maintained the defensive. The combat proceeded but coldly–Willmington tried every skilful pass and cunning trick. He had contrived to edge his sword, as he imagined, imperceptibly to Appadocca, within but a short distance from his adversary's hilt, and was just inclining his hand inwards to thrust home, when Appadocca met the inclination by an opposite movement, and by a sudden jerk again unarmed his adversary.

"Sir, destiny seems to favour me at these. I presume you have pistols, shall we try them?" inquired Appadocca.

"It strikes me you are longing for my blood?" remarked young Willmington.

"By no means," answered Appadocca, "I have waded through too much of that already. But I am willing to give you the greatest opportunity of redeeming your father. Then am I to understand that you will fight no more?"

"No more," answered young Willmington.

Appadocca drew forth a small silver whistle, he blew it, and in a moment the pavilion was again surrounded by his men.

"Sir," said Appadocca, on the arrival of the men, "the safety of my followers require that you should be rendered incapable of alarming the town. You must consent to be gagged and bound. Ho! outside there."

Three or four pirates entered the room.

"Gag and pinion him," said Appadocca, and pointed to young Willmington.

In less than a few minutes the order was executed upon him.

"Take him to the remotest room in the house."

Young Willmington was carried bodily out of the apartment. "Ho! Jack Jimmy," cried Appadocca.

That individual immediately rushed into the room, trembling with excitement.

"Rummage the whole house, and bring all the silver and gold, Pedro, help him."

"Yes, massa," Jack Jimmy answered, and hurried out of the apartment.

While Jack Jimmy and the other man were intent on searching for whatever valuables the villa contained, Appadocca seated himself on the same chair that still stood at the head of the table.

His eyes had become gradually more and more intently fixed on the two beautiful children, who clung in wakeful unconsciousness to their pale and still insensible mother.

They seemed actually petrified with fear, while their large interesting eyes were firmly rivetted in a vacant stare on the terrible being whose coming had brought so much horror to the happy villa.

"Yes, it is too true," muttered Appadocca, "the sins of the fathers are visited on their children.* Were it not for the injustice of your father, my little ones, I should not be here to-night to terrify you with my fierce and unfriendly looks. If my heart had not been long seared, if there was still in it one single portion that continued as fresh as once the whole was, your silent looks, your unspeaking terror, would move me more than the eloquence of a thousand glib-tongued orators. Nay, I might, perhaps, forget my vow.

"How poisonously bitter are the cups that others season for our lips? Still, may heaven preserve in your minds the deeds of to-night, and when you shall have grown up, always recollect this sad retribution, and speak a word whenever you may be able, and say that you know, by the experience of a scene of your childhood, that certain creatures who are branded and repudiated by society are beings who possess feelings, and who claim the same measure of justice as is meted out to all."

"Me get all, massa," said Jack Jimmy, who now came in with an air of serious importance.

Appadocca rose and pointed to the door; the two men then walked off from the villa, and were immediately followed by the captain himself.

The villa which, but a short time before, presented a scene of domestic happiness, was now left in the desolation of death, with the lights still burning, and the superfluity of luxury still scattered about. The gate was heavily drawn after them by the three persons that had just passed through, and silence settled over the place.

The pirates, who with their prisoner and booty, awaited the captain in the road, were drawn up in order, and after saying a few words to an officer, Appadocca gave the word to march, and they silently went down the road. He himself remained behind.

CHAPTER XXVII

"How now, you secret, black, and midnight hags,
What is't you do?"

MACBETH

IT was dark, on a certain evening, to which the attention of the reader is now called, when, amidst the rocks and bushes of the mountainous district that flanks Port-of-Spain on the east, and that is known by name of Lavantille, two female forms might be perceived.

---

* "the sins of the fathers . . . ": Exodus 34:7.

They were following a rough and narrow path which led up to the mountains through a thousand rugged ascents and yawning and frightful precipices. The two travellers seemed foot-sore and exhausted, and were compelled now and then to grasp a root or twig of the guava-bushes that grew here and there to assist them, as they arrived at a more broken and difficult part of the small road. The air was also oppressive–the rocks were still radiating the beams which the sun, that had not long set, had shot full upon them as it was sinking in the west. Nature was hushed: but the distant and faint barking of the cur that guarded some invisible hut, and bayed at some imaginary danger, fell on the ear.

The two persons still followed the path, and ascended still higher and higher up the mountain that overlooks Port-of-Spain.

"You are tired, madame," said one of the persons, whose dress indicated an humble condition in life, and who was evidently conducting the other.

"Yes," replied the other, who appeared to be of a different class.

"We shall not have very much farther to go," said the guide.

"The place is certainly a great distance from town," remarked the other.

"Yes, it is, and the path is very rough and unpleasant; but we shall presently come to a beautiful spot, where we shall be able to rest for a few moments."

"No, no," answered the other; "it would be better to proceed at once: the night is now quickly coming on, and we do not know what dangers there may be among these solitary rocks. What, if robbers were to attack us?"

"Robbers," replied the other; "madame needs not fear robbers; bless me, people would not take the trouble to come and remain here for the purpose of robbing others. Robbers are never heard of in Trinidad, I assure you."

"Indeed," replied the other.

"Yes, indeed: I know persons who have traversed this place at all hours of the night. I myself have passed here on one of the darkest nights, and quite alone, also: you need not be under any fear I assure you."

In the meantime the wayfarers arrived at a small level piece of ground that was covered with grass. It was quite an "oasis" in those rough and flinty parts.

"Ah," cried the guide, "here is the place, let us rest here," and sat down on the grass. The lady did the same.

"This is a beautiful little spot, is it not, madame?" remarked the guide interrogatingly.

"It seems so," answered the lady.

"If it was day, you should be able to see the whole country round from this," proceeded the guide: "on that side is Caroni, where we first settled when my master and his family came from Carriacou; a disagreeable and muddy place, madame; there is Maraval, a sweet pretty spot, with beautiful hills and scenes, and straight before us lies the sea. If it were light, you would be able to perceive the five islands, and the large bay where Admiral Appadocca–"

At this name the lady started suddenly.

"What is the matter, madame?" asked the guide.

"Nothing, nothing," hastily replied the lady.

"Do not be alarmed; it is, no doubt, a cricket, that has jumped on you. There are not many snakes here: Caroni is the place for them," observed the female cicerone.

"Well, as I was saying, madame,–what was I saying?–I was telling you about the large bay where Admiral Appadocca–"

The lady started again, but more slightly than before.

"Let me drive it away for you," said the guide, "these crickets are sometimes very troublesome; but they are a sign of good luck–they are a sign of good luck. People say, those on whom they may happen to jump, are sure to have money–plenty of money. Where is it? Let me catch it."

"Oh, never mind, never mind," the lady said hastily, "continue, continue your story."

"When Admiral Appadocca, I was saying, set the Spanish ships on fire, at the time when the English took the island, I remember the blaze they made. People say they were laden with gold; what a pity that was."

"Why did he set them on fire?" inquired the lady.

"Because he would not let the money fall into the hands of the English," answered the guide.

"And what became of the admiral himself?" the lady inquired again.

"I really cannot say," answered the guide.

A short pause ensued.

"Had he any son, do you know?" asked the lady after a time.

"I do not know, madame," answered the guide.

"The money that I spoke of just now, has been all lost. They say that sometimes the fishermen manage to bring up a portion. I don't think that is true," said the guide.

"Do you not think we had better go on," inquired the lady–"I wish very much to see that old woman, as soon as possible."

"Come, then," answered the guide, and the two travellers continued their journey. As they proceeded, the path became still more rough, steep, and trying. They, however, went on.

"I should be very much disappointed," said the lady, "if after all this trouble and labour, the person that you tell me of, should not be able to give me the information I require."

"Never fear that, madame, never fear that," replied the guide, "she is a wonderful woman."

"Do you know of any instance in which, what she said, turned out to be the truth?" asked the lady.

"Bless me, yes, madame, great many, I can assure you. She has often foretold what would happen, and what she said, proved as true as possible."

"She may be able," said the lady, "to speak about what is to come, but can she say anything about the present?"

"All," replied the guide.

"Do you think, she will be able, to give me any information, about the person whom I am now seeking?" inquired the lady.

"I am sure she will," answered the guide.

"Let us walk faster," said the lady, and, at the same time, quickened her pace.

"I should not advise you to walk faster, madame," said the guide, "we have still a considerable way to go."

"True," said the lady, "and fell again into the measured and leisurely pace of the guide.

"You are sure she will give me the information, you say?" observed the lady.

"Quite sure," answered the guide, dryly, "I can point you out a hundred families in town, who were landed here as poor as myself, and who made the great fortunes they now possess, only by consulting her. In the time of slavery, when a planter lost any of his slaves, he had nothing else to do, but to come to her, and she would send him to the very corner, where he would be sure to find his run-away."

"Indeed!" cried the lady.

"It is true,"–replied the guide, "beside, she can cure all sorts of disorders. Those that are pronounced incurable by the doctors in town, resort to her, and are sure to be restored to health.

"I remember one case in particular," said the guide, seriously, "of a man who had been suffering for two years, from a hand that was swollen to a very great size. He could not get any rest, either night or day, but groaned continually. He consulted every doctor–they did everything in their power but could not relieve him. His hand grew daily worse and worse: and he was reduced to the size of a nail. Well, some one told him about this old woman, and he came to her. She examined the hand, then pressed the fingers; from under the nails of each she took out a rusty pin. Next day the hand was perfectly cured."

"Impossible," said the lady.

"Quite true," replied the guide.

"There is another case," continued the guide, "that is as striking. There was once an unfortunate man who was afflicted with madness; sometimes he was quiet, at others he would break out in the greatest violence and beat his wife and children almost to death. All the doctors saw him and said he was quite gone, there was no curing him. His illness daily gained ground upon him, until at last he went violently mad. His friends were grieved on his account, and were at last persuaded to take him to the old woman. They did so: as soon as she saw him, she took a little stick and struck him on the head; his skull opened: she took out twenty small fishing hooks that were stuck into his brains; and closed the skull again. In a few moments the man was cured."

"Is that possible?" exclaimed the lady.

"It is remarkable," observed the guide.

"Did you see the cure yourself?" inquired the lady.

"No, I did not," answered the guide, "but every one in the town knows it."

The path in the meantime became more rugged, broken, and steep.

"Ha, we are now arrived," said the guide, taking a long inspiration.

The travellers made two or three steps forward, and they immediately perceived a faint light that glimmered indistinctly through the brushwood.

"Now, madame, you must disguise yourself, or else she won't speak to you," said the guide.

"Why so?"

"Because," replied the guide, "there is a law in this country against those who tell fortunes. If it was to be known that she told anything to any one, she would be burnt alive. Leave your veil here, madame, there, so, and hide your comb with it. That's it, that's it; now take this handkerchief, tie it round your head–let me do it."

The guide tied and adjusted a Madras* handkerchief on the head of the lady.

"Now let us go: and recollect let me speak."

The two travellers diverged into a still narrower part that was almost entirely hidden by the bush which grew thickly and fully about it.

---

*Madras handkerchief: Madras, a city in India; a madras handkerchief is a large, bright-colored, cotton kerchief, often worn as a turban.

The angry barking of a dog was now heard. The travellers still went on, until they could now distinguish the outlines of a low and narrow hut, in the open part of which the embers of a wood fire still smouldered. By its faint light was to be indistinctly seen, the form of the wakeful watch-dog, that stood determinedly a little way in front of the hut, and barked fiercely and fretfully.

The two women stood, afraid of approaching nearer. The dog still barked noisily.

"Ho, Mother! Mother Celeste," called the guide. "Mother Celeste!"

No one answered.

"She does not hear," observed the lady, "she is asleep; call louder."

"Ho, Mother Celeste! Mother Celeste! it is I, it is I," repeated the guide. Still there was no answer,—the dog barked still more loudly.

"Heavens! I hope we have not come all this way for nothing," exclaimed the lady, in a voice that faltered with anxiety.

"It is to be hoped not," answered the guide, and she began to call out more loudly than before: "Mother Celeste! Mother Celeste!"

"Who is it that comes to disturb me at this lonely hour of the night?" said a weak and obscure voice, that came from within the fragile hut.

"It is I, it is I, and another person, who wish to see you," answered the guide.

"You cannot see me to-night. I do not know what you have to see me about," answered the same voice.

"We have come a great distance, and we cannot return without seeing you: let us in."

"I cannot open my door at this hour of the night," replied the voice: "return."

"That we cannot," replied the guide. "Call your dog, Mother Celeste, and open the door to us; you will see what a present we have brought you."

"What present can you bring me this time of night?"

"Fifty dollars, Mother Celeste, fifty dollars."

"I can't open to you," replied the voice, "I can't open to you."

"Say a hundred," said the lady.

"Well, a hundred dollars," cried the guide.

"It is very late, I do not know who you may be; I shall consider—I shall consider," said the same voice.

"She will open now," said the guide, "that is what she always says, she is now hiding all her things."

Truly enough, in a short time, the voice from within was again heard.

"Approach, my children; come and tell me your woes," it said.

"But the dog, the dog," cried the guide.

"True," replied the same voice, "Fidele, Fidele," it called, and the dog immediately became silent and disappeared.

The two females now approached the hut. It was a little cabin, that was built of a few pieces of round timber, which were now black with smoke. Palmetto* leaves formed a slight covering to it. A few reeds roughly fastened to the primitive posts, fenced in the part which lay in the direction from which the wind usually came. The other, or inner part of the hut, however, was fenced entirely in, and covered, as the sleeping apartment.

"Wait until I strike a light," said the same voice.

In a few moments a rudely constructed old door opened.

"Enter, enter, quickly, my children," said the same voice.

The lady hesitated a moment.

"Go in, go in, madame," said the guide, and gently pushed her.

The two travellers entered.

The hut presented as peculiar an appearance on the inside as it did on the outside. The rough pieces of palmetto bark that boarded it, was hung with drapery of spiders' webs, that either floated black with time and dust, or was still spread in the process of extension, under the industry of the master insect himself. From crooked nails, that were driven into this primitive wall, a number of bottles, of peculiar fashions and makes, hung suspended by cord that had long lost its colour under the many dyes which it may have received from the black, yellow, green, brown, and bluish liquors which those bottles seemed to contain.

In one corner stood a rough bed, that seemed constructed of four branches of a guava-bush; and around, a number of nasty, greasy, barrels were ranged, and had their heads carefully covered over by pieces of plastered old canvas.

In one of the deep angles of the hut there burnt a lamp, constructed of a hollow gourd, in which some cotton and some oil were adjusted, and was made to throw around a dim light, whose faint radii did not extend farther than a foot or two beyond its centre.

At the side of this lamp was huddled up a being which at first view, might appear to be one from whom life had long departed, and whom the veneration of friends or kindred persisted in still retaining among them. She was a little black woman of diminutive size, with an old greasy dress, that lay slack

*Palmetto leaves: low-growing fan palms.

and loose about her. Her knees were drawn up to her jaws, which protruded largely and hideously. Her skin was shrivelled and dry, and seemed to flap as she moved her toothless jaws. A Madras handkerchief was tied carelessly round her head, and from a corner, or a hole here and there, her short gray and matted hair peeped out.

"Good night to you, Mother Celeste," said the guide, as she drew a three-legged stool for the lady, and sat, herself, on the ground.

"Good night to you, my children, good night," said Mother Celeste.

"I have brought this friend of mine," said the guide, "to see you on a matter of great importance."

"To see me? to see me, my child," mumbled Mother Celeste: "what can I do for her, poor old woman as I am, except give her my blessing?"

"She wants some information about a person she is seeking," said the guide.

"How can I give it, how can I give it, my child?" answered Mother Celeste.

"Try, mother, try," remarked the guide.

A pause ensued, during which Mother Celeste seemed thoughtful.

"What friend of yours is this, my child?" inquired Mother Celeste.

"She is from the Spanish main," answered the guide.

Mother Celeste raised the rude lamp to the face of the lady: "Yes, yes," she muttered, and replaced it on the ground, and then grasped her hand: the lady started when she felt the rough, hacked skin of the sorceress.

"Do not start, my child," said Mother Celeste, "do not start; and now tell me your story, she mumbled. Will you go into the front awhile?" she added to the guide.

The latter opened the little door, and went out.

"I love," said Feliciana, whom the reader may have recognised before this, "I love a man—a stranger to me—I cannot tell you how I love him. He was taken to my father's house, from the beach on which he was found half-drowned. I loved him the very first moment I saw him, he is so handsome. He suddenly left my father's house, and now I wish to know where to find him. Do tell me: there are a hundred dollars for you."

The sorceress clutched the money and pressed her flabby lips to it again and again, then tottered towards her rude bed and laid it under her pillow.

"Yours is a difficult case, child," mumbled the old woman.

"What is the man?"

"Alas, mother," answered Feliciana, "I fear he is a pirate."

"Is he short or tall?"

"Tall."

"Dark or fair?"

"Pale."

"Retire for a moment, child," said mother Celeste.

Feliciana went out of the small apartment.

An hour passed. During this time, Feliciana and her guide were alarmed by the horrible noises that were heard from the room of the sorceress. Now the most fearful yells – now the most heart-rending groans broke forth – the violent stamping of several individuals were at one time heard, at another, the strangest jargon grated harshly on the ear, while, at the same time, the stench that penetrated through the chinks in the partition almost suffocated those without.

Feliciana and her guide trembled in utter fear.

"Shall we run away?" said one to the other.

"No, no," answered Feliciana, her whisper almost inarticulate with terror.

Even at this trying moment the thought of Appadocca was the most powerful in her mind. The hope of finding him, sustained her against all terrors.

At the end of the hour the little door of the hut was violently opened, and the little sorceress was seen standing in a body of flame.

"Seek your lover, amidst the tombstones to-morrow, at the lonely hours of night," she said, and the door was violently closed.

This uncertain answer fell on the ears of Feliciana like a thunderbolt.

"Oh, he is dead – he is dead," she cried, and wept bitterly.

The guide stood aside and allowed the young lady to give vent to her sorrow.

"Who knows, madame," she said, after a few moments, "the answer may not mean that."

The young lady raised her head for a moment, a new thought seemed to strike her.

"Let us ask," she said, "let us ask?"

"Oh, she will not open the door now, for the world," the guide replied.

"Will she not? Mother Celeste, Mother Celeste," cried Feliciana.

The barking of the dog that now reappeared drowned their voices.

"I tell you, madame, she will not open the door," said the guide. "I ought to know her, since I bring people to her almost every day."

Feliciana remained buried in thought where she was for a moment. "Let us go," she shortly said.

The two travellers began to retrace their steps towards Port-of-Spain. Feliciana was sad and pensive; the guide was less talkative than before, and after half-an-hour's walk, the barking of the dog still reached their ears.

CHAPTER XXVIII

- "Who's there?
Who is it that consorts, so late, the dead?"
ROMEO AND JULIET

APPADOCCA stood for a while, and watched his men, who, in military order, were marching down the dark and solitary road. When even their footsteps could no longer be heard; he cast one more look on the desolated villa, that still shone resplendently under the many lights which burnt within, and that now presented the appearance of a place, in which the pleasures of a marriage feast, may have been broken in upon, by some unexpected and chilling calamity.

What ever reflections he may have made, while he gazed at the house before him, were short and transitory and perhaps unpleasant, for he suddenly turned away his head, and bent his steps rapidly towards the beautiful Savannah, that opened before the splendid house of James Willmington.

Having immediately approached the Savannah, Appadocca climbed over the iron rails that enclose it, and got within.

The night was one of a peculiar sort. It was dark, but the air was soft and dry, and the numberless stars that shone, seemed to twinkle more, and more, and more brightly, and by their brilliant light, the imaginative, may have seen, or fancied to have seen, to a vast depth into the bluish ethereal fluid, in which they were suspended. Appadocca directed his steps immediately across the Savannah. He walked on pensively and moodily, without even raising his head for a moment, to gaze on the stars above; or, to listen to the faint and peculiar insect-sounds, that might now be heard, amidst the general calm and lull of nature.

When he had arrived at the western end of the Savannah, he again climbed over the railing, and found himself in the road which runs parallel in that direction, with the Saint Ann's road, on the opposite side. He then diverged towards the left, and continued down the road, until he had arrived *in* a certain street, which ran to the right.

Appadocca walked along this street, and was obliged to stop from time to time, in order to drive away the numbers of dogs that followed, and that kept up an unceasing noise at his heels.

The street opened on the extensive cemetery, that lies to the westward of Port-of-Spain, and that looks picturesque and beautiful by day, under the grove of magnificent trees, that shelter it; but which, by night, looks as dark and as gloomy, as the thoughts themselves which it calls up.

Appadocca stood for a moment, and looked over the wall; no one, nothing was to be seen, save a few white and spotted goats, that silently cropped the grass at a distance, or frisked capriciously over the tombstones.

He scaled the wall, and held his way straight down the road, which lies concealed beneath the thickly knotted branches of the trees that overhang it, and that unseen, leads into the innermost parts of that long and lasting home of thousands.

Having reached the utmost end of this road, he turned towards the left, into one of the many cross-formed paths, that bisect the cemetery. He walked carefully along, and examined attentively every tomb that he passed, until he had arrived at a simple grave, that with a plain cross at its head, lay sheltered beneath the rich spreading foliage, of a thick cluster of bamboos. Here Appadocca stood, and remained motionless and entranced, at the foot of that unornamented tomb; his arms were folded over his breast, and he was in the attitude of one whose thoughts were veiled in an absorbing and holy feeling.

In a moment he approached nearer and nearer; then seated himself down at the head of the grave, and remained there, his brow resting on his hand, as if his spirit was in communion with that of the body which the grave contained.

Time fled, still the pirate captain remained in the same position. The deeds of a whole life-time, one would have said, were returning in rapid succession on his memory. The pursuits, the pleasures and pains, the endearments and enjoyments of childhood, of boyhood, of youth, of all, seemed to fly back like administering angels, or like fiends of hell upon his mind; for his recollections were freshened, his sensibilities were awakened by his mother's grave:–his mother's grave, which he approached now a different man from what he was, when he bade the farewell which proved the last on earth to that mother. He had left her with the halo of those virtues, which she had taught more by example than by precepts, still surrounding his head, with his spirits fresh and expanding, with his heart good and at ease, with his intellect aspiring higher and higher; now he revisited her in the cold tomb, with a callous indifference either to virtue or to vice, with a heart that was poisoned to the centre, with spirits lacerated and torn to shreds and tatters. How to wreak retribution now engrossed his whole intellect–retribution on the man whom that mother had once too fondly loved, and whose placid nature had, no doubt, long long forgiven. How could he be certain that her spirit now looked down upon him with pleasure, the spirit of her whose life was a speaking lesson of patient endurance.

Such might be the feelings and thoughts of Emmanuel Appadocca, whose manhood could not restrain the tears that trickled down his cheeks, and flowed, as it were, in mockery over the hilt of the sword that lay across his knees, and moistened the mound before him.

The fleeting hours glided by, Appadocca was in the same position. The brilliant stars shone beautifully above him, the fire-flies played about the tombstones, the tall dark trees rustled, and the pliant bamboos creaked melancholily before the gentle night breeze.

"I may not look upon you again: still, let me–let me perform, perhaps, the last office that I may be permitted," said Appadocca, as if speaking to some one by his side, and began to pluck the weeds that grew over the grave.

Time passed quickly. His labour was completed. Appadocca took one last and earnest gaze at the grave, then muffled his cloak leisurely around him, and turned moodily away.

He followed the same path that led to the grave, and came out on the wide gravelly walk. His footsteps echoed in the silence of the hour, and he proceeded with his eyes fixed upon the ground. From time to time, however, he raised them to look at the morning star. He had now done so, when he beheld before him a tall female form, that was clad in black, standing under the branches of a rose-apple tree, which edged the road.

"Heavens!" muttered Appadocca, "is there, then, such a thing as spirit?"

He stood for a moment.

"Oh, human mind," he cried, "how weak thou art in all thy greatness! how imperfectly thou canst cut away the indifferent portions of thyself. Behold, whither imagination now hurries thee. Can there be such a thing as a spirit?"

Appadocca began again to walk. The form began to advance towards him. They met.

"Appadocca," it cried, and grasped the hand of the pirate captain.

"Feliciana! impossible: my ears play upon me," said Appadocca.

No, no: it is–it is Feliciana; Feliciana, who has tracked you from her father's humble house, and who will still follow you as long as life continues under the labours she will undertake for you, and the privations she may have to endure on your account."

"At this place, and at this dismal hour!" remarked Appadocca.

"Better this place with all its horrors than the palace in which I could not find you," answered Feliciana.

"Strange devotedness," muttered Appadocca.

"But how came you to know that I was here," asked Appadocca.

"A sorceress told me you would be," answered Feliciana. I entered this cemetery. Heavens, how I trembled! and trod its solitary walk and examined each whitened monument until – until – I – saw you – at – at – a grave. Return, return, with me, let me pray with you, let me join my prayers with yours."

On saying this, Feliciana proceeded down the walk, and led the unresisting captain after her.

Arrived at the simple grave, she threw herself on her knees, and began to pray. Appadocca stood by, now resting on his sword.

"Oh grant," said the lady, in conclusion to her prayer; and she repeated the part aloud, "grant that his heart may be turned from the unholy pursuit which now throws his soul into the hands of demons, and let the spirit of his mother inspire him with the thoughts that she possessed."

This loud conclusion sounded solemnly in the silence of the night. The sternness of Appadocca's character could scarcely resist it.

"Come and join me; say you renounce the life you now lead," said Feliciana.

Appadocca made no answer.

"Come, come – for your mother's sake, come," said Feliciana.

"Pray you, senora. I will not pray, and I cannot renounce."

"I entreat you: imagine you behold the mother that you have loved so much, making the same petition to you. Could you refuse her?"

"Senora, speak no more on this theme, I say I cannot renounce; my vow is made."

"Heaven looks not upon unholy vows; not on vows of vengeance," said Feliciana, "renounce your life and forget that oath."

"Senora, the morning star is sinking; my followers must be growing impatient. I must go;" and Appadocca moved a step.

Feliciana sprang from her knees and grasped him by the hand; "do not go from this spot the same man as you came to it. Wash yourself by prayer from the blood which you may have shed, and ask – ask her spirit to forgive you, if you offended it."

Appadocca drew his hand quickly across his brow. "Feliciana, you are ungenerous, unkind: my–feelings–require–no–further laceration. Life and my miseries have already made me too, too well acquainted with anguish. Spare me, spare me the thought of an offended mother–the only–the only–the only–friend that I had in this bitter, bitter, world."

"Say–say not so," quickly rejoined Feliciana, still more melted by the grief of one who appeared always so indifferent. "You have still, still a friend. Oh fly, fly with me to some wilderness; there enjoy your thoughts, your silence, your feelings. I shall be your slave, your dog, that will gather the inkling of the wish from your very eyes. My *fallucha* is by the shore; Appadocca will you go?"

A pause ensued.

"No, no, Feliciana," said Appadocca; "I shall not: lean not, good, good girl, upon a broken reed. To me all things, save one idea, are stale and indifferent. My life is gloomy, dark, and troublesome: my existence is already a heavy, heavy oppression. My soul, like the cumbrous* tower, fell but once, it can never rise again. Your presence would create a new grief in me, for I could not see you love one whose blood was chilled."

"I require no love–I require no love," quickly rejoined Feliciana, "I shall be your slave."

"That, I shall not endure; my idol is woman. I ought to worship, not she."

"Still you will let me follow you?" eagerly inquired Feliciana.

"No, no, my career may still lie through blood," answered Appadocca.

"Speak no more of blood," cried Feliciana, "forswear your vengeance."

"Never," answered Appadocca sternly.

"Say, why doom yourself for ever," Feliciana was going to inquire–when–

"That the world may profit by my conduct," answered Appadocca.

"But the world will not know, will not attend to what you do."

"I care not, I care not," answered Appadocca, "my word is passed and I shall fulfill it. I am resolved, the sacrifice must be made.

"But see, the morning star is sinking fast. I must away."

"But do not–"

"Come, come, let me lead you hence," so saying Appadocca grasped the arm of the faint Feliciana, and hurried out of the cemetery.

They walked down the street that runs from north to south on the western side of Port-of-Spain, and soon reached the principal landing-place, where the crew of the Black Schooner were impatiently waiting for their captain.

"Feliciana, I bid you a long, long adieu," said Appadocca, as they stopped

---

*cumbrous: heavy, ponderous.

under one of the almond trees that form the shady walk we have already mentioned.

"Do not say so," said Feliciana indistinctly, as she leaned against the tree, "oh do not say so."

There was no answer, not a word.

"Feliciana let me ask you–to–to–place this near your heart, and whenever you gaze upon it, let one thought return–to–to–the–the sick man of your father's house." So saying, Appadocca drew his sword and cut off a lock of his flowing hair, and presented it to the lady.

"Look–look–there," she cried faintly, as he received the token.

Appadocca turned round and beheld a crowd of people who, with torches and lanterns, were following a company of soldiers that were marching quickly down the walk.

"Flee," cried Feliciana.

"One more request," said Appadocca. "Forget not, Feliciana, the place where you first saw me to-night. If foul and rank weeds grow upon it, pluck them as you pass by. Farewell, farewell."

Appadocca walked down the wharf and was received by his men.

"Shove off," he cried, as he threw himself on the stern sheets of the boat, and folded his cloak around him.

The soldiers arrived at the wharf just in time to see the boat disappear in the gray light of the morning.

They fired–the air resounded with their repeated volleys.

CHAPTER XXIX

"Go back again thou slave, and fetch him home."
COMEDY OF ERRORS

It was not until an early hour of the morning, when Mrs. Willmington recovered from her swoon, that it was possible to give any alarm of the outrage that had been committed at the villa of James Willmington.

When the lady recovered from her state of insensibility, and saw before her the scattered and disordered furniture, the flickering wax candles that had now burnt down to the very sockets, and her children, who, after the departure of the pirate party, had fallen asleep around her, recollections of the supposed apparition, and of the terror of her husband, flashed across her mind. Alarmed at the silence that reigned around, and not being able to understand why she had been permitted to remain in the same place where she had fainted away, she rushed impulsively to the bell, that lay on the sideboard, and rang it violently.

No one came.

She rang again—no one came: she rang again, and again, more and more violently; still no one came.

She then looked out of the parlour, and beheld the whole house still lighted up. She ventured out a little, and still a little farther, until she summoned sufficient courage, traversed the court yard, and entered the servant's apartments.

In the principal room nothing was to be seen. Mrs. Willmington raised the light high up, while she stood at the entrance, and looked into every corner and hole. She could see nothing.

"Good God! can I be abandoned here with my children," she said in a low tone, fearful to hear even her own voice, in such a silent and deserted situation.

She entered the room, and proceeded towards a door, which opened into another apartment. She turned the handle, and went into that room also; nothing was to be seen. She was turning to leave, when a low groan was heard. Mrs. Willmington started two paces backwards, but raised the light and looked back intently towards the part from which the groan came. In a dark recess, that lay in a remote corner of a room, two white shining balls seemed to glare upon her. She started still farther back: another groan was heard; she raised the light still higher; it fell upon a part of the recess, and discovered the shining face of the individual to whom the eyes belonged and from whom the groans proceeded.

"It is Jack, it is Jack!" cried Mrs. Willmington, and walked up towards the recess.

It was, indeed, Jack, who had his mouth as well filled with grass and cloths as it could possibly hold, and whose arms were as tightly tied behind his back, as mortal arms could be: and whose short legs were stretched straighter than they had ever been stretched before in Jack's life. He was lying on his side, and his eyes were playing in their sockets like those fierce-looking things which German ingenuity has designed to represent the visual apparatus of man, and which are to be seen every day in some of the back streets of London in full play, to the infinite excitement and gratification of the awe-struck and wondering urchins.

"Jack, cook!" cried Mrs. Willmington, "what state is this you are in?"

"Jack, cook," groaned, and his eyes played still more rapidly.

"How can I assist?" said Mrs. Willmington, "I think of it!" she ran hastily out of the room, and returned a few moments afterwards, with a large knife.

With this, she cut the cords which bound the limbs of the unfortunate Jack. A task of no little labour, for those who secured him, had done so with a marvellous amount of skill and success.

"Do the rest for yourself, now," she said, when she had completed part of the work.

Jack required no exhortation, but as soon as his arms were free, he began with all his might to pluck out the number of things, with which his not incapacious mouth had been filled.

"Tenk Gad," he cried, as he nimbly jumped on his legs, and shook himself like a Newfoundland dog* coming from the water.

"Where is your master?" quickly inquired Mrs. Willmington.

"Me massa, ma'am!" answered Jack in the manner that is rather peculiar to his class.

"Yes, your master; and where are the other servants?" Mrs. Willmington asked again.

"Dem gane?" asked Jack again, in his turn.

"Who, goue?" inquired Mrs. Willmington.

"De paniole, ma'am:" answered Jack.

"Tell me, Jack, will you; tell me quickly," said Mrs. Willmington, now waxing impatient, "where is your master and the other servants?"

"Let me see if dey gane," said Jack, and he walked on tiptoe towards the door, then carefully and cautiously peeped out, then ventured a little way into the courtyard, then ran hurriedly towards the great gate, and bolted it and rebolted it.

"Awh!" he cried, "Garamighty! Dey gane now! awh! me, neber see such ting in all my barn days. Wha dat? Me hab time foo blow now: put big, big, bundle so nan me mout! tap my breath, awh! But me can blow now–tshwh, tshwh!" and Jack took a long breath in the fashion which seems to be peculiar to his people–a fashion which compresses a vast quantity of air, and sends it vehemently forth, so that the same hissing noise which the steam makes when it comes through the valve of a railway engine, is produced. A fashion which, be it said within parentheses, may be very economical, inasmuch as it affords a certain large amount of respiration within a certain small period of time.

This soliloquy, in the making of which, the illustrious cook by no means

---

*Newfoundland dog: a breed of large, strong, black-and-white or black-coated dogs.

limited himself as to time, being over, and after having cast searching glances about the gate, and having looked and relooked above, below, sideways, before, and behind, Jack then, and not till then, deemed it proper to return to his mistress, who had also come to the door, and was endeavouring to discover what the cook was about.

"Me shet it, ma'am, me shet it," cried Jack, as he returned.

"Now, perhaps, you will tell me what I ask," said Mrs. Willmington, getting still more excited and angry, "where is your master?"

"Tap, missus," answered Jack, "I'll tell you all bout it."

"Make haste, then."

"Yes, missus," said Jack, and began to tell all about it. He had the preliminary caution, however, of looking carefully round to see if no more 'paniole,' as he called the pirates, were concealed thereabouts. Being for the time satisfied on that point, he proceeded–

"Last night, ma'am–no, the night before the night, ma'am, ee already dis ma'aning, Bekky come in, and find me da smoke me pipe. 'Good night–' "

"What has that to do with Mr. Willmington, Jack? Tell me where your master is, will you," said Mrs. Willmington, still more angry.

"Me da tell you, missus," answered Jack. " 'Good night, buddee Jack,' say Bekky, says she. 'Good night, sissee Bekky,' me say, says I. 'Awh! Jack!' Bekky say, 'wha tobacca you da smoke dey Jack, ee smell bad! da–' "

"No more of this, Jack," said Mrs. Willmington; "tell me."

"Tap, missus, tap, if you plase; me da come to it, me da come to it now," said Jack.

Mrs. Willmington looked resignation itself.

" 'Da tobacca I buy dis ma'aning, Bekky,' me say ma'am," continued Jack; 'and dat was all. Last night wen me finish de fowl, and bin da clean the kitchen, who me see, but Bekky. 'Good even, buddee Jack,' she said, says she. 'Good even, sissee,' I say, says I. 'Look, some good tobacca a bring foo you, Jack,' she say; and give me a bundle tobacca. So last night, when I sen in the dinna, I went into the garden foo try dis tobacca."

"Me sit down under de bread-fruit tree; me tink me see somebody walk in de garden. Garamighty! me say, wha jumbee want early, early so. Me look agin, and me see de purson hab big, big beard like Paniole. Me frieghten! Da who you, me bin go halla out, and bin da go run away, when somebody hold me fram behind, and chucked grass and ivery ting into my mout, tie me han an foot, and trow me into the little room way you fin' me ma'am."

"And where is your master?" asked Mrs. Willmington.

"Me no know, ma'am," answered Jack.

"And where are the servants?"

"Me no know, ma'am," again answered Jack.

"Rummage the house, you simpleton," said Mrs. Willmington, and lighted him the way to the other parts. Jack went cautiously, and turned his head round in all directions.

They entered another room. "Garamighty! Jim, dey tie you, too," exclaimed Jack, as his eyes alighted upon the "Jim" who was exactly in the same predicament from which Jack himself had but a short time ago been delivered.

The only intimation of intelligence that Jim could make was, rolling his eyes about.

All the apartments were now searched, and the servants were found, one here, the other there, among them. They said that they were all simultaneously laid hold of by a number of "panioles," and were gagged, bound hand and foot, and deposited separately in the different rooms.

"And where is your master; and your young master?" asked Mrs. Willmington.

"Dey carry old massa away pon their shoulders, ma'am, and dey took young massa up-stairs."

"Heavens!" cried Mrs. Willmington, "and was it not then a spirit?" she asked.

"He looked more like a paniole than a pirit, ma'am," said the individual who gave the information, who was the chief servant in the house, and whose especial destiny it had been to be gagged and otherwise dealt with in his pantry, wherein he was at the moment busy about some particulars connected with his avocation.

"Run up stairs. Go you, Edward, to–to–Mr.–, the magistrate; alarm the town; tell the soldiers at the fort," exclaimed Mrs. Willmington, while she herself pushed upstairs with a servant.

Young Willmington was found duly gagged and tied in the favourite style of the pirates. He was immediately released, and he got up from the bed on which the kind consideration of the unwelcome visitors had laid him. He exhibited less pleasure at his freedom than one would have expected to see.

"What is the matter with you, James?" said Mrs. Willmington, not a little surprised at the strange calmness of her son. "Do you know that your father has been carried away from his house?"

"Yes, mother, I know it."

"Then why not make more haste, James, and go to see about it?" rejoined Mrs. Willmington.

No answer.

"I shall go," said young Willmington, after a pause, "but my mind misgives me about this whole affair. My father ought not to have concealed the truth from us. The man who came into the house, last night, is my brother."

"Your brother!"

"Yes, dear mother: he possesses the family peculiarity," answered James. "However, I shall go and alarm the authorities."

The magistrates were awakened, the alarm was given at the forts, and the whole town was shortly in commotion. The streets were searched, but no pirates could be found. A body of soldiers was then marched down to the wharf, as the reader already knows.

At early dawn the magistrates went alongside the English man-of-war, and related to the commander what had taken place.

"There is not much mystery about all this, gentlemen," said the commander, after he had reflected a moment, "I shall promise you, that when it is clear, you will be able to see a long, sharp, and strange-looking schooner in these waters. I have, unfortunately, been made too familiar of late with the boldness of that set of pirates. I am so certain of what I am telling you, that I shall at once give orders for weighing anchor: so that I shall be ready, as soon as it is light, to give chase, and I shall see," muttered the commander to himself, "if I cannot get to windward of those fellows this time."

True enough, the pirate schooner was seen in the light of the morning opposite the harbour of Port-of-Spain, but at an immense distance out at sea.

The heavy sails of the large ship then began leisurely to ascend its encumbered masts, in preparation for the chase of the pirate vessel.

CHAPTER XXX

"The deed is done."
MACBETH

WHEN Appadocca with his party had gained the schooner, he immediately ordered the prisoner Willmington to be taken to the torture-room and to be there kept in custody: at the same time the men were summoned to the main deck, and the booty of the previous night, was distributed in the same manner as we have described at the beginning of this tale.

In the meantime the morning dawned more brightly, and the waters of the gulf lay smooth and shining before the piercing rays of the morning sun, unbroken as they were by the faintest breath.

The heavy sails of the man-of-war were still seen to ascend one by one, and fall, as they were spread, heavily against the masts.

They reflected the sunbeams from their white and clear surface, far and wide: and amidst the number of vessels in the harbour, the huge ship-of-war, with all its canvas spread, and its stern decorated with the fiery ensign of England, looked like a gigantic monarch of the sea that floated at the head of its smaller subjects.

She was now ready to weigh anchor, and was now evidently only waiting for the wind which was certain to spring about the hour of ten in the forenoon.

When Appadocca had superintended the division of the spoil amongst his followers, he ordered the young midshipman to be brought before him.

That individual, in a few moments, made his appearance. He had scarcely as yet recovered from the effects of his torture; he was pale, and appeared still weak and emaciated. Yet in his eye there could now be read a more earnest seriousness – the fruit of the self dependent position in which he had for some time so accidentally found himself, and the consequence of the example to whose power he had been exposed, in the stern and manly society into which he had been thrown.

From a boy whose yearnings had been continually after excitement and pleasure, he was suddenly transformed into a man, whose thoughts began to be characterised by the seriousness of purpose which alone can be worthy of the highest of the animal creation.

A change was marked on his face, and his demeanour was more subdued and more self-possessed.

"Young man," said Appadocca, as he stood before him, "I set you at liberty, you shall have a small boat, which will in a moment be ready for you, you will be able to scull to your ship. I cannot, I am sorry to say, spare any of my men to help you. I see she is preparing to weigh anchor. Take my compliments to the commander himself, and tell him, to take the advice of one, who has experienced much kindness at his hands, and by no means to move from his anchorage to-day. Ask him to consult a calculation which I made on the partition of the cabin in which I was confined, and he will know the reason. Before you leave the schooner, ask the officer of the watch for a letter which I shall send to your commander's son."

Appadocca then descended into his cabin and wrote thus:–

"DEAR HAMILTON,

"The consummation of my existence is now fast approaching; I, therefore, write to you, as I fear it will be the last time that I may have the opportunity of communicating with a dear friend, from whose heart I have experienced so much consideration, and from whose hands I have received so much kindness! It is scarcely necessary for me to tell you, that destiny preserved me from the perils from which few could have hoped to escape.

"I am at the head of my faithful followers once more, and it rejoices me to think that my escape was effected entirely by my own efforts and quite unknowingly to one on whose escutcheon I should not have even virtue itself accidentally to paint a blot. I shall lead the men who have followed me so bravely, and who have served me so faithfully, to some remote spot on the fertile and vast continent that lies on our right, and build them a city in which they may live happily, quietly, and far removed from the world, whose sympathy they cannot hope, and care not, to possess. For myself. . . . . Receive, my dear Charles, the sincere good wishes of one who esteems you.

"EMMANUEL APPADOCCA"

"N.B.–Recollect and prevail upon your father not to set sail to-day. Remember the tempest of which I spoke, it will come within these twenty-four hours.

"E. A."

The young midshipman was withdrawn and in a few moments he pushed off gladly from the schooner, and was soon seen gradually leaving it behind.

Ten o'clock came, and with it the steady trade wind. The placid gulf curled before it–the vessels at anchor in the harbour, swung to and fro on their long cables, as they felt its force, and the vessel-of-war sheered off under her canvas that swelled and looked full and turgid with the wind. The sprays flew about her broad bows, and she was bearing straight down on the schooner with the wind on her quarter. Every sail that could be hoisted was set, and her commander seemed again determined to make another powerful effort, in order to have a chance of bringing his batteries to bear against the Black Schooner. As for that vessel herself, she remained in the same place where she was, and seemed quite indifferent to the movements of the man-of-war.

Appadocca pensively paced her deck, and looked from time to time towards the eastern shore.

"The rash and fiery old man," he muttered, with an expression half anxious, half indignant, when he saw the large vessel fall off from her anchorage.

When the wind had become fairly settled in, the order was given to set sail.

With the usual rapidity, the masts of the schooner became sheeted in her ample sails, her small kedges were let go, and she turned gracefully to the wind. Her bow pointed to the southern outlet of the gulf–the Serpent's Mouth.

The calm and placid picture which the two vessels presented, as they sailed in the same direction, bore in itself but a faint resemblance to the fierce passions that might animate their crews, or the bloody deeds which might be done if once they came within gun-shot of each other.

The usually quiet gulf smiled under the freshness of the morning: the two vessels sailed smoothly on its even bosom. There was no labouring, no plunging, no heaving of terrible seas, to call forth any feeling, akin to terror.

The dark blue waves appeared through the thin vapours of the morning like a landscape in a picture, and the light slender fishing canoes, with their feather-like sails, which seemed to play on the waters, like butterflies in the beams of a sunny day, added a peculiar and peaceful appearance to the scene.

The high and solitary mountain of Naparima, with a few scattered and scathed trees on its crown, rose in the distance; while the low sloping shores before, seemed entirely to enclose the gulf, and to hem it round against the violence of intrusive winds. Upon the whole, a beholder, on seeing the two vessels together, with the thousand sailing boats and sloops that followed in the wake of the man-of-war in order to witness the exciting scene of an action, might have taken them to be the pleasure ships of luxurious lord-lings, who had launched forth on the deep to seek another subject of excite-ment, in order to cheat monotony of some of its victim-days.

The pirate schooner held its course with an indifference that would not have led one to believe she was pursued. The watchful chief stood by the shroud of the mainmast, with his arms folded on his breast, calm and im-passable as he was at almost all the moments of his life.

Not so the pursuing man-of-war. Ever and anon, as any of the small sailing vessels that navigate the gulf came in sight, signals upon signals went up her masts, to intimate that the vessel ahead was a pirate, and to command it to be harrassed and hindered in its course. But all these were lost on the simple skippers of those simple crafts.

The chase continued. The terrible rock that is known by the name of the "Soldier," and that true to its appellation, seems to guard with unsurpriz-able vigilance the passage of the Serpent's Mouth, was passed. Point Icacos, too, was doubted, and the two vessels were now riding on the Atlantic billows, with the low Orinoco marshes on the right and the rocky and wild coast of Trinidad on the left.

The sun was setting, when, suddenly, as if some monster screen had been abruptly raised from earth to heaven, in order to keep one part of the globe from the other, the wind fell, and the sails lay like humid sheets against the masts.

"Nature will now begin to speak," said Appadocca to himself, with a certain air of contentment now lighting up his stern brow, and then looked aloft and around.

At his order, the spars were instantaneously armed with steel spears, from whose feet, conducting wires hung down along the shrouds and dipped into the sea. At another order, the large jibs, foresail, and mainsail of the schooner were stripped from the masts, and in their place, small narrow sails, which, from their size, could not have been supposed to be capable of having the least effect, were set.

The guns were doubly secured in their places, and the arms were fastened with even greater care than usual in their cases, in the bulwarks.

The two vessels now lay on the ocean, that now heaved as if from its own convulsions; for the lightest vane hung straight and stiffly down. There was not a breath of air. The vessels turned round and round helplessly on the seas, and as they rose on this wave, and were beaten athwart, or astern by the other, for the billows rolled at this time in no regular course, they fell into the troughs, or rose on the brows of the waves with such sudden and straining movements, that the wood and iron that formed them, seemed scarcely strong enough to hold together.

Night closed in; with it came a darkness that in itself was awful. No man could see his hand before him, shipmate could not see even the shipmate that stood at his side; which was the sea, which the deck, no one could tell, save when some counter-running wave broke suddenly on the side or bow of the schooner, and threw up the myriads of shining insects that inhabited its full and swollen bosom.

Those that were obliged to move about, clung cautiously to the bulwarks, and set one foot carefully before the other, that they might not throw themselves over.

The cries of the terror-stricken sea-birds, as they wandered on the still and suffocating air, with even instinct failing to lead them to their resting place on the shore, sounded hoarse and ominous to the ear.

Not a sound was heard on board the schooner, except the creaks of the straining cordage, as the vessel violently and madly plunged.

Now, like molten lead, the rain began to fall in large, heavy, and leisurely drops. Then distant sounds, like the groans of a labouring world, when earthquakes shake it to its base, were heard. A sudden and faint gush of wind, like the fluttering of gigantic wings, came and turned the schooner round and round, and passed away, leaving the deadly calm as it was before. Flash–flash–the lightning came, and by its lurid light, the ocean to the southard shone in one sheet of foam.

"How is your helm?" inquired Appadocca of the steersman.

"Very slack, your excellency. She does not feel it," the man replied.

The sounds increased; they approached nearer and nearer; they came, and like a toy in the hand of a giant, the schooner was suddenly thrown on her beamends. The water washed one-half of her long deck, and the first gust of the hurricane swept with a terrible noise, over the prostrate vessel, and seemed to crush her, like a mountain that had fallen from its base, and had met some paltry obstacle in its way, while it was rolling along to find its level.

"Luff," cried the chief to the steersman.

"Luff."

The schooner lay on her side for a few minutes, as if she would never right again: at last, like an impatient steed, whose course has been arrested by some temporary barrier, after sustaining the violence of the gust, she sprang forth into the face of the wind, and seemed like a thing of passion and pride, roused to brave the power of the overwhelming hurricane.

With the scanty storm sails, which the foresight of Appadocca had had bent, she shot through the mountain billows with her usual speed, cleaving them through, and throwing the sprays mast high.

On–on, she went, as if actuated by the bold spirit of the man who commanded her, she sought to penetrate the very bosom of the hurricane.

Her slender masts bent like willows to and fro, as she mounted the mountains of rushing water, that struck and shook her to the very keel.

By the flashes of glaring and frequent lightning, the fierce sailors could now and then be seen standing stolidly at their respective stations, their red caps drawn far down over their puckered brows, and their black beards dripping with spray and rain.

A rope fastened each man to his post, and unmoved, like carved wood, they stood in the terrors of the howling winds: the bonds of discipline were still on them.

As for Appadocca himself, far from evincing any anxiety, he seemed to take pleasure in the terrible convulsions of nature. With the dark heavens above him re-echoing far and wide with the rolls of the loud and never ceasing thunder; with the balancing ocean below him, and the terrifying howls of the devastating hurricane around him, he was the same unimpassioned, collected, intrepid man, as when the schooner rode on the calmest sea, under the most smiling sky. He seemed to take pleasure – if his nature could receive pleasure – in the awe-striking scene. Ever and anon he took up his red cap, and pressed his hand over his brow in apparent delight.

The schooner still laboured in the seas that now began to grow higher and higher, and heavier and heavier. The lightnings came and played about her masts, like the spirits of the tempest, that seemed marking her as their victim; but the fluid glided down the wires, and lost itself in the foaming deep.

Still on – on – on she went. A terrible gust . . . . She was laid on her beams again. The wind was gone: the air was calm and close: not a breath; – her narrow sails hung to her masts, and she was tossed about without wind enough to feel her helm.

At this frightful interval the echoes of rending broadsides were heard towards the north. They were the reports of the man-of-war's distress guns.

"Take in the fore and mainsail," cried Appadocca, in a voice that seemed to sound solitary and lonely amidst the terrors of the night. "Reef the jib."

The order was scarcely executed, when the rumbling sounds were again heard. It was coming – it was coming; the schooner was thrust forward, as if some immense rock had been let to fall against her; her bows were dashed through the approaching billows; as she emerged for a moment, the same power thrust her backwards; her stern sank under the volumes of water that washed over her decks; and then, as quick as thought, she was lifted from the surface, and twisted, and twisted, and turned reelingly round in mid-air, and was let to fall with a tremendous crash again. Crack – crack – her two tapering masts snapt from the deck. They were overboard, and the lately resisting schooner was now borne with the rapidity of lightning before the hurricane.

"Get up the anchors," the voice of Appadocca was again heard, as he recovered from the concussion of the whirlwind.

The prostrate sailors scrambled from the corners into which they had been thrown; the hatches were raised, and the only hope of the schooner, – the anchors – were quickly drawn on deck.

The hurricane was now at its height. Like a feather on the overturning currents of an overflowing cataract, the vessel was furiously borne away before the sweeping wind.

The anchors, with their immense coils of chain-cable were thrown overboard, to arrest the progress of the vessel for a time, until jury-masts could be rigged.

It was of no avail. – Fast – fast – before the wind the schooner went; and then a grating noise, and a dreadful shock; – every man fell on his face – she was ashore – on the rocks.

"Save yourselves, my brave men," the deep-toned Appadocca cried, as he stood boldly prominent amidst the surrounding rack and ruin.

The ocean was fringed with foam, as it broke on the rocks of Trinidad, on which the once beautiful schooner was at this moment being dashed to pieces.

The sailors now thought of saving themselves. The distance from dry land was not much, and it might be gained on the crest of the waves, if no rock dashed to pieces the daring fugitives in their attempt.

Each bold pirate watched his time, and leapt boldly on the crest of the billow, as it came washing by, and in the twinkling of an eye, was thrown up high and dry, alive or dead, on the top of the rocks.

Already every man had left the schooner, and had perished or been tossed up alive.

Appadocca still stood leaning on the bulwarks, contemplating the sad remnants of his once all but animated vessel.

Lorenzo and Jack Jimmy drew together imperceptibly to his sides. They stood around him silent, and unperceived.

The schooner was breaking up; still Appadocca stood where he was.

"Will not your excellency go on shore?" Lorenzo at last ventured to say.

Appadocca started slightly, as if awakened from a dream or reverie.

"Yes, Lorenzo; but save yourselves first. Watch the wave; here it is – jump in – you, too, Jack Jimmy, quickly, so, so."

The two men jumped on the billow as it swept by the schooner, Appadocca followed, and they reached the shore.

Now the wind suddenly ceased as before.

Appadocca, with Lorenzo and Jack Jimmy, were sitting on the top of a lofty rock: they were viewing the last struggles of their vessel.

"A terrible night, this is, Lorenzo," said Appadocca.

"It is, indeed, your excellency, a frightful night! for – hark! What cry is that? It is from the schooner," cried Lorenzo, as he stood up.

A supernatural shriek fell on the ear. It came from the schooner. Again it came – again – and again – as she was battered against the rock.

The three persons were silent.

"Oh, I know," cried Lorenzo.

"It is the prisoner – I may save him yet – I may save him yet," said Lorenzo.

They were the shrieks of James Willmington, who was still battened down in the narrow torture-room, into which he had been thrown, and was undergoing more than a thousand deaths; dying as he was, thus cooped up in a dark narrow cabin, and the vessel breaking asunder under him.

The cabin was so close, that his terrified shrieks could not be heard before; but now, when the seams were opened, they alone, prolonged, and agonizing as they were, were now to be heard in the lull of the wind, on the silent, close, and death-strewn air.

Lorenzo rushed down the rock, but ere he could devise a means to rescue him, the schooner broke in two, and the unhappy Willmington sank for ever, still a prisoner in the torture-room.

The schooner went to pieces, and soon the billows rolled on the rocks over her once graceful form.

Appadocca silently watched the gradual destruction of his vessel, and silently listened to the shrieks of his father.

When not a timber of her remained above water, he heaved a heavy sigh. The first, that Lorenzo had ever heard from him. It was the sigh that came from a hurricane of feelings within him, which equalled the raging hurricane of nature without.

CHAPTER XXXI

"I 'gin to be a weary of the sun,
And wish the estate 'o the world were now undone."
MACBETH

"LORENZO," said Appadocca to his officer who had returned *from* the wreck, "that was a good and faithful vessel."

"Ay, your excellency," replied Lorenzo, sorrowfully, "she was."

"All things must end, Lorenzo," continued Appadocca.

"True, your excellency," answered Lorenzo.

"If so, Lorenzo, the honours and greatness of men are scarcely to be longed after. The pursuits that engross us during an entire lifetime, and lead us too frequently, to sacrifice health, happiness, and sometimes even drag us into crime, must all – all end in this – in nothing."

"True, your excellency," answered Lorenzo.

"You know not, Lorenzo, how different the world appears to me now, from what it did when I was a happy student of eighteen. It was then tinged with golden hues, and shone in whatever light I viewed it. Greatness: oh, greatness, seemed so captivating to me! My nights were devoted to its attainment, my days the same. Now, the world is charmless, scarcely tolerable, and my beautiful dreams have all passed away like the crystal dew before the sucking sun."

"There is still hope, your excellency," remarked Lorenzo.

"What among all things seems the most deserving of preservation, Lorenzo," continued Appadocca, "is our honor, our consciousness of acting right. How many a mind that is curbed down by misfortune and sorrow, finds its own little relief in the simple idea, that it has acted up to the dictates of its honor."

Lorenzo made no reply, he saw that his chief was deeply affected.

"Lorenzo," resumed Appadocca, after a pause, "there is destiny–there is destiny–there is synchronism of events and a simultaneousness of the actings of nature's general laws that constitute destiny; against which no man from the absence of any power to read the future can provide. Thus, in the whirlwind, that raises in mid-air the light feather, there is to be seen the hand of destiny, for there is the synchronism of the feather's being separated from the bird with the acting of the law of nature that produces the wind. It would have been as impossible to the bird, granting that its reasoning powers were less limited, to have provided against the falling of its feather and the eventual taking of it up by storm, as it was impossible to foresee the whirlwind that overcame the schooner which was made to pass through every danger."

"Too true, your excellency," answered Lorenzo.

"So that it follows," continued Appadocca, "that since men are subject to the former of this destiny, their most strenuous efforts must always prove impotent in restraining its action, and that they are liable every moment, whether they are good, or whether they are bad, to be subjected to misfortune and calamity. And this corroborates what I have already said, that the only thing which we are bound to consider in life, is our honor, which alone is, or ought to be, the source of satisfaction or misery to us."

Lorenzo assented to the philosophy of Appadocca.

"If ever I should be suddenly overtaken by the hand of this destiny recollect, beneath the solitary fig-tree that grows on the Island of Sombrero, you will find a treasure. Devote half to the erection of a college for abandoned children, and with the rest provide for my men who have served me truly. Do not forget that peculiar old servant," he said in a low tone, and pointed to Jack Jimmy.

"Your excellency is growing melancholy," observed Lorenzo, with some anxiety.

"No, no," replied Appadocca. "Still, who knows how soon destiny may end his days."

"For you, Lorenzo, you have acted towards me in a manner that I have duly appreciated," continued Appadocca, while he grasped his officer's hand, "here is my sword, wear it, and may the time soon arrive when you may use it in the cause to which you are pledged, farewell!"

With a spring Appadocca jumped from the rock and threw himself head-long into the thundering waves below.

His movement was so sudden that Lorenzo, and Jack Jimmy, who sprang to their feet at once, were too late to hold him back and save him.

The little negro silently returned to the spot where he had sat since he had come on shore, and his his face in his hands. Not a word–not a sob escaped him. His grief was too deep and strong for tears.

Morning dawned on the devastated scene of the late hurricane.

Like a strong man who is recovering from illness, nature presented a smiling, though languid look. The billows still ran high, but unlashed now by the wind, they rolled heavily against the rocks.

High and dry lay the bodies of the dead, their pallid faces still locked in the grim passions which had attended the departure of life.

The dawn had scarcely come, when Jack Jimmy might have been seen moving totteringly along the ruffled beach, with a dead body on his shoulders. Away into a solitary recess of the picturesque little bay, he bore his burden. He laid it down, and then slowly began to scoop a hole.

Solemnly he worked–his arms rose and fell like his heart–heavily.

But who comes to interrupt the sacred work! Lorenzo! It was Lorenzo. He had followed Jack Jimmy to the spot. The officer began to dig, too.

"Tap, massa–tap," said Jack Jimmy, solemnly grasping his arm–"let me one do it."

The hole was dug:–Jack Jimmy adjusted the uniform and hair of the corpse, composed its features, and laid it carefully in it.

His arms again rose and fell as heavily as before:–the grave was closed, and made even with the ground. Jack Jimmy knelt at its foot, raised his eyes to heaven–his lips rapidly moved, and a heavy tear fell on the simple grave of the pirate captain.

It was about this time that a little *fallucha* came labouring over the still perturbed waves under four powerful sweeps. At its stern sat the captain and a lady.

Attracted by the signs of the shipwrecked pirates, she drew towards the shore.

The tale of the wreck was soon told. The lady raised her hands and held her forehead as if it were about to split asunder. She landed, and walked along the strand and studied each dead man's face that she passed by. She arrived at the spot where Jack Jimmy was completing the grave, and was adjusting each tiny pebble in its proper place.

Her heart sank within her. Quickly she approached the one who was toiling in so sad a mood.

"Whose grave is this?" the lady quickly asked.

"My young massa's," Jack Jimmy slowly answered, without raising his eye from his work.

"What was his name?" again asked the lady.

"Emmanuel Appadocca," again answered Jack Jimmy, as slowly as before.

"Emmanuel Appadocca!"

The lady raised her hands to her burning brows, and pressed her eyes. She remained for a few moments in this position. Then her arms fell languidly by her sides, an expression of vagueness spread itself over her face, she looked absently around, a ringing laugh broke forth from her lips, her jaws then hung mopingly. Feliciana fell mad over Appadocca's grave.

CHAPTER XXXII

"Of that, and all the progress, more and less,
Resolvedly more leisure shall express:
All yet seems well; and if it end so meet,
The bitter past, more welcome is the sweet."
ALL'S WELL THAT ENDS WELL

FELICIANA was taken to her *fallucha,* which immediately changed her course, and returned to Trinidad.

Lorenzo built a camp on the shore for the protection of his men, until he should be able to send a vessel to their rescue, and then began to traverse the island under the guidance of Jack Jimmy, whose excitability had now yielded to a melancholy and dull sombreness.

One evening the sun had set, the twilight was passing away, and gloom was settling over the forests, when Lorenzo, exhausted and fatigued, thought of going to ask shelter on a plantation, which he knew to be near at hand, by the repeated crowings of cocks, that noisily vented their loud farewell-clarions to the departing day.

"Jack Jimmy, do you know who is the proprietor of the estate which I think we are approaching?"

"No, massa," answered Jack Jimmy.

"Do you think they would give us shelter for to-night?" inquired Lorenzo.

"Yes, massa," answered Jack Jimmy.

"Then will you endeavour to find your way to it?"

"Yes, massa,"

In about half an hour, Lorenzo and Jack Jimmy came out amidst a number of flourishing gardens, that lay smiling at the back of a village of labourers' houses.

The two travellers quickly crossed there, and opened into a long lane that was shaded by tall tamarind and sappodilla trees.

An ecclesiastic was seen calmly pacing this umbrageous retreat, while his lips rapidly moved as he pored over the dark and riband-marked breviary, which he held open before *him*.

The father was so wrapped up in what he was reading, that he did not perceive the two strangers until they had almost met face to face.

The priest started back, as he came on Lorenzo. "Mercy on us! the pirate officer!" he cried.

"What, what new deed is it, sir," he said, after a pause: "which now tarnishes your soul again, and draws you to this peaceful and quiet retreat?"

"Pirate officer no longer, good father," answered Lorenzo, "and I bring no outrage on your peaceful retreat. My spirit now itself requires too much calm to break it wherever it already exists."

The priest folded his arms across his breast, and looked silently and sympathisingly on the unhappy man before him.

"My son," he said, with a countenance that beamed with charity; "my son, there is one above that can relieve our bitterest woes. Seek consolation in the afflictions which press upon your soul from his hand."

"I am now in your power, good father," said Lorenzo. "The schooner is wrecked on these shores; Appadocca is no more."

"Is he dead?" cried the priest.

"Yes."

The priest turned towards heaven, and prayed for the soul of the pirate captain.

"God forbid that I should ever refuse charity to the afflicted: come with me, sir, and my good patron will, I doubt not, afford you hospitality."

The three persons walked up the lane, and discovered a comfortable planter's house, that stood in an open space amidst a number of orange trees. They quickly approached the house; and Agnes, who was sitting at the open window enjoying the evening breeze, fell senseless to the ground, as she beheld Lorenzo.

"Accommodate the stranger as soon as possible," said a fiery looking old man, whose gray hair floated over his shoulders, and fell over a large and turned-down collar, while the boots which had not crossed the threshold for many a day, still shone with heavy and immense silver spurs.

"Accommodate the stranger, and get him a guide as soon as possible," he said, as soon as the priest told him of Agnes's illness, and had no doubt expressed his own surmises.

The time for Lorenzo's departure, approached. He was informed that a guide and a mule awaited his leisure.

"I must see the master of the house," he said.

The servant withdrew, and shortly afterwards conducted the officer into the presence of the old man, who stood up as well as he could, bowed, and asked Lorenzo to be seated.

"Sir," said Lorenzo, speaking without any preliminaries; "your daughter and I love each other."

"What, sir! mention my daughter!" cried the old man, furiously, without hearing any more. "Sir, the mule and guide are ready."

But there was a softening balm even for the inflammable spirit of the old gentleman. He, like all other men, had the particular point by which he could be led!

The pirate officer immediately disclosed that his real name was not Lorenzo, but St. James Carmonte; and that he was the lineal descendant of the Carmontes, who fell fighting for the Prince. He went on to explain that his people before him had vegetated in a number of corners all over Europe; but that he and the others that then survived had been eventually expelled from France at the epoch of the great revolution. That he had then taken to the sea, there to seek adventures; as he imagined he had been long enough on the enduring side.

"What! the descendant of Carmonte," cried the old man, who was touched in a sensitive part: "Carmonte, whose fathers fought at the side of mine. How can you vouch this, sir?"

Lorenzo presented a ring.

"The word, sir."

Lorenzo said something.

"Agnes, Agnes, come hither, Agnes," vociferated the old man.

The young lady appeared. She was still pale and emaciated.

"Take her, take her, man," cried the old cavalier. "May God bless you, and preserve you to see the day when the king shall enjoy his own again."

The priest blessed the union, and Lorenzo, after disposing of Appadocca's followers, lived happy in the retreat of the plantation.

Jack Jimmy served the officer of his young master with fidelity. A smile, however, was never seen more on his face; and when the winds howled more loudly than usual, the drops calmly fell from his now aged eyes.

In a certain city of Venezuela, Feliciana might be seen in her white veil, and her sombre dress, amidst the abodes of the heart-stricken and afflicted; she was known as the "Succouring Mother." Twice a-year she might also be seen on her pilgrimage to Trinidad, when she plucked the weeds from off his mother's tomb, and tended the sea-grape tree that grew over the lonely grave of EMMANUEL APPADOCCA.

THE END

Afterword:
Emmanuel Appadocca, the First
Anglo-Caribbean Novel

SELWYN R. CUDJOE

It hardly seems possible that never more will the stalwart upright form [of Maxwell Philip] be seen in and about the Court House.

And yet never again shall we see him with stately steps entering the Court House, his torn gown gathered up in his left hand behind his back, towering a head and shoulders above his fellows.

Never more shall we see the courtly bow and hear the suave "good morning to you."

Never more shall we hear those brilliant sallies of creole wit, which used to delight all who knew him.

Never more will he be seen rising at his place at the bar, to plead the cause of his client in sonorous tones and well-rounded phrases pregnant with deep and earnest thoughts.

Never more will he address the Council upon some knotty point of law or to explain some fact of by-gone history.

Maxwell is dead and is gathered to his fathers, and all that is left is a little mound in the cemetery and the mark he left upon the political history of his country and his influence upon those who knew him. Long will his memory remain green in the hearts of each true son of *Trinidad.*

"Elegy on Maxwell Philip's Death," *Public Opinion,* July 3, 1888

> Pity me not, but lend thy serious hearing,
> To what I shall unfold.
> WILLIAM SHAKESPEARE, *Hamlet*
> (Quoted in *Emmanuel Appadocca*)

Introduction

Michel Maxwell Philip, one of the most important Caribbean intellectual-activists of the nineteenth century, stands out because of his pioneering contributions to the social, legal, and literary life of the Caribbean in general and Trinidad and Tobago in particular. A significant figure in Carib-

249

bean literary history, he helped to shape the culture of nineteenth-century Caribbean and left a profound and illuminating legacy that has sometimes been ignored.[1] Although he was forgotten soon after his death, understanding his life and work is indispensable for understanding Caribbean society, especially the intellectual, political, and literary giants that the society produced.[2]

One has to place Philip in a historical context to get a more comprehensive idea of his intellectual contributions to his society.[3] In *Main Currents in Caribbean Thought,* Gordon Lewis noted that the animus against Caribbean intellectual thought "obscured the fact that from the very beginning there grew up a genuine Caribbean historiography, a Caribbean sociology, a Caribbean anthropology; in brief a movement of ideas at once created by European ideologues concerned with the New World, by Europeans residents in the islands, and, later, by a Caribbean intelligentsia itself. But it all had to struggle against the myth of cultural philistinism."[4] Philip and other Caribbean intellectuals worked in a climate that expected very little from them in terms of intellectual and philosophical thought. As early as 1774, Edward Long argued, "In general they [the negroes] are void of genius and seem almost incapable of making any progress in civility or science. They have no plan or system or morality among them. Their barbarity to children debases their nature even below that of brutes. They have no moral sensations, no taste for women; gormandsing, and drinking to excess; no wish but to be idle."[5] In 1791, as he compared those Africans born in Africa with those who were born in the Caribbean, Thomas Atwood made very much the same case against African people in the Caribbean:

> The Creole negros [sic], that is to say, those who are born in the West Indies, having been brought up among white people, and paid some attention to from

1. Although Gordon Lewis devoted two pages to the works of J. J. Thomas in *Main Currents in Caribbean Thought: The Historical Evolution of Caribbean Society in Its Ideological Aspects, 1492–1900* (Baltimore: Johns Hopkins University Press, 1983), the seminal work that traced the intellectual development of Caribbean society, he makes no mention of Philip's novel. See also Elsa V. Goveia, *A Study on the Historiography of the British West Indies* (1956; Washington, D.C.: Howard University Press, 1980), for an examination of the major historical writings that have shaped our understanding of the development of the British Caribbean.

2. See Donald Wood, *Trinidad in Transition: The Years after Slavery* (London: Oxford University Press, 1968), 41–42, 229–30. Although Wood mentions Jean-Baptiste Philippe and devotes two pages of his work to J. J. Thomas, two other outstanding Trinidadian intellectuals of the nineteenth century, he does not mention Maxwell Philip at all.

3. In an illuminating introduction to the present edition, William Cain places Maxwell Philip within an Atlantic/American context.

4. Lewis, *Main Currents in Caribbean Thought,* 25.

5. Long, quoted in Goveia, *Historiography of the British West Indies,* 60.

their infancy, lose much of that uncommon stupidity so conspicuous in their new negro parents; and are in general tolerably sensible, sharp, and sagacious. But there is actually something so very unaccountable in the genius of all negros, so very different from that of white people in general, that there is not to be produced an instance in the West Indies, of any of them ever arriving to any degree of perfection in the liberal arts or sciences, notwithstanding the greatest pains taken with them; and the only thing they are remarkable for attaining to any degree of perfection is Musick."[6]

This tradition of denigrating Caribbean people was engaged in by Anthony Trollope, Thomas Carlyle, James Anthony Froude, and William Pringle Livingstone, each of whom argued that Caribbean people were inferior beings, lacking in intellectual capacity and incapable of political self-governance. As had Long and Atwood before them, Trollope, Carlyle, Froude, and Livingstone saw the British colonizing presence as a civilizing force for African people.[7] Philip Curtin, in his introduction to *Two Jamaicas: The Role of Ideas in a Tropical Country,* and V. S. Naipaul in *The Middle Passage* offered contemporary versions of a similar animus and vilification of Caribbean intellectual thought.[8] Despite these attempts at vilification, there emerged an indigenous Creole intellectual strata that espoused views that reflected the sentiments of their people, particularly as they struggled against the hegemony of colonial rule.[9] It is within this latter tradition that the contributions of scholar-activists such as Maxwell Philip, Jean-Baptiste Philippe, a cousin of the former, and J. J. Thomas ought to be

6. Thomas Atwood, *The History of the Island of Dominica* (1791, London: Frank Cass, 1971), 267.

7. See Anthony Trollope, *The West Indies and the Spanish Main* (London, Chapman and Hall, 1860); Thomas Carlyle, "Occasional Discourse on the Negro Question," *Frasers Magazine* (1849); James Anthony Froude, *The English in the West Indies or, the Bow of Ulysses* (1888; New York: C. Scribner and Sons, 1900); and William Pringle Livingstone, *Black Jamaica: A Study in Evolution* (London: Sampson Low, Marston and Company, 1899). Lewis argues that Livingstone utilized scientific arguments to buttress his racist arguments (*Main Currents in Caribbean Thought,* 311-12). For a fuller discussion of this important point, see William Cain's introduction to this volume.

8. In a somewhat ambiguous statement, Philip Curtin noted: "Nineteenth-century Jamaican ideas are not often worthy of notice for their own sake, and the principal interest is not in the intellectual effort of the exceptional person. It is the outlook of the ordinary man, even though this must often be approached through the works of the not-so-ordinary men who left some record of their beliefs" (*Two Jamaicas: The Role of Ideas in a Tropical Country, 1830-1865* [Cambridge: Harvard University Press, 1955], xi). Picking up on English thought of the nineteenth century, Naipaul noted: "History is built around achievement and creation; and nothing was created in the West Indies" (*The Middle Passage* [London: Andre Deutsch, 1963], 29). For a different reading of Naipaul, see Stefano Harney, *Nationalism and Identity* (London, Zed, 1996), 139-68.

9. See Lewis, *Main Currents in Caribbean Thought,* for a splendid discussion of the growth of Caribbean intellectual thought from 1492 to 1900.

judged. More important, a careful examination of *Emmanuel Appadocca* suggests the brilliant insights Philip possessed about his society. Such an examination is the subject of this afterword.

Emmanuel Appadocca: A Myth of Beginnings

Although *Emmanuel Appadocca* was not the first novel to deal with miscegenation, it was certainly the first Anglo-Caribbean novel to do so from the point of view of the colonized person.[10] A product of the larger current of writing at the time, *Emmanuel Appadocca* was informed by the African American slave narrative, the historical romance, and the ideology of organized piracy. Indeed, it is Philip's dexterous ability to weave these three traditions within his novel that accounts for its splendid literary tapestry.

In the first instance, *Emmanuel Appadocca* relies very heavily on the slave narrative. When, for example, we recognize that Philip not only wrote his book in solidarity with the African American liberation struggle but used it to denounce the Fugitive Slave Law of 1850, his identification with the sufferings of the African American struggle becomes clearer. In his preface, Philip announced that his work "was written at a moment when the feelings of the Author are roused up to a high pitch of indignant excitement, by a statement of the cruel manner in which the slave holders of America deal with their slave-children."[11] His indignation at the way African Americans were treated (and I don't think the term "slave-children" was used accidentally) shows that Philip was fully acquainted with the narratives of African Americans, especially William Wells Brown's "A True Story of Slave Life," written by one of the most famous fugitive slaves of the time.[12] Published in *The Anti-Slave Advocate* in London in December

10. See, for example, E. L. Joseph, *Warner Arundell: The Adventures of a Creole*, 3 vols. (London: Saunders and Otley, 1838), which discusses the life and adventures of Warner Arundell and examines the question of interracial love.

11. Maxwell Philip, *Emmanuel Appadocca: or, Blighted Life* (London: Charles J. Skeet, 1854), preface. All subsequent quotations are taken from the current edition, unless otherwise noted.

12. Philip was acquainted with the discussions taking place around slavery and more specifically, the Fugitive Slave Law of 1850. He was also aware of the works of Frederick Douglass, William Wells Brown, Solomon Northtrop, Harriet Beecher Stowe, and other slaves whose activities were carried in the Trinidad newspapers. Aspects of the debate on the Fugitive Slave Law was published in the *Trinidadian* in August 1850 while some of the pernicious consequences of the law were published in December 1850.

On August 1, 1850, during the observances of Emancipation Day on New Grant Estate (in close proximity to the estate where Philip was born), Rev. George Sherman Cowen, head of the

1852, "A True Story of Slave Life" contained many of the ideas that were examined in Brown's *Clotel: The President's Daughter,* published in London a year later.[13] *Emmanuel Appadocca* is very similar to *Clotel.* Each novel treats the problems of slave children, their abandonment by their wealthy and prominent white fathers, and their mothers' despair. Each novel advocates the use of force to gain one's freedom. Both Philip and Brown were concerned about the impact of the Fugitive Slave Law and how it intensified the brutality of slavery. Thus Brown wrote:

> On every foot of soil, over which *Stars and Stripes* wave, the Negro is considered common property, on which any white man may lay his hands with perfect impunity. The entire white population of the United States, North and South, are bound by their oath to the constitution, and their adhesion to the Fugitive Slave Law, to hunt down the runaway slave and return him to his claimant, and to suppress any effort that may be made by the slaves to gain their freedom by physical force. Twenty-five million whites have banded themselves in solemn conclave to keep four millions of blacks in their chains. In all grades of society are to be found men who either hold, buy, or sell slaves, from the statesmen and

---

Baptist Missionary Society in Trinidad, read passages from Frederick Douglass's "graphic story of his famous narrative . . . which stirred in the breast of many [former African-American slaves who had settled on the island] present recollections of their past history" (*San Fernando Gazette,* August 7, 1850).

In 1853–54, after Philip left the island to study in England, the newspapers were saturated with stories of *Uncle Tom's Cabin.* On January 1853, the *Trinidadian* published the preface to the German edition of *Uncle Tom's Cabin*; on January 7, 1853, *The San Fernando Gazette* published the preface to the French edition; and on March 23, 1853, the *Trinidad Free Press* ran the first chapter of *Uncle Tom's Cabin.* On September 17, 1853, the *San Fernando Gazette* announced the publication of the eight edition of *The Illustrated Edition of the Life and Escape of William Wells Brown* and published one of Brown's lectures from *The Liberty Bell* (1848). An active promoter of the Trinidad Literary Association, Philip must have been aware of the conditions to which the American slaves were subjected and the narratives that recorded their life-stories.

13. Invited by the English abolitionists to visit Great Britain and chosen as a delegate to the Paris Peace Congress of 1849 by the American Peace Society and also by the Colored Convention of Boston, Brown sailed for London and Paris in July 1849 and remained in Britain until September 1854. After the Peace Conference in Paris, Brown was greeted by Victor Hugo, the Abbé Duguerry, Emile de Girardin, and other Paris notables. In England, he was welcomed by some of the most influential abolitionists in the country and "from nearly all the cities and large provincial towns he received invitations to lecture or address public meetings. The mayors, or other citizens of note, presided over many of these meetings" (William Wells Brown, *Clotel, or the President's Daughter* [1853; New York: First Carol Publishing Group, 1989], 48). During his stay in Britain, Brown traveled more than 20,000 miles, addressed 130 public meetings, and lectured to twenty-three mechanics' and literary organizations. Philip would have known about the work and activity of this very famous fugitive. It also explains the sentiments expressed in the preface of his novel for those slaves such as Brown who were being persecuted under the Fugitive Slave Law.

doctors of divinity, who can own their hundreds, down to the person who can purchase but one.[14]

Brown was also aware of events in the Caribbean having visited Cuba in 1840 and Haiti in 1844. He noted in *The Rising Son* that he had read "everything of importance [about Haiti] given by the historians." He also wrote about the development of African people.[15] As a result, he was able to link what transpired in the slave societies of the Caribbean and the United States. More important, he was just as angry at Carlyle's comments about the ex-slaves of the Caribbean as Philip was about the passage of the Fugitive Slave Law. As he traveled in an omnibus with Carlyle in London in 1850, Brown observed what he described as "a forbidding and distasteful frown" on Carlyle's countenance "that seemed to tell one that he thought himself better than those about him." Speaking in solidarity with Caribbean peoples, Brown noted: "I had read his *Hero-Worship* and *Past and Present,* and had formed a high opinion of his literary abilities. But his recent attack upon emancipated people of the West Indies, and his laborious article ["Occasional Discourse on the Negro Question"] in favor of the reestablishment of the lash and slavery, had created in my mind a dislike for the man, and I almost regretted that we were in the same omnibus."[16]

As a Caribbean person, Philip also wanted to add his voice to the chorus of dissenting abolitionists who were upset by the dehumanizing practices of slavery. Philip seemed to be distressed by three aspects of slavery: the way the slave children were treated (he was himself a slave child), the manner in which slave mothers were abandoned by their white lovers, and the cruel manner in which slavery ignored the natural bonds of humanity. In his novel, he also examined what should constitute the correct response of slave children to the unnatural and unfilial acts of their nonslave fathers in his discussion of the implications of the *lex talionis,* which becomes a subtext of his novel. As he noted in the preface of *Emmanuel Appadocca:*

> Not being able to imagine that even that dissolver of natural bonds—slavery—
> can shade over the hideousness of begetting children for the purpose of turn-
> ing them out into the fields to labour at the lash's sting, [I have] ventured to

14. Brown, *Clotel,* 15.

15. William Wells Brown, *The Rising Son: or the Antecedents and Advancement of the Colored Race* (1874; Miami: Mnemosyne Publishing, 1969), 140. Like Philip, Brown demonstrated some knowledge about ancient Africa even though his analysis embodied European biases about Africa.

16. William Wells Brown, *Sketches, Places and People Abroad* (Boston: John P. Jewett, 1855), 199–200. Brown also prided himself on the fact that *Sketches, Places and People Abroad* was "the first product of a Fugitive Slave as a history of travels" (iii).

sketch out the line of conduct, which a high-spirited and sensitive person would probably follow, if he found himself picking cotton under the spurring encouragement of "Jimboes" or "Quimboes" on his own father's plantation.

It is also to be remembered that the degrading fate of Clotel, reputedly the daughter of President Thomas Jefferson, the father of the American Declaration of Independence, was to be enslaved despite her father's position. Both Brown and Philip tried to answer a similar question in their novels: What was the proper conduct for a high-spirited and sensitive person in such a situation? *Emmanuel Appadocca* attempts to tell that story from the Caribbean perspective, using the activities of the buccaneers—he says the story is grounded in truth—to do so. In the circumstances, it is not coincidental that *Clotel* and *Emmanuel Appadocca* are the first novels in their respective literary traditions and that each draws on the techniques of the slave narrative and the romantic novel.

In turning to the tradition of organized piracy to set his narrative, Philip drew upon an important aspect of the social and political history of the Caribbean. As an organized aspect of the political economy of the early Caribbean, piracy was used by most European states to supplement their wealth. Indeed, many buccaneers brought fame, glory, and income to their European patrons by their activities. For example, while Queen Elizabeth "publicly excused or disavowed to Philip II the outrages committed by [Sir John] Hawkins and [Sir Francis] Drake, blaming the turbulence of the times and promising to do her utmost to suppress the disorders, [she] was secretly one of the principal shareholders in their enterprises."[17] Gordon Lewis concludes that piracy was "at once, an economic institution and a social organism."[18] The ideology of piracy, therefore, offered Philip two important metaphors (economic and political ones) that he used to structure his novel.

In the first instance, the activities of the pirates offered a model of economic independence and a scrupulous adherence to honesty. In *The Buccaneers and Marooners of America* A. O. Esquemeling, an eyewitness to the activities of the pirates, noted that:

> They [the pirates] observe among themselves very good orders; for in the prizes which they take, it is severely prohibited, to every one, to take anything to themselves; hence all they take is equally divided, as hath been said before; yea, they take a solemn oath to each other, not to conceal the least thing they find among the prizes; and if any one is found false to the said oath, he is immediately turned out of the society. They are very civil and charitable to

17. C. H. Haring, *The Buccaneers in the West Indies in the XVII Century* (New York: E. P. Dutton, 1910), 31.
18. Lewis, *Main Currents in Caribbean Thought*, 70.

each other; so that if any one wants what another has, with great willingness they give it to one another.[19]

It is conceivable that the buccaneers felt that there was little wrong in their emulating the organized state which, in many instances, encouraged and safeguarded its own pirates.[20] Not only did the British have recourse to the use of the buccaneers to combat the maroons of Jamaica in the latter part of the sixteenth and seventeenth centuries under the command of Henry Morgan, they even made open alliances with them. Edward Long felt Jamaica "stood indebted" to the valor of the buccaneers and observed that "it is to the buccaneers that we owe the possession of Jamaica at this hour." In defending their gallantry, he observed that preceding the treaty that Britain signed with Spain in 1670, the buccaneers, "attacked only their declared enemies, the Spaniards, who had done their utmost to extirpate the English from this and all the other islands in the West Indies." Hence he commended their acts: "The general name of *pirates,* given to these persons, loads the memory of some among them with an undeserved opprobrium; considering the many wonderful and gallant actions they performed, the eminent services they effected for the nation, the riches they acquired to their country, and the solid establishment they gave to so valuable a colony."[21]

Morgan, one of the most notorious of the buccaneers, eventually was knighted and became the governor of Jamaica in 1670. Long described him as "the most celebrated of all the English leaders, . . . equal to any [of] the most renowned warriors of historical fame, in valour, conduct, and success." He lamented the fact that "this gentleman has been unhappily confounded with the piratical herd."[22]

In the second instance, the ideology of piracy was attractive to Philip because of the "rough" democratic dimension of the enterprise. In her

19. A. O. Esquemeling, *The Buccaneers and Marooners of America,* ed. Howard Pyle (London: T. Fisher Unwin, 1891), 82.

20. Howard Pyle argued that the piracy of the early eighteenth century evolved from the "semi-lawful buccaneering of the sixteenth century." Moreover, he noted that "there was a deal of piratical smack in the anti-Spanish ventures of Elizabethan days. Many of the adventurers—of the Sir Francis Drake school, for instance—actually overstepped again and again the bounds of international law, entering into the realms of de facto piracy. Nevertheless, while their doings were not recognized officially by the Government, the perpetrators were neither punished nor reprimanded for their excursions against Spanish commerce at home or in the West Indies; rather they were commended, and it was considered not altogether a discreditable thing for men to get rich upon the spoils taken from Spanish galleons in times of nominal peace" (ibid., 17-18).

21. Edward Long, *The History of Jamaica,* vol. 1 (London: T. Lowndes, 1774), 300, 304, 300-301.

22. Ibid., 301.

study on the historiography of the British West Indies, Elsa Goveia noted that the phenomenon of piracy reflected "the individualism, and the courage which went to the making of West Indian history in the seventeenth century."[23] Following the lead of Goveia, Lewis argues that organized piracy represented "a tradition of rough, quasi-democratic self-government characteristic of early Caribbean frontier conditions."[24] Thus, it seems plausible to argue that Philip located his novel within the frame of organized piracy because it drew–albeit partially–on the Robin Hood legend of stealing from the rich to give to the poor and the aspect of rough democracy that this tradition embodied.[25]

Because organized piracy presumed its own values, bespoke a particular kind of autonomy on the part of the pirates, validated a sense of courage in the pirates' undertakings, and cultivated a righteous indifference toward official society, Philip found it a fitting vehicle to carry forward the slave's sentiments about his condition. Because organized piracy inverted the notions of justice sanctioned by the civil state–that is, the purported respect for private property (which included slaves)–it offered Philip an apt metaphor to advance an alternative system of values that differed from that of the slave-owning class. In other words, while the slave-owning class robbed Africans of their lives, as depicted by Philip, the pirates robbed the slave-owning class of its illusions about their system and themselves and sought to destroy them at any cost.

Philip was also influenced by the specific character of the revolutionary, nationalist tradition of nineteenth-century intellectual thought in Trinidad. When he came across *Free Mulatto,* the work of his cousin,[26] he pursued it "with that earnestness and enthusiasm which that immortal work inspires in those who are in the least connected with the African race."[27] We are asked to believe that when Maxwell Philip returned from Europe in 1855, "he landed on the very spot where the celebrated author of the *Free Mulatto*

23. Goveia, *Historiography of the British West Indies,* 31.

24. Lewis, *Main Currents in Caribbean Thought,* 81.

25. This Robin Hood aspect of piracy seems to be supported by the remarks of one Captain Bellamy, the leader of a buccaneer group, who is reported to have told his followers that "organized society robs the poor under the cover of the law while they, the pirates, plundered the rich under the protection of their own pirates' courage" (cited in ibid., 80).

26. See [Jean-Baptiste Philippe], *An Address to the Right Hon. Earl Bathurst* (London: S. Gosnell, 1824). This address was reprinted by Allers and Blondel in 1882 as *Free Mulatto,* which is what it is usually called. It outlines the grievances that the people of color harbored against the English, especially under the rule of Sir Ralph Woodford, governor of Trinidad from 1813 to 1827.

27. L. B. Tronchin, "The Great West Indian Orator," *Public Opinion,* December 18 and 21, 1888, p. 5.

had landed more than a quarter century before, holding in his hand the famous dispatch of Lord Bathurst to Sir Ralph Woodford, with reference to the civil rights of coloured people." Such an apocryphal association demonstrates the continuity in the actions of these two creole cousins–and one could certainly create a scenario in which Maxwell heard his parents talking about the older relative–and also suggests that the Philips were committed to the liberation struggle of black people, a commitment of which Maxwell would have been aware. Significantly, *Free Mulatto* was republished in Trinidad in 1882 when there was a similar rise in nationalist sentiments.

Such a connection gains credence when one notes Philip's association with the nationalist struggle that was taking place when he began his novel. We know that Philip was interested in the questions of liberation and the historic conditions of black people when he left Trinidad in 1850. L. B. Tronchin reports that around 1849 or 1850 "at the annual banquet for the celebration of the anniversary of the abolition of slavery in the West Indies, he [Philip] delivered a speech which was received with the greatest demonstration of approbation by the audience, prognosticating as it did, those marvelous orations with which he gratified his country a few years afterwards."[28] Many of Appadocca's disquisitions on the problems of his race suggest that Philip was also aware of the contributions of ancient Africans to world civilization. The pangs that he must have felt at the announcement of the Fugitive Slave Law deepened his sensitivity to the conditions of his brothers and sisters in the United States.

Essentially, *Emmanuel Appadocca* is a quest-romance, concerned with the desertion of the protagonist's mulatto mother by his white father, a wealthy sugar planter from Trinidad, and Appadocca's subsequent attempt to vindicate his mother's dishonor. It was necessary for a mulatto protagonist to come to terms with the shame that the European half of his ancestry inflicted upon him. Northrop Frye notes that "translated into dream terms, the quest-romance is the search of the libido or desiring self for a fulfillment that will deliver it from the anxieties of reality but will still contain that reality."[29] Like *Free Mulatto*, *Emmanuel Appadocca* outlines some of the grievances that the colored people felt against European men who dishonored and debased black women and then abandoned them.[30] Such treatment

---

28. Ibid.

29. Northrop Frye, *Anatomy of Criticism: Four Essays* (Princeton: Princeton University Press, 1957), 193.

30. I have argued in another context that Philip's approach to this question is in direct opposition to that of Joseph in *Warner Arundell.* See Selwyn R. Cudjoe, *Literary Trinidad: 1805–1940* (forthcoming).

on the part of white men demanded that the black man uphold the honor of the women and children of his family. It is the enormous desire for retribution that drives Appadocca to give up all other pursuits in order to punish his father for betraying his mother and himself, the illegitimate product of the union. It is, then, to fulfill or realize himself that Appadocca pursues his father.

Emmanuel Appadocca, a great adventure story written with enormous style, eloquence, and subtlety, contains all the major tenets of the romance. Frye notes that "the complete form of the romance is clearly the successful quest" that results in "the recognition of the hero, who has clearly proved himself to be a hero even if he does not survive the conflict." Generally, the protagonist (or hero) is associated with order, fertility, vigor, and youth whereas the antagonist (or enemy) is associated with disorder, sterility, darkness, and a moribund life. *Agon* or conflict is the "archetypal theme of romance, the radical of romance being a sequence of marvelous adventures," whereas the central concern of the quest-romance is what Frye calls "the dragon-killing theme," which is clearly present in *Emmanuel Appadocca.* Although Frye argues that "in every age the ruling class tends to project its ideals in some form of romance, where the virtuous heroes and beautiful heroines represent the ideals and the villains the threats to their ascendancy,"[31] in *Emmanuel Appadocca,* Philip demonstrates how a member of the oppressed class can invert the form to project what he thinks the ideal response of a high-spirited slave child should be to enslavement. In other words, in *Emmanuel Appadocca* Philip is concerned to show how an enslaved person ought to behave under the crushing weight of slavery.

Set primarily in the Gulf of Paria, the Caribbean Sea, St. Thomas, Venezuela, and Trinidad, the novel tells of the activities of a company of men, denizens from different nations, who find a sense of security in the presence of one another and take the law (of vengeance) into their own hands. More specifically, it seeks to counterpoise the moral heroism of Emmanuel Appadocca, the protagonist, against the villainy of James Willmington, the antagonist. As we view the motley company of pirates as they rejoice at the booty they had plundered from the *Letitia* of Bristol, an English ship, we get a good sense of their condition and their attitude to the world:

> Those [were] fierce men, who had abandoned the entire world for the narrow space of their small vessel, and the inhabitants of the vast universe for the few kindred spirits who were their associates—that had separated themselves, by their deeds, from the world, the world's sympathy, and the world's good and

31. Frye, *Anatomy of Criticism,* 187, 192, 189, 186.

bad, that had actually turned their hand against all men, and had expected, as they had probably frequently experienced, that the hand of all men should be turned against them, could not restrain their feelings of welcome, and three loud and prolonged cheers resounded, far and wide over the silent ocean, as they were wafted, in undying echoes, over the crests of the heavy and heaving billows. As comrade rejoined comrade, their grim and bearded faces appeared to relax from their wonted habit of ferocity, under the influence of a prevailing sense of joy: such a joy, those, alone, can experience who have seen every natural tie break asunder around them—who have felt the heavy hand of a crushing destiny, or have been hunted and driven, by the injustice and persecution of friend or relative, to seek shelter in that desperate solitude, which is relieved, but, by the presence, and cheered, but, by the sympathy of the few, who, like themselves, have been picked out by fate, to suffer, to be miserable, and to be finally, cast forth from the society of mankind. (43–44)

These sentiments, a reflection of the ideology of piracy, demonstrate how well Philip integrated this vision into his work. More important, it shows how thoroughly these men had rejected the oppressive slave system of their masters and the outlines of a society in which they hoped to live. Although the society proposed by Philip may have been utopian by design, it offered an alter-native vision of what, to the native son, constituted a desirable way of living.

Thus on the *Black Schooner,* the ship on which the pirates lived, each man was considered an equal as long as he followed the discipline of the ship. These men also maintained "a strict sense of honor," convinced "that the least breach of honesty among themselves, would be the end of their individual security, and the dissolution of their society" (57). Because their feeling of abandonment condemned them to establish their own values and to follow their own rules, they considered the piracy to which they had committed their lives "more like adventures, in which men of spirit could engage with as much honour, as in fighting under the banners of stranger kings, for the purpose of conquering distant and unoffending peoples" (57). To these men, piracy in booty was considered to be just as legitimate as piracy in men, a reflection of the sentiments echoed by Captain Bellamy earlier.[32]

32. See n. 25, above. It is significant that the plight of an abandoned young mother and her child, ready to throw herself and her child into the Thames of London (echoes of Clotel throwing herself into the Potomac) finally led Emmanuel to devote himself to a life of piracy. Harriet Beecher Stowe makes the connection between slavery and piracy when she notes that "the slave-trade is now, by American law, considered as piracy. But a slave-trade, as systematic as ever was carried on the coast of Africa, is an inevitable attendant and result of American slavery. And its heartbreak and its horrors, can they be told?" (*Uncle Tom's Cabin* [1852, reprint, Harmondsworth: Penguin, 1981], 622).

It is this abandonment, then, of which James Willmington is accused. Thus the son reviles his father:

> "James Willmington, before God, and in the presence of these men, and in the name of Nature, I accuse you of having violated one of the most sacred and most binding of her laws; of having abandoned your offspring; of having neglected the being whose existence sprang from you, and for whom you were bound by a holy obligation to care and provide. . . .
>
> " . . . The tiger will tear to pieces the bold intruder that menaces, nay, that approaches its cubs, and, fiercely fighting, will die for the protection of its young. The solitary bird of the desert will open its vein, and make its parched young one's drink of its life blood, then die; the venomous serpent will writhe and twist under the fiercest foe for its hatchling; but you, unlike the tiger, the bird, or the serpent, not resembling even the most ferocious brute, or the lowest reptile that crawls upon this earth, you cast away from you, and shut out from your mind and heart, until a cowardly consideration for your own safety made *you* remember it, the blood of your blood, and the flesh of your flesh, which even the common affection that you have for yourself–your very essential selfishness itself–should have made you love and cherish; or, at least, feed and water. I am your son; I charge you with having abandoned me from childhood; what defense can you make? I give you ten minutes to reflect and to answer" (61-63)

In this novel, as in *Clotel,* a respect for natural law ("by certain feelings which are implanted in us, and which are considered the laws of the Creator" [62]) predominates. On the *Black Schooner,* only "great Nature's" laws prevailed. In *Clotel,* Thomas Jefferson, president of the United States and father of Clotel, could have been indicted for the same crime of violating and abandoning natural feelings for which Willmington was indicted.[33] Appadocca charged his father, and by extension other such fathers as follows: "You have prostituted the law of nature to your own selfish gratification, perjured yourself, and given that life for which you neglected to provide and care" (63). The author seems to suggest that abandoning natural feeling and natural law, which were enshrined in "the laws of the land," and to which Willmington appealed, was the predominant motif of the age and had led to the "spoilt and blighted existence" (64) of these men of the sea and all others so circumstanced. Hence the title of the novel, *Emmanuel Appadocca; or, Blighted Life.*

But, as the novel asks, when these laws are violated, who has the responsibility to correct the crime and how should it be done? Resorting to an updated interpretation of the *lex talionis,* Appadocca suggests that man has

33. It should be noted that Thomas Jefferson was a strong believer in natural law. Many of these ideas, inculcated in the Declaration of Independence, are alluded to in Brown's *Clotel.*

an obligation to correct these violations and uses this ground to justify his actions.[34] After he notes that law exists in all of nature, he concludes:

"Man, as well as all other beings, is subject to it, and the penalty which its violation entails. If you establish false systems among yourselves, and consent to postpone to an imaginary period, this penalty, which ought to be made to follow closely upon every violation of the law, surely Heaven is not to be blamed. Duty is poised between the reward of virtue and retribution:–man has the license to choose, between either meriting the former, or bringing down the latter, upon himself. The great error of your social physics is, that you remit this penalty to a period of time, which it were even unimagined, would fail to afford the principal and best effect of retribution,–the deterring from crimes." (105)

He notes further: "Know that man himself, by law, is the avenger, the retributionist on himself or others." It is to the principles of *lex talionis,* as he interprets them, that Emmanuel turns to vindicate "the law of nature that has been violated in me, and in your child; and I swear, by the Great Being who gave me reason, that I shall not rest until I have taught my father, that the creature to whom he has given life possesses feelings and sensibility, and is capable of taking vengeance" (106).

Yet the most intriguing aspect of Appadocca's (and by extension Philip's) interpretation of the *lex talionis* is his belief that this theological law was an integral part of ancient Africans' philosophical and theological system (that is, "those who dwelt on the banks of the Nile of old"), even though Europeans came to associate it with Hebraic law. He seems to suggest that this African theological borrowing is applied inadequately within the Judeo-Christian system. As he says to Hamilton, "You forget, in your social system, the wisdom of the race which you affect to despise, while you cherish the theological philosophy which you were eager to borrow from them, and tie the hand of the avenger, and blunt the double-edged sword of retribution" (106). Indeed, it is plausible to argue that by insisting on this earth-based notion of retribution, a "now-orientation" of this theological concept, Appadocca was expressing what Mervyn Alleyne calls "an African religious and world-view continuity [that] underlies the strong desire to

34. Although the *lex talionis* has been interpreted variously as the law of vengeance or the law of compensation and retaliation, it certainly has its origins in what constitutes the correct relationship between a master and his slave. Nahum M. Sarna writes "the *lex talionis* strove to achieve exact justice: only one life for one life, only one eye for one eye, and so forth. In pursuit of this goal, however, the laws allowed physical retaliation and vicarious punishment and did not accept the principle of equal justice for all but, rather, adjusted penalties according to social class" (*The JPS Torah Commentary Exodus,* commentary by Nahum M. Sarna [Philadelphia: Jewish Publication Society, 1991], 126). In Roman jurisprudence, the *lex talionis* came to be interpreted as the law of just retribution.

remove the inequalities and injustices of the status quo which is commonly found in Afro-Jamaican religious movements."[35] In this sense, there is a continuity of religious sentiments in African Jamaica as there was in African Trinidad.

In advancing his thesis of how social and religious life ought to be ordered and the appropriateness of the *lex talionis* within the context of the slave system (in this case, the relationship between a master-father and his slave-son), Philip intends a broader indictment of Western civilization and colonialism which he notes is nothing more than a "licensed system of robbing and thieving" around which "the civilized world turns" (113). Thus, in the defense of colonized peoples, Appadocca makes an important statement that bears repetition:

"The barbarous hordes, whose fathers, either [by] choice or some unlucky accident, originally drove to some cold, frozen, cheerless, and fruitless waste, increasing in numbers, wincing under the inclemency of their clime and the poverty of their land, and longing after the richer, and more fertile, and teeming soil of some other country, desert their wretched regions, and with all the machinery of war, melt down on the unprovoking nations, whose only crime is their being more fortunate and blest, and wrench from their enervated sway the prosperous fields that first provoked their famished cupidity. The people which a convenient position, either on a neck of land, or the elbow of some large river, first consolidated, developed, and enriched, after having appropriated, through the medium of commerce, the wealth of its immediate neighbours, sends forth its numerous and powerful ships to scour the seas, to penetrate into hitherto unknown regions, where discovering new and rich countries, they, in the name of civilization, first open an intercourse with the peaceful and contented inhabitants, next contrive to provoke a quarrel, which always terminates in a war that leaves them the conquerors and possessors of the land. As for the original inhabitants themselves, they are driven after the destruction of their cities, to roam the woods, and to perish and disappear on the advance of their greedy supplanters. Nations that are different only in the language with which they vent their thoughts, inhabiting the same portions of the globe, and separated but by a narrow stream, eagerly watch the slightest inclination of accident in their respective favours, and on the plea, either of religion–that fertile theme, and ready instigator–or on the still more extensive and uncertain ground of politics, use the chance that circumstances throw into their hands, make incursions and fight battles, whose fruits are only misery and wretchedness. A fashion springs up at a certain time to have others to labour for our benefit, and to bear 'the heat and burthen of the day' in our stead: straightway, the map of the world is opened, and the straggling and weakest portions of a certain race, whose power of bodily and mental endurance, ren-

35. Mervyn C. Alleyne, *Roots of Jamaican Culture* (London: Pluto Press, 1989), 105.

ders them the likely objects to answer this end, are chosen. The coasts of the country on which nature has placed them, are immediately lined with ships of acquisitive voyagers, who kidnap and tear them away from the scenes that teem with the associations of their own and their fathers' happiness, load them with irons, throw them into the cruel ordeal of the 'middle passage,' to test whether they are sufficiently iron-constituted as to survive the starvation, stench, and pestilential contagion which decide the extent of the African's endurance, and fix his value. This, my dear friend, is an abstracted idea of the manner in which the world turns." (113-14)

In this incisive disquisition of how Europeans treated Africans and other "weaker" races, Appadocca outlines a myth of beginnings: a narrative of the colonial encounter. He notes that first, Europeans rushed to discover warmer and more productive climes. Initially the natives welcomed them—especially by sharing their meager food supplies. Gradually, misunderstandings arose between the two parties. As a result, violent conflicts ensued, which the Europeans perceived as treachery on the part of the native peoples. In the aftermath, native people were dispossessed. In 1986, Peter Hulme described this pattern of behavior:

> There seems little doubt that as far as the Amerindians were concerned the turning point [in their relationship with the Europeans] was always the realization that their 'guests' had come to stay. The Europeans were blinded to this by their failure to comprehend that what confronted them was an agriculturally based society with claims over the land. Unable to understand the effects of their own behavior, the only narrative that they could construct to make sense of both the hospitality and the violence was a narrative of treachery in which the initial kindness was a ruse to establish trust before the natives 'natural' violence emerged from behind the mask.[36]

It is to Philip's credit that as early as the 1850s he understood that Europeans' discourses about their civilizing mission, their notions about the pacification of savage peoples, and their vain mouthings about their Christianizing endeavors were nothing less than the invention of so many disguises to rob and enslave native peoples whose only crime was "their being more fortunate and blest . . . [with] prosperous fields that first provoked [the colonizers'] famished cupidity." Although Appadocca offered a romantic alternative of social development ("The mind can thrive only in the silence that courts contemplation. . . . Commerce makes steam engines and money—it assists not the philosophical progress of the mind" [116]), he understood that a system that depended on the brutalizing of others to achieve greatness and encouraged human beings to exhibit the worst as-

---

36. Peter Hulme, *Colonial Encounters: Europe and the Native Caribbean 1492-1797* (London: Methuen, 1986), 131.

pects of vice and wickedness could not be construed as being civilized or Christian.

It is also to Philip's credit that he understood that Africans "gave philosophy, religion, and government to the world, but [they] must now themselves stoop, to cut wood, and to carry water, when, by the common rules of justice, they should be permitted to enjoy the land from which they have sprung, and to participate in its dignities" (114). That an inhabitant of Trinidad, in the middle of the nineteenth century, should make the careful distinction between instinct and reason and argue that "there are no such things as instincts in man: he alone is distinguished from the rest of organic beings by the indefiniteness of his mind and sensibilities," that he should speak so perceptively about the law of revenge and make such an important case against slavery, must be considered a remarkable achievement. Such stunning observations from a man who came from a "backward country" reflect a mind that was willing to explore difficult questions and was not afraid to advance serious ideas about the way the world turns.

Emmanuel Appadocca, therefore, offers an important philosophical explanation of slavery and its attendant sin, racism. It also suggests that enslaved Africans should have responded in a spirit of "manliness" to the system of oppression. To some degree, Philip believed that the enslaved should have followed the example of the buccaneers. For no matter how hopeless the situation looked (it is important to remember that Philip was looking at the American slave system in which oppression was rife), these people had an obligation to take on the slave system and fight for a noble cause. Like William Wells Brown, Philip believed that one should confront the social order, and so he has his hero argue in full romantic splendor:

> "Take the furious bull–society, by the horns, and though its lurid eyes shine fire upon you, nay, though it gore you, shout out your truths still higher than its bellowings; and when its madness-fit is over, your truths shall live, nay, ride it even as a broken-spirited ass.
>
> "Men of such boldness there have been, who, Lycurgus-like, have exiled themselves from all to throw their truths into the world. Society may have branded them, starved them, cursed them, and driven them into hovels, there to perish and to rot, but they have ever re-risen in their thoughts, and now their names receive, on the bended knees, the unbounded veneration of mankind. (123)

Appadocca also believes that the most important thing in life is the courage to preserve "our honour, our consciousness of acting right," a central virtue in the buccaneer's code. Such honor, he believes, could be achieved only by dedicating one's life to avenging (justly retaliating for) the cause of one's displeasure and one's shame. It is within this process that one fulfills one's destiny, a complicated notion of what he calls a "synchronism of events and a simultaneousness of the actings of nature's general laws; . . . against which no man from absence of any power to read the future can provide" (243). Although Appadocca chooses to end his life after having completed his destined objective, he has clearly proven himself a romantic hero and is exalted by his faithful followers.

In its own way, *Emmanuel Appadocca* can be read as a nineteenth-century response to the philosophies of slavery, racism, and European arrogance. In many ways, the ideas in the novel resonate with what V. Y. Mudimbe calls "the romantic possibilities of otherness which flourished in Europe in the nineteenth century." It also anticipates Blyden's arguments on racial identity, the theories of Negritude and Pan-Africanism. Like Blyden's, Philip's thesis represents "an emotional response to the European process of denigrating Africa [and Africans] and an opposition to the exploitation that resulted from the expansionism of Europe from the fifteenth century" to the time when Philip was writing.[37] As such, the passage of the Fugitive Slave Law, in reaction to which this text at least in part was written, proved to be the final humiliation of the African in the New World.

To the degree that *Emmanuel Appadocca* exposed the cruelties of the slave system, it opened up many important and exciting possibilities in Caribbean literary and intellectual thought. As Mudimbe notes, however, because "the racial moment is always the promise of another step, another contradiction,"[38] *Emmanuel Appadocca* represented the continued struggle of African American peoples against colonialism and imperialism and acted as a foil against their being falsified and depersonalized, major objectives of the colonialist project. It is Philip's concern with these important social and philosophical questions that anticipates the works of Sylvester Williams, J. J. Thomas, C. L. R. James, and Eric Williams and suggests a specific Caribbean angle of vision for examining these questions. The works of Stuart Hall, Paul Gilroy, Hazel Carby and other such thinkers continue to extend the trajectory of Philip's ideas.

The Language of *Emmanuel Appadocca*

One important aspect of *Emmanuel Appadocca* is the introduction of Jack Jimmy and Jack, distinctly Afro-Trinidadian voices, into the body of the

37. V. Y. Mudimbe, *The Invention of Africa* (Bloomington: Indiana University Press, 1988), 132.
38. Ibid.

literature. In the novel, at least three distinct voices are reflected in the patterns of speech. Because language is accented differently by different groups, the different voices (languages) in the text represent the struggle of various social groups for power. As the literature develops one is able to see the evolving nature of social relations via the language used by various characters in other novels.

The first distinctive voice in the novel is Appadocca's, the formal English of a colonial person–a creole–who has had the benefit of a European education and who knows and understands the more important currents of Euro-American intellectual thought.[39] He is resolute, intellectually sophisticated, articulate and thoughtful. It is to this voice that Philip entrusted the moral tenor of the novel.

The second voice in the text is that of Willmington and Hamilton, members of the dominant class, who reflect the standard English of the colonizer. While Willmington represents the grosser manifestation of the colonial enterprise (he is a wealthy planter), Hamilton, having studied at a university, represents the more refined and thoughtful dimensions of the colonial class. Although the latter accepts hierarchical distinctions in social life, he recognizes a common bond of feeling with Appadocca. Intended to be contrasted with Appadocca, the radical and oppositional dimension of the colonial system, Hamilton represents the enlightened wisdom of his age. Identifying with Appadocca, although he disagrees with his reasoning and disapproves of his goals, Hamilton tries to free Appadocca against the wishes of his own father.

In Jimmy, Philip introduces an Afro-Trinidadian who uses lower-class colloquial speech. At the phonological level, Jimmy's dialect resembles the speech of an Afro-Trinidadian in both its lexical dimensions and syntactical qualities. Theoreticians of black English and creole language studies have identified his voice as black speech. Moreover, the syntax, diction, and vernacular rhythms, the flow of the prose, the structure of the mental process, and the memorable manner in which Jimmy's speech registers even with a contemporary audience demonstrate its resemblance to the emerging language of the black Trinidadian. And even if Philip had no conscious desire to reflect Afro-Trinidadian speech in a complimentary manner–Bridget Brereton notes the negative fashion in which Philip describes Jimmy–the

---

39. Alleyne defines the term *creole:* "Originally meant of European origin, but born in the colonies, and referred to persons, animals, trees, plants. It then came to designate persons of African descent born in the New World, and from there, the language related by vocabulary to the European language, and which was spoken by African creoles in the New World and on the west African coast" (*Roots of Jamaican Culture,* xi).

directness, lucidity, and exuberance of his language make it quintessen-
tially black.[40] Indeed, the emergence of this distinctive Afro-Trinidadian
voice reflects an important aspect of the creolization process of Africans in
Trinidad and represents, as Mervyn Alleyne notes in another context, the
first major step toward the Trinidadization of the culture.[41] In Jimmy we see
one of the earliest attempts to render the speech patterns of an Afro-
Trinidadian in print, a voice that rings out eloquently when, in digging
Appadocca's grave, Jimmy asserts: "Let me one do it."

In trying to understand the impact of Jimmy and his language within the
context of Trinidadian literature, Ralph Ellison's observation about Jim,
the major character of *Huckleberry Finn,* seems appropriate: "Writing at a
time when the blackfaced minstrel was still popular, and shortly after a war
which left even the abolitionists weary of those problems associated with
the Negro, Twain fitted Jim into the outlines of the minstrel tradition, and it
was from behind this stereotype mask that we see Jim's dignity and human
capacity–and Twain's complexity–emerge."[42] Reading between the lines or
beneath the surface of the text–in spite of Philip, as it were–one sees a very
human figure in Jimmy, someone who is fed up with the system–that is why
he stayed with Appadocca–and whose essential being seems to be weighted
down by an oppressive system. In Jimmy, we see a black man who is willing
to give his life to a cause and to follow his compatriot faithfully. He too is
committed to the eventual overthrow of the colonial system. Like Stowe
with some of her characters in *Uncle Tom's Cabin,* Philip may have had
negative feelings about Jimmy–although we do not know this for sure.
Nonetheless, the attributes that Philip gives to Jimmy undercut any attempt
to interpret him as merely a racist caricature.[43] It is only through an examination of Jimmy's language that we can discover who Jimmy was.

40. Bridget Brereton, "Michel Maxwell Philip (1829–1888): Servant of the Centurion,"
Antilia . . . Journal of the Faculty of Arts (University of the West Indies) 1, no. 3 (1989). In a
similar context, Twain's understanding of language and the role it plays in the construction of
characters is very important. He says: "I don't believe an author, good, bad, or indifferent,
ever lived, who created a character. It was always drawn from his recollection of someone he
had known. Sometimes like a composite photograph, an author's presentation of a character
may possibly be from the blending of . . . two or more real characters in his recollection. But,
even when he is making no attempt to draw his characters from life . . . he is yet unconsciously
drawing from memory" (quoted in Shelley Fisher Fishkin, *Was Huck Black? Mark Twain and
African-American Voices* (New York: Oxford University Press, 1993), 34–35.

41. Mervyn Alleyne, "Language and Empowerment in the Caribbean," in Kari Levitt and
Michael Witter, *The Caribbean Tradition of Political Economy* (Kingston: Ian Randle, 1996).

42. Ellison, *Shadow and Act* (New York: Random House, 1953), 50.

43. In a seminar on Trinidad and Tobago literature held during the summer of 1996 at the
Rudranath Capildeo Learning Resource Center, some of the participants agreed with Brereton's conclusion that Philip did indeed depict Jimmy in a racist manner.

The Reception of *Emmanuel Appadocca*

The evidence is that *Emmanuel Appadocca* did well financially. Tronchin notes that the proceeds from his novel "were of the greatest assistance to [Philip] under his difficult circumstances" while C. L. R. James suggests that the proceeds enabled Philip to travel throughout Europe. Although some critics felt that the hero was too hard on his father and treated him in a very unnatural manner, Tronchin noted that the novel "was well-received in the literary world." In defense of the novel, he argued:

> A grave accusation plausible to a certain extent, but altogether unfounded in reality, has been formulated against the author of that sensational novel with reference to the unnatural sentiments he ascribed to his hero, who heartlessly exposed his own father to certain death in the open seas. But little reflection will be sufficient to justify the course adopted by the author in applying a cruel punishment as retributive of an unheard crime.
>
> The *lex talionis* is frequently resorted to in works of fiction where the imagination is allowed considerable latitude without necessarily interpreting its extravagance in a manner detrimental to the personal character of the author.[44]

Tronchin's task, it seems, was to demonstrate that *Emmanuel Appadocca,* a fictional piece of work, did not reflect the author's character or personality. He suggests that the *lex talionis* allows for a freedom of imagination that may not necessarily be present in a novel with a different central theme. More important, though, he distinguishes between the integrity of the text (which allows for literary freedom and license) and that of the author (whose opinions may not necessarily be those of his characters). Nonetheless, some critics thought that Philip had overstepped his bounds (the danger inherent in treating the law of just retribution) and that aspects of his personal philosophy may have influenced the novel unduly. Certainly, Appadocca's final confrontation with Feliciana, a Spanish woman who falls in love with him and who pleads with him to renounce "the unholy pursuit which now throws [your] soul into the hands of the demons," leaves the reader somewhat troubled. That his life ends up being "gloomy, dark, and troublesome," his existence, "a heavy, heavy oppression," and his soul, feeling "like the cumbrous tower . . . [that] can never rise again" suggests an eerie association with Hecuba's fate. Of course, it is also likely that his interpretation of the law of just retribution, sometimes reduced to the law of vengeance, did not make members of the ruling class feel very comfortable.

Brereton, a distinguished historian, has argued:

44. Tronchin, "The Great West Indian Orator."

> The novel is an extremely bad one, the plot absurd, the characters incredible, the prose turgid; the whole production is a fourth-rate 'Gothick' romance by a very young man with high-flown literary pretensions. . . .
>
> Philip's portrait of the comic black, Jack Jimmy, who closely resembled a "rolled up ouran-outan," stresses his extreme "Negroid" features–protruding jaws, huge eyes, "miserably abbreviated and flat nose," kinky hair–and presents him in fact as a uniquely ugly and ridiculous figure. In a simile which anticipates J. A. Froude [*The English in the West Indies*], he writes "the movements of the little negro were as brisk and as rapid as those of a monkey." The novel has no real literary merit; but it illustrates the young student's ideas at the time and it has a certain interest as a curiosity: it is almost certainly the first novel published by a Trinidadian.[45]

Such an unusually harsh judgment does not take the literary aspects of the text fully into consideration. It may also reflect Brereton's understandable dismay at the verbiage, vague abstractions, highflown sentiments, and grandiose turns of phrases in the novel. The same argument could be made against *Uncle Tom's Cabin*. Indeed, the very nature of the convention depends on the use of the marvelous and the incredulous to drive home the point of the text and, with Jimmy's language, the emanation of a particular kind of Trinidadian. One has to read within the convention of the form (that is, within the tradition of the romance) to understand how the novel works. In *A Key to Uncle Tom's Cabin* Stowe cited the many sources upon which she drew to create the character Uncle Tom. And although many of Stowe's racist beliefs did undercut the strength of her message about slavery's inhumanity, the novel certainly dramatized the unchristian nature of slavery, the larger theme of the novel. A similar case can be made for *Emmanuel Appadocca*. To Brereton's contention that *Emmanuel Appadocca* anticipates the stereotypes used in Froude's *The English in the West Indies,* it only needs to be pointed out that whereas the former is a novel, the latter was a social commentary that did not abide by similar standards of judgment. More important, one cannot arbitrarily ascribe the fictional voice of *Emmanuel Appadocca* to Philip as one can the nonfictional assertions that are made in *The English in the West Indies* to Froude. As Ellison notes in another context, "The identity of fictional characters is determined by the implicit realism of the form, not by their relation to tradition; they are what they do or do not do."[46]

In trying to understand the place of this remarkable novel at the beginning of Anglo-Caribbean literary history, we must realize that rather than reproducing the conventional ideals and values of romanticism and the

45. Brereton, "Michel Maxwell Philip," 6–7.
46. Ellison, *Shadow and Act,* 57.

slave narrative verbatim, Philip attempted to defamiliarize the cultural and social milieu in which he wrote to better highlight the specific problems of his society. Although Philip used some of the linguistic structures of the Anglo-Saxon romance, he also included the voice of Jimmy, a specific product of Trinidad. And, by foregrounding the judgments of Appadocca, Philip attempts to demonstrate the specific problem to which a slave and a colonial person was subjected. Although Philip drew on the conventional wisdom of the time (such as the principle of natural rights and the role of reason) to make his larger point, he surely brought those theories to bear on the specific dimension of what can be called the Caribbean problematic. The novel used aspects of romance and the slave narrative, but in its finished form it represents the beginning of the Caribbean novel.

For reasons unknown to us, Philip withdrew the novel from circulation some years after it was published.[47] Five years after he died the novel was republished in Trinidad (the first edition had been published in London) with a short, laudatory sketch of the author's life. This would suggest that the reading public wished to have the work placed before them once more. Also, it might have been that the public had seen and known what Philip could not necessarily see or know: that is, that "novels are never content to deal with fiction; they must pretend to deal with the truth, the truth behind the discourse of ideology that gives them form. So paradoxically enough, the truth with which they deal is fiction itself."[48] Moreover, it was an acknowledgment that the citizens of Trinidad recognized and appreciated what Philip had accomplished and knew that truth lay behind the fictional interpretation of Trinidadian society.

The Importance of *Emmanuel Appadocca*

It has been common wisdom to locate the beginnings of Anglophone Caribbean literature in Jamaica at the turn of the twentieth century, a schema that conveniently forgets the important autobiographical works of Mary Prince, Mary Seacole, and a host of writings by the slaves themselves.[49] *Emmanuel Appadocca* alerts us that there exists a series of works written in the nineteenth-century Anglophone Caribbean to be recovered if we are to make that literature more complete. Gordon Lewis noted that Caribbean

47. José Bodu, *Trinidadiana* (Port of Spain: A. C. Blondel, 1890), 83.
48. Roberto Gonzalez Echavarria, *Myth and Archive: A Theory of Latin American Narrative* (Cambridge: Cambridge University Press, 1989), 18.
49. See, for example, Kenneth Ramchand, *The West Indian Novel and Its Background* (London: Heinemann, 1983); Bruce King, ed., *West Indian Literature* (Hamden, Conn.: Archon Books, 1979); and Cudjoe, *Caribbean Slave Narratives* (forthcoming).

literature has always been activist, in part because the forces unleashed by "the tremendous revolution of the sixteenth century."[50] *Emmanuel Appadocca,* therefore, has to be seen as one work that organizes itself around the trope of Caribbean resistance as its author tried to determine the most appropriate response to the forces unleashed by the Atlantic slave trade and slavery. More important, Philip's attempt to locate the concept of *lex talionis* within the context of African jurisprudence extends the connection that Caribbean scholar-activists of the nineteenth century were making with Africa. This connection was reflected in the works of scholars such as Baron de Vastey of Haiti, who, in responding to a wave of "European Negrophobia," defended the African race and argued that "Africa has been traditionally the cradle of civilization–Carthaginian, Ethiopian, Egyptian, Phoenician predating the European forms by some 1500 years" or Antenor Firmin, who, in his thesis about the equality of the races and the sociopolitical basis of human development, seemed equally to have been responding to the preevolutionary justification of scientific racism that was taking place in the United States at the end of the nineteenth century.[51]

Just as important, Philip's use of the ideology of piracy, the slave narrative, and the romance demonstrates just how much his novel was part of a sensibility that was emerging in the Atlantic world of the nineteenth century. Sidney Mintz has argued that the great task of the serious student of Afro-Americana is to probe the conscious life of the slave masses as they "sought to make comprehensible the destinies imposed on them by brute force. The daily job of living did not end with enslavement, and the slaves could and did create viable patterns of life, for which their pasts were pools of available symbolic and material resources. . . . The glory of Afro-Americana inheres in the durable fiber of humanity, in the face of what surely must have been the most repressive epoch in modern world history. It has depended upon creativity and innovation, far more than upon the indelibility of particular culture contents."[52] *Emmanuel Appadocca* allows us to examine the thoughts and sentiments of a nineteenth-century Caribbean

50. Lewis, *Main Currents in Caribbean Thought,* 60. See also Selwyn R. Cudjoe, *Resistance and Caribbean Literature* (Athens: Ohio University Press, 1980), which argues for the role of resistance as a fashioning aesthetic in Caribbean literature.

51. Vastey quoted in Lewis, *Main Currents in Caribbean Thought,* 256. See also Antenor Firmin, *De l'égalité des races humaines* (Paris: Levaine Cotilon, 1885). See also J. Stephen Gould, *The Mismeasure of Man* (New York: Norton, 1981), chap. 2, for a discussion of scientific racism in the United States.

52. Sidney Mintz in his foreword to *Afro-American Anthropology: Contemporary Perspectives,* ed. Norman E. Whitten, Jr., and John Szwed (New York: Free Press, 1970), 8-9.

intellectual-activist as he tried to make sense of a life over which he had little control; a life that was shaped very much by the slave and colonial systems.

Conclusion

From 1854 to 1888, Philip devoted himself to the practice of law and he became famous for his oratorical gifts. As Sir William Robinson, governor of Trinidad at the time of Philip's death, noted: "He certainly was possessed of a most wonderful memory, and he had to the full extent, what is called 'the Heaven born gift of Eloquence' " (9). Although the consensus is that Philip was the finest lawyer of his time, Brereton has some reservations about his commitment to his race and she sees 1871, the year he was appointed solicitor general, as a critical turning point in his life. She argues:

> The picture of Philip before his permanent appointment as Solicitor-General in 1871 is one of a liberal, advocating constitutional reform, seeking to promote the interests of non-whites, and confronting the Establishment. When he became a member of that Establishment, the picture was bound to change. Just before his appointment, Governor [Arthur] Gordon left, and under two immediate successors conservatism seemed once more in the ascendant. Philip's position was perilous. He was an adviser to the Government, but conservatism, of the kind practised in West Indian Crown Colonies, was alien to his political beliefs and to his commitment to the people. He remained in office. He was still a liberal, but it was bound to be a tortuous path; and it was resented by many of his "people," the educated coloureds. At the same time, because of his colour and his liberal past, he was both useful and suspect to the Government which he only too faithfully served. He was useful not only because he was a loyal and able supporter of the Government, but because, as Governor Sir Henry Irving wrote in 1879, "for many years past he . . . has exercised a most useful influence amongst a class whose tendency is towards agitation and mischief." In other words, he had effectively helped to control and neutralise discontent among the educated coloureds. For the Crown Colony regime, this was the most useful role to be played by Philip and other prominent coloured officials, who had visibly succeeded within the system and had come to enjoy some of its privileges and honours.[53]

Brereton contends that although Philip continued to support certain demands of the people (objecting to the chants by the Trinidad stickfighters,[54] criticizing absentee landlords for doing little for the island where they made

53. Brereton, "Michel Maxwell Philip," 12.

54. Stickfighting, one of the African martial arts that was brought to Trinidad and practiced by Afro-Trinidadians, was usually accompanied by chants such as "bois" by the participants and the onlookers. During the latter part of the nineteenth century, efforts were made by the colonial authorities to outlaw such activities.

their wealth), there was a feeling among a few persons that he helped "to carry out policy with which he often disagreed." Some of the stands he took, and for which he was condemned (for example, supporting the resolution to make Tranquillity Square private), seem questionable. Yet, it is clear that Philip responded in much the same contradictory fashion as most of the coloreds of his time: with a feeling of ambivalence toward their aspirations for the privileges that whiteness conferred, which were counterbalanced by the allegiance they owed to the other half of their heritage.[55] Today we can guess that he found himself in a treacherous social and political situation that was difficult to navigate.[56] Suffice it to say that this ambiguity resided more at the nonfictional, real-life level than it did in his fiction.

Nonetheless, when Philip left for a visit to London in 1873, J. J. Thomas, one of the most eminent of his contemporaries, observed that "owing to the numerous and all but insuperable obstacles presented by certain peculiarities of our social system to the advancement of certain individuals, it has been with intense interest and gratification that your fellow-Trinidadians, and indeed all men of liberal principles, have contemplated your career."[57] So while it is correct to suggest that Philip encountered difficulty in trying to keep his warring halves in harmony, it is also true that he was able to achieve much in a society that would have preferred that he stay in his place.

Whatever the ultimate judgment, Philip distinguished himself among his contemporaries in a way that made them feel at his death that they lost one of their "great patriots" and a "great West Indian orator." When death "paralyzed those noble faculties, sealed forever those eloquent lips and arrested the pulsations of that patriotic heart, which during so many long years vibrated in accordance with the aspirations of his native land," great indeed was the sorrow. In oratorical flights that befitted the dignity of this great son, his eulogist lamented that "it may justly be said that a great citizen has disappeared from among us and no occasion is more propitious than the present one to renew the lamentations which Zion echoed after the death of Judas Machabeus; 'Weep Jerusalem weep, for a great man has

55. See my introduction to *Free Mulatto* (Wellesley: Calaloux Publications, 1996).

56. David Trotman takes exception to C. L. R. James's laudatory comments on Philip. He argues that James adopted an "overly sympathetic view" of Philip (*Crime in Trinidad* [University of Tennessee Press, 1986], 309). See also C. L. R. James, "Michel Maxwell Philip: 1829-1888," in *From Trinidad: An Anthology of Early West Indian Writing*, ed. Reinhard W. Sander (New York: Africana Publishing, 1978), 253-69.

57. Thomas quoted in Brereton, "Michel Maxwell Philip," 13.

fallen today in Israel!' " Given such feelings of sorrow and loss among his compatriots, it is only fitting that we conclude this appreciation of his literary life by reechoing their poetic celebration of his life:

> Yes! Trinidad's illustrious son is gone,
> Thy victory now is sure, thy work is done.
> O thou implacable and cruel death
> Revengeful for with foul Lethean's breath,
> That bringest here desolation's bitter tears
> To patriot's eyes, whose soul unknown to fears.
> In times of yore defied the tyrant's yoke,
> And liberty the blessed day evoke.
> But no! O death thy victory is vain
> And Philip's memory will still remain,
> Enthroned in love within the grateful heart
> Of those to whom the voice of faith imparts
> Sweet consolation, heavenly balm;
> O yes, his memory lives secure and calm
> Among the young who hailed his fame so fair,
> Who would not blush to weep for one so dear.
> When the eternal spark forsook its shell
> His memory lives and history will tell
> His work, the battles fought to freedom's name,
> When impious tyranny imposed its fame
> And timid liberty conceals its head;
> Assailed at last! by legitimate dread.
> O sweet breeze of the Naparima's plains,
> Repeat at times in thy melodious strains
> the name of Philip to the distant hills
> Where oft are heard the distant thunder peals!
> And you, O friends, let not oblivion's womb
> Conceal in darkness, veil the hero's tomb.[58]

Although *Emmanuel Appadocca* has been virtually unknown for close to one hundred and fifty years, it remains a significant achievement in Caribbean and African American literature and intellectual thought. Scholars of Caribbean, African American, and American literature need to revisit this magisterial text as they attempt to expand and refashion the meaning of the Atlantic sensibility.

Wellesley/Aix-en-Provence

58. Tronchin, "The Great West Indian Orator."